ZOE BRENNAN,
FIRST CRUSH

ZOE BRENNAN, FIRST CRUSH

LAURA PIPER LEE

UNION
SQUARE
& CO.

NEW YORK

UNION SQUARE & CO.

NEW YORK

UNION SQUARE & CO. and the distinctive Union Square & Co. logo
are trademarks of Sterling Publishing Co., Inc.

Union Square & Co., LLC, is a subsidiary of Sterling Publishing Co., Inc.

ISBN 978-1-4549-5522-1 (paperback)
ISBN 978-1-4549-5523-8 (e-book)
ISBN 978-1-60582-459-8 (galley)

For information about custom editions, special
sales, and premium purchases, please contact
specialsales@unionsquareandco.com.

Printed in Canada

2 4 6 8 10 9 7 5 3 1

unionsquareandco.com

Cover illustration by Vi-An Nguyen
Interior design by Christine Heun

Dedication TK

CHAPTER ONE

I t's eight a.m. on a brisk March morning, and there's a man in my mouth.

An *annoying* one.

"Open wide for me, baby. You can take it."

"*Teddy.*" I growl around the mouthful of metal and cotton he's loaded into my face, then gag as something pointy hits my tonsils.

"Come on now, Zoe!" Teddy's futuristic dentist spectacles flash as he roots around inside my face like it's the junk drawer, and he's hunting for the last triple A battery. "I know you lesbians don't have a lot of practice, but surely you can open wider than *that*. Think boa constrictors. Unhinged jaws."

There are downsides to being best friends with your inappropriate gay dentist.

This is one of them.

After Teddy retrieves the last of his clanking oral probes from my mouth, he picks up my chart and frowns, vigorously drawing several large circles on various teeth in the diagram.

I arch an eyebrow. I can see where this is going a mile away.

"Bad news," Teddy says gravely. "Some of these cavities are so deep, they're forming a tunnel network. Have you ever heard of fistulas?" He swats his hand at me, like *never you mind*, and gets up and opens the door. "George? Prepare the shots! We're going to need them *all!*"

Teddy's hygienist materializes in the doorway like a ghoul, eyes delighted, gripping a large metal tray cluttered with needles.

I remove the wad of wet cotton from my mouth and smile politely. "That won't be necessary, George. Thank you."

Teddy's theatrical frown turns genuine. "You're no fun, Zoe Brennan. You know that? All *well-adjusted* and *calm*."

I get the feeling I'm supposed to be insulted.

George's face falls as he realizes the shots aren't needed after all. I watch him shuffle back to his station from the corner of my eye. "You ever worry about George?"

"He brings a certain unhealthy enthusiasm for the job, yes," Teddy says simply, his back turned to prepare the next round of tortures.

"So what's this '*red-hot emergency business meeting*' I had to drop everything and come in for?" That's usually Teddy's code for fresh gossip, but every now and then, he legitimately wants to talk business. As the go-to lender for my family's vineyard, Teddy considers himself my "silent partner," which is hilarious because nothing about Teddy is silent.

Teddy swings back around with a set of whitening trays and a suspiciously innocent face. "You mean other than your red teeth, you unrepentant vampire?" He butts the upper tray against my mouth, and I reluctantly open wide enough for him to shove it in. Is this what blow jobs are like?

"You're lucky I got a shipment of the good bleach in." He *tsks* and jams the lower tray in next.

"Pitfalls ah running a winn-yer," I say as dignified as I can around the two trays. "'inking wine ih my yob."

"That's funny, I could've sworn *making* wine was your job."

"Same 'hing. Now 'pill it." I give him my best *don't fuck around* look, but I'm still wearing those giant black safety glasses and drooling, so it's less effective than usual.

"Mayor Esposito's aide was in yesterday—Elisa?" he says with feigned nonchalance. "You know the girl. Class one malocclusion? Well, she mentioned that the *Bon Vivant* has chosen to host their annual wine festival in Blue Ridge this year."

Even Teddy's reflexes can't stop the trays from shooting out of my mouth. "*Everyday Bon Vivant?!*"

"Ms. Brennan, this is expensive bleach, you want me to charge your ass double?"

"*TEDDY!* Tell me everything!" I rip the black safety glasses off.

The grin spreading beneath his dental specs is positively evil. "Not so calm now, are you?"

I blink against the chair's overhead spotlight, head spinning. *Everyday Bon Vivant* magazine is *the* word on exemplary—but accessible—wine. I've gone to their traveling annual festival a few times, whenever our vineyard can afford to send me, and it's always an amazing time. It draws thousands of visitors from around the world for three blissful days of eating, drinking, and fun events, and when it's over, the area picked to host is officially on the map. As a small wine-producing region, Blue Ridge can't compete with Napa and Sonoma; wine connoisseurs don't even know we exist. But if it hosts *Everyday Bon Vivant,* it would change everything—for our wine scene, our town, and especially for the lucky vineyard chosen to host the opening showcase.

"When?"

"This fall, after harvest at the tail end of tourist season. They'll start scouting locations right away."

I sit back, mouth hanging open long enough for Teddy to jam the trays back in.

"It's time to put on that clever thinking cap of yours, baby." Teddy dabs at the drool on my chin affectionately with the paper towel clipped to my chest. "This is Bluebell Vineyards' big opportunity to level up."

He's not wrong. Most people don't know this, but running a small vineyard isn't the most profitable venture. The pandemic hit our region's tourism hard, followed by two drenching, grape-killing rainy seasons back-to-back. Teddy's loans, local music nights, family picnics, business 101 classes—I've had to pull every trick out of my hat to keep the lights on and the grapes growing. Some days it feels like a miracle we're open at all, and the stress keeps a perpetual grip around my throat.

Bluebell Vineyards was my mom's dream—she and my dad built it from the ground up. But Mom died when I was twelve, and I vowed to continue her legacy by pouring my love and energy into the business the way she and my father always had. Watching sales decline these last few years fills me with a panicked desperation that keeps me up at night. Dad's been so down lately, too. Our money situation stresses him out, though I try to protect him from the worst of it.

But if Bluebell gets the *Everyday Bon Vivant* showcase? Dad might even be able to retire one day. We've always assumed he'd be out there pruning to the very end, but this could change everything.

"Did Elisa mention any vineyards the mayor's considering endorsing?"

Teddy grimaces, and I already know the answer.

"Into the Woods. Who else?" he says.

Our neighboring vineyard run by my best-friend-turned-enemy Rachel Woods.

Of *course*.

It's a shame, really. Rachel's parents Molly and Ezra Woods are my dad's closest friends, her older brother Chance is an all-around nice guy, and her big sister Charlaine? An absolute *goddess* and star of all my teen-age fantasies.

Rachel, however, is a stone-cold bitch.

Rachel, Charlaine, Chance, and I all grew up together, our houses on neighboring properties nestled between rows of young vines and tucked away in the lush, rolling woods of Gilmer County. I was at the Woods's house every day for years, until things with Rachel went to hell in a handbasket. Now here we are, twelve years after high school graduation, all still working in the wine business. Charlaine went to California to study viticulture and never came back, while Rachel and Chance stayed on at their family's vineyard. Thanks to Chance's wine-making skills and Rachel's insufferable knack for making money, Into the Woods is our biggest competition and the snobbiest vineyard in town. They spell *classic* "*classique*" for no good reason and generally make me want to throw things.

"Rachel better stay out of my way. That showcase is *mine.*" The decree slurps out around the trays.

Teddy's smile returns with fiendish glee. "I love it when you're business evil, Zoe Brennan!"

My mind's off to the races already. It's the beginning of the spring season, and vineyard operations will grow busier until the first grapes appear. Then work transitions to pure chaos, which reigns through harvest. If *Everyday Bon Vivant* is scouting soon, I've got to put together a plan for winning the showcase *now.*

The bleaching timer goes off, and I yank the trays out and set them on the counter, ignoring Teddy's disgusted demands that I rinse. My hand's already turning the doorknob to leave when he calls out, "Wait, dammit! There's one more thing!"

I sigh impatiently. I've got a date with Microsoft 365, two shots of espresso, and my entrepreneurial cunning. "Make it quick, Teddy."

"Harlow Benoit rolled into town yesterday—Diego and I saw her when we were out for dinner." Teddy levies his finger in my direction. With his dental specs still on, he looks like a very stern gem dealer. "Do *not* text her, Zoe! Remember your New Year's resolution!"

Harlow. Her name alone brings a flush of heat to my neck. Harlow Benoit, wine buyer for the prestigious Bouche à Bouche restaurant group, rolls into Blue Ridge a few times a year to sample new wines and negotiate supply deals. She's a human tornado disguised as a five-foot-two pan-sexual party girl who always manages to destroy my calm and upend my carefully curated feelings. She's fun, extraordinarily sexy, and pushes my limits until I let go, willingly, of all the things I'm trying to control at any given minute. I absolutely crave the release I feel in her arms.

The problem is she always leaves. She's an employed vagabond, based in New York City for a few months a year, then on the road for the rest of it. I get two or three days of sexual bliss, then she's gone, and I'm left desperately trying to remind myself that I don't *want* a real relationship. Why bother wanting what I can't have? The queer community in Blue Ridge is thriving thanks to all the gay transplants—it was even named the friendliest LGBTQ city in Georgia a few years ago—but the lesbians who move here are already coupled up, and the few who *aren't* hooked up with me, then settled down with each other.

Which is *fine*. None of them were right for me, anyway. And Harlow isn't, either. I know this, I do . . . but then she rolls into town, and the desire to be touched overwhelms me. I break all my resolutions for one more round of sex followed by the brief whiplash of loneliness being with her always kicks up. But not this time. Teddy's sick of the emotional hangovers I have after she leaves, and I am, too. This past New Year's after a *particularly* incredible Christmas rendezvous when she kissed a snow-flake off my nose—*ugh*, it was *so* romantic—I vowed I'd stop for good. It's easier to be alone than to have these periodic moments of intimacy, show-ing me what life with another person could be like.

"Relax, Teddy. I won't." I smile, confident that the words are true this time. Who has time for amazing meaningless sex when the biggest busi-ness opportunity of all time just landed in your lap?

Even Harlow Benoit can't compete with that.

After a quick pilgrimage to Office Depot to stock up on my favorite thinking supplies—a new binder, graph paper, and approximately two hundred colorful gel pens—I turn the vineyard's old truck onto the long, winding road that curls its way through our forest. Like a sea of green parting, the forest dips back to reveal our rolling valley striped with vines. Into the Woods's extensive property is first, streaming past my window in all its pastoral bounty, and I deny the urge to flip it off. I hate what Rachel's done to her family's vineyard since taking over operations. *Hate.* It was Rachel's decision to renovate the old farmhouse into a "modern Tuscan" theme, even though a real, live Tuscan family operates the vineyard next door. *We* manage to restrain ourselves from curling ironwork and decorative plates with roosters on them. Why can't she? Every time I see their Tuscan palazzo by way of T.J. Maxx, my Italian heritage cringes.

The worst part is that Into the Woods is thriving under Rachel's tacky, unoriginal hands. They host five weddings for every one we do, their lush vineyards are triple the size of ours and put out some of the best grapes in the region, and their parking lot's full every weekend. They have money to expand their land, hire more workers, and make more wine, giving them *more money.* Meanwhile, Bluebell Vineyards can't afford to grow, buy new equipment, hire new people, *or* make more wine, and despite my best efforts, we can't seem to budge out of the same profit/loss cycle every year. As our vintner, farmer, and primary fieldworker rolled into one, Dad will *never* get to retire, unlike his best friends Molly and Ezra Woods. Chance, Rachel's brother, took over for their father Ezra as lead vintner a few years ago, and from my palate's perspective, the transition's been seamless. Into the Woods consistently makes the same good (if boring) wines every year. Respectable reds and whites that respectable wine aficionados enjoy drinking. I particularly love their crisp Chardonnays, not that I'd ever admit it publicly. Who could ever take over for Dad?

Not me. I can wither a succulent just by looking at it.

That's why we have to get the showcase. It's the one thing that could break us out of our boxed-in position and let us finally grow. Then maybe we could breathe a little, take a goddamn day off here and there. Into the Woods doesn't need the showcase like we do, yet that won't stop Rachel's manicured nails grabbing for it.

I just have to grab it first.

As I pass the hand-carved sign for Into the Woods, a white Lexus SUV appears from the opposite direction, blinding me. My jaw snaps shut.

Rachel Woods, Director of Operations for Into the Woods, former best friend, and current pain in my ass, slows down until her aggressively polished vehicle reflects the chipped paint of mine. God, she's *obsessed* with her car. Behind the wheel, she's in an expensive sports-bra-shirt thing I'm convinced runners wear as an excuse to be half-naked in public. I don't mind normally, but this is Rachel, and thus, everything she does is inherently the worst.

We lock eyes as our vehicles inch past each other, like two sharks lurking over a contested feeding ground. Her long brown hair is pulled into a high ponytail so tight, it lifts the corners of her eyes, making her look even more feline and cruel than usual. Her fingers visibly tighten around her steering wheel as she mouths exaggeratedly, *Helloooo, bitch*, and caps it with a frosty smile.

Rachel doesn't know about *Everyday Bon Vivant* yet! If she did, her savage competitive streak would be on full display, and I wouldn't have received such a pleasant greeting. I raise two fingers to my brow in salute, then smile all the way home.

"Hey, Dad?" I slam the truck's door shut with my hip, arms full of sweet, sweet office supplies. "I've got *ne-ews*!"

I dump my stuff in the office and enter the winery, where the magic happens. The sharp scent of fermenting wine permeates the air, rushing me like an excited puppy as soon as I step in, followed by the smooth sigh of oak from the barrels racked along the back wall. Our winery is smaller than what you'd find at most vineyards, but I've always loved it in here. The wooden rafters crisscross above my head like steepled fingers, and the steady hum of the air conditioners keep it a brisk sixty degrees year-round. I squeeze down a narrow aisle of massive plastic bins filled with aging reds to reach our cold room in the back, where I find Dad standing in front of a bin of Vidal Blanc, foot tapping, holding a clipboard.

"Ahhh! Questo vino mi sta sui coglioni!" He makes a rude gesture at the bin that raises my eyebrows.

"Um, Dad? Something wrong?" I don't speak much Italian, but I know enough to clock that he just yelled at the wine for standing on his balls. Cosimo Rossi Giuratraboccetti came to America for college, met Julie Brennan of Blue Ridge shortly thereafter, had a little bambina they decided was too tiny for such a big name, then never left again. Most of the Italian Dad speaks now is reserved for when he's deep in his cups and feeling sentimental, or angry at inanimate objects that defy him, so my grasp on our mother tongue is spotty at best. But if you want someone to moon over you, then curse you out? *Prego!* I'm your *donna.*

He whips around, startled, and smiles hastily at me, pulling his clipboard to his chest. "Zoe Nicoletta! No, no, it's just this wine"—he pauses to give it a dirty look—"is *still* not ready for bottling. I'd hoped to do it before . . . well, before now." His face droops into its normal pensive state.

I follow him out of the cold room and over to his worktable where he plops into his chair, muttering about *Brix* and *acid* and *just a simple farmer* as I swoop in to give his bearded cheek a kiss.

"Well, I hope our whites stop squishing your balls soon, but Dad, I've got amazing news." I brush a lock of his once smoky black, now generously silver hair out of his eyes. "You won't *believe*—" I stop suddenly. His worktable, normally neat as a pin, is covered with scattered papers, and his clipboard sports a checklist a mile long, with over half its to-do items crossed off. "What's all this?"

Dad's large, dark eyes meet mine. "I have some news, too, Zoe Nicoletta."

I frown. Dad's been even more distant than usual lately, staying late at the winery, avoiding me in the tasting room. He hasn't cooked us dinner in over a week. I chalked it up to Mom's impending birthday, which always brings him low, but this feels like something else. Something more.

I pull up a stool to sit beside him.

"What is it, Dad?"

He takes off his small round glasses that look unfairly chic on him and slips them into his shirt pocket. "Paolo called. It's Nonna, Zoe Nicoletta. She's sick." His voice cracks on the word *sick*, and my hand flies to my mouth. I don't have many memories of my Nonna, but the ones I do have are good. When I was little, we'd visit her in Montepulciano, a small town in Tuscany where most of my Italian family lives, once every few years. My grandfather died before I was born, so as far back as I can remember, it's only been my beautiful Nonna. She never remarried. She once told me there are a million kinds of love, but you only need a few to get by. I hold that close on my lonelier days.

"Oh, Dad. How sick is she?"

"She's had a stroke, a serious one. She doesn't want to be at the hospital, so the family is taking turns caring for her at home." Dad takes both my hands in his. "I have to go to her, Zoe Nicoletta."

My mouth parts, the news landing in my stomach like a hot, heavy brick. The notes, the checklist, the preparations—it makes sense now. It's a bad time of year for us to leave the vineyard, but then again, it's always a bad time. That's why we haven't visited Italy since Mom died. With Dad running the vineyard by himself until I graduated college and came back to take over operations, it's been a near round-the-clock endeavor to keep the vineyard open. Even with both of us, it's beyond full-time. We could swing one, maybe two weeks, away, but anything more and the financial hit would be brutal.

Dad sits there watching me realize how difficult this is going to be and squeezes my hands.

And then I hear what he's really saying. *He* needs to go.

Not *we.*

My heart contracts painfully at the idea of never seeing Nonna again, but I haven't seen my grandmother since my own mother's funeral. It feels wrong to place my grief on the same level as Dad's right now. This is *his* mother. I swallow and nod numbly. "Of—of course, you should go. I can take care of things here while you're gone."

He purses his lips in a smile so soft, it's almost a grimace. "I know you can, my sweet Zoe Nicoletta. You won't be on your own, though. I've already arranged for someone to take my place while I'm gone."

"A replacement? Is that necessary?" My forehead knits together. Josiah, our vineyard hand, will gripe about it, but he can handle the farming work for a few weeks. "How long will you be gone?"

"As long as she needs me, Zoe Nicoletta."

"Dad." I stare into his woeful eyes, my heartbeat picking up in rhythm against my will. "What are you saying?"

"Paolo and the others cannot handle this on their own. They have lives in other towns, small children. Nonna deserves to die in peace, in the house she loves where she's spent her life. I can give her that."

"So you're—what . . . going to buy a one-way ticket?"

"I already have," Dad says softly.

"For when?" My voice cracks, the feelings rising like floodwaters within me.

"Saturday."

"That's two days from now!" I stand up so fast, the stool crashes behind me, and Dad jumps a little. "I'm sorry, I'm sorry, it's just . . ." I run my hands down my face. "This is all so fast. When were you going to tell me?"

He sighs and rubs the ridge of forehead above his eyebrows. "I wanted to wait until I had the replacement lined up so you wouldn't worry, Zoe Nicoletta. It's taken me longer than I thought, but I found someone who can handle the growing *and* the winemaking while I'm away. Someone extremely qualified." He smiles wistfully. "More than I am."

I blink at him, my thoughts and feelings clashing into each other like tectonic plates. How am I going to train some novice wannabe winemaker on top of everything else I already do? I *sell* wine, I can't make it. And no matter what Dad says, this replacement can't be anyone other than a total reject. I know this because we can't afford to pay anyone with real skill to take over Dad's responsibilities. Dad and I don't even pull down salaries— we just take what we need to live, and the rest goes back into the vineyard.

How the hell am I going to get the showcase now?

"Zoe, I'm so sorry, but Nonna needs this. I do, too." He stands and reaches for me. I let him pull me into his arms and press my hot cheek into his warm, soft chest, like he did when I was small. His forever smell— freshly baked bread and the sharp, sweet tang of crushed grapes—fills my nose, but instead of bringing me comfort, guilt roils inside. Here I am, panicking about business and timing and when Dad will return, as if that's not counting down the remaining days of Nonna's life. But this vineyard has always been more than a business to me. It's Mom. It's our family.

It's all I have.

"Okay, Dad." A single tear rolls down my cheek, and I pull away. "I've got a lot of work to do before my shift starts in the tasting room. We'll talk more later, okay?"

"Okay." Dad regards me with that soft, sad look, and I shuffle back to my office.

No three-ring binder can rescue this day now.

Cool winds whip around my ankles as I trudge up the hill to my little cottage at the back of the vineyard. It was a torturously slow day in the tasting room. I tried halfheartedly to brainstorm pitches for the showcase, but it's hard to be creative when your only grandparent is deathly ill, and the core of your business is leaving the country indefinitely. Dad promised to bring his replacement by to meet with me tomorrow, but I was too numb to ask any of the questions beating at the back door of my brain. Like who is this person? And even more importantly—how are we going to pay them? I heard Angry Bear Vineyards just fired a senior farmhand for stealing from the till—Robbie? Bobby? I guess I'll find out tomorrow when Dad brings him round because who else could it be? The Blue Ridge wine scene is *tiny*. If someone qualified was looking for work, I'd know. This is an absolute disaster.

I shoulder open my door and drop my bags of fresh, forgotten office supplies on the small table. I brought them home in the hopes that inspiration for the festival would hit but looking at the colorful page tabs still encased in their packaging is only making me feel worse. There are no ideas to organize. No brilliance to divide. *Fuck.* I know I'm wasting the precious head start Teddy gave me, but how can I plan when I don't know how I'm going to keep our doors open? If Dad is gone more than a few weeks, Bobby McThief will be responsible for bottling next year's whites in addition to nurturing our vines from leaf to bud to grape. If Dad's gone for a few months, this schmuck will have to blend our reds, too. And if Dad's gone until harvest . . .

I can't even *think* about that. It's practically a death sentence for this season's output, and whatever happens this year affects next year, which affects the following year, and the year after that. One bad year can wipe an unprepared vineyard out.

And a vineyard without a vintner? It doesn't get more unprepared than that.

I collapse onto my loveseat, letting the backs of my knees hang over the armrest, feet dangling lifelessly over the edge. When life's thrown me curveballs, I've always had our vineyard to pour myself into. That's the family way, after all. Dad turned his grief into work, and now I do, too. But when the vineyard's in trouble, where do I put this grief?

My phone buzzes from my pocket, making me flinch. I half expect it to be Rachel crowing she's found out about the festival, but it's . . .

Oh, shit.

FOR THE LOVE OF WINE, ZOE, HAVE SOME GODDAMN SELF-RESPECT

> Guess who's in town . . . 😉

Teddy got into my phone and changed my contact names again. I sigh out a small laugh that sounds anything but happy. After a second, I unlock my phone.

Zoe

> Hey, Harlow.

And then, after a pause:

Zoe

CHAPTER TWO

The tips of my short black hair are still wet from my shower when I arrive, chilled by the night air and curled against my neck. That's why I'm shivering at the door of Harlow's Airbnb. Definitely not from pre-bad-decision nerves. Her texts swim over me again, sending heat prickling up the back of my thighs.

FOR THE LOVE OF WINE, ZOE, HAVE SOME GODDAMN SELF-RESPECT

I have a proposition for you, darling.

FOR THE LOVE OF WINE, ZOE, HAVE SOME GODDAMN SELF-RESPECT

You, me, and my lovely friend from out of town.
Two blindfolds. One king-size bed. Tonight.

Zoe

👀

FOR THE LOVE OF WINE, ZOE, HAVE SOME GODDAMN SELF-RESPECT

Sending the address now. 🎭 🎭 🎭

A *threesome.* I've never had one before. So many breasts, one mouth. For once, the idea of multitasking thrills me.

But it's still a threesome with *Harlow.*

My fist hovers near the door. I feel so sheepish for abandoning my promises. Defeated, once again, by the siren song of being held by someone who knows me. Even though I know how this story ends, with Harlow on a plane and me in my office, filling the relationship-sized hole in my life with work until I forget it's there again, I knock anyway. There are a million kinds of love, and this is one of the only kinds I get.

A soft, tinkling laugh answers from within, then murmured talk. Footsteps. I try to banish all my feelings with a short, sharp exhale. When Harlow answers, it's with a smile so mischievous, so delightfully *familiar*, excitement stirs within my belly and my heart squeezes with fondness.

This is why Harlow's so dangerous. The fact that her petite frame is dressed in nothing more than a matte gray silk slip, her cheek resting lightly against the door as her stormy eyes travel over me, doesn't help.

"Come in," she commands, and I step across the threshold. She wraps her arms languidly around my neck, chills traveling up my back as she brings my face down to hers and takes my bottom lip gently into her mouth. She tastes like champagne feels: bubbly, electric, bright. I sigh into her and wrap my own arms around her waist, bringing her hips against mine. The skin-warmed silk glides beneath my cold fingers, aching for the heat of another.

She tilts her head back, breaking our kiss with a sly grin, and holds up a long strip of black. "Are you ready to meet my friend?"

"Is this a—I mean, so we're definitely going to wear—" My thoughts can't seem to cohere into sentences as she slips the blindfold over my eyes.

"It helps, when it's your first time." She nips at my earlobe and finishes tying it on. "I'll be there to guide you. You're safe with me."

And this is why I can never tell her no. I didn't admit this would be my first threesome, but I didn't have to. Harlow always meets me where I'm at, then gives me exactly what I need to escape my own skin. Like a rope thrown down into a deep, dark well, she rescues me from myself.

If only for a little while.

She leads me by the hand to the bedroom, her fingers entwined with mine. All I know about Harlow's friend is that she's a hot butch sommelier Harlow met out west on a "little break." Lina. *She's amazing,* Harlow had promised. *You'll love her.*

I'm less sure. I don't go for butches usually—not because I don't find them attractive, I *absolutely* do—but Charlaine Woods has always occupied that spot for me. My first queer crush was also my first butch. Soft curves smoothed down by sports bras and boyish hips hugged by men's denim, her high cheekbones kissed by sunshine and nothing else. She was beautiful on her own terms, not society's, and it felt completely radical at the time. To be yourself, to *like yourself,* in high school? Unheard of. No one else could really compare.

Can this other *she,* this Lina, see me right now? I fumble for my blindfold, but Harlow catches my hand, bites my palm. I gasp, and she whispers in my ear, sending heat to my center. "Don't worry, she's wearing one, too. Tonight is for feeling each other. Not self-consciousness." She pulls me inside the room and begins to undress me. "*Trust me.*"

My black jean jacket clatters to the floor, louder than I expect, but all my senses are heightened right now. Harlow dips one small hand beneath the rim of my jeans, and a sweet, urgent wish blooms in my belly. She uses the other hand to unbutton my jeans and push them to the floor. Her hands ripple over my body, finding the tension in my muscles, the fear. "Let *go.*"

Maybe it's because I'm the boss 24/7, in charge of everything in my life, making decisions and decisions and *always more decisions* nonstop. But nothing turns me on more than relinquishing my control to someone who's going to boss *me* around for once.

Someone who's going to make me come.

"Yes," I whisper, relaxing into Harlow's touch. She's got me down to my panties and white T-shirt, the black-and-white image of Stevie Nicks stretched across my breasts. When I picked out what to wear, I felt like the matron saint of hot women with big fuck-it energy would watch over me tonight. No bra because Harlow loves the look of my breasts barely constrained by thin cotton. I can feel her staring at me, and it feels *good*. The thought of Lina waiting on the bed, warm and present and *ready*, electrifies my blood. I want to find her. Feel her, too.

So I'm a threesome person. I had no clue.

Harlow guides me to the bed. When my bare knees bump against the soft duvet, I reach out and find other hands waiting for me, new hands. They're strong, supporting me as I climb onto the bed on my knees. Harlow groans softly.

"You two are so fucking hot." I can hear the rustle of her gray slip sliding over her short, white-blonde hair, then landing on the floor with a whisper. She scrambles onto the bed, laughing as she jostles us both by accident. We're facing each other, a triad on our knees. Harlow's laugh stops short, turns into a sharp breath in, as my left hand lightly trails down the slope of her small, upturned breast. Her skin rises to meet the soft brush of my knuckles, pebbling tight beneath my touch.

"I'm a goddamn genius," Harlow breathes, and whatever she's doing to Lina on her other side makes her groan low in agreement. Then a mismatched pair of hands finds each of my own breasts. Lina's strong hand is trembling and gentle, tracing the shape of my right breast, cupping it in her hand, while Harlow's touch is fierce and sure, a sharp pinch followed by the soft suck of her mouth through the shirt I'm still wearing. Familiar meets unfamiliar. The dichotomy of sensation thrills across my skin, my belly levitating within me. I don't have to touch myself to know that I'm slick and hot and ready to *go*.

Fuck New Year's. *Fuck* resolutions. Fuck denying myself this one thing I can have. I rip off my shirt, and then both of Lina's hands find me, palming my bare breasts with a gasp of desire. They fit in her hands almost perfectly, overflowing enough that her head dips forward into me; pressing her mouth against them in wild half-kisses, half-bites. My hands find the shaved sides of Lina's head, smooth like suede until they reach a flop of soft length. I dig my fingers in, trawling down her scalp as she ravishes my chest. I arch my back into her kisses while Harlow moves behind me. Her hard nipples blaze into me below my shoulder blades, explosions of feeling emanating from where her peaks press against my skin. When her small hands slide over my hip bones, traveling at diagonals down my panties, my hips thrust forward involuntarily, a cry escaping my lips. The pressure on the bed changes quickly, and then I feel Lina's soft hair brushing between my spread thighs, hot breath gusting upward before her teeth bite into my panties, pulling them down.

A liquid, molten tension tugs within me, begging for pressure, relief. Lina's on her back, her head between my legs. And so help me, if she licks me gently right now, a soft swipe of beaded tongue flirting with my need, I'll *scream*.

But Lina has mercy.

The ridge of her nose drives into me as she slides a finger inside, then two. I clench around them, crying out in gratitude while Harlow roughly yanks my panties the rest of the way off. The elastic band snaps against the tender flesh of my ass, and I like it so much, she does it again. Truly getting double-teamed right now, and I may not survive.

My hands clench into fists, needing to grab onto something—for balance, strength, the sheer desire to claim someone else's flesh for a while. With one hand, I stroke Lina's round, muscular shoulder, squeezing the firm skin hard, then running my hand across her chest. There the skin is slightly raised, my fingers unconsciously tracing the scar of a design inked into her skin.

Oh *god*, she's got chest tattoos? I practically purr as she moans into my swollen clit. With my other hand, I find Harlow behind me and slide my finger along her wet split, already spread wide in her kneeling position. Her clit responds to me first, tensing before her mouth whispers *yes, yes, yes* against my neck. She writhes against my back as I stroke her rhythmically in the way I know she likes, and this is intimacy, it *is*. It fills me to the brim with heat and longing and joy, real *joy*, when she comes wildly against me.

"I'm about to fuck you senseless," she rasps into my ear before standing. "I'll be back—getting my favorite dick."

I hear Harlow scamper out of the room, leaving Lina and me alone. For an instant, I hesitate—are we supposed to wait for her? The disappointing thought disappears, though, when Lina takes my entire clit into her mouth and *sucks*. It's such a punch of pleasure, I fall forward, into her, between her legs, greedy to have her all to myself. I'm so used to my blindfold now, so aware of *her*, I yank off what feels like cotton boxer briefs without any trouble at all. She lifts her ass, helping me along, and I catch the first smell of her. I moan into her flesh as I lick, overwhelmed with the heat of this stranger whose touch ignites my every nerve ending. How can you know someone this intimately yet have no idea who they are?

Lina feels amazing, and I can't help myself from exploring the hard planes of her stomach, the strong, thick thighs cradling my head. God, I've been an idiot avoiding butch women this long. It's more than just looks, obviously—I can't even see her. It's the rough grip of her hands on my hips, guiding me with a confidence that tells me we *will get* to where we're going. If Harlow's movements are teasing and lush, Lina's are commanding: focused, deliberate, burning with want. My body melts against her. I wrap my hands beneath her, and her ass is perfect in my grasp. I squeeze it again and again as I lick her front to back, learning where she likes my touch, then punishing her for giving me that knowledge. The way she vibrates against me, this butch wants to be teased. She's in charge, but longs to be undermined, so I toy with her, my tongue so close to the ache I'm building that she whimpers. My fingers scrabble around the curve of her ass until they reach her wet pussy, tugging, pulling her apart, forcing her to give all of herself to me. She can't help but obey.

It sends her *flying* over the edge. Lina's tongue goes erratic against my clit as she comes apart beneath me, her groan ecstatic and furious.

She didn't want to come first, and I am in trouble for it. I can tell by the renewed command she exerts on my hips, the frenzied determination with which she pins me down, making me squirm with want for her. Her strong hands put me exactly where she wants me, not playing now, and she attacks me with broad, fierce licks with the flat of her tongue and sharp, focused sucks, and then I am coming, too. Coming *hard*, relentlessly, grinding into her chin for relief. I cry into her, keening as each wave of electric pleasure travels from my epicenter in both directions, to the roots of my hair, the tips of my toes.

"Li-*Lina*!"

She laughs softly against me, her voice low and smug and husky. "It's Laine, baby."

Laine. *Laine?*

Ice-cold adrenaline shoots through my veins before my brain can pinpoint what's freaking it out. So I didn't get her name right, so I—

It's Laine, baby. That voice plays again in my head, terrifyingly familiar. I gasp and roll off her, expecting the bed to catch me.

Instead, there's a long fall to the wooden floor.

Oof!

I land on my naked ass, the cabin's smooth, wooden floor spanking me hard like the gym coach's paddle when he caught me skipping class with Rachel that time (corporal punishment in school persisted way too long in Georgia). Rachel had texted her sister to pick us up, but we got caught before Charlaine rolled into the parking lot.

I rip off my blindfold, breathing too quickly.

Lina—no, *Laine*—sits up, and I watch with horror as the absolute sex-bomb that just fucked me better than I've ever been in my life takes off her own blindfold. Her soft brown eyes rove over me, concerned. "Shit, are you okay?"

"Oh. My. God," I hoarse out, then scoot backward on my sore ass. *"Charlaine?!"*

Charlaine Woods, Rachel's big sister, my first crush, the First Lesbian I Ever Perceived for God's sake, stares down at me, confused as hell. Her eyebrows furrow as she tilts her head. "Do I . . . know you?" Her lips quirk to the side. "I mean, from before just now when I made you scream the wrong name." She reaches down from the bed, offering a hand to help me up. Pure boss energy rolls off her, and I want to hide under something.

I stare at her outstretched hand, my mouth slightly open, unable to think of what to say. I couldn't talk in front of Charlaine when we were in high school, either. She reduced me to a pile of jittering nerve endings every time, but I'm an adult now, and that quiet, insecure Zoe is years behind me. Come on, brain. *Think!*

But then Harlow bursts into the room wearing the most impressive strap-on I've ever seen outside of a catalogue, and modern language is out of my reach.

"Hey," Harlow exclaims, putting her hands on her hips. "You took your masks off!"

Maybe it's being eye-level with a giant rainbow dick, but that shocks me out of my stupor. I scramble to my feet.

"What's your name again?" Laine squints as she tries, and fails, to place my face.

I momentarily consider lying. Lying could work. Then Harlow's dildo grazes my ass, and I remember she's here, too.

Lying won't work.

"Zoe. Rachel's best friend growing up?" The words fall out in a jumble.

Laine's frown grows. She doesn't remember me at all? I know she pretended we didn't exist, but I was at her house every weekend of my young life. Laine drags a hand through her doe-brown hair, shaved on both sides. The move highlights the lean line of muscles in her arm, and my belly flips involuntarily. But her face remains firmly confused.

A piece of young Zoe's heart crumbles inside of me.

I run my hands down my face because I know the one thing that'll make her remember in an instant, and I don't want to own it. At all. "Rachel's friend that went to prom with Chance. The one who—who went to the after party and drank too much?"

Laine's eyes widen with a jolt. "Oh fuck!" She covers her mouth and laughs. "Oh my god, I remember you now. Chop Chop, right? You're *gay?*"

"Whoa, whoa, whoa." Harlow waves her hands at us. "You *know* each other?" She hiccups out a delighted laugh. "I didn't know you were from Blue Ridge, Laine!"

"Yeah," Laine says slowly, beginning to grin. "Zoe dated my twin brother in high school."

"You *what?*" Harlow's laughing harder, and my whole body's turning red, which everyone can see because I'm still *naked*. "I didn't think you had a straight bone in your body, Zoe Brennan!"

"It was just prom the one time, and I—*ugh*—you told me her name was Lina!"

"No, I definitely said Laine. You must've read it wrong."

Laine suddenly stops laughing, her face going pale. "Wait. Zoe *Brennan?*"

There it is. She remembers who I am now, all right. All my personas have compiled. The adoring neighbor kid who stared at her like she held all the answers to every question. Rachel's scrawny best friend. The confused drunk teen who humiliated herself in front of everyone at prom. Standing here naked, all the past versions of me that I've purposefully banished are pulled out on display once more in front of the perfect *Charlaine Woods*. I feel like the ground beneath an avalanche—breathless, cold, trapped.

"Zoe! Don't freak out," Harlow manages between laughs. "It's just a funny coincidence!"

"I—I'm sorry, I've got to go. Big morning tomorrow!" I stammer out as I jump up and down trying to squeeze into my jeans only to realize one leg's half turned inside out. I throw my jacket on over my topless breasts and grab my T-shirt—*thanks for nothing, Stevie Nicks*—and step into my black boots, not bothering to zip them up. Harlow runs after me, but my last glimpse of Laine is her sitting with her back pressed against the headboard, eyes fully spooked. I can't get out of here fast enough.

Fuck, fuck, *fuck!*

CHAPTER THREE

The knocking on my cottage door feels like somebody pounding on the lid of my coffin, summoning me from the dead.

This zombie does *not* want to rise.

I groan and roll over, curling into a ball of human *ughhhh*. I couldn't escape last night's mortification even in my melatonin-induced coma. Dream after dream replayed the event from different angles, torturing me. The amazing sex, Laine's horrified face, Harlow laughing while her rainbow dick swayed like a gay elephant's trunk.

I gingerly run my hand over my bruised backside and wince. Last night literally kicked my ass.

And yet, the knocking continues. I squint at the clock—eight a.m.—and sigh. I'm usually an early riser. I love working in the morning, when my brain's freshest and the day's problems haven't crowded out my creativity yet. But I took enough melatonin to bring down that gay elephant, and I feel hung over. From the sleep aid, from embarrassment, from the most mind-blowing sex of my life. I grab the water bottle by my bed and drain it. Being that thoroughly turned on dehydrates a woman.

"Zoe Brennan, are you alive in there? Why aren't you in your office organizing your highlighters?!"

Despite everything, I smile. Hannah Tate is the only person in the world I can handle seeing right now. She's well acquainted with feeling like a disaster and always manages to walk me back from whatever dark mood's gripped me that day.

I hobble to the door and find her standing there, a giant three-ring binder pressed to her chest.

"Good morning," I hoarse out as I let her in, then move into my tiny kitchen to click the electric kettle on.

"Sweet Jesus on a biscuit, what happened to you?" Hannah looks vaguely alarmed as she takes in my mussed hair, two-legged limp, and dead eyes. She shuts the door behind her, which is good because I'm still in my tiny Stevie Nicks T-shirt and a pair of panties. At least those are fresh.

Fresh-ish.

"Long, horrible story." I make a cup of Darjeeling tea before throwing an extra pillow on the couch and easing my sore ass onto it. "You don't want to hear."

"Of course I want to hear!" Hannah tosses the binder down and sits across from me.

I frown at her. "What's that?"

"Oh, this?" Her words peter out into a sigh. "River's inspiration material for our Tolkienesque wedding so you can start the planning here." She air quotes *Tolkienesque* as though the term's been debated mightily.

"He's really sticking with that, huh?"

Hannah blinks. "I thought he was joking at first, but 'he has a vision.'" She checks her watch. "Come on, Brennan. Spill the story and make it fast. You've got a vineyard tour in thirty minutes."

I let out a sigh that excavates my insides. The treehouse my cousin River built and Hannah now manages for us must've been booked last minute. I should be grateful for the extra revenue, but all I feel is depleted. I sip my tea, weighing the pros and cons. I don't usually like to share personal things like this, even with Hannah. It's not about trust or privacy— it's just that talking about feelings always has the unfortunate side effect of making them *real* to me.

But last night was so mortifying, it needs an exorcism. I take a deep breath. "Did I ever tell you about Charlaine Woods—Rachel's big sister?"

"No. Why?"

"Well. Charlaine was the 'First Lesbian' I ever knew, and last night I fucked her by accident."

Hannah's eyebrows rise. "There's a lot to unpack there. Proceed."

Most queer folks have the same set of core stories—when they first knew, how they came out, the first crushing discrimination they experienced—but my favorite tale is hearing about the First Lesbian, the Alpha Queer, the first person you recognized as living the outer experience that matched your heart's inner longing.

And mine's Charlaine Woods. Star soccer player, effortlessly cool, completely aloof in this charming way that made you want her golden-brown eyes to stop their wandering and settle on you. What got me most of all was how entirely in control she was—of herself, how she felt, the situation. She was more self-possessed at seventeen than most adults I know, and *God*, so ambitious. I was obsessed with her. Rachel's perfect older sister, the subject of my queer longing before I even knew what the word meant. All I knew was that something rang a bell within me every time I saw her, some note of shared existence. The First Lesbian. *My* Alpha Queer.

Maybe I wasn't alone, after all.

The story of last night's threesome spills out the way the juiciest confessions to priests must, desire and carnal lust burdened with shame and regret. When I'm done, Hannah sits back and whistles.

"I can't believe you had sex with your first crush—the *First Lesbian*, no less," Hannah says in awe. "That's like accidentally climbing Mt. Everest, emotionally speaking."

I give Hannah an annoyed look. "She was my first queer crush, that's all."

Hannah snorts. "You just told me more about Charlaine Woods than anyone you've ever dated. Well, except for Harlow Benoit, maybe. For you to have a threesome with those two?" She crosses her arms behind her head and smirks. "You should go ahead and vow your abstinence now. Nothing's ever going to compare to last night."

I start to argue but can't. "*Fuck.*" I cradle my tired face in my hands. "It was so mortifying, Hannah. I never want to see Laine again."

"Do you have to? Doesn't she live out west?"

"Yeah, maybe she'll leave soon." I wonder how long I need to live underground until she returns to California, and I can live in peace again.

"What exactly is so embarrassing for you, anyways? Is it the association with the prom thing?" Hannah uncrosses her arms and sits forward eagerly. "Are you *finally* going to tell me about what happened with Chance Woods that night?"

I eye her warily. "If I tell you, do you promise to never bring it up, ever?"

"I promise." Hannah crosses her heart, then pulls her wavy hair into a pile on the top of her head and secures it with a pen. "Gotta hear every word of this," she explains. "Go ahead."

"So Chance and Charlaine are twins and two years older than me. I was a sophomore their senior year."

"Were you still friends with Rachel then?"

"No." I huff out a breath. "Once she realized I had a crush on Charlaine, she stopped talking to me altogether."

"She friend-dumped you because you're *gay*?"

"No, pretty sure it was because I was gay *for Charlaine*, which to Rachel was as good as sleeping with the enemy. Aunt Bri had started to suspect I was queer, too." River's mom, my Aunt Bri, had stepped in to help care for me during my dad's darkest days after my mom died, and while she meant well, she was a gun-toting conservative. When her suspicions about my sexuality were confirmed years later, she disowned me, and River stood up for me, leading to the dissolution of their own relationship when she wouldn't welcome me back into the family because of her "values." Which I guess amounts to Dicks and Vaginas 4-Eva, because Aunt Bri shoved me toward any boy that showed interest in me prior to that. Starting with Chance Woods.

"Why? How did Bri know?" Hannah asks gently. While she's had her own issues with her mom, Trish, over the years, Trish has never judged a person in her life, and Hannah's sensitive to how much Aunt Bri, my mother's only sister, hurt me.

"There were some . . . browser windows I left open on my laptop." I clear my throat. "Aunt Bri had my password. I didn't know."

"Shit."

"I was able to lie my way out of it, said they must have been pop-up spam. But she watched me after that, and when she heard Chance asked me to prom, she came over that night with a big, poufy dress and a bag full of new makeup."

"Saying no wasn't an option," Hannah murmurs, and I nod.

"So I went, and it was fine. Chance is a good guy, and he mostly hung out with his friends anyway. It was the after party when things went to hell."

I take a deep breath, the cringe already rising within me like the tide. "I'd made this dumb decision when I said yes to Chance. He's Charlaine's twin, right? They're not identical obviously, but they look a lot alike. He was nice, into me, and the socially acceptable version of who I really wanted. I thought, maybe I should have sex with *him* and finally prove whether I'm gay or not. But I was nervous, so when someone handed me a red Solo cup full of beer, I drank it. And another. And another."

Hannah leans forward. "That asshole didn't do anything to you, did he?"

"No, no, no. It was me. I did the . . . things." I squeeze my eyes shut. "I found him outside playing beer pong, and I pulled him aside. And in front of the entire senior class, I said . . . I said . . ." I groan at the ceiling.

"Come on, Zoe. You can tell me."

"I said, 'Okay, let's go have the sex.'"

"*No.*" Hannah's eyes bug wide. "*The* sex?!"

"Then I clapped my hands, Hannah, I *clapped my fucking hands*, and said, 'Chop chop.' And then, I threw up in the pool."

Hannah doesn't let go of my hands, but her mouth falls open. A startled laugh escapes. "Chop . . . *chop*? Oh, Zoe!"

"Charlaine was right there, she saw everything. Everyone did." I throw back the rest of my hot tea. "They called me Chop Chop for the rest of high school."

Tears are streaming down Hannah's cheeks as her chest quakes with the effort of holding back laughter. "That's *terrible*, Zoe, oh my GOD!"

I breathe deeply through my nose, then snort, and that's all it takes for Hannah to fully lose control.

"I'm—so—sorry," she says between gasps, "to laugh at your—your—*trauma!*"

I roll my eyes. "It's not trauma. Well, not anymore at least." Chance and I have even laughed about it at local wine events. Most people who knew me then and know me now as the proud, hot lesbian that I am think it's pretty hilarious and was an obvious sign of what was to come. But it doesn't change the fact that Charlaine saw me say *that* to her twin *brother* and knows me better as *Chop Chop* than Zoe.

"Okay, babe." Hannah stands up, wiping away the tears from her eyes. "If you want to shower before the tour, you better go now."

I grumble into my empty mug, and Hannah extends a hand to me. "Come on." She bites her lip, the words hovering there, and I glare at her. "*Hann—*"

"Chop Chop," she squeaks, then absolutely loses it.

Hannah giggles all the way down to the vineyard's parking lot. I forgive her, but only because I love her. She hugs me tight.

"Don't think about the embarrassing parts, Zoe." She pulls away and runs her hands over my hair. "You're amazing, and I guarantee you that's all Laine and Harlow are thinking about right now. Not the fact you—"

"Han-*nah*! You promised you wouldn't bring it up all the time."

"—ever . . . said . . . things," she finishes brightly. I give her a scathing look, and laughing, she waves goodbye.

Hannah's words provide comfort, though. The sex was objectively amazing, and Laine's a big-time vintner out west. She's probably visiting her folks for a few days before the growing season starts, then she'll disappear into the sunset again. Who knows? Maybe she'll look me up next time she's in town, too, and I'll have another chance to make her see stars. The idea heats me up from the inside out.

I hustle over to the tasting room where our tours usually begin, feeling more in control of the situation already. A few minutes pass, though, and nobody shows up. There's a rental car parked near the treehouse, but the guest isn't here, and neither is Dad. Maybe they already started? My phone buzzes from my pocket, and I pull it out to check the message. Could be the guest.

WARNING, it's that bitch Rachel

The jig is up, Brennan. I found out about the Everyday Bon Vivant festival.

WARNING, it's that bitch Rachel

Might as well prepare your concession speech
now because that showcase is mine.

I suck a deep breath in through my nostrils. Head start officially squandered.

And I have no vintner.

I mouth *Fuck!* at my phone. I can't show weakness, though. Can't let her know anything's wrong. I'm not ready to concede *yet*.

Zoe

It's on, Rachel.

Zoe

P.S. T.J. Maxx has decorative roosters on
sale 2 for 1, thought you should know.

I shove my phone in my pocket and speed-walk along our normal tour route, but there's nobody in the vineyard blocks, either. A murmur of voices escapes from the winery, making me frown. While we bring guests into the front of the winery to get a glimpse of the racks of pretty barrels and the precious few stainless-steel tanks we have, the voices are coming from the back, behind the plastic sheeting divide, where Dad's worktable and the uglier plastic tote bins that comprise most of our wine storage are. There are exactly zero selfie-backdrop opportunities in there. What's Dad playing at?

As I draw closer, I catch a snip of conversation:

"—it's the Pinot Noir. My wife blended it with our Norton crops just so . . . Most beautiful body on your tongue—a few bottles left, yes . . . treasured, you see, and very important to Zoe . . ."

That's even stranger. Dad *never* mentions Mom to vineyard guests. It's too loaded a subject for him, too painful, so we go through life pretending that every inch of this place isn't imbued with her spirit, memories, and laughter. I push aside the plastic sheeting and see a flop of light brown hair bobbing thoughtfully to what my dad's saying.

Laine? Laine's our treehouse guest?

A strangled sound of alarm rumbles in my throat, and both their heads turn in unison.

She *is*.

It's unfair how good some people look. Last night, all I saw of Laine was her tanned skin and the inky tattoos that drape across her muscular frame like they're grateful to be there, but it was in the middle of an existential crisis. It's a wonder my brain didn't explode on the spot. Her slim, athletic build always made me sigh in juvenile longing in high school, but years spent working in vineyards under the California sun have filled her out. She's in a pair of tight, straight-legged trousers, subtly textured, a camel-brown leather belt cinched around her narrow hips. The shirt is a pale blue button-down, cut slim and made of a matte, buttery fabric that appears structured until I realize it's the line of her strong shoulders holding it so perfectly in place. A pair of thick, tortoiseshell glasses sits on her long, straight nose, her doe-brown hair waved perfectly to the side, and I involuntarily suck in a breath at how blazing hot she looks.

Professorial butch, a pro*found* new weakness. Noted.

I'm suddenly aware of my bare face, my black bob left wavy from the quick shower, and the truly giant sweater I'm currently retreating into. Laine adjusts her glasses slowly, her eyes tracking it all, and a blush wraps around my neck, flooding my cheeks with heat.

"Ah, Zoe Nicoletta! There you are!" Dad gestures for me to join them. "Do you remember little Charlaine Woods from down the road?"

A flash of muscle memory *zings* from my core up my spine, like every nerve ending in my body decided to squeal *yes!* all at once.

"I do." The echo of last night's ride against *big Charlaine Woods* makes my words come out low and breathy. "Hello, Charlaine."

A kiss of peach appears high on her cheekbones, her deep brown eyes heating.

"It's Laine," she says, a real-life déjà vu, only this time she doesn't call me baby. Her lips twitch, as though she's not sure whether to smile. Why is she here? Our vineyard tour is optional for our Treebnb guests—she didn't need to sign up for the first slot. Unless . . .

She *wanted* to see me?

Excitement tugs low and warm in my belly.

"I still remember when Molly and Ezra brought you and Chance home from the hospital," Dad says, a sentimental twinkle in his eyes, completely oblivious to the sexual energy thrumming between us. "And now, look at you! All grown up."

My eyes linger on her full mouth, before flickering up to meet her gaze. "Sure are."

An eyebrow lifts barely, amusement flashing on Laine's face before disappearing beneath professional neutrality. She clears her throat. "Cosimo was about to show me where you age your whites."

"Here, of course—this is our cold storage area!" Dad points to the window A/C unit rigged to blast cold air at 55 degrees year-round, then to the plastic sheeting flaps that keep the cold air in. "Much more cost effective than a glycol system, eh?" Dad winks.

Laine startles like a patient on the operating table who's just realized her surgeon got licensed virtually from Phoenix University. "How resourceful." She stares at the plastic totes with clear dismay. I sigh.

This is why we don't bring guests back here. People don't want to know how wine gets made at scrappy little vineyards like ours. It's not pretty.

"A little different from Le Jardin's winery operations, I imagine." I give her a little smile, trying to telepathically assure her that we know we're small potatoes compared to the ultra-prestigious Napa vineyard she's used to.

But Laine winces at my words. She quickly recovers with a tight nod, but I saw something there. Before I can make any sense of it, Dad laughs and shakes his head. "A Le Jardin vintner, here in our winery! Just think of it!"

I snap my head to look at him as he steps between us, placing a hand on each of our shoulders. "You'll be a *fantastic* replacement for me as Blue-bell's chief vintner. Welcome aboard, Laine!"

CHAPTER FOUR

Queer Mountaineers Who Occasionally Drink Beer

Queer Steering Committee

Diego

This is good news, right? You need a new vintner, and your dad hired a very sexy, very competent one. I don't see the problem!

Zoe

As a woman of business, I don't sleep with my employees.

Tristan

Can confirm. 👍

Teddy

I canNOT believe you texted Harlow!

Zoe

I didn't! She texted ME. And I was upset about my Nonna.

Hannah

Aww, Zoe. Next time text me! We'll come give you hugs.

Zoe

Not the kind of hugs
I was hoping for last night.

Tristan

She wanted vagina hugs.

Hannah

. . .

Zoe

. . .

Zoe

I'll let that one slide, Stan, since you're
not versed in sex with women.

Teddy

 Giving you a gap between your teeth next time you come in.

Tristan

Okay. Vulva hugs.

Hannah

There ya go, champ. 💯

Zoe

Hannah, why didn't you tell me a
"Laine Woods" booked the Treebnb?!

Hannah

I didn't know, I swear! Your dad entered the booking himself.

Zoe

Wait.

Zoe

How long is the booking for?

Hannah

He blocked the calendar for the next eight months . . .

Zoe

WHAT?!

Zoe

WHAT?!

Zoe

WHAT?!

Diego

Uh-oh. You broke Zoe.

Hannah

Doesn't mean Laine will DEFINITELY be staying in your treehouse for all that time. He probably blocked it off until after harvest to be safe.

Zoe

"Dad, listen. We need to—" I burst through the office door, then stop cold, the words dying on my lips. Because it isn't Dad leaning casually against my desk.

It's Laine.

"What are you doing in here?" I quickly shut the door behind me, which is a mistake because now the room's even smaller. Laine's tall, confident presence fills it til it's overflowing.

"Waiting for you," Laine says simply. "We should talk. About last night."

Now my entire body's blushing. I press my back against the door, as though creating space between us will make this less awkward. But this is *my* office. *My* vineyard. I can't let her walk in here and control me with her gaze. I stand up straighter, then move with conviction past her to my desk and sit. "Yes, we do. Please, have a seat."

There, boss-bitch status restored.

Laine sits, and I almost wish she hadn't. The way she spreads her legs, leaning forward to rest her elbows on her knees, looking at me through those professor glasses, makes me want more vulva hugs. I clear my throat, but before I can speak, she launches in.

"Look, I don't know what that was about back there"—she gestures behind her at the winery where I *clearly* faked getting a call and ran away to scream-text my friends—"but you need me to take this job, so let's figure this out and get past it, Brennan."

I fold my arms and sit back in my chair. For as long as I can remember, Charlaine Woods has rendered me unable to speak in her presence. Part of the reason she didn't know who the hell I was until I ordered her brother to get an erection in front of her senior class, probably. But I left that sweet, shy little Zoe behind years ago, and Zoe Brennan, Director of Operations for Bluebell Vineyards, isn't taking *any* of her shit. "I'm well aware of what I need, *Woods.*"

Laine's head is cocked to the left, her face thoughtful as she tries to decipher my words. Perhaps I should be clearer. I let the chair spin to the side so that I can cross my legs, noticing how her gaze follows their long line.

Mm-hmm. Exactly as I suspected.

She catches *me* catching *her* look, and I raise both my eyebrows, point made. "How are *we* supposed to run this vineyard together as professionals after last night?"

"It was an accident." Laine blushes. "I *swear* I didn't know who you were until I heard your last name."

I huff. "Yes, I remember your look of horror when you finally realized who I was, too."

Laine puts her face in her hands and sighs. "I'm sorry. I don't usually fuck my new boss the night before my interview."

There's something about the words *fuck* and *my new boss* coming out of Laine's full lips in reference to *me* that sends a wave of heat crashing through me. My sore ass tingles beneath my cuffed jeans, as if to say *what about now? Do you fuck your new boss* after *your interview?*

"Why do you even want this job, though? What about Le Jardin?"

Laine sits up straight and clears her throat. "I'm on a temporary leave of absence from Le Jardin. I'm not coming back to Georgia to relocate or anything." She says *relocate* like it's physically unpleasant to taste. "I just . . . came into this free time, and I've missed my family. When my parents asked me to do this favor for Cosimo, it seemed like the right time to come home and reconnect, get to know Chance's kids better." She shrugs, but her voice is tight, constrained, like whatever feelings bubbling within her about this development have been fermenting for a while.

I blink at her and the windfall she's presenting. A favor to my family exactly when we need it most? And it's not some disgraced vineyard hand that'll be making our wines, either—Laine's a trained and celebrated young vintner who works at one of the most prestigious vineyards in the country. The timing is almost unbelievable.

"Wait. When *exactly* did you learn about my dad leaving?" I lean forward, hands flat on the desk.

Laine squints, considering. "About three weeks ago?"

Three weeks? Dad knew three weeks ago that he was leaving, and he waited until *yesterday* to tell me?

"Hey, are you okay?" Laine reaches out to put her hand on mine, bringing me crashing back into the present. The concern in her golden-brown eyes makes a knot rise in my throat.

"I'm—fine. It's just you knew before I did." I swallow. "I found out yesterday, actually. It's part of why . . . last night I needed to . . . Well. It's been a lot to process."

"Oh, shit," Laine breathes out, and her shared surprise at how Dad's handled this feels validating, but also suspiciously like pity. I pull my hand back, and Laine straightens in her seat immediately.

I blow out a breath and get my business face back on. "Okay, here's the deal. We need a vintner to make it through this harvest with the vineyard intact, and you're the only option we have unless I want to hire Bobby the thief."

"Bobby the *who*—?"

"What did Dad promise to pay you? He doesn't usually handle the money, and I'm concerned I may not be able to honor whatever he's promised you."

Laine bites her lips, a crack of nervous energy spidering its way across her cool demeanor. "He said I could stay in the vineyard's treehouse rent-free plus forty hours a week at minimum wage."

My mouth drops open a degree. *That's all?* I can't believe Laine agreed to work for so little, but then again, with housing included, it's not a horrible deal . . . Kudos to Dad, too, because it's one we can afford. Barely, but still. "And that . . . works for you?"

"For now, yes."

"Okay. Deal." I hold my hand out to shake, then yank it back just as Laine reaches for mine. "On one condition, though."

Laine looks at me warily. "What?"

"Your sister is my sworn enemy. I need to know you're loyal to Bluebell Vineyards, that you'll work hard for us and put our interests first, especially when it comes to getting the *Everyday Bon Vivant* showcase. Does that affect your decision?"

Laine's face tenses, and a flash of anxiety illuminates her eyes, disappearing just as fast. "*Everyday Bon Vivant* is coming here? To Blue Ridge?"

Napa-trained Laine is nervous about *Everyday Bon Vivant*?

"Yes, for their annual festival after harvest," I say slowly, trying to unpack the confusing emotions scuttling across her face. "Bluebell has a good chance to win the local showcase spot. It's my top goal this year, and if you work here, you're on *my* team, not your family's, favor be damned. If you can agree to all that, then we have a deal."

"Deal," Laine agrees, but the hesitation lingering in her voice unsettles me. What part of what I said is holding her back? *Everyday Bon Vivant* or being on my team?

She reaches out, and her hand shakes mine like it wasn't *inside* me last night. A small, perfunctory smile appears on her face. "I'm going to make this vineyard shine, wait and see."

I frown. "We already shine." Sure, our sweet, simple wines are for basics, but basics love wine, too. Bluebell Vineyards believes in providing accessible happy juice for everyone, not just sexy California wine snobs.

Laine opens her mouth to say something, but my *you-sure-about-that?* expression makes her think better of it. After a long pause, she says, "Sure."

Still feels like an insult.

"Oh, and about last night . . ."

My pulse picks up in speed. "Yes?"

Laine smiles down at me. "We're both adults, and we can leave it in the past and forget it ever happened. Sound good?"

My grip on her slackens, the handshake losing momentum. The tentative smile, the hope in her eyes, her entire body posture's begging me to be cool about this. And why shouldn't I? I've certainly had enough practice with flings that go nowhere, with being set aside.

"Yeah. Of course." Young Zoe couldn't handle Charlaine Woods so much as looking her way, but I can rise to this occasion. Laine tending to my vines, making my wine, living on my property?

No problem. It's not like I have a crush on her *now*.

Her palm is warm against mine, but it still sends tiny shivers up my arm and through my core. She lets go of my hand abruptly, as though she just realized she was still holding it.

Rich, buttery smells greet me as I jiggle the door open to the house I grew up in. Dad's making my favorite comfort food—a decadent butternut squash lasagna—for our last dinner together before he leaves.

I slide into my chair at the small pedestal table that's sat in the corner of our kitchen for as long as I can remember. The table's set for two tonight, but Mom's chair is still there, painted in the sunset's last pink rays filtering in from the big window overlooking our vineyard. God, it's a sight out there. The newly budding vines are kissed by gold, the hills beyond limned with lavender and the coming night. Mom's memory is etched into the view itself. How many times did we sit here, staring out into all that's ours, waiting for Dad's latest culinary adventure to arrive at the table? My heart aches as it always does knowing she's no longer here to share it, but over the years, the hurt's grown soft and pliant, its sharp, jagged edges worn smooth by time. If anything, the ache of losing her has become part of Bluebell's beauty. This place was always part of her, but now, she's part of it, too.

I could never leave. I used to think Dad felt the same, but his old, leather suitcases are waiting by the door.

A bottle of red sits in the middle of our table, along with a corkscrew. The label is yellowed and crumbly at the edges, one of the last remaining bottles of Mom's famous red blend, vintage 2004. The best season, best grapes, best batch. There are only a handful left.

This is Dad's custom on special occasions—he places one of our last treasured bottles on the table as an invitation, but I rarely accept. The last one we opened was after my college graduation eight years ago, when I returned to take my place at the vineyard beside him. While Dad leaving for Italy is certainly momentous, these last tastes of Mom's genius should be in celebration, not consolation. I get up and pull a half-empty bottle of C'est la Grigio out of the fridge and bring it to the table instead. Maybe I'll open one of Mom's reds to celebrate if we get the showcase.

No. *When* we get it. A small smile blooms on my face, and I feel a little better. My old ambition is a warm blanket wrapped around cold shoulders. I simply don't know how to be myself without it. These last few days, the March winds cut deeper, the weak, watery daylight unable to banish the chill that set in with the news of Nonna's illness and Dad's indefinite trip. But sitting in our cozy, humid kitchen, ringed with bookcases stuffed with Mom's old wine journals and Dad's spy novels, my ambition stirs again. We have a vintner. And a real chance.

With oven mitts up to his elbows, Dad sets the steaming lasagna onto a folded towel on the table. He returns carrying a simple arugula salad with shaved parmesan, dressed in truffle oil and lemon, and sighs with satisfaction as he slides into his chair.

"Dad, this smells amazing. Thanks for cooking."

He waves a hand at me and mumbles *it's nothing!* in the obligatory Italian way, even though he's been in the kitchen for hours. We tuck in quietly, the evening now purple and dreamy outside.

After a few minutes of thoughtful chewing, Dad asks, "So, what's this news you have?"

"Hmm?" I'm deep in food admiration right now.

"Before I told you about Nonna." Dad reaches for his glass of wine. "You had news, too."

"Oh, right." I twist my fork in the lasagna. "Do you remember when we went to the *Everyday Bon Vivant* food and wine festival in the Finger Lakes? When I was a kid?"

Dad's face slackens as the memory inhabits him. "What a trip that was. Your mother discovered ice wine. You discovered poutine." He huffs, a rueful sound. "I'm not sure who vomited more."

"Right . . . Well, remember how much fun it was? *Before* the vomiting?"

"Of course." His gaze has turned fully inward now, eyes welling at the memories of my mother when they were young and in love, our family whole. I know the look well. He wears it every day, after all.

I exhale a small, patient breath and take his hand, willing him to rejoin me in the present. This is what it's like living with Cosimo Rossi Giura-traboccetti. Half loving father, half living memorial to my mother. He says it's our Italian blood that makes him so romantic, but I'm half Italian and I've never said *I love you* to someone I don't share DNA with. I haven't even gotten close, my longest relationship spanning a whopping two months.

"Dad, *Everyday Bon Vivant* is coming here, to Blue Ridge. They're scouting for vineyards to host the local showcase." I gently shake his hand, like I'm trying to wake him without scaring him. "I'm going to convince them to have it here."

"That's wonderful," he says, returning to me at last. "We should collaborate with Into the Woods, see if together we can nab the spot."

"Dad, *we* need to win, not Into the Woods. I can't collaborate with *Rachel*."

Dad shakes his head sadly. "You used to be so close. Maybe it's time you made up?"

I roll my eyes. "For the millionth time, Dad, Rachel's the one who woke up one day and decided she hates my guts. Besides, we don't need Into the Woods's help to win."

He frowns. "But their wines are better than ours."

"So?" I cross my arms. "Our vibes are better. Our views are better. We're more fun, more accessible, more creative." My voice is rising in both pitch and volume, but this gets under my skin more than any of Dad's other bullshit. He should be loyal to *our* vineyard. But when Mom died, Dad's love for this place started to, as well. This was their dream, the magic they made together in the warm Appalachian sun. But doesn't he realize that I made this my dream, too? That it's all I have?

Dad's frown softens. "Yes, all that is true, and it's because of your hard work, Zoe Nicoletta. I'm sorry. Of course I want them to choose Bluebell Vineyards." The corner of his mouth quirks up, though it's not with a smile. "It's a good thing Laine came along when she did. Maybe with her making our wine, we'll have a better chance."

My jaw tenses, and he takes my hand. I'm still angry Laine knew Dad was going to Italy to be with my sick grandmother before I did. *Weeks* before.

"Why didn't you tell me earlier, Dad?"

His calloused hand closes around mine. "I wasn't sure I'd go through with it if I couldn't find someone to take care of you."

A sigh exits me with force. "Laine isn't taking care of me. She's going to keep the vines happy and make some wine. That's it."

"Yes, yes, but I know how important Bluebell is to you, Zoe Nicoletta. I couldn't leave without knowing it would be well-cared for, because that's how I take care of *you*."

I swallow, surprised, though I guess I shouldn't be. I've been showing my love for Dad through the vineyard for ages. Not many twelve-year-olds spend their Saturdays cleaning wine barrels, but after Mom died, when I had no clue how to help my grieving father, I'd sit next to him and scrub until my arms ached. I didn't realize he'd been doing the same for me. That to him, Laine could readily fill the needs in my heart created by him leaving.

It's sweet and naive and incredibly wrong.

"Zoe, promise me you'll give Laine a chance." Dad looks over the rim of his round eyeglasses. "Laine is a different vintner than I am, or your mother, and that's a wonderful thing. Let her vision guide her, give her your faith. Okay?"

"As long as her vision is tasty and accessible and she follows our recipes to the letter, she can express herself however she wants."

Dad's big brown eyes crinkle at that, the closest he ever gets to a real smile anymore. I desperately hope Italy will be good for him, that it'll wake up the part of him that's been sleeping ever since Mom died. But I can't shake the fear that it'll only make things worse. That maybe, this grief will break him for good.

"The vines grow through Laine's heart, too, Zoe Nicoletta. Just like yours. She'll be good for Bluebell if you let her."

I nod, promising whatever he wants, but the conversation leaves me unsettled. The more Dad tries to prepare me for his departure, the longer this indefinite trip feels like it will be.

"Don't stay away too long, okay, Dad?" I say through the feelings tightening in my throat.

"Oh, Zoe Nicoletta. I'll miss you so much." Dad strokes the apple of my cheek with his coarse thumb, then stands and brings me in for an all-encompassing hug, as though he's trying to tell me that I have nothing to worry about. That this vineyard won't sink without him, and neither will I.

After his plane leaves the next morning, the world feels quieter. Newer, and uncertain, too.

But I've promised to make the best of things, and I will. More than ever, I want to defeat Rachel Woods, host the *Everyday Bon Vivant* showcase, and represent the town I love to the world's wine scene. If that takes teaming up with Napa-snob Laine Woods, the First Lesbian, Alpha Queer, verifiable sex goddess who I cannot lick ever again, then so be it.

I'll survive.

Though I'll be masturbating a *lot*.

CHAPTER FIVE

cap my gel pen and lean back to admire three days' worth of cunning. The mega-binder on my kitchen table is organized and divided by each stage of my multipronged plan to win the showcase, with an Excel spreadsheet on my laptop so detailed it'd get the sternest accountant wet. If this were a heist movie, I'd be the mastermind steepling her fingers at the beginning of the montage where I set all my diabolical plans in motion.

I'm feeling good. Even better, I'm feeling *ready*.

I send a quick text to Teddy to stop by after work. I need his funding to get a few initiatives off the ground, and with the empire of dentistry he's built in Blue Ridge, he's an excellent businessman in his own right. I want his feedback on my plan.

Movement in the nearby block of Chardonnay grapes pulls my focus from my work and directs it out the window toward a strong set of shoulders. Like a sunflower shining amid the twiggy winter vines, Laine Woods tromps around my vineyard in work boots. She comes to a halt at the end of the block. Young Zoe would be fritzing out right now from sheer proximity to her idol, but I, mature, grown-up businesswoman Zoe, am beyond such things. I casually observe that she's clad in a slim flannel shirt rolled up to reveal lean forearms, bronzed from sun. Likewise, it's of no import that she's wearing high-waisted Levi's that hug the straight line of her hips, kissing the curve of her muscular ass. And it is with scientific detachment alone how I note the beat but satisfied slant to her shoulders, the unmistakable posture of *quittin' time*. It is almost four p.m., after all.

I wonder what she's doing later. Does she have plans? Will she stop by the treehouse to shower, scrubbing her skin until all the hard work of the day washes off?

The idea is strangely disappointing.

At first, I thought Laine might resent the farming demands of being our vintner. It's so different out west, where the big corporate vineyards have whole crews of farmhands. But in the week since she started, she's applied herself wholeheartedly. I've always admired that about her—Laine's singular focus when she wants something, that determination and steady will to succeed. I saw it growing up when she'd spend evenings doing soccer drills after a long afternoon of team practice, then camp out at the dining table after dinner until her homework was finished. In high school, when showing effort at anything was considered mortifying, Laine's utter lack of self-consciousness about crushing her goals stood out like a shining beacon over dull, gray waters. The ambition in me saw the ambition in her and was *drawn* to it, charged by it.

As I watch her intently inspecting a leaning trellis, then setting it to rights, it occurs to me that Laine brought that same drive to conquer to making me come.

My cheeks warm as heat pulses down my spine, pooling between my legs at the memory.

I snap the binder closed with a sigh. I've already checked off *masturbate* on the day's to-do list, and I'm running a tight ship here.

I pick up my phone, determined to get back to work, but bring up Laine's number instead. My fingers hover over the screen, a small burst of self-consciousness alighting in my chest. But it makes sense to invite her to the meeting today. After all, she's going to play a pivotal role in my plan to win the showcase, and this is work.

> **Zoe**
>
> Everyday Bon Vivant planning meeting at 4:30 p.m. in the tasting room.

I hit send and watch Laine where she's still hunkered down fixing the trellis. Will she stop to read the text? Will she resent my business tone? Should I have asked and said *please*?

I forcibly put my phone down instead of waiting for the screen to light up with her reply. Naturally, this results in me staring out the window at her instead.

Laine pauses, sets the pliers on the ground, and reaches for her back pocket. I inexplicably hold my breath as she glances at her phone's screen. Her face is impassive as she rattles off a quick reply.

> Laine Woods, Interim Vintner
>
> Depends.

> Laine Woods, Interim Vintner
>
> Are you going to give me a taste?

My mouth drops open. This is a business meeting! A workplace matter! The phone's in my hand in an instant, my fingers flying with righteous indignation:

> **Zoe**
>
> Come thirsty.

I stare at the message, blinking rapidly, as it's sent, delivered, read. What am I *thinking*? A tiny smirk perks up one side of Laine's mouth before she shoves the phone into her back pocket, packs up her tools, and walks off, and my pulse becomes erratic in my veins.

I leap out of my chair. I've got to get dressed for the meeting.

The thought of seeing Laine after that flirty round of texts makes my momentum stutter, but like an old engine turning over, it eventually catches and vrooms again. While I'm over the debilitating crush I had on her growing up and fine keeping things professional after our accidental threesome, I can't help feeling excited to show off Bluebell's offerings to her tonight. Sure, Laine's used to more sophisticated fare, but our white wines are sweet, simple, and true to our mountains. Every sip feels like a Blue Ridge afternoon. She's from here, too; she'll see that. Then maybe the snooty disdain for our vineyard that her manners don't quite mask will be dispelled for good, and together, we'll come up with ideas to transform our struggling red line, making Bluebell Vineyards stronger than ever.

I shimmy into a tight pair of dark jeans and pick a soft black shirt that dips in a V so low, it shows off the hollow between my breasts, the swell of flesh in stereo. Side boob is great, but in-between-boob? Goddess tier. A bold red lip, a touch of cat-eye, a pair of black heeled ankle boots later, and I'm ready.

I immediately frown at the hot lady in the mirror. Ready for *what*, exactly?

This is date-night Zoe, or more accurately, pre-fling Zoe. Not workplace Zoe. I shake my head like there's water in my ears instead of pent-up sexual energy and knot a heavy plaid shawl across my chest.

There. That's better.

I set off for the tasting room, strolling through the same Chardonnay block Laine was in earlier. The vines are already starting to bud, and in a few short months, their canes will push out a heavy drape of lush foliage. The Chardonnay vines are always the first to awaken from the vineyard's long winter sleep. It seems so foolish to push out new life when frosts still regularly threaten our cold mountain nights, but that doesn't stop the Chardonnays from sticking their necks out and leaving their survival to chance.

Stupid grapes.

In the large, airy tasting room, the lighting's warm glow mixes with the pale afternoon sunlight painted across the floors. The public-facing part of our winery is framed out with tall windows that let in the sun and gentle breezes riffling down from the mountains and are original to the structure. But while Mom and Dad may've scored with the windows, the 1990s were otherwise alive and well with cherrywood everything and those frosted overhead lights that popped from the ceiling like nipples when I first took over operations. Now the floors are finished in pale maple, the U-shaped bar topped with waxed butcher block below and white marble above, trimmed in a thin band of brass, and the lighting is pure vibes. Globe lamps hang in a line, gently illuminating the people drinking below and highlighting everyone's best features. River's always been my favorite cousin, but after helping me make this place magical, he's become nothing short of a blood brother.

Tristan appears from the back, holding a fresh crate of glassware. He eyes my outfit, complete with plaid shawl, with an eyebrow jacked damn near to his hairline. "Ah."

I narrow my eyes, daring him to continue. "Ah, *what*, Stan?"

But then the big double doors open from the back patio, and Laine saunters in. "Here for the meeting, boss."

"*Ah*," Tristan replies again as if that's all the answer that's needed, then starts unloading the crate, looking smug as hell.

When Laine draws near, the earthy smell of a day's work outside tickles my nose—soil, sunshine, and the scent of her sweat, surprisingly familiar. Dirt is streaked across her cheek; the knees of her faded jeans are tinged with earth. The urge to knock her flat, push her down in the grass, and get the backside of her just as dirty floods my system.

"Thank you for coming to this business meeting." The words rush out, a little too loud for the space. I clutch my shawl tighter. "A colleague will be joining us, but he's not here yet."

A small smirk appears on Laine's face, as though she sees right through my efforts at professionalism. "Sure, boss."

Annoying. I breathe deeply through my nose, spin on my heels, and march toward the bar. Growing up, Laine spooked me in a way no one else ever has, but I'm no kitten scared off by the big tomcat. Not anymore.

I'm the big pussy around here.

A vaguely crazed snort ripples through me at the thought, and I swing behind the bar, plunk an empty glass in front of Laine, and grab the first bottle. The shawl constricts my movement, though, and the corkscrew's being a real bitch.

Laine's smirk grows. "Need help, boss?"

"No, I've—got it—" Somehow, I've driven the cork in sideways, like I don't do this a hundred times a week.

Laine folds her arms behind her head, clearly amused, as I break a sweat. "I thought you worked here."

"It's this—shawl, too *tight*," I grind out.

"Sure."

When the cork nearly severs in half, I groan. In one slick movement, Laine leans forward and grabs the offending bottle by the neck. Her hand curls around mine, the rough pads of her fingers hot against the sensitive skin of my wrist. My hand opens willingly to her, relinquishing the cork-screw. It's still hanging there dumbly when she hands me the open bottle, cork removed with zero effort.

Fucking *athletes.*

"You okay, boss?" Laine's grin is intoxicating, and I'm drunk with the desire to wipe it *right off* her face.

I untie the knot of the strangling shawl, letting it fall to the ground. "I am now."

Her grin softens as her gaze slides down my throat, across the smooth skin of my chest, to the vale between my breasts. It's so visceral I feel it like the trail of fingertips. Now it's my turn to smile, and it fills me with a satisfied heat. I pluck the shawl from the floor and hang it on a hook. Laine swallows, her mocking bravado mysteriously disappeared.

Well, well. Look at that.

"Now how about that taste?" I lower my eyes to the glasses I've set before her, the pleased smile still lingering on my lips, and deftly pour a spread of seven wines because I *do* work in this damn vineyard. I've included three of our most popular whites, followed by a rosé, then a bit reluctantly, three reds. "You've got to learn our offerings since you'll be making them soon."

"Mm-hmm," Laine agrees absently, eyes lingering near my collarbone.

I push the first glass forward, Electric Daisy, our lightest white. It's a honeyed Traminette that tastes like a bouquet of lightly carbonated wild-flowers. I *love* it.

With effort, Laine redirects her gaze to the glass in her hand, which she swirls, the wine lightly swishing within. She assesses the way it clings to the glass, then brings it to her nose and breathes in deeply. Eyes closed, she tastes tentatively, swallows a miserly amount, then blinks open.

"Sweet," she pronounces flatly, the taste shaking the fog from her expression.

Disappointment tears through the excitement I'd felt, thinking Laine might appreciate what we have to offer. I push the embarrassment down and the second glass forward, rattling off our Pinot Grigio's attributes like a parent whose child made honor roll, but C'est la Grigio fares no better.

"Somehow? Also sweet." Laine flicks her tongue out, like she can shake the taste off by force. The memory of it sliding between my breasts makes my cheeks heat, then heat more because I'm thinking about that instead of how she's insulting my wine. "Imbalanced. Next?"

My fingers involuntarily flex around the stem of the third glass, and I push it forward a little too hard, nearly tipping it over. "This is Bluebell's signature blend, (Wish They All Could Be) Georgia Girls. It's a mix of estate-grown Catawba, muscadine, and peaches. The stone fruit—"

Laine sniffs the wine and expels a loud cough, then looks incredulously into the glass as if I've offered her a fresh batch of toilet wine instead of our bestseller. She squeezes her eyes closed and throws back a quick swallow, which is not *at all* how you're supposed to taste wine.

"*Extremely* sweet." She reaches for a napkin and wipes her tongue with it. "People like this?"

"People love it." I coax my expression into something cool even as warm hurt curdles in my gut. My chin lifts of its own accord. "It's our most popular wine.".

Laine shakes her head, like she just learned her little cousin Jimmy was back in jail again.

I can't hide my irritation any longer. I huff out a short, unamused laugh and start cleaning up a little too vigorously.

Laine arches an eyebrow as I snatch up her used tasting glasses, still full. "Look, I can't turn off my palate just because you make"—she pauses to pick up the bottle of Georgia Girls, eying it with dismay—"bachelorette party wine."

"It is *not* bachelorette party wine!" I look to Tristan for backup, but he's busy tending bar. "Also, that's a weirdly sexist thing to say."

"Okaaaay. It's white-cis-het-ladies-in-pushup-bras-throwing-down-wine wine. Better?"

I put my hands on my hips. "At least it's not *your* stuffy crap with notes of curdled lemon and—and—gasoline!"

Laine has the gall to look impressed. "Oh, so you've had Chilean Rieslings?"

I throw my hands in the air just as the door twinkles open, followed by a chorus of laughing, gleeful women, their heels merrily tapping toward the bar. They're wearing dresses the color of cotton candy, except for a bubbly woman in a minidress covered in stiff white lace.

Fuck it all to hell. She's got a sash on.

"*Helloooo*, ladies." Laine grins at them, earning a rowdy round of *wooooo!!* for her efforts. Tristan plunks three cold bottles of Georgia Girls in front of the cheering women, and Laine turns back to me, *I told you so* etched into every dimple of her face.

I suck a deep breath in through my nose, willing myself not to lose it. "Well, so what if it's bachelorette party wine? Look around you, Laine." Folks have been pouring into our tasting room ever since the clock struck five, the pleasant buzz of Friday happy-hour conversations surrounding us. I lean over the bar right into her face. "Our wine makes people *happy*."

"Wine for people who don't like wine, maybe." Laine says, then gives one of the bridesmaids a little wave.

I grip the bar, ignoring the irrational jealousy that wave kicked up. "Don't they deserve wine, too?"

The fact is, the gentle clatter of bottle against glass, happy sighs after sips, and laughter dispelling a long day of work is louder than her condescending Napa bullshit. It doesn't escape me, though, that the glasses raised in toasts and cheers are almost uniformly pale gold in color. I straighten, grit my teeth, and push the first of the reds toward Laine. If she thinks our ultra-popular whites are bad, this is going to be downright painful. She eyes the red warily, then sips, her eyes meeting mine over the rim of glass.

"This is—"

"—boring, I know." I cut her off, not giving her a chance to insult me any further, and push the second glass toward her, then the third. Her expression grows grimmer with each taste of our red offerings. They're not disgusting or anything, they're just profoundly *unspecial*. Basic. Clunky. The kind of wine you don't bother to finish. "Think you can do better?" The words come out clipped, but I can't help it, she's pissed me off, and worse, hurt my feelings.

"Of *course* I can." The words accompany a spark in her eyes, a glimpse of July lightning on this chilly spring night. "Though that's not saying much."

"Good. Because I'm gonna need you to bring every ounce of this"—I pause, gesturing at the entirety of her haughty demeanor—"big vintner energy and pour it into my wine."

Some unknowable emotion swirls across her face, chasing the arrogance away. Fear? Reluctance? Laine drops her eyes and pinches the stem of her wineglass, rolling it between her thumb and forefinger, her voice carefully neutral. "What do you mean?"

"Our grapes are good, our base wines solid. But we're missing that just-right blend of tart and sweet, mellow yet bright, the casual boldness all the best reds have. And I need *you* to find it for us. Fast."

"What, the clitoris?" A voice booms from my right as Teddy strolls in, loosening his bow tie and cackling to himself. His ability to make an uncomfortable entrance is truly unparalleled, but I'm grateful he's here to buffer. If I hear one more dig from Laine, someone's gonna need to take this corkscrew away. He sits next to Laine, who's staring at him with mild alarm.

"Meet Teddy," I explain, "town dentist, Bluebell's informal financier, master of inappropriate jokes."

Teddy leans in toward her. "And her best friend, though Zoe only cops to it half the time." He sits back suddenly, frowning. "Wait a minute—an outdoorsy butch sporting an uncanny likeness to our nemesis Rachel Woods? You must be the new vintner, Laine."

I am infinitely relieved he didn't include *Zoe's latest fuck* in that list.

One of Laine's brows quirks up. "Pleasure to meet you, Teddy."

"You may call me Money bags, since that's why I'm here." He slaps both palms against the bar. "Now, give me a glass of Electric Daisy before you shake me down."

I pour him a good one, open my binder, and begin.

"As one of the most popular vineyards in the greater Blue Ridge area, Bluebell Vineyards is already well positioned to snag *Everyday Bon Vivant*'s showcase. Our line of white wines reflects the local terroir and region's tastes, our mountain views are breathtaking, and best of all, we know how to throw a great party. But"—I hold a hand up—"these strengths are not enough. Not if we're going to compete against Into the Woods and win."

Laine appraises me, the faint stain of our subpar Pinot Noir blend lingering on her full lips. "You want to eliminate your weaknesses, too."

My back stiffens, but I can admit where we need improvement.

Just, I'd rather it not be to *her*.

"Yes. We're going to remove every good reason there is *not* to choose Bluebell. Laine, you'll tackle our red blends. We were known for having excellent reds until my father took over, and it's gone downhill ever since. You're going to change that for us. Be as creative as you want, just fix them."

Intrigue and apprehension swirl in her eyes in equal part. I can't blame her—creating a solid line-up of reds in one season using existing base wines with almost no aging time won't be easy—but the air between us seems to change; *she* seems to change. At least, how she looks at me has.

"Our next big weakness is lack of infrastructure around the property. With River and Hannah's wedding in July, it's the perfect time to build external fixtures that will turn *Everyday Bon Vivant*'s heads. I'm talking a bandstand, movable staging, and patio overlooks highlighting our best views." I flip to a section of my binder entitled *Comparators*, thumbing through pictures of previous festival locations. "For the last eight showcases, *Everyday Bon Vivant* chose vineyards with multiple bar locations on-site, along with picturesque selfie opportunities, romantic viewpoints, and the kind of hideaways that can be transformed into VIP experiences for higher-paying guests." I tap my finger on the pictures. "We can do all that, too."

"Which is where Ol' Money bags comes in," Teddy says, all business now. "Is River running the builds?" A quick nod from me, and he *hmm*s appreciatively. "That'll keep our costs low—down to labor and supplies with no overhead."

"The increase in wedding business alone will pay back your investment with interest by the end of the fall, if not sooner."

"But what's the story going to be?" Laine asks, her undeniable interest taking over. "How does Bluebell Vineyards represent a true showcase of what Blue Ridge has to offer?"

"It's our existing partnerships—our *friendships*—with local businesses that matter here. Every single stand in our Saturday farmers' markets could add to our appeal. Fresh butter from Mountain Farms' creamery spread across crusty loaves of sourdough from Dana's bakery. Old Pete's boiled peanuts stand set right next to Mercier's apple pies and hot cider. We'll have something for everyone because we're *friends* with *everyone*."

"When you're here, you're family!" Teddy announces.

Laine frowns. "Isn't that . . . Olive Garden?"

"*No*," he says indignantly, as though he doesn't drive an hour to get his unlimited breadsticks on cheat days.

I point at him. "It absolutely is, and you know it. But I'm thinking more like: *Welcome home to Bluebell Vineyards. Welcome home to Blue Ridge.*"

"Hear, hear!" Teddy says, then knocks his glass of wine back. "Go on and take my money!"

"Gladly." Teddy's enthusiasm smooths over my grated mood, and a real smile lifts the corners of my mouth. I chance a look at Laine, willing her to put aside her snobbery and apply her singular focus to helping me win the showcase.. So, she doesn't like our wines. So I want to throw her out a window. That doesn't mean we can't be on the same team, right? The way she returns my gaze, steady, cautious, and grudgingly respectful, makes my heart lift an inch in my chest. This time it's *my* ambition drawing her in, charging her up.

Maybe this will work out, after all.

"Step one is getting an endorsement from Mayor Esposito." I tap my finger on the timeline in the binder and grimace slightly. "Rachel's number one fan."

CHAPTER SIX

With each ring of the phone in my ear, I groan a little louder. I've been trying all week to reach Elisa, Mayor Esposito's aide, to get on her calendar. I've called, emailed, left messages with the receptionist, and filled Elisa's voicemail box to the brim, but no luck. All I need is a measly five minutes to present my pitch for the showcase, but I'm starting to think Elisa's screening my calls.

For the hundredth time this week, I curse myself for mentioning the showcase as the reason for my calls. I've never had trouble getting time with the mayor before, and Elisa's as diligent as they come. If she's not answering my messages, she's either dead or doing it on purpose.

The rings stop, and Elisa's automated message clicks on. I'm pondering switching tactics with my message—perhaps a Bigfoot sighting will get me a call back—when a bubble of laughter sounds from outside my window. A blur of blonde curls about knee-high giggles by, followed by my cousin River. He's doing some kind of gorilla-armed chase after little Bowie, while Hannah stands there, hands pressed to her stomach and laughing.

I smile wistfully at their sweet little family, then go out to meet them.

"Hey, fam!" I call out, glad that it's true. A grunt and a delighted squeal later, Bowie's hanging upside down laughing hysterically over his soon-to-be-stepdad River's back, and River's grinning, too, if winded.

"I swear, I'm gonna get one of those kid leashes and strap you to my side, boy," Hannah says, wagging her finger playfully at her son, who now sits atop River's shoulders looking pleased as hell. Bowie got that cloud of golden curls from his mama, but right now, they're making him look like a mischievous clown child.

"If the suspect has been secured, I can show y'all where I'm thinking for the ceremony and reception, and we can talk infrastructure."

"Lead on, cousin," River says, his face the picture of easy happiness. With his hands cupping Bowie's little legs to his chest, we set out into the lovely March afternoon, wending our way through rows of vines.

"I've been thinking about the VIP experiences you mentioned." Hannah pulls out a fat sketchbook from her tote bag and flips to a dog-eared page somewhere in the middle. "With your theme of 'Welcome Home to Bluebell Vineyards,' you're presenting this idea of modern southern hospitality, right? And I thought: what if we built a line of firepits flanked by open-front canvas tents with cozy seating, mood lighting, and blankets? We could stock them with s'mores kits and hot chocolate, and if we set them up here"—Hannah stops to gesture at the stretch of unused land on the hill nearest to the winery—"the VIP guests would still feel a part of the festivities but with just enough privacy to feel special. What do you think?"

I throw my arm around Hannah's shoulders and squeeze her tight. "I think you're a genius, Hannah Tate."

Hannah flushes a little and smiles. "I've got more ideas, too, for the viewpoints' designs."

It's been so gratifying seeing Hannah embrace her inherent talents and taste, her confidence and business acumen growing by the day. It's like watching a flower bloom in fast motion. "I want to hear them all."

We walk past the western edge of our vineyards, past the newly budding Seyval Blanc and Catawba vines, to where the hill dips into a beautiful clearing, the old-growth pine and birch forest towering behind it. I step ahead and walk backward, arms raised.

"Most weddings want the mountain views, but with your Tolkien-esque theme, I figured the forest backdrop would be more appropriate."

River's face breaks into a delighted sunny grin. "Tom Bombadil-approved." He offers me a fist bump, which is so surprisingly 2000s I actually bump him back before I can ask who the hell Tom Bombadil is.

River sets Bowie down, and with a firm grip on his tiny hand, walks him around the area explaining his ideas for the platform he's going to build for the ceremony. When they return, River says, "Okay, this spot is a winner. Bowie gives two thumbs-up." To confirm the statement, Bowie lifts his hand and flips us all off.

"He's working on it," Hannah explains, smiling with such love, it makes me laugh.

"We could set up the bride and groom's tents over there, flanking the entrance of the ceremony area, with a makeshift stable for our horses set up *here*—"

I hold up a hand. "Whoa, horses? Just how far is this Lord of the Rings theme going?"

"He keeps begging me to wear elf ears," Hannah says, smirking at River like he's the biggest dork she's ever seen, yet still wants to bone him.

"I have a vision, that's all." River pulls her close, then brushes one of her curls behind her ear.

"An elven vision, though?"

"You'd be such a hot elf, baby."

Hannah rolls her eyes but gives him a kiss before joining at my side again.

"You're not really going to wear elf ears, are you?" I ask under my breath.

"Maybe on the honeymoon. If he asks reaaaaal nice."

I make a face, and she grins like the imp she is. We all walk back to the winery, listening to River's less eccentric ideas for the wedding, like the beautiful arched canopy he'll build for the ceremony, and Bowie's ideas for slides around the property. Bowie's got a point—a rustic, wooden playground that doesn't scream plastic in loud primary colors would definitely draw families in, if our budget can go that far. I'm so excited to see what River does. This wedding will benefit us in a big way, with River building all the outdoor infrastructure needed for his vision that we can then use to win over the *Everyday Bon Vivant* team and bolster our wedding business going forward.

The sharp snip of pruning shears makes me stop short, and I whip my head around, looking for the source. There, two rows away, is Laine, busily hacking off all but two buds from each of the Seyval Blanc vines.

My eyes widen. "Laine! Stop!"

She doesn't hear me thanks to a pair of absurdly large headphones hugging her head. I run toward her up the hill, panting, waving my arms and cursing my abysmal cardiovascular health. When her eyes meet mine, a weariness surfaces that's unmissable. It stings, a little. We haven't seen each other much since the tasting a few weeks ago, but when we do, it's a run-in in the truest sense of the word. My will seems to collide with hers at every turn. No matter what request I make, or how gently I broach it, it always resolves into bickering. It's been disappointing honestly. While the tasting got off to a rocky start, I thought I'd gotten through to her about the showcase and that she was finally on *my team*, but that comes with conditions, apparently.

The main one being I do *not* tell her what to do.

"STOP. PRUNING!" I yell, punctuating each word until Laine finally slips off her headphones. With a stubborn twist of her mouth, she cuts off another precious bud, and we both watch it fall to the ground.

"Why?" she asks, a sullen edge to her tone.

"Because," I say, still panting a bit, "we aren't past the last of the frosts yet. We've got to keep insurance buds, enough to make sure that at least two will survive until the weather stabilizes."

"Oh, so now you're gonna tell me how to farm, too?"

I know she's thinking of how I busted in on her bottling the whites last week, forcing her to consult the checklist Dad made for her instead of whatever she was doing. But she doesn't seem to get that a vineyard our size lives season to season. A single mistake could be our last, and this is one of the worst ones she could make.

"I'm not telling you how to farm, Laine, I'm telling you how to farm *here*. Our weather dictates different techniques, that's all." I frown, wondering where the confident, astute Charlaine of my youth is right now. She was always eager to learn, improve, excel.

This Laine just wants me to shut up.

I put a hand on her arm. "It's okay not to know everything, you know," I say softly.

"I know enough for this rundown vineyard." Her eyes flash to where my hand is, and I drop it as though burned. She shakes her head and raises the shears to snip another one, but I reach out again and grab her by the wrist, nothing soft about it this time. Because this time, *I'm* angry.

Does she not believe me?

Or does she not respect me?

"I said, *stop!*"

The challenge in her eyes beams at me like a laser, cutting through my calm, professional demeanor with searing precision. If I didn't need Laine to keep Bluebell operational, her ass would be so out of here. She's rude, condescending, and her belittling opinions feel like an attack on *me*. *My* vineyard. Which is basically my family.

My grip on her wrist squeezes tighter. "Now you listen to *me*. Ask any vineyard in Blue Ridge—nobody's pruning all the way down to two yet. It's too soon!"

Laine stops and pretends to think, positively swelling with that big vintner energy. "Let me get this straight: you're director of operations, marketing, and sales; bottling manager; and now you're the fucking chief viticulturist, too?"

"Don't forget *your boss*," I say, my voice dropping low and dangerous, redirecting the challenge right at her. "I'm also very much *your boss*."

Laine's face hardens, hot fury sliding beneath it. She lifts her chin, leveling the full weight of that destructive gaze on me. Heat floods up my back, enveloping every nerve ending with crackling energy. I stand my ground as she steps into my face, vaguely aware I'm still clutching her wrist. My fingers can't seem to let go.

"*Are* you my boss?" she breathes down at me, her frame filling my entire field of vision. The words are laced with pure sexual dominance, and it's so surprising, my jaw drops open even as every string in my core writhes, aching for the pressure of her thumbs against my hipbones, that chin smashed against my pussy.

I'm overcome with the urge to *whimper.*

Hannah *ahem*s into her hand, and I suddenly remember we're not alone. My face flushes, this time in embarrassment, and I let go of her wrist. I have a whole session in Small Business Owners 101 on treating your staff with compassion and respect that both Hannah *and* River took, and now they're seeing me do the exact opposite. I suck in a breath and step firmly out of Laine's face.

Especially since she's still clutching shears.

"I'm sorry," I say to Hannah, River, and Bowie, and *definitely* not Laine. "Just talking . . . farm stuff." I swallow around the knot of desire and fury lodged in my throat.

"Farm stuff, huh," River says. Laine and I both shift our gazes, a bit sheepishly. Hannah, bless her, smooths the tension over with a bright smile. "Laine, right? I don't believe we've met. I'm Hannah Tate, and this is my son Bowie. You already know River?"

Laine pauses and punches out a short breath. "That I do. Hey, River, good to see you, man." Her eyes flicker over to Hannah, and a spike of jealousy surges inside me as Laine's gaze softens. "Nice to meet you, Hannah. I'm sorry, too. Me and the boss here don't always see eye to eye." Laine shrugs, then gives Hannah a crooked, cocky smile. "Guess I'm used to doing things the Napa way."

Oh, *look*. I want to murder her again!

"Yes, Laine often forgets we're in *Blue Ridge*, which has an entirely different *climate*. We get frosts well into May here in Northern Georgia. Which funnily enough,"—I raise a finger to the sky—"is *not* California!"

I'll be professional next time.

"That's for fucking sure," Laine mutters through her clenched jaw. Then, with a smile that looks like an insult, she says louder, "Okay, boss. I'll delay the rest of the pruning if you say so."

"I say so, *Beave*."

Everyone frowns until I explain. "Big Vintner Energy? BVE?" Is there anything more awkward than having to explain a bad joke. *Ugh*. Nothing to do except own it now.

Laine raises both hands with a *fuck this* smile and walks away from me backward. "Got it. If you don't mind, I've got more farm stuff to do."

I hope she trips. But not with the shears. That'd be too graphic.

"See you around, Laine!" Hannah calls. "If you're free, some of the local queer community's meeting up at the new wine bar downtown later this week."

I spin on Hannah as Laine salutes and turns away.

"Hannah!"

She grimaces. "Sorry, but she's new here, and I know how hard that can be. Besides, maybe you two just need to bond?" She laughs nervously, grabs Bowie, and books it toward the winery.

I sigh, emptying my soul into it. I know she can't help it. Hannah's physically unable to be rude. It's cute most of the time, but the Queer Mountaineers is *mine*. I refuse to share another sacred thing with Laine, only for her to hate it, too.

After Hannah, River, and Bowie leave, I stew in my office, puzzling over the encounter again and again. What was with that boss comment Laine made, anyway? Did she think I'd say *no, haha, never mind, I'm your sweet little bottom, sorr-eeee!*

Or did she *want* me to say yes? Did she want me to say *yes, I'm your fucking boss, now do as I say*, then grind her beneath my heel? The thought makes my mouth go dry as a trail of goose bumps alight on my arms because I—I think she *did*.

The sound of stomping feet passing by my office toward the winery snaps me back to present. They land with a distinctly pissy quality, telling me who it is before she passes my open door.

"Laine, come in. Need to talk to you."

Laine heaves a sigh from the hallway. "Don't worry, boss. I won't go to your little queer club," she says, enough ice in her tone to make me shiver. "Now, can we be done for the day, or are there more things you'd like to criticize?"

"Come *in*," I repeat, refusing to take the argument-bait she's dangling in front of me. "Please?"

Laine pivots on the spot with rigid compliance and moves a miserly inch into my office. "What."

"*Goddammit* Laine, just come in and sit down." She's not making this easy on me, that's for sure. These hot and cold reactions leave my head spinning. She absolutely hates being told what to do until suddenly, out of nowhere, it seems to . . . turn her *on*? She goes from *fuck this* to *fuck me* and back so fast I'm not even sure it happened.

Judging by the muscle ticking in her jaw right now, she's firmly in *fuck this* territory, and I have about thirty seconds before she leaves, whether I'm done talking or not. She drops into the chair across from me, folds her arms over her chest, and spreads her legs wide, taking up as much space in my small office as she possibly can. This is intimidation, pure and simple.

I wish I didn't like it so much.

Like applying pressure to a bleeding wound, I try to staunch the horny thoughts flowing right now. But Laine's words out there rattled me, igniting an electric energy between us that refuses to dissipate—half *wanna fight*, half *wanna fuck*, and 100 percent *try me*.

I *want* to try her. I want to stand over her, lift my boot to her shoulder, and press her furious face against the throbbing pulse she's caused between my legs. The sheer intensity of that want is so alarming, my heart's rhythm is thudding in fear and anticipation both, as though I might do it. The moment stretches between us, air charged, and Laine's eyes snag on something in mine. Want? Anger?

Or fear?

She leans forward, eyes hungry and searching. Terrified, I snatch my phone off the desk and bring up my contacts. "My friend Jamal is the vintner at Fightingtown Vines and head of our local vineyard association. I've given him a call, and he's agreed to bring you up to speed on how things are done in Blue Ridge."

If I thought I'd seen Laine mad before, it was nothing compared to the hellfire burgeoning from her eyes now. "I don't need anyone to bring *me* up to speed, *boss*."

"I'm not concerned with what you think you need." The words are cool and calm, impersonal, and with each one, I feel my strength returning. "Your inexperience today could've cost us our entire crop of Seyval Blanc. You've got a lot to learn about how wine is made in this region, and you're not going to do it by jeopardizing my family's business just because *you think* you're better than this town and everyone in it."

The words land like a blow to her stomach, visibly taking her aback, and for a second, I regret having gone there. Then I remember the casually dismissive way she looks at Bluebell Vineyards, like everything I have on this earth is beneath her. Like I'm beneath her, too.

And I don't feel sorry at all. This is *my* business, and I can't let whatever these feelings are between us make me forget that.

I walk around the desk to where she's still sitting and put the slip of paper with Jamal's number directly into her hand.

"Call him. *Today.*"

CHAPTER SEVEN

Hey, Zoe.

I'm sorry I accidentally set up a threesome for us with your old friend from high school. I get that it was embarrassing, but I had no way of knowing. Are you going to hold it against me forever?

And after I spend all day ignoring Harlow's texts:

I guess so.

My phone buzzes against the table with Harlow's last text flashing across the locked screen. I sigh and pick up my iced tea instead. It's not the first time Harlow's reached out since she blew my carefully ordered world apart and left me lying dazed in a pile of rubble. I haven't responded. It's not that I'm angry with her, but what's there to say? *Hi, Harlow, I've finally learned my lesson that you + me always = extremely distracting emotional turbulence. Let's just . . . not. Okay?*

The sweet tea slides down my throat, ice gently clinking against my teeth, and I sigh again, looking out onto town from my spot on The Dogwood's porch. It's a sunny afternoon, the kind of warm that grows flowers, so I couldn't resist grabbing my laptop and going out for lunch. Plus, I haven't eaten a real meal in a week, instead turning the contents of my kitchen into sad imitations of charcuterie boards whenever I get hungry. The dregs of tortilla chips, bananas just past their prime, a lone slice of leftover pizza. How did food get so depressing? I needed delicious tots to ease my troubled mind.

I'm just . . . tired. So tired of feeling a thousand variations of *alone*. I always get emotional hangovers after a Harlow visit, but this one's rising to new heights, aided by the rest of my life going slowly insane. It's been over a month now since Dad's left, and our weekly calls leave more ache than comfort. I miss him, his sad eyes and gentle smile and how much simpler my life was when he was vintner instead of the prickly butch I can't manage. Even pursuing the showcase hasn't been able to fill me up lately. Laine's negativity is like a black hole roaming around our vineyards, sucking up all my good energy whenever she gets too close. I thought she was going to be on my team, and now, I just feel stupid.

Laine's not on my team—I'm not sure she's on *anyone's*. She'd mentioned this temporary leave of absence was so that she could reconnect with her family, but as far as I can tell, she hasn't gone to Into the Woods once. Before work begins, she does soccer drills up and down the vineyard rows, dribbling the ball back and forth between her feet, or practices kicks with a small foldable goal she set up by her Treebnb. After work, the lights flick on up there and stay on until late into the evening. The next day repeats, not that I'm spying on her or anything. I just keep waiting for something, some clue to help me understand her better, why she's here, and why she seems so angry all the time.

So far, I've got nothing.

The door to the restaurant opens, and a high, twinkling laugh exits first. I glance over my shoulder, and a burst of adrenaline lights up my body. Rachel Woods, in all her ironed country club glory, holds the door open for Mayor Esposito. She's laughing her fake ultra-femme laugh, not at all like the hilarious throaty burble she had when we were kids. I've been trying to get a meeting scheduled with the mayor for weeks now, but when I finally cornered her assistant Elisa in the Ingles parking lot the other day, she claimed the mayor was booked through summer. I distinctly remember Elisa saying she'd be on vacation this week. In *Reno*. You remember when someone says they're vacationing in *Reno*.

Torn between elbowing Rachel out of the way so I can pitch Bluebell Vineyards for the showcase and disappearing into the ether, ultimately I choose the ether, slumping down in my seat as they pass by. I shouldn't be surprised. Flor Esposito, a strong-jawed Latina who rose in political prominence on her platform of *Doing the Unexpected!* and positioning Blue Ridge as an innovator in the tourism industry, struck up a friendship with Rachel after Into the Woods hosted a successful event for Flor when she was a struggling real estate agent with mayoral ambitions. Rachel's been one of her most active fundraisers ever since, which is admittedly a decent use of Rachel's toxic perfectionist energy. Mayor Esposito is great, but her success and loyalty are tied to Rachel in an incredibly inconvenient way for Bluebell Vineyards right now. Of course the mayor doesn't want to meet with me, Into the Woods's biggest competitor. She doesn't want to tell me no.

Ugh. The tots-induced happiness has turned into a flat, greasy despair. Getting the mayor's endorsement for the showcase isn't a must-have, but it'd demonstrate to *Everyday Bon Vivant* that the town is behind us, implicitly confirming that we'd experience no interference from the permitting office or city council.

I just need to rethink my strategy, that's all. Some way to bypass the mayor or approach the permitting office first. I throw back the rest of my tea and settle the bill, ready to hole up at my desk until I solve this problem, but halfway to my car I stop dead.

Rachel's parked two cars down from mine, and she's leaning against the back of her sparkling SUV, rapidly typing something on her phone. Her large sunglasses lift, spotting me before I can detour out of sight. She gives a small huff of recognition, like *Oh. You again.*

"What are *you* doing here?" Rachel folds her arms, her long, brown hair reflecting the sunlight straight into my eyes. She's wearing calf-high leather riding boots over dark skinny jeans and a slim-cut white button-down tucked neatly in, all cinched together with a matching leather belt. A Ralph Lauren ad in 3-D, if Ralph Lauren only hired bitches.

I wave a hand behind me. "At a restaurant? You're really asking me what I'm doing at a *restaurant?*"

"You heard me."

I sigh, fully aggrieved now. "I was doing tots, Rachel. *Tots.*"

She looks at me over the rim of her sunglasses. "You weren't spying on me with the mayor, were you?"

"What for? So I could steal your secrets for kissing ass?"

Rachel barks out a laugh. "You *wish* you had as much access to her ass as I do."

I tilt my head, eyebrows raised, until a furious blush envelops Rachel's high cheekbones.

"You know what I mean!" She straightens up, grabbing for her keys in her purse. "Well, you can quit stalking Flor because she's endorsing Into the Woods for the showcase. It's a done deal."

"I don't need her endorsement to win the showcase," I say with more confidence than I feel.

"Maybe not, but you do need decent wine and a vintner who can actually make it, and on that front, you're *screwed.*" Rachel smiles sweetly, steps up into her vehicle, and throws her SUV in reverse, claiming the last word.

She's always been like this. Stubborn, demanding, and viciously competitive. The only difference is she used to be on my side. We spent our

childhoods running back and forth between our families' vineyards, playing hide-and-seek among the vines, tasting unfinished wines from the
taps, and pretending to barf all over each other. Rachel always had a hard
time with other kids; they got one taste of her bullish ways and avoided
her thereafter, never bothering to get to her soft, ferociously loving heart
within. But she was there for me when my mom died, when my dad could
barely string a sentence together without collapsing in grief. Her happy
home became *my* happy home, where I could escape the sadness that hung
over my motherless house like a shroud. I was as shy as she was confron-
tational, but even still, we were so alike back then. Awkward, ambitious,
and full of yearning—me for the family I'd lost, and her to be different,
to be liked. To be just like Charlaine.

We were Charlaine's number one fans. We went to all her soccer
games, painted her number on our cheeks, and cheered like little mani-
acs. Whatever music she listened to, we listened to. If she liked a show, we
made that show our entire personalities. She was simply the coolest, and
most of Gilmer County agreed. Rachel wanted to be just like her, going
so far as to quit our quiz bowl team to play soccer instead. While Rachel
was never as fast or naturally coordinated, she tried just as hard, huffing
her way onto the junior varsity team in high school in ninth grade.

It was the August before our sophomore year when everything went
to hell. Rachel was trying out for the varsity soccer team that she wasn't
ready for, but Charlaine was varsity captain, and Rachel was *convinced*
she'd put her on the team. I came out to support her, wearing Rachel's
JV number on one cheek and Charlaine's on the other, and watched with
mounting unease from the front row as Rachel scrapped, kicked shins,
intercepted balls, and mercilessly drove them all the way to the goal. She
didn't pass the ball once, but she passed plenty of elbows, accepting whistles and reprimands from the coach like Girl Scout badges until finally,
they called her off the field.

Rachel jogged off, red-faced and exuberant, stopping on the sidelines where Charlaine and the coach stood talking, and me sitting just behind the fence.

"How'd I do, Captain?" she'd asked Charlaine, her face this terrible mix of excitement and hope.

It was the coach that answered. "You're excused, Rachel." He blew his whistle then, initiating another drill.

"Charlaine?" Rachel said, frowning as tryouts continued for everyone else.

"You heard him, Rachel, you're done." Charlaine rubbed her forehead. "Go on home."

"What do you mean, I'm done?"

"I *mean* you showed your ass out there, hogging the ball like that. You gave Sadie a bloody nose! What were you thinking? That you're Megan Rapinoe?" Charlaine had turned then, shaking her head with disgust, and Rachel just . . . imploded. All the excitement and pride on her face, all the love and adoration for Charlaine, all the hope of ascending to her big sister's status contracted inward, then disappeared as Rachel collapsed in on herself in a fit of furious tears. She stormed off the field. I rushed to follow, picking up the towel she threw, her water bottle. I held her while she bawled all that night, vowing revenge on Charlaine, on the coach, on poor Sadie and her bloody nose. When the varsity picks were announced the next day, omitting her name of course, Rachel quit the JV squad on the spot.

She was destroyed. Overnight, everything Charlaine did became criminal, and I was suddenly the sole member of our Charlaine fan club. All my positive regard had to go into hiding, which wasn't easy because somewhere along the way, my feelings toward Charlaine had grown . . . complicated. While Rachel wanted to be her, I craved being *near* her, always wondering where she was when I came over. Would she walk by in her sports bra and emerald-green Umbros? Would she climb onto the stool next to mine at the kitchen counter, grabbing a banana while I suddenly lost the ability to breathe?

Then one Saturday, Rachel and I were in the middle of watching the BBC version of *Pride and Prejudice* when I decided we needed more snacks. It was late, so I tiptoed through the dark downstairs not to wake anybody. But when I flipped on the kitchen lights, there, sitting on the counter with her shirt off, was Ava Sanchez, goalkeeper for the varsity team. Her legs were splayed wide, bookending Charlaine between them, whose mouth was wrapped around one of Ava's exposed nipples.

"Oh, *shit!*" Ava thrust Charlaine's face away when the lights came on. Charlaine whirled around to face me where I stood with my hand still hovering over the light switch, open-mouthed, eyes wide. Charlaine's hair was mussed and free, her lips swollen. She looked beautiful and wild and hungry, and it stabbed me, seeing her like that.

With someone *else*.

After that, it was like a bomb detonated within me. But instead of blowing my adoration apart, my explosion was more volcanic—hot, intense feelings surged out of me from deep within, burning down everything I knew, leaving unfamiliar landscapes in their wake. Creating new land.

And Rachel noticed.

She started watching me around Charlaine. Her eyes bored into me whenever Charlaine loped into the kitchen, wearing a tight tank top and cutoff shorts. If we bummed a ride to school from Charlaine and Chance, I'd sit stock-still in the back and stare out the window for fear of giving anything away and pissing Rachel off more. I was trapped between this intense crush and what it meant for who I was becoming and my best friend, and I couldn't talk about it to anyone. Mom was gone, Dad was emotionally out to sea, and I knew, undoubtedly, that if Rachel found out how I felt about Charlaine, she'd never talk to me again.

A few months later, she did. Just like that, our friendship was over.

It hurt so much. To be so close to someone, then lose them like that. But it made me angry, too. Because when I developed a crush on her big sister, Rachel took all that history—all those laughs and spend-the-nights and days exploring our woods—and threw them away.

And for what? Nothing even *happened*. I could barely speak around Charlaine, she made me so nervous. She left for college on the other side of the country without ever knowing how her little sister's sad, half-orphaned friend next door felt about her. Or that those feelings eventually drove Rachel and me apart, once they became too big for me to smother.

I heave a sigh, then climb into my own truck. Rachel's words dig into me for the rest of the afternoon, chasing every idea I jot down with *it's a done deal* and *you're screwed*. I scratch out everything until my pen nearly rips the paper. What did Rachel mean by implying Laine can't make our wine? She might hate her guts still, but Laine's worked at some of the best vineyards in the country. Rising to the top of Le Jardin as a young queer woman couldn't have been easy, but she did it.

Of course she did. She's Charlaine Woods, young Zoe's voice says in my head. *She's a star.*

More like a mean butch who despises me. How Rachel would *love* knowing just how badly we get along. I snort, but it's a sound bordering on despair. I lean my head into my hands, clutching at my hair. I knew winning the showcase wouldn't be easy, but I didn't expect it to be so hard, either.

My phone dings, reminding me of the Queer Mountaineers hang. I shuffle into my bathroom and stare into the mirror at my face, bare except for all these feelings. But I don't *want* to feel these feelings right now, or preferably, at all. I want to be Zoe Brennan, Director of Operations and Boss Bitch of Bluebell Vineyards. Not high school Zoe whose best friend dumped her, or post-college Zoe, burdened by the bad business decisions her father made, or even current-day Zoe, forced to work with her first crush who now hates her. I want to be in control again. I *need* to be in control again.

I pick up my eyeliner and turn it over in my hand, staring at its well-worn nib. I should go tonight, it'll be good to see friends, but who says I need to get fixed up? It's just a Queer Mountaineers hang where everyone's already coupled off or otherwise unavailable. My friends love me with or without cat-eyes. I zip up the makeup bag and put it back on the shelf, then find the coziest sweatpants I own.

This is my sweatpants era.

"Good lord, *sweatpants?*" Teddy exclaims when I putz into the wine bar twenty minutes later. He slaps the counter to get the bartender's attention. "Get this sad lesbian a glass of Petite Sirah."

I smile despite myself. Teddy knows I drink the darkest red available whenever I'm depressed. He pats my back as I lean onto the bar next to him. "Drink what you want, baby." I'll put you in for a whitening next week."

"Love you, Teddy," I say, low enough for only him to hear. Teddy doesn't really do displays of genuine, non-sarcastic affection, but beneath his silky athleisure ensembles and brash exterior, there flows a kindness and generosity that's gotten me through some of my roughest times. After Rachel friend-dumped me, it took me years to open up to somebody else. I had friends, sure, but they bobbed on the surface of my life just like everything else. But when Teddy started moonlighting at Bluebell while he was getting his dental practice off the ground, his playful ribbing graduated into real conversations and over time, we made it past each other's defensive obstacle course of protective barriers and coping mechanisms. When we met, he hadn't found Diego yet, and we bonded over our shared, secret fear of being hopelessly single in a tiny queer community. Watching

Diego and Teddy fall in love, then *stay* in love, casts a warm, comforting light over the shadows I'm still lost in, a bit of hope that maybe my perfect match will move to Blue Ridge one day, too. Most importantly, though, Teddy's concern for me never feels like pity. It just feels like love.

He looks both ways, as though he doesn't want to be caught being my best friend, then leans in and whispers, "Still charging your ass."

The place is packed with the local queer community, and I give little nods and salutes to different tables of my former flings as I pass. Kai is here with her wife Charlie, both of whom attended the Zoe Brennan Finishing School for Young Lesbians, Kai class of 2019, Charlie 2021; both remorseless dropouts. Jojo and her wife are here, too. Only had one date before Jojo stopped texting me, but kudos to her for picking up that text thread with zero shame two years later to ask about our wedding rental rates. Her eyes travel down my outfit, and not in a good way.

Coulda had *all this*, Jojo.

We head back to my friends' table, thankfully free of my former dalliances. When Tristan eyes my outfit this time, his beard twitches around his smile. "This look's giving big *don't-look-at-me-motherfucker* energy. Guess you're over your crush on the new vintner?"

I squeeze my eyes closed. "For the love of god, I don't have a crush on Laine!"

The whole table stops to stare at me with frank disbelief. Teddy just says, "*Baby.*"

I shrug and reach for my wine. "I accidentally slept with her—there's a difference."

Tristan arches an auburn eyebrow. "O-kaaaay. Are you over accidentally sleeping with the new vintner then?"

I think back to the last few weeks—the arguing, all of Laine's snobby digs, her disdain for Bluebell Vineyards that drips continually from her very essence. "You know what? I'm *so* over it."

As blazing hot as Laine is, her attitude toward Bluebell Vineyards has cooled any feelings I might've had for her. I'm almost grateful she sucks so plentifully, come to think of it. Falling for my interim vintner would've been aggressively stupid.

"Look, I need her help to keep the vineyard running until Dad comes home so I can snag the *Everyday Bon Vivant* showcase. If I didn't, I'd have fired her weeks ago."

"So if she were standing behind you, right now, you wouldn't care?" Tristan says, his smoky-rimmed hazel eyes flicking over my shoulder to the door.

I whip around so fast, I nearly sprain my neck.

And . . . there's no one there.

"You *asshole!*" I hit Tristan on one of his thick arms, and everyone starts laughing. I roll my eyes, but I'm laughing now, too. The best part is, I *keep* laughing. Diego launches into a funny story about a nurse he works with at the local hospital getting caught stealing bedpans (*I mean, is there a black market for bedpans??*), then our stalwart softball lesbians Maeve and Gloria show up, looking as disgruntled as I've ever seen them.

"What's this all about?" Diego gestures with both hands, gently encompassing their ragamuffin appearance and downtrodden expressions.

Maeve sits down. "Saving animals, that's what. Whole petting zoo got dropped off."

Teddy arches an eyebrow. "I'm guessing you don't wanna pet them."

Gloria sits beside Maeve and sniffs. "No, sir."

"What happened?" I bite back a smile, but they're so comically peeved. I've known Maeve for years, and she's as bighearted as they come, taking in all manner of critters for her animal rescue. She ends up adopting half of them herself, but that's to be expected when you're a big softie like Maeve. She used to try to foist the poor orphan fur-children onto me, but I rebuffed her every time, showing my support by regularly donating to her rescue instead. I refuse to attach my heart to anything with less than a seventy-five-year lifespan.

Maeve heaves a world-weary sigh. "The zoo owner got arrested. Turns out he was on the run from the Swiss government."

Tristan mock-gasps. "And here I thought they were neutral."

Maeve side-eyes him. "Laugh it up, junior. I've got snakes to re-home."

Tristan's laugh dies in his throat as Gloria grits her teeth. "Snakes aren't the problem. It's the goat." She growls, legit *growls*. "Ate my softballs."

"A criminal, just like his human father," Maeve adds somberly, and I'm dying. Laughing so hard, the tears roll freely down my face. With each sip of wine, every story shared, friend-after-friend's appearance at our ever-growing table, the stress of the last month undergoes an alchemical reaction, leaving me awash with a relief so palpable, it wraps around my soul like a big, cozy blanket. I hadn't realized how much I needed to be surrounded by my friends and laughter. While I often joke about the lack of available women in the Queer Mountaineers, being part of a group that doesn't care about your sexual value or relationship potential, that loves you for the whole, complete person you are in this world, is its own special reward. I need to remember that.

Diego pokes me in the arm. "So are we gonna get the details of what went down with the hot butch vintner you're totally over or what?" I shoot dagger eyes at Hannah, but she lifts her hands in innocence.

"I've told them nothing!" She crosses her heart, but she's a few deep, too, so it looks more like swatting a bee. "Promise."

I lift my glass to the group and say, "I am a lady of discretion and grace," which is greeted with whoops and vehement pshaws. "But let's just say I was inspired to buy this baby after." I flash my phone at the table, where the shipping notice of the giant rainbow dildo Harlow had is displayed. "It's my special occasion dick. Double-headed for *both* lesbians' pleasure!"

"Um, Zoe?" Tristan says, eyes wide. "Laine just walked in."

"Not gonna get me this time, *Stan*." I snort and throw back the rest of my Grenache. At this point in the evening, my teeth are probably full-on vampire. "You can't hold me *or* my giant rainbow dildo back! I just need to find a *new* sexy butch to use it on."

"*Zoe!*" Hannah hisses, but I'm not stopping now. I stand and lift my empty glass, getting into it like I'm one of the Founding Fathers, and this here's my statement of the union. "I need someone with *pizzazz*." I've never said *pizzazz* in my life, but I say it now with gusto. "Someone with a less annoying face! But most importantly, someone who has a healthy relationship with constructive criticism!"

I wait for them to applaud, to whoop and support me like my fellow colonists should, but all I hear is a husky voice clearing behind me. From *immediately* behind me.

"Room for two more?"

Tristan hides his face behind his hands while Teddy's booming voice fills the wine bar, and my heart seizes in my chest. "There's always room for more queers! What're your names, pronouns, and thoughts on giant rainbow special occasion dicks?" He clearly doesn't understand the catastrophe-in-the-making.

A soft hand lands on my arm, and I freeze as it slides away. "Harlow Benoit, she/they." She smiles gently at me as she slips around the table. "Pro—giant rainbow dick, for regular *and* special occasions."

"Oh, *shit*," Teddy slurs, squinting at her, then Laine. "I did not see you there." He runs a hand down his slack face, then leans over and checks my pulse. "Zoe, you still breathing, baby?"

Good question. I wish I wasn't.

"I'm Laine Woods, also she/they, and I'm *pro—not-being-an-oversharing-drunk-asshole*," she says pointedly at me. Laine pulls up two chairs for herself and Harlow and squeezes them in at the opposite corner, as far as she can get from me. She salutes the rest of the table. "Nice to meet y'all. Thanks for the invite, Hannah."

Someone whispers, "Is she the—"

"*Yep*," someone else says quickly.

Hannah laughs nervously. "Sure thing!" The group murmurs subdued *hello*s to the newcomers as they send me covert glances, asking *are you okay?* with their eyes. I should be. I'm over the threesome with Harlow and Laine, *I am*. But God, did they have to hear me bragging about my new dildo and renouncing Laine's annoying face? I watch soundlessly as Harlow and Laine take their seats, Laine draping her arm over the back of Harlow's chair.

A wave of nausea crashes over me.

"So, Laine," Maeve begins, then clears her throat. "Do you have any use for a goat?"

Laine frowns. "What kind of goat?"

"You said you weren't coming!" The words blurt from my mouth before Maeve can begin her sales pitch.

"I changed my mind, boss. That okay?" Laine's voice is strained, like she's struggling to keep her contempt for me from erupting all over the table. She's barely looked at me since last week when I instructed her to contact Jamal, but she shows up now? Why? To show off Harlow and shove how much she doesn't like me in my face? Ruin the only other safe space I have?

I slide clumsily out of my chair, its legs screeching backward against the cement floor. I can't look at either of them. My sweatpants, my unwashed hair, my mom's old T-shirt blotched with years upon years of wine stains and a rip in one armpit that I wear when I'm feeling down. I didn't feel self-conscious before because my friends love me, but in the eye-melting sexual glow of Harlow and Laine, I feel like an old-timey story-book villain, drawn extra ugly so everyone will hate me and feel justified in doing so. The unreasonable boss. The lonely spinster. The tacky, drunk kiss-and-tell.

I make it to the sidewalk before the tears come.

The door slams behind me, then reopens just as fast. Footsteps hurry toward my turned back. I don't know which of my friends is checking on me, but I really wish they wouldn't. The mayor's snubbing, the run-in with Rachel, and now humiliating myself in front of Harlow and Laine? I need to cry this instant, need the release like steam fighting to escape a kettle.

"What the *hell* is your problem?" Laine spits from behind me.

Fuck. There goes the comfort hug I would have secretly gladly accepted. My back stiffens, and I don't turn around. "There are many problems," I reply, hating the tear-clogged sound of my voice. "To which are you referring?"

"You, Zoe Brennan, *you!* I'm doing your family this huge favor, and you treat me like I don't understand what the hell I'm doing!"

"Well, do you?" I fold my arms over my chest protectively, still staring out into downtown Blue Ridge, quiet now as the minutes tick toward closing. "You treat my vineyard like it's nothing, but don't you understand it's *everything* to me?"

"I don't—I mean—can you just look at me?" Laine grips my shoulder and turns me around, forcing me to meet her eyes. But when she sees my tear-streaked face, her anger melts into confusion. Her tight grip releases, her hand sliding slowly down my arm, until it stops where it circles around my wrist. "God, Zoe," she says softly, frowning in dismay as her eyes track across my face and the misery collected there. "Do you really hate me so much?"

I force myself to lift my chin, my breath catching in my throat. Because that's the problem, isn't it? After all the mean things she's said, the way she belittles the place I love most, after she casually moved from fucking me to loathing me and expects me to be fine with it?

"No. I don't." The truth of it barrels between us, along with all the words I don't have to say. Laine breathes sharply inward, and her hand tightens around my wrist. She pulls me toward her, the furrow between her brows deepening, and me? I've stopped breathing. Her other hand lifts tentatively, like she's either going to brush away my tears or push *me* away, unclear. Either way, I wish it would happen. Some kind of period to punctuate this standoff, cut it off and make the agony end. We're staring at each other so hard, she doesn't even notice the red Chevrolet that pulls up alongside us, its passenger window rolled down.

"Zoe Brennan? Your Lyft's here."

CHAPTER EIGHT

The hangover from the worst Queer Mountaineers gathering in history lasts a full two weeks. Tristan claims that's impossible, but how else to explain the headache that's gripped me ever since I drunk-sobbed all the way home in the one ride-share car in town? The driver blared heavy metal to give me some privacy, and maybe all that excessive guitar soloing helped, because eventually my tears transformed into righteous anger at all the many ways Laine sucks. The only way I've gotten through these last two weeks is that she literally turns and walks in the other direction as soon as she sees me. Which, good. Great.

The fact is this arrangement with Laine isn't working out. While she hasn't made any more rookie errors since she started meeting with Jamal, having her help isn't worth the physical *illness* I feel knowing she thinks my vineyard isn't good enough for her. The threesome just makes everything more complicated, leading to weird moments like outside the wine bar where her hate and my hurt mix with leftover lust, and I'm so tired of feeling broken and confused in the one place that's always given me strength. The day after the Queer Mountaineers gathering, I finally put out discreet feelers for someone to take her place. She can't wait to leave, so why make her stay?

I'm stepping out of the shower when my phone buzzes on the bathroom counter.

Gloria

U HOME 2DAY

Then, an instant later:

Gloria

I STG, ZOE, I SWEAR. TO. GOD.

Zoe

Yeah, I'm home. What's wrong?

Gloria

SEE U SOON

Huh. I try asking Gloria, then Maeve, what's going on a few more times, but they both leave me on read. I'm still puzzling down at my phone when it rings in my hand, right on time. It's Wednesday at nine here, but three p.m. Dad's time in Montepulciano, and we have a standing date to chat.

"Hey, Dad." I pull my wet hair out of the way and cradle the phone to my ear. "How are you? How's Nonna?"

"Zoe Nicoletta! It is so good to hear your voice," he says, just like he does every week, his words like a warm, lingering hug. "I am doing well, and your Nonna is having one of her better days." He says that every week, too, which makes me wonder about all the bad days he doesn't tell me about. I want an honest report, for him to finally give me some details about what's going on over there, but just like *I* do every week, I bite the questions down, too scared to ask. I never know how far I can push Dad before he'll topple over and shut down completely.

Once, a few days before the first anniversary of Mom's death, I asked him if we could do something special for her. I had this idea that we'd take her ashes and sit beneath her favorite tree. From dawn until dusk, we'd tell our favorite stories about her, and then maybe, after the moon rose, her ghost would come and visit with us. Mom believed in ghosts, after all, and I thought maybe the strength of our memories would pull her back to us, if only for one night. I was twelve, incredibly maudlin, and I'd just lost my mother. It seemed like the best idea I'd ever had. Life took her away, but what if magic could bring her back? Then Dad would be better, and I would be better, and after a long, wretched year of feeling disjointed and wrong, everything would finally *be better*.

It took me all day to summon the courage to share my idea. Maybe some part of me knew he couldn't handle it. When I finally did, he just . . . left. It was like the person inside his eyes slammed a door, shutting me out and locking himself in. He didn't speak for two whole months after that, and *I* became the ghost in our house. He didn't look at me, or talk to me, or anything. I could be standing right in front of him, but he didn't even *see* me.

It was terrifying.

I wasn't sure what scared me more—losing Dad, too, or being lost from him myself. When the anniversary came, I took Mom's ashes and sat beneath her tree alone. I told story after story about her to our vineyard and the birds singing in the trees, until my voice was hoarse, and I had to whisper the memories into the night. I sat there late, waiting for the moon to rise and for Mom to come back and finally make us whole again. But the moon never rose, and of course, Mom never came. Her urn was warm in my arms, but the heat was from *my* flesh and blood. Not hers.

I've walked lightly around Dad's grief ever since.

"So, how is the vineyard? Is Laine enjoying the work?" Dad prompts, and I let him change the subject away from the harder things. Like always.

"Honestly, Dad? It's going terribly."

"*What?* No, I can't believe it! Laine is such a lovely person, so qualified!"

"She's a complete wine snob, Dad." I comb my fingers through my still-dripping hair, then blot it with the towel, weighing whether I should confess I've put out feelers for a replacement. He'd *definitely* disapprove, and do I want his opinion?

Hard no.

"It's not snobbery to have standards for your wine, Zoe Nicoletta."

"Standards are one thing, messing with how we make our best-selling wine is another." My thoughts drift back to the one interaction we've had since the wine bar, when I happened to catch her doing some weird shit to (Wish They All Could Be) Georgia Girls. Dad always ensures that the finished product goes into the bottle crystal clear and free from any unpleasant particulate, but instead of following his directions, Laine was bottling up wine the color of cloudy gold.

"It strips the flavors if you over-filter, boss," Laine explained in this tight, miserable tone when I confronted her about it.

"Not everybody likes a mouthful of sediment when they're drinking wine, Laine," I'd replied, and she'd heaved a sigh and started over. But what would've happened had I not decided to lightly stalk her progress through the bottling? An entire season's worth of our bestseller would've been unrecognizable to our customers' palate, the strange organic cousin that brings pickled beet kombucha to the church potluck and gets hurt when nobody tries it.

"So what if she's shaking things up a bit? Bluebell Vineyards needs a fresh outlook in its wine offerings, Zoe. My heart hasn't been in it for some time, and I'm ashamed to admit that it shows in our declining quality."

I squeeze my eyes closed, willing my blood pressure to fall. I get that every day, Dad holds himself up against what Mom could do and finds his work pitiful in comparison. I understand that's the baggage he carries to his work, his own personal impostor syndrome.

But it still completely pisses me off.

"Dad, I've got to go. Busy day and all."

Dad exhales into the phone's receiver. After a long pause he says, "Okay, Zoe Nicoletta. I miss you."

"Miss you, too, Dad. So much." I sniff, the tears prickling against my will. "Give my love to everyone, especially Nonna."

"I will. Ciao, Zoe."

After the call disconnects, I let my head fall back onto the couch cushions, not caring about the wet spot it'll leave. Despite the conversation leaving me sour, Dad sounded lighter than usual. Brighter, even. Maybe things with Nonna aren't as bad as we initially suspected. Maybe she'll make a full recovery, and Dad doesn't want to jinx it by talking about it. Then Dad could come home, and this purgatory with Laine would finally end without it having to mean something terrible for Nonna. The thought is so comforting, I hold onto it for a little longer, letting myself imagine it into being.

Loud cursing erupts outside, followed by a crash of metal, and inexplicably, *bleating*. A barrage of frantic knocking sounds upon my cottage door., I open it to find Gloria who, still wearing her softball gear, is clutching a leash attached to a belligerent, bucking goat.

"What the hell's going on?" I tie my bathrobe tightly around my waist, looking between Gloria fuming on my step and Maeve running up the path to my cottage, desperately trying to catch up.

"Zoe, you've gotta take this goat RIGHT NOW!" Gloria's tanned face is tomato red, sweat beading all over. She thrusts the leash at my hands, which I stupidly take.

"What do you mean, take the goat?" My eyes widen as the goat does a double backkick and *baa*s aggressively at Gloria. "Take it where?"

"Good morning, Zoe!" Maeve wheezes, fully out of breath. "Turns out we're in dire need of a foster for this here goat!"

An incredulous huff of laughter bursts from my mouth. "Can*not* do, my friend."

"Temporarily?" Maeve pants. "For my marriage's sake? Come on, Laine already agreed!"

"No, she didn't!"

"You have to take 'im, Zoe!" Gloria yells like an angry umpire calling an out, right in my face. "He ate my best mitt!"

"Baby, I told you, I'll get you a new one," Maeve says, as much in the doghouse as the goat.

"That mitt was three hundred dollars, Maeve!" Gloria spits out. "*Three hundred dollars!*"

"Y'all know I love you, but I can't take your goat. Where would I even put it?" I try to shove the leash at Maeve, but she's grabbed Gloria's arm and is dragging her backward. Panic bubbles in my chest. I don't know the first thing about animals. I don't *do* pets!

"You've got a barn! Goats *love* barns! Laine'll know what to do!" Maeve says, then hisses something to Gloria, and they both break into a full run back to their truck. "Thanks, Zoe! We'll get this goat out of your hair ASAP!"

"Don't you leave me with this goat, Maeve Jenkins!" I holler, but the screech of tires drowns me out, and Maeve and Gloria disappear in a cloud of dust.

I stare at the goat.

It stares back and worse, has the audacity to remain my problem. "Goddammit, come on." I slip on my tennis shoes and tromp down the rows of vines, still in my damn bathrobe because how could I possibly change? Bring the goat into my cottage? Leave it to wander in my vineyard? Not happening. The goat trots behind me willingly enough until he sees the tempting new leaves on the Chardonnay vines.

"Come on, goat!" I tug the leash, trying to get him to leave my vines alone. Miraculously, he stops and turns his goaty chin toward me. With an ominous bleat, he rears up suddenly on his two back legs, yanking the leash from my grip. When he lands, he angles his head down, those demonic eyes flashing. I have a split second to notice his curvy horns before I realize they're pointed at *me* and quickly approaching.

A shriek rips out of me as I take off down the rows, my short bathrobe flapping in the wind. Am I faster than a goat? Only time will tell.

"HELP!" I shout as I run pell-mell toward the winery, the goat hot on my tail. "MAD GOAT!!"

Tristan peeks his head out the glass patio doors, spots me, and his eyes jack wide open. "Why's there a goat chasing you?"

"WHO THE FUCK CARES, GET IT OFFA ME!!" I wheeze-shriek as I beeline toward the barn next to the winery. It's full of barrels and other equipment in storage, but goats like barns, apparently.

Tristan takes off after us both, but while he's strong, he's not fast. My survival is up to me. The barn doors are right ahead. *Just a little farther, Zoe!*

I push my lungs to their limits, and with a last burst of speed, I fly through the planked door, its rusty hinges screaming. I hit something painfully solid on the other side of it, a *person*, knocking the air from my lungs with a loud *oof* as I tumble to the ground on top of them. Their hard stomach and soft chest, heaving and rustling beneath me, trapped.

Oh god! No. NO! I squeeze my eyes shut.

"What the—hell?!" Laine grunts from underneath me, trying to push me off. My mouth's still opening and closing like a fish, trying to suck in air that my lungs momentarily refuse to accept, like *haha, air, what's that?*

I manage to push myself up to sitting, still gasping for breath that won't come. Laine's angry face quickly turns to concern as she hoists herself onto her elbows, still beneath me. "Are you okay? Why are you—" Her eyes flicker down to my chest, where my pink bathrobe gapes wide open, exposing my breasts, the smooth line of skin all the way to my navel, thighs spread on either side of Laine's hips. The fact I'm not wearing any panties is *quite* evident. Color darkens her high cheekbones, and we both realize at the same time that her hands are gripping the sides of my thighs.

That does it. The sheer mortification forces air into my stubborn lungs, and I scramble to close my robe and gasp out, "Mad—goat! Chasing—me!" I make curly finger horns and hold them up to my head, unable to recall the right word, probably due to prolonged lack of oxygen.

Laine's brow furrows, and she peers past me, out the open barn door, to where the devil goat stands peacefully grazing on some overgrown grass. She turns her dubious gaze back on me.

"He was—chasing me!" I wheeze. "I swear!"

"Sure, boss." Then, she has the nerve to smirk. It's not lost on me that neither of us has moved, and is it my imagination, or have her hands slid higher up my legs? Heat emanates from where her fingers rest against that tender space between ass and leg, just enough pressure there to part me good and proper. She bites the corner of her lower lip, staring up at me, that blazing firelight returned to her eyes. I'm spread wide open against her, and it feels so good, it *hurts*. Apropos of nothing, her breathy, intense words from the pruning debacle spring to mind: *"Are you my boss?"*

My hand itches to dive into her hair, pull her head back, and slide my tongue up the tender skin of her neck till I wipe that smirk off her face.

"Um, Zoe?" Tristan says, hands on thighs and breathing heavily, having finally arrived on the scene.

"Hmm?" The voice that answers sounds dreamy, far away. I can't seem to rip my eyes from Laine's right now.

"That goat's running down the road."

"Fuck!"

"Well?" Laine's voice holds an urgent edge to it as she hunches over the steering wheel of my truck, her eyes scanning from left to right and back again. "Do you see him?"

Of all the things Laine Woods could care about, I did *not* see Maeve's devil goat coming. But Tristan barely got the words out that he was cantering down the road before Laine was scrambling up off the barn floor, bringing me with her.

"Come on! We've gotta catch him!"

"Us?" I'd asked incredulously. "*Why?*"

"He's from that petting zoo Maeve rescued, remember?"

"Yeah, so?"

"That means he's *domesticated*, Zoe! He can't survive out there!"

I'd started to say *nope* that I'd call animal control or better yet, Maeve, to come fix the mess she'd made, but Laine looked so worried in that moment, her eyebrows raised in a fitful rainbow of concern, that I . . . couldn't.

"Can I change first?" We'd both seen what was under my scanty bathrobe, aka nothing.

"*No!*" Laine yelled like I was the world's biggest idiot for asking, then threw herself into my truck and revved the engine to life. And that's how I ended up here, riding shotgun in nothing but a bathrobe and sneakers, while Laine barrels down the highway on the hunt for a damn goat.

But I don't have to like it. I glare at her.

"Don't look at me, look for *him*!" Laine demands.

I groan and lower the passenger side window. "Slow down! If he wandered into the woods, I won't see him with you flying down the road like this!" I tuck my legs beneath me, rise to my knees, and stick my head out the window.

"What are you *doing*?" Laine yells at my ass, which is probably fully on display judging by the breeze I'm feeling.

"What do you think? Here, goat!" I yell out at the blur of green, but no goat appears.

Hmph. So much for domesticated.

"If you lean much farther out that window, you're gonna fall out." Laine's voice breaks in over the choppy air beating against my face. "Saying it now: I will not be held accountable!"

"Just take your heavy ass foot off the gas pedal, and I'll be fine." I clasp my pink bathrobe a bit tighter around the neck, as if that will magically transform it into appropriate, ass-covering attire.

It doesn't.

The truck swerves suddenly, then corrects, sending me jolting upward in the window frame with an *oof*. "*Jesus.* Are you trying to hit every pothole in Georgia?" I glare over my shoulder at Laine. "I said slow down!"

She waves wildly with one hand at my ass without taking her eyes off the road. "You're distracting me! Can't you aim that thing somewhere else?!"

"It only points in one direction, Laine."

But then, a dark blur darts from the edge of the road across Into the Woods's parking lot. "There! Up ahead!"

Laine slams on the brakes, taking the turn into the parking lot with too much speed, and the sudden shift in momentum sends me falling backward, ass first, right into Laine's lap as the truck comes to a screeching halt.

We sit there a minute, both breathing heavily with the truck idling as I process that once again, I'm bare-assed atop Laine Woods. When I landed on her, her arms went around me protectively, wedging me between the old, knobby steering wheel and her. This close, I can feel the rapid patter of her heartbeat against my shoulder, and the intimacy of the sensation tugs something deep in my core.

Our eyes meet like magnets, my south pulled inexorably to her north, however unwillingly. A lock of the golden-brown hair she usually keeps swept to the side tumbles over her forehead, and my fingers yearn to touch it, push it back, *insist* it keep a business-professional posture here. That achingly soft wave of hair. How dare it so casually remind me of Laine mussed up from sex, her long limbs stretched languidly across the bed? But I can't trust my hand to correct. Not when that impulse's evil twin is right there, too, commanding me to bury my fingers into that naughty lock of hair and pull her to me, crushing my mouth to hers. Laine's watching me, breathless, like she's waiting to see what I'll do, too.

"You drive like a batshit maniac," I murmur, thoroughly annoyed at the cacophony of feelings she manages to produce in my once-quiet life. She doesn't deny it. Instead, she leans her head back against the headrest, eyes locked on mine. The strong line of her eyebrows and nose, her high cheekbones casting a light shadow across the hollows of her face—all these perfect, angular features contrast so starkly against the lush pout of her lips, so full and soft and sensuous it strikes me as obscene and entirely inappropriate. Laine Woods may be an insufferable snob who's upended my life, but she is inconveniently gorgeous. My head feels light.

"We've got to find him," she finally says, her voice so low it thrums in my belly.

"Who?"

The corners of her mouth lift, just a bit. Her eyes slide away from mine, down my neck, her arms flexing subtly to pin me in place, tighter. When her gaze returns to mine, it's like melted chocolate, sticky and rich and delicious and wonderfully *messy*.

"Our goat, boss." The words slowly drawl across my skin.

"Wait." My chin jerks at an angle. "*Our* goat?" When Laine doesn't immediately answer, my brow creases into a demanding line. "Laine Woods, what did you do?"

She shrugs, a sly smile appearing. "Goats are amazing at clearing brush." Then she slides out from beneath me for the second time today and out the car door.

My eyes widen. "I thought Maeve was lying! Tell me you did *not* adopt that goddamn goat—" I jump out of the cab after her when a loud banging sound, like hooves upon metal, comes from up ahead.

Rachel's sparkly white SUV is parked alongside the employee entrance to their tasting room, the trunk hatch open, revealing the telltale brown of grocery bags. Something loud crashes from within the car.

Oh, *shit*.

The employee door swings open, and there she is in expensive leggings and impeccably white tennis shoes, her hair pulled up into a long, swinging ponytail. She reaches the trunk before we do. Rachel grabs the last two bags while staring at us.

"What the *hell* are you two doing here?" Rachel pauses to squint at me, then clicks a button on her key ring that closes the trunk automatically. "And why are you in a bathrobe?"

A shadowy figure darts around the back seat, visible through the windows behind her.

Laine and I exchange a quick glance. *You tell her*, her gaze seems to say. *No way, it's your damn goat!* I glare right back.

Laine clears her throat. "Um, Rachel? There's something of mine in your car. I need to get it out real quick."

One of Rachel's eyebrows quirks as she heads for the driver's door. "Like hell there is."

"Please, Rachel, I'm *telling* you—"

"Look, I don't know what you're up to, but I'm not letting you root around in my car." She opens the door, still shaking her head, and hoists herself inside. "Now, leave. The winery is not open to the public right now." She aims that barb at Laine before slamming the door shut..

One second passes. Two. The ignition turns, then the car starts to pull out. My breath stutters in my chest. Doesn't she realize there's a *goat* in her back—

The brake lights blink on as the car lurches to a stop.

A scream. *"WHAT the FUCK!"*

The door opens and Rachel tears out of her fancy SUV, loud bleating behind her. Laine grabs the leash as the goat rips past, horns now aimed at Rachel's ass. But Rachel doesn't realize the suspect's been apprehended, because she's still running screaming her head off, all the way to the road.

I press a hand to my mouth.

"You assholes!" Rachel screeches from thirty feet away. "You put a *wild animal* in my car!"

"Not on purpose," Laine says, which makes a single, wild laugh burst through my fingers. Laine's chest rumbles once, her mouth quivering as it desperately wants to grin. I have to turn away, or I will *lose it.*

Rachel rage-stomps back to her SUV where the door's still open, the engine idling. Her eyes grow wide. *"My car!"*

I peer in after her and grimace. Squashed bananas in the back seat, a distinctly chewed headrest, the overall *eau de goat* lingering in the air . . .

She wheels on us, her face a riot of fury. "I'm calling the police!" She squeezes both hands into fists.

"Oh my GOD!" I exhale another laugh, my blood heating. "You left your trunk open, and the goat climbed in! It was an accident!" I fold my arms over my bathrobe. "Or karma, can't rule that out."

Rachel's eyes flare wide before narrowing, and she steps forward. "You just can't handle that Mayor Esposito has endorsed Into the Woods over your crappy vineyard for the *Everyday Bon Vivant* showcase, you jealous, little *bitch*."

"Rachel." Laine steps in front of me. "You need to stop talking to her like that, *right now*. Do you understand me?"

Rachel barks out a small, hard laugh, and like the minutes before a storm, the air is thick with vicious current. "Oh, I see." She flicks a finger up and down at my skimpy bathrobe, then at Laine's messy appearance. "The Hayseed Vintner and Lady Wine Cooler, rolling around in the barn when you're not making shit wine. What a match!" She turns those heartless eyes on me. "Just like you always wanted, *eh, Zoe*? Still got that box of yours?" Her teeth glisten through her sneer.

My heart threatens to stop beating altogether. "Rachel, *shut up*."

"You even tried to fuck our brother just to, *what*, squint your eyes and pretend you were really with Charlaine?"

"*Stop it*." Laine snaps.

"No, really, I'm happy for you both! It took Laine imploding her entire career out west before she'd look at you, but it's all working out!" She flings a hand at Laine. "Now you're working minimum wage at the illustrious Bluebell Vineyards, but hey, at least you get to fuck your boss while you shake down your family, right?"

I suck in a breath. What about Le Jardin? I search Laine's eyes for confirmation, but they dull and deaden on the spot.

A burst of fury *engulfs* me. Good thing the river's miles away because I have the sudden urge to throw Rachel into it.

"Come on, Laine." I tug at her arm, and after a second, her body complies. The goat trots willingly behind her.

"You may've fooled Mom and Dad, but I see you plain as day, Charlaine!" Rachel yells at our backs, still desperate to wound. "All you do is *take*, but I'm not giving you shit! D'YOU HEAR ME?!"

Laine hands me the truck's keys without meeting my eyes. "I'll walk him home." Before I can protest, she disappears down the road, the goat trailing beside her. I want to yell after her to come back, that Rachel's stupid, and for some reason, that everything's going to be okay.

But Laine Woods doesn't need my comfort.

Does she?

CHAPTER NINE

"Mwreah?" I flop up in bed, flailing about for the ringing thing that woke me from a *very* good, if problematic, dream where I was inexplicably a 1950s secretary taking dictation from a suited Laine on a loud, clicking typewriter. Only, her mouth was on my ear, breathing the words into me from behind while she grabbed my breast with one hand and fingered me hard in time with the clicking of the keys with the other. I groan, wishing for the secretary dream to come back, but somebody's shouting at me.

Oh, right. My phone. I find it on the nightstand and yank the charging cord out. The ringing finally stops. *Bliss.*

"Zoe! You there?" A voice that sounds both far away and too close makes me snuffle awake again. I grab the phone and put it against my head.

"What."

"Zoe? This is Jamal. Don't tell me I woke your ass up."

"Jamal?" I pull the phone back and squint at it before resting it haphazardly on my face. "It's two a.m. What the hell?"

"This is your friendly neighborhood frost warning. You've got approximately twenty minutes to get your smudge pots going before your buds are killed! Now go get Laine—she isn't answering her phone!"

That wakes me *all* the way up. A late spring frost is the worst-case scenario. The low temperature kills the buds and can wipe out entire crops, which would devastate a vineyard the size of ours. We can't afford to buy replacement grapes like the richer vineyards can, nor can we go all out and hire helicopters to fly over our vines all night, keeping the air moving and preventing the frost from forming like Into the Woods does.

No, us poor outfits do smudge pots.

I leap out of bed, chilling my bare feet as I race around my cold bedroom, throwing on my warmest pair of jeans, boots, and a thick sweater. I grab my coat and scarf, and for the second time today, race down the rows of my vineyard, this time heading for the Treebnb. I haven't seen Laine since she left Into the Woods on foot with our new foster goat, and I pray she's home. The cold air assaults the few inches of my exposed skin, slicing through my layers until I shiver. Ironically, these icy winds streaming down the mountains will protect our higher-placed crops from frost forming on their baby buds and tendrils, but they can't reach the vines located lower on our property.

I take the steps up the spiral staircase to our Treebnb two at a time, clutching the rail. "Laine?" I beat at her door. "Wake up!" Running smudge pots requires all hands on deck, and right now, there are only two sets of hands: mine and Laine's. Josiah, our vineyard hand, would normally handle these with Dad, but he's out of town. Not only do you have to haul out your propane-fueled smudge pots—metal chimneys speckled with holes that emit heat from the fire raging inside—you've gotta get the fires started, too, then stand guard over them until the frost passes. We only have about five working smudge pots, which means Dad and Josiah end up lighting fires in big steel drums strategically placed around the property to cover the rest.

It's a lot of work, and with less than twenty minutes? We'll be lucky to protect half the crops. Damn, this frost came out of *nowhere*.

"LAINE!" I bellow, briefly considering using my master key to break in and haul her out of bed when shuffling steps approach the doorway, followed by a string of cursing. She's at the door a minute later.

"What is it?" she garbles, eyes barely open. There's something wrong with her face, like her teeth are too big for it.

"Frost!" I exclaim, then realize what's so weird. "Are you . . . wearing a retainer?"

"What?" Laine's eyes widen and she ducks out of sight, spitting hard. "*No!*"

I literally hear the bulky dental device clatter against the floor, and despite the dire situation, a smirk tugs my upper lip. "You *were*."

"No, I wasn't!" Laine snaps over her shoulder, leaving the door open for me to come in after her. She's wearing a sports bra and thermal jammy pants that hug the muscular curvature of her body, but all I can think about is the fact that Laine Woods is embarrassed about something.

My smirk grows into a full grin. Laine narrows her eyes at me as she yanks on a sweatshirt, then grabs her jeans from the floor. "What are you looking at?"

"Your beautiful teeth."

Laine groans, then shoves past me. "Let's go!"

Two minutes later, we're running to the barn, stepping lightly past the devil goat all nestled in his stupid hay to get to the smudge pots.

"Have you ever used a smudge pot?" We heave it onto the hand truck, the propane sloshing in its tank below. Thank God Dad preloaded them with fuel for the season.

Laine grimaces. "Nope."

I exhale a sigh. "Right. Napa. Okay, just follow my lead."

Together we manage to get the smudge pots in place, setting each one ablaze, but as the temperature continues to drop, it's woefully clear that we need way more fires across the property to save the buds. I'm drenched in cold sweat beneath my clothes from the labor, but we don't stop until the steel drums are positioned in all the low-lying areas of our property. The fires in those are harder to light, but we split up, and an hour later, Bluebell Vineyards is a dark sky with a constellation of fiery stars flickering merrily. I finish lighting the last one and find Laine where she's collapsed beneath a big tree, her back against its trunk and legs sprawled out.

The image twists beneath my skin, squeezing my heart. It's Mom's favorite tree, where I sit vigil on her birthdays to this day. Not from dawn until dusk like I used to, but I spend at least an hour at twilight there every year, telling myself my favorite stories about her and holding them close. I do it in part because it's tradition, but also because I'm terrified of forgetting them. I haven't sat here for any other purpose since Mom died, but I ease down onto the ground next to Laine, my body singing a symphony of aches and pains.

It's quiet for a long minute as we stare out onto the vineyard lit by fire below. I get why Laine picked this tree to sit under—there's a sweeping view of our entire property from up here. That's why it was Mom's favorite, too.

"I'm sorry," Laine says so quietly it's almost drowned out by the winds still whipping down the mountains at our backs.

I turn and frown at her. Her features are displayed in shades of grey instead of her usual golds and browns, but she's as bold in this monochrome moonlight as she is in color. "You're . . . sorry? For what? Adopting a damn goat without asking?"

Laine blinks, then huffs out a small laugh. "That, too, I guess. God, everything. For being such a pain in your ass. For being wrong all the time and refusing to acknowledge it. For being such a liability here." She riffles a hand through her hair, which I've noticed she does when she feels uncomfortable. "A late-season frost, just like you said." She huffs, and it's filled with self-loathing. "Thank God you stopped me from pruning that day. I could've really screwed things up."

"Yeah, well." I shrug, unsure how to feel now that I'm finally receiving all the remorse I've felt owed ever since Laine showed up. Not sure I want it anymore, though. Not if it comes with the potent disgust for herself underlying all her words. "You didn't."

Laine draws her knees up, her eyes watchful over the fires. She looks defeated, a word I don't associate with Laine Woods. "In California, everything I did was too Georgia. In Georgia, everything I do is too California." She shakes her head, her frustration with herself evident and painful to see. "I don't fit anywhere."

"What about . . . Missouri?"

She looks so affronted it makes me laugh.

"What? Right in the middle." I squint an eye and poke a finger at an imaginary map. "You could be a Branson dyke."

Laine scrunches up her face and huffs out a single incredulous laugh. "Okay, first? Missouri isn't in the middle of the country, look at a map sometime; second, what the hell is a *Branson dyke*?"

I shrug again, ridiculously pleased to have gotten a laugh out of her. "Oh, I don't know. A lady that enjoys themed minigolf, riverboat gambling, and breasts?"

"I do enjoy breasts." Laine tilts her head to the side. "And minigolf."

"All Branson dykes do," I explain, the new authority on this thing I just invented. "See? You'd fit right in."

"Next stop, the city of freshly chlorinated waterfalls," Laine says, but her tone's too wistful for chemically blue water.

"You fit here, Laine," I say softly. She side-eyes me, one eyebrow high, as though she knows I'm full of shit. "Or you could, at least. If you wanted to."

"I don't know what I want anymore," Laine murmurs, more to the vineyard than to me. "Rachel was right—my career out west imploded. Everything was going so well, I thought—" She pauses to swipe at a single tear rolling down her cheek. "I thought I was invincible. Destined for the top."

"What happened?"

"After years of making Le Jardin's signature line, I'd finally earned the right to experiment with a new white for the label. It's a big deal, you know, they don't put their name on just anything, and I was so eager to make *my* wine for once, I just—" Laine pauses to shake her head. "I aimed for the fences. Tried the organic processing method I'd been dying to implement, experimented with a new blend of grapes, too much new all at once, and it was . . ." Her shoulders drop, along with her gaze. "Not great. This wine critic Benjamin Soren attended an early tasting and wrote a scathing review for *Vinitopia* magazine. 'The Hayseed Vintner,' he called me, the Georgia bumpkin who made wine that tasted like a barnyard. Le Jardin fired me a few weeks later."

"Over one review?" I can't keep the shock from my voice. "That's crazy!"

"That's Le Jardin. They don't keep losers around."

"Laine, you're *not* a loser. So you made something that one asshole didn't like—"

She holds up a finger. "Lots of assholes didn't like it, to be fair."

"So what? At least you made something! At least you *tried*." I shake my head. "So many people go their whole lives without ever taking a chance on themselves. Too afraid to speak up, or stick their necks out, or God forbid, be seen *trying* to do something. To them, being embarrassed or disliked is scarier than never being anything at all. *That's* losing to me. So you tried something, and it didn't work out. That doesn't make you a loser. It makes you brave."

The words hang in the air around us, like little stars burning brightly. I huddle closer into myself, into the comfort of my ambition. "We have this one life, Laine. If we're not brave enough to try and live it, to give ourselves and our dreams the benefit of the doubt, then what's the point?"

Laine looks at me sidelong, surprise changing the architecture of her expression. It warms my cheeks, the way she watches me, as though I might say something profound that she really wants to hear.

It's ironic since she's the one who taught me this lesson. This almost-religious faith in trying is what drew me to her in the first place, all those years ago.

I duck my chin into my scarf.

"But what if you fail so spectacularly, you're not sure you know how to try anymore? What if trying feels like failing, and everything feels wrong? How do you keep going then?"

"Maybe because it's your dream?" I offer slowly. This is unknown territory, this *conversing* with Laine—not fighting, or bickering, or feeling so in awe of her that I couldn't speak at all. Maybe this foreign terrain is only accessible under the light of the moon and the magic of a dozen tiny fires, but . . . I want to explore it. "Maybe because you know, deep down, that trying is hard, failing is harder, but giving up what you love would be hardest of all."

Laine looks at me then, long and assessing. "Is that how you feel?"

"About Bluebell? Yes." I lean my head against the tree trunk and look at her, too. "This place is special. My mom knew it, my dad knew it, and they built our whole lives around this small, beautiful piece of the universe. I feel a moral imperative to keep it going, to cherish it, to share it with others."

Laine considers me thoughtfully. "I'm sorry about that, too. I've been a real dick about Bluebell Vineyards."

"Yeah. You have."

Laine drags a long breath in. "Would you believe me if I said it wasn't about Bluebell at all?"

"I would, because this place is magical, and any problems you have with it come from you." I intend the words to be playful, but Laine's frown only grows.

"You're right." She looks sheepishly up at the moon now, like she's asking it for forgiveness instead of me. "I told myself coming home was only temporary, but even still, it feels like surrender. Been working through some resentment about how it all went down, and—I don't know. It was easier to put all those bad feelings on C'est la Grigio than take owner- ship of my fuckups, you know? Because I did fuck up. Everything in that review is true. I *am* difficult to work with. The wine I made *did* taste like a barnyard." She looks down at our vineyards with such regret, it catches in my heart. "But I swear I'm a better vintner now, and I can do better. I *will* do better, for you."

And I'm—*impressed*. I'm *floored*. Here Laine is, spilling out her feel- ings, and I don't know what to do with it. I've spent so long living in a house of deferred sadness, Dad and I both moving around our grief gin- gerly, cautiously, as though one loud footstep might wake it up, and it'd devour us for good. Ignoring our feelings has become a way of life. When I feel sad, angry, or hurt, I turn those feelings into work. But now, under Mom's favorite tree, Laine's shoulder gently pressed against my own, stay- ing silent about my own crimes seems . . . well, criminal. A violation of everything about this moment that's made it so meaningful. I don't want to leave Laine out here in truth-land alone.

"I do know," I say softly. "What it's like, I mean. To lay a big bag of bad feelings at the wrong doorstep and light it on fire."

Laine frowns. "Is that—a burning dog shit metaphor?"

"Well, it fits, doesn't it?" I shake my head irritably. "Listen, I'm sorry for making things difficult for you here. I'm viciously protective of Blue- bell as you've noticed, but the tension between us stems from more than that." I swallow, the words suddenly difficult to find, but I want to pay Laine's courage and honesty back to her and prove that I'm ready to make things better, too.

"It's just, I'm used to being set aside, okay? I've hooked up with every queer woman in Blue Ridge only to watch each one of them move on and find somebody else. But I'm not used to facing that feeling of being discarded every day, here, at my favorite place on earth. You criticizing Bluebell Vineyards after what happened between us snowballed into one big uncomfortable rejection for me."

"You feel . . . rejected?" Laine asks.

"Well, yeah." My cheeks are on fire, and my mouth has suddenly gone bone dry. "Part of me has been punishing you for your negative opinions about the vineyard and our wines, but—about me, also. You hit me on two fronts." I turn to her now, ready to face her. The mild shock in her expression makes me feel a little better. At least my petty bullshit hasn't been totally transparent. "I'm sorry for being so unprofessional, Laine. I know we said we'd put what happened behind us, and this time, I really will."

In the cold, dark night, our bodies creating our own force field of warmth, I wait for Laine's reaction. I desperately want her to tell me it's okay, that she likes it here and that our wines are actually good. And if I'm honest, that she's struggled with keeping things professional between us, too. Those scorching moments, when her desire to dominate collides with my own, they couldn't have all been in my head.

Could they?

I see her full lips part, hear the intake of air, but the space between that breath and the words that follow stretches on. When my eyes flick upward, her expression's unreadable.

"Was all that true? What Rachel said about . . . how you felt back then?"

For an instant, I consider owning it. Telling her just how much she meant to me as a young queer, the massive space she's occupied in my psyche since I was a wee tween. Would she understand then how hard it's been having her here, hating me? Would it change anything?

"Nah." I shrug. "It was just a little crush."

We have departed truth-land, and it shows. *God.* That wouldn't convince a wall.

"Uh-huh," Laine says.

"I didn't even know I was gay."

Sure, Zoe. Let's double-down on the bullshit.

"No, no. Makes sense," Laine deadpans. "Wanting to kiss other girls is *surprisingly* unclear."

"How would I know?" My voice rises. "What if I was just a Charlaine-o-sexual?"

Laine frowns. "I thought you were Italian, not Irish."

I throw my head back and laugh, Laine's ember eyes twinkling above her own pleased smile.

"You were my best friend's older sister." I shrug again, as if that's what this moment needs—more ambivalent body language. "You were like a celebrity to us." My body is on fire in this cold, starless night, burning from the inside out, and I point my gaze at the vineyard blocks instead, willing my heart to stop hammering in my chest. "Now you know why it blew my mind when I discovered that Lina, the dead-sexy butch in the blindfold, was actually *Charlaine Woods*, #27 of the Gilmer County Bobcats. Star student and queen of Blue Ridge who could do no wrong."

I wait for her smug smile, for that *damn right, next time you better remember who you're dealing with* attitude to flare. Her lips twitch upward before melting into a frown. "That's not who I am anymore."

And dammit if that's not worse than the arrogance I'd expected.

I swallow hard. "Well, celebrity or not, you didn't even remember who I was that night at Harlow's."

Laine blows out a long breath. "Yes, I did."

I cut a disbelieving glance at her, and she quickly amends. "I mean, I didn't immediately connect the dead-sexy *Amélie* type hyperventilating in the nude with my kid sister's best friend. Even after you said it, my brain refused to compute." Her smile is faint, but playful. "In my defense, you *were* naked. But I remember you. Of *course* I remember you."

The words fill me to the brim, like a glass of overflowing champagne, the feelings they create fizzing over me in bubbling streams. Down my neck, my chest, my arms, across the tight buds of my nipples. She *did* remember me. And she thinks I'm sexy, too? *Swoo—*

I stop mid-swoon.

"Wait. Just as Chop Chop?" I raise an eyebrow.

Laine laughs. "More than that. You used to come to all my games, like this bonus member of my family fan club. This sad, shadowed girl, but you always lit up in the stands." She shrugs. "And here I thought you were just really into soccer."

I snort. "Not so much."

"You always painted my number on your cheek. I loved that." Laine smiles fondly, and somehow, I know that smile is for young Zoe. It ricochets around my heart, searching for its home until it lands, warm and soothing against a spot that's ached for ages. "It always made me feel special, you looking up to me like that," she says quietly. "It's . . . hurt, watching you change your mind. Feeling so dumb every time you called me out for my lack of experience here. Knowing you wouldn't want me near your vineyard after you found out about the review."

I twist to face her, and before I can think better of it, my gloved hands grip her by her upper arms. Her muscles tense beneath my touch. "Let's get one thing straight, Laine Woods. I don't give two shits about that review. You are incredibly talented, and no critic can change my mind about that, because I *see* you. All that matters to me is that you try while you're here. Try to learn how we do things in a Georgia vineyard and try to make our wine as good as possible."

Her eyes search mine, like she's hunting for any trace that I don't mean the words I'm saying. I lift my chin. "Can you do that for me?" My thumb rubs a light circle against her arm until I force myself to stop.

"I will," she says, her voice a vow.

"Good. And maybe try to keep more of an open mind, too."

"About what?" Laine's forehead creases a little. "I'm open-minded."

"About *everything*, Laine. Living here, working here. Georgia Girls." A small smile settles on my face. "How good it tastes."

"Don't you mean how good *they* taste?" The corner of her mouth lifts wickedly, and a current zips from her arms into my hands. I realize I'm still gripping her, but instead of letting go, my fingers momentarily tighten, like I mean to drag her to my mouth, taste her all over again.

Her eyebrows lift into a playful bend, but her eyes are dark and hungry. It steals the air from my lungs.

"I'm sorry. I just promised you I'd be professional," I breathe out into the small space between us, feeling my temperature rise, "but you're making it difficult."

The apology would be more effective if I could let go of her. Laine's smirk deepens, her chest broadening between my hands, like a lion about to teach a lesson to the kitten swatting at its nose. "You saying I'm asking for it, boss?"

Are you? I want to demand, shake the answer I want from her like apples from a tree. *Are you asking for it?*

Or am *I*?

My fingers finally release her, a jolt of shame retracting them like bolts in a lock. "I'm sorry, *Jesus*. I'm a *terrible* boss."

She clocks the change in my demeanor, and her own smirk softens.

"Now let me get something straight with *you*, Zoe Brennan," she says, meeting my eyes. "We've only worked together for a few weeks, but you're already the best boss I've ever had. You're creative and kind and, god, this sounds corny, but you're *inspiring*." Her words drip down my spine like warm honey, settling between my legs. "So I'm gonna do my best for you, and together, we're gonna win that showcase. Got it?"

I swallow and nod. Laine, who dominated every Gilmer County spelling bee, soccer game, and goddamn *limbo* contest, on my team. *Truly* on my team. Whatever hesitation I saw when I assigned her the red wine renovation is long gone now, as though she couldn't access her signature determination until we banished the specter of that horrible review for good.

Laine smiles and leans back against the tree, her shoulder pressing warmth into mine as we quietly watch the fires dotting the vineyard like the first fireflies of summer. The thick cover of clouds spackling the night sky has begun to peel away, revealing cracks of cold, silvered moonlight. As the night passes us by, the heat swirling within me finally cools, but down below, our fires burn bright.

CHAPTER TEN

Day always comes too soon after a night spent under the stars. Worse, I drank so much coffee last night, it seems to have lost any effect. I lay my head down on the bar in our empty tasting room then jolt upright when my phone buzzes from my back pocket.

WARNING, it's that bitch Rachel

> Your goat did $1,382.47 worth of damage to my car. Here's the itemized breakdown.

Three photos come in quick succession showing a bill for the many tasks required to de-goat Rachel's SUV. I groan.

Zoe

> $250 for a ceiling shampoo?
> Was that really necessary?

WARNING, it's that bitch Rachel

> There were HOOF MARKS on my CEILING.
> Send it to my Pay-Me app. ▦

I snort despite the hit my checking account's about to take, then transfer the funds over less two dollars and fifty-two cents, an amount I pick at random, because the discrepancy will bug her to no end.

WARNING, it's that bitch Rachel

> Received.

A second later, the *typing . . .* notification pops up, then disappears, pops up again, my petty smile growing until another text arrives.

WARNING, it's that bitch Rachel

Stay away from Charlaine.

I stare down at the phone in disbelief.

Zoe

Being that she's my vintner . . . no.

WARNING, it's that bitch Rachel

Romantically, asshole.

Zoe

Why, you got dibs or something?

WARNING, it's that bitch Rachel

 She will destroy you, Zoe, and you know it.

WARNING, it's that bitch Rachel

Also, you owe me $2.52.

I put my phone down and slowly lower my forehead to the bar again. I'm too tired to think about Rachel's ominous words, and now too broke to feel joy.

"Am I interrupting your nap?" Tristan cruelly flicks each switch on as he enters for his afternoon shift. He's got charcoal eyeliner on today, which means swooning will occur in this tasting room tonight. The smoky gray brings out the grassy centers of his hazel eyes, and he knows it. Right now, those babe magnets are fixed on me in a decidedly *are you kidding me* posture.

Ungrateful subordinate.

"Yes."

He sighs through his nose as he readies the tasting room for our Thursday crowds. And by crowds, I mean Ms. Betty's cross-stitch club that comes here every week to drink and embroider until someone gets hurt. He puts out an assortment of tapestry needles, spare hoops, and embroidery floss in discount colors at their usual table by the windows. All he needs are the butt cushions from the back to pad the chairs for our genteel guests and their long-suffering asses and a healthy stock of chilled Georgia Girls, and we'll be ready for a long, rowdy afternoon with the ladies.

Laine enters through the patio doors, the epitome of bright-eyed and bushy-tailed, which *how?*

"Good afternoon, boss!" She hops onto a barstool and beams at me. It's enough to make my dead pulse stammer in my veins. Before when she called me boss, it was snide, a reluctant acquiescence to whatever dumb thing I was demanding of her. But this time, it's friendly and light, a nod to our new understanding forged beneath the canopy of my mother's tree. A door creaks open inside me, just an inch.

I try to smile back, but it collapses into a yawn. "Bad afternoon. Sleepy afternoon." Broke afternoon more like it, but despite Laine's pivotal involvement in yesterday's goat debacle, I'm not asking her for money to help cover it. Not sure why, exactly.

Laine scoffs and drums her hands happily on the bar. "Get some coffee and come right back. I've got an idea I want to run by you."

I'm too busy frowning to move, though.

"Go on," she adds, a devilish smile on her face. "*Chop, chop.*"

"Ex-*cuse me, Beave?*"

"Oh, you done it now," Tristan drawls as he spools some loose floss.

Laine lifts her ass off the barstool and leans over the bar. Her eyes are alight with mischief, a small, satisfied smirk dancing on her lips. She's so close, I can smell the crisp citrus notes of young wine wafting off her skin. It fits her, highlighting her real scent like a perfume. My mouth waters.

"Sorry for callin' you names, boss," Laine says, inches from my face, though she doesn't sound sorry at all. Her smirk's now a grin, and my ears flush. It's hard to hold up this mock outrage when her warm breath slides down my throat, prickling the skin there. "But I was there that night, so I've got rights." Laine hovers there for a moment, that wicked grin jacking up my heartbeat like caffeine hasn't managed to all day. Can I drink two cups of *her* every morning? Sweet Jesus.

She points to the back. "Go on now. We've got work to do!"

I stumble when I stand up, accidentally kicking a bucket, an empty crate, and for some reason, the *wall*, on my way to the back, where we keep our coffee stash right outside my office. I've drunk so much coffee today it tastes like water now, but I can't tell Laine no. Not when she's looking at me like that.

Quite troubling, really.

The blush has worked its way down my entire body, and I hate myself a little for physically responding to her casual flirting. Because I know why she's doing this—I'm an expert in this field. This is good, old-fashioned *throw her a bone* sympathy. When two people come to an understanding that, *yes, we hooked up, and no, we're not gonna do it anymore,* but it's not quite mutual? This is what happens: pity-flirting.

The rejector pity-flirts with the rejectee, and while it may *look* convincing, the message is clear: *hey, maybe it could happen again! But we both know it won't, so don't try anything and accept this light flirting for your bruised ego so I don't feel bad about never wanting to see you naked again, okay? Thaaaaanks.*

I'm extremely familiar. So familiar that, when Hannah first moved here, she didn't believe me when I explained nobody in town wanted anything to do with me.

"What're you talking about?" she'd exclaimed as Kai blew me a kiss in Das Kaffee Haus. "Everyone's been winking and wagging their eyebrows at you all day!"

"It's pity-flirting, Hannah. I guess some might still find me attractive, but they've all had their taste—"

"A conscious word choice, here for it."

"And chose not to have seconds or thirds and *why* am I talking about myself like I'm a meal?"

"Because society has trained us to think of women as something to be consumed."

"Fucking society." We'd clinked gingerbread lattes at that (that woman can*not* drink plain coffee to save her life) and carried on with our day, Hannah pointing out every instance of empty queer flirtation, and me, dryly outlining the series of unfortunate events that got me there like some sad lesbian Lemony Snicket.

Still, I can't be angry with Laine for throwing me a bone. It's better than the sour looks and frustrated sighs she's doled out ever since she started working here. I just need to keep my head on straight about what it means, that's all.

When I return, she's busily gesturing to Tristan while he stands by, arms folded, a big frown on his face.

"I don't know," Tristan says, unconvinced. "Zoe doesn't like to sweat."

"What in the world are you talking about?" I step up to their little duo, peering between them.

Laine turns to me, her face like sunlight. "Mayor Esposito's Field Day fundraiser is next weekend."

"Yeah, so?" My tone turns frosty. Rachel plans the Field Day fundraiser in the mayor's honor every year, which is a great idea, but that's the problem—throwing an all-ages field day was *my* great idea before Rachel stole and repackaged it as her own. She even schedules it the same weekend in spring I used to schedule mine, forcing our events into a direct head-to-head popularity contest—which I lost when she tacked on a fundraiser for Mayor Esposito. From what I hear, Rachel prances about like Queen Spandex when she's not viciously elbowing children out of the way to win all the events.

"We should sign up as a team."

"I'd rather drink red wine vinegar."

"You need time to pitch to the mayor, now's your chance. Plus, what does Rachel hate more than anything?" Laine's smile stretches across her face, pure Grinchian connivery, and my lower belly hums in response.

I clear my throat, but my voice still comes out in a rumble. "Um, losing?" I pose it like a question, but there's no question about it. I once saw her self-destruct over Candyland.

She was fifteen.

"That's right." Laine's eyes shimmer like caramel in a pan—hot, sweet, sticky—as they track down my face to my mouth, then back again. *"Especially* to me. Doesn't that sound like fun, boss?"

Laine Woods is business evil, and boy, do I *like it*. A flood of warmth streams down my spine as I feel my cheeks burn.

Yes. Yes, it does.

The best part of being a baseball player is having your own theme song play as you walk up to bat. I've *always* wanted one. Something that'd automatically start rolling whenever I enter a room, letting everybody know that *I'm Zoe Brennan, and I'm about to kick some ass.*

I wouldn't have chosen "Let It Go" from the *Frozen* soundtrack, yet that's what's playing as our ragtag team of Bluebell Vineyards employees and friends saunters onto the field, dressed in matching tie-dye shirts from the gift shop and a *can-fuckin'-do* attitude. Teddy's in front with the Bluetooth speaker, running slightly ahead so that Tristan can't tackle him and change it to "Bad Blood" by Taylor Swift and Kendrick Lamar.

I glance over at Laine, and she smiles. Her glasses have been tucked away for the day, and she's sporting a smear of yellow paint across each cheekbone, like the eye black football players wear to reduce glare, but less useful since Teddy insisted we go full rainbow.

After all, how often do you have an all-queer field day team?

Our grand entrance turns heads, and soon a mob of children is singing along to the wildly complex anthem Teddy's chosen for us. It feels good to slap their little palms as we jog toward the contestants' area, and when Rachel sees us from the stage, straight-up delightful. She looks *pissed*, and a rich, sultry satisfaction blooms in my chest.

Laine leans in, her warm breath tickling my ear. "Go on and say it."

"Say what?" I turn my head, halting when I realize any farther would bring us lip to lip.

Laine's eyes twinkle. "That I'm a genius for signing us up."

I shrug coyly. "That remains to be seen." My eyes drift back to the stage, where Mayor Esposito stands straight-backed in a royal blue skirt suit next to Rachel. If I manage to finally get the mayor alone to deliver my pitch for hosting the showcase, I'll call Laine anything she wants.

Rachel hits the mic in a rapid, woodpecker attack, *thwick-thwick-thwick*, until we take our places among the other contestants. A too-big grin transforms her expression from murderous to psychopathic. "Hello there! Welcome to Blue Ridge's favorite field day festival"—she throws that grenade at me before letting her gaze travel across the crowds—"in honor of everybody's favorite mayor, Flor Esposito!" She lifts her hands in a dainty little clap, like exerting too much noise might be considered masculine. That's Rachel in a nutshell, though—deeply self-conscious, restrained, but *vicious*.

"Team captains, please report to the sign-in desk to get your squad's schedule of events and remember," Rachel says, her dark eyes glittering beneath the rim of her faux-aged mauve baseball hat, "*have fun!*"

Tristan shudders. "Why did that feel like a threat?"

We nominate Laine as our captain, and when she returns with our team's schedule, she's grinning.

I raise an eyebrow. "What have you done?"

Laine shrugs. "Oh, nothing. Just made sure that our team is competing against Rachel's in every challenge. We're gonna kick some Woods ass." Our team erupts into cheers.

"Now, now," I say, raising both hands. "Rachel's right—"

Booing ensues.

"—we *are* here to have fun, but also corner the mayor so she can't hide from me anymore. Winning is optional."

Laine laughs and pats my back. "Right. Sure. *Anyway*, we've got to play to our strengths if we're going to sweep this thing—which is *mandatory*. Teddy, I hear you're the Peloton champ of Appalachia?"

"These hips hinge like a nutcracker, baby." Teddy slaps his thighs. Everybody's eyes flick to Diego, out of concern or morbid curiosity or some mix of both, but he's too busy beaming at his husband to notice.

Laine nods as if that settles things. "Great. Nutcracker, you're on the tricycle race. Tristan, Diego, and I will take tug-of-war."

My brow furrows. "Hey! I'm strong." It's a stretch, but I can't take Laine's truthful assessments without putting up a fight. "Ish."

Diego smiles kindly at me. "Honey, you arm-wrestled Bowie and lost."

"He's two!" My eyes bug out with indignation. "What was I supposed to do, smack a toddler down?"

"Yes," Teddy, Diego, and Laine all say in unison.

"At least, for today." Laine grins. "But don't worry, you're doing the balloon race, and that requires no toddler fighting."

I don't know what the balloon race entails, but I'm relieved it's not the human wheelbarrow. Halfhearted protests aside, my workout routine consists of removing corks and zipping up my own dresses. But luckily, Laine's decided she and Teddy will do the human wheelbarrow, which basically requires someone driving you by the ankles while you attempt an extended plank. *No, thank you.* The only plank I can do is the pirate kind.

Someone sounds an air horn, and the teams scatter to their respective events. The mayor immediately disappears from the stage, and my lips form a thin line.

"Look alive, Brennan!" Laine yells from up ahead, and I straighten immediately in response to the stern coach vibes she's putting off. First up for the Eager BV-ers is the tricycle race. Teddy's a small-statured man, but even he looks huge on the shiny blue trike, knees flared wide on either side of him like he's on the world's squattiest potty. The race begins with a loud *Ahhoooga!*, and the children competing stream forward, leaving the awkward adults cursing in their dusty wake, Teddy included. Representing the Woods Winners (real clever, Rachel) is Chance's daughter, Darla, who just turned six and has definitely inherited the family's competitive streak. With a bloodthirsty grin, she pedals her trike, squealing around the track. Teddy looks ready, willing, and able to take out the gaggle of children flanking him on all sides, but luckily Darla screeches across the finish line before mistakes are made. Despite being Gulliver on a Lilliputian vehicle, Teddy comes in second.

"You'll get 'em next time, Nutcracker!" Laine claps Teddy on the shoulder as he limps past. Rachel and the rest of the Woods Winners are busy congratulating little Darla, but Rachel stops long enough to give me a predatory smile.

My blood runs cold. I drag our team into a huddle. "Okay, listen up, BV-ers. We *cannot* afford to place second again."

"We can't?" Laine asks, her tone teasing.

"No!" I frown at her, hard.

"But we're here to have fun, boss." Her smile is so playful now I feel the urge to push her down and lick it off.

"That was before I had to see *that*." I thumb over my shoulder in a rough approximation of where Rachel still stands with her shit-eating smile. "Now it's about total annihilation. *And* team building."

Laine's smile turns up a notch. "Well, you heard the boss, team!" We each put a hand in the middle, and on the count of three, yell, "B-V, BV-ERS!"

My pep talk must be working because the BV-ers absolutely crush Chance, his wife Betsy, and one of their farmhands in tug-of-war. The moment Chance and Betsy fall into the dirt, Tristan and Laine do a running chest thump while Diego beats his pecs and crows at the sky. Rachel, now an alarming shade of fuchsia, marches up to her fallen teammates.

"What *was* that, Betsy?! I thought you taught Pilates!" Rachel yanks their team's schedule out of Chance's hands and begins scribbling furiously on it, then huffs over to the sign-in table, who accepts her team's substitutions with a mild look of concern.

"It's working." Laine points at Rachel. "Rachel's gonna compete in every team event for the rest of the day. She can't stand other people losing on her behalf. After this next event, you'll be free to find a Rachel-free mayor."

My eyebrows lift, impressed.

"Am I a genius yet?"

I squint in assessment. "You're getting fives on your AP exams, but genius remains to be seen."

Sure enough, as we line up for the balloon race, I note that instead of Betsy and Chance competing against Laine and me, it's now *Rachel* and Chance.

After a few seconds' studying, it appears the *goal* of the balloon race is to position a balloon between two people's bodies without popping it, letting it fall to the ground, *or* dying of embarrassment.

"So, um." I clear my throat. "How do we . . ." I motion between the two of us as we take our places at the starting line. A helpful teenager approaches with a basketful of balloons, takes one look at us and, grinning, presents us with the smallest one he has.

Laine gives me a sly wink. "Whatever it takes. Right, boss?"

She nestles the balloon in the dip between her breasts, then beckons me forward with a finger.

"Laine, I—"

"Want to win, don't you?" Her eyebrows are raised, infuriatingly jolly. "That's what I thought. Stop worrying about being professional and get over here." Her voice this time is low, a command, and I step forward, willing myself not to gasp a little as I press my chest into hers, pinning the balloon in our wall-to-wall cleavage.

"This is obscene," I whisper. She locks her arms under mine, clutching my body to hers. Slowly, I do the same. Can she feel my nipples hardening against the swell of her breasts? "How on earth do they let children play—" But I stop abruptly to turn and stare at Rachel and Chance, both horrified and *delighted* to see how an adult sister and brother could possibly make this work. Rachel snagged the biggest balloon she could, which they're currently trying to pin between their sides, but it keeps slipping out.

"Gotta go butt-to-butt, baby!" Teddy yells, to the crowd's glee.

"She did *not* think this through," I murmur, making Laine shake with laughter against me. Betsy must have the same thought, because she's standing on the sidelines, smirk fully on display at her cursing sister-in-law.

"On yer marks, get set, *GO!*" An old-timer hollers, and we're off. First with Laine jogging backward, hauling me with her, but it trips me up too much, so we move to a shuffling, sideways motion. She holds me so close, her pulse ticks against my flesh, the places where our bodies press together becoming slick with sweat in the day's growing heat.

"That's it—shuffle right, shuffle right." Laine's instructions come in between fits of our giddy, wheezing laughter. It's impossible not to lose it with Chance and Rachel struggling to keep it PG next to us.

"*Fine!*" Rachel screeches when they've still barely managed a few steps forward. "Butt-to-butt!" Wide-eyed but resigned, Chance starts rolling the balloon carefully from his hip to his ass, which he's stuck out at a ridiculous angle.

"Breathe!" Laine commands between her own sobs of laughter. "Zoe, you're turning red! You've gotta breathe!"

"I don't know if I—can," I hiccup out, eyes streaming, "ever—breathe—again!"

"Stick your butt out, Chance, farther! *Farther*, are you—Chance!" Their balloon gets halfway around Rachel's own ass before it pops loudly, speared by a brassy grommet on her jean shorts. "*Dammit!*"

"Woods Winners are deee-qualified!" the old-timer announces through his megaphone just as Laine and I fall cackling across the finish line. He gestures at us where we lay on the ground. "These here Eager BV-ers win!"

Laine's still laughing as we face each other, long, ticklish spears of grass pressed into our cheeks. Her arms are still locked around me, our pink balloon cradled between us like a heart. A sweet, effusive joy blooms in my chest, dampened only slightly when Teddy's face appears upside down above us.

"Good job, lesbians!" he yells into our faces. "Next up, human wheelbarrow!"

If Rachel was feeling the competition before, she's out for blood now. She pulls on fingerless weight-lifting gloves one at a time, then cracks her neck like an ominous maraca, but I'm not worried. Laine and Teddy are our fittest members. Teddy can do a hundred push-ups drunk on sangria, and Laine lifts barrels we use hand trucks for. I'm about to go find the mayor when I hear a loud yelp from behind. Teddy's on the ground, grabbing wildly at his groin. Diego rushes over.

"I must've sprained something going around that last curve," Teddy moans, massaging at the spot where crotch meets thigh so aggressively, it makes Tristan blush. Teddy looks up at Laine with mournful eyes. "I can't do it, coach."

One by one Laine assesses Tristan, then Diego, before settling on me with a sigh. Tristan and Diego are both big guys—while they could wheel Laine no doubt, she wouldn't be able to make the return trip holding up their heavy bottom halves. That's why Teddy had been the perfect choice—small, but strong. Now she's left with only one *extremely* imperfect choice.

"You strong?" Though Laine's frowning at me, the look somehow still feels tender.

"Ish?" It comes out as a question.

"We don't have to do the event," Laine says so the others can't hear. But all it takes is one look at Rachel doing warm-up planks to fill me with determination.

"Hell *yes*, we do! We can't let her win without a fight."

We get in our lane, and gingerly, I get down on my hands and knees. Rachel's next to us, about to be driven by her sister-in-law Betsy, and my *god* what a weird game this is.

The referee blows the whistle, and suddenly my back half is levitating into the air so fast, I don't have time to brace my arms. My chin hits the dirt hard, grass entering my nose and mouth.

"Oh, shit, are you all right?!" Laine asks, but I can barely hear her over Rachel's demonic snorting to my left. I spit the grass out and glare at Rachel, who's crawling forward on her hands like some kind of horror movie beastie.

"I'm fine!" I bark out.

"You don't look like you're fine, Brennan!" Rachel yells over her shoulder.

"Well, you look like the girl from *The Ring*!" I twist my sore neck as far as it'll go. "Move it, Laine!"

Laine hikes my ankles up even higher around her hips, and I make like a scorpion outta hell, willing my screaming shoulders to comply as we lurch forward. It's a short stretch, accounting for the fact most Americans don't have functioning abs, but it's still long enough to constitute torture. By the end, I'm forking along on my forearms, Laine hunched over so she doesn't warp my body at an unnatural angle. But we make it, passing Rachel and Betsy already on their return trip. When it's my turn to carry Laine's legs, my arms have turned to jelly, but I'll be damned if I'm giving up now. I tuck her feet against my sides, and we power forward. Rachel and Betsy cross the finish line before we're even halfway there.

"THAT'S RIGHT!" Rachel whoops, jumping up and down and grabbing a bewildered Betsy's arm into the air.

"*Dammit!*" Laine runs her hands through her hair, hot anger reddening her features. "If I hadn't dropped you, we'd have won!"

Doubtful, but Laine looks like she could overturn a Gatorade table, so I'm not gonna argue. She turns to me, her frustration evaporating into the air.

"You okay, boss?" Laine's fingers gently tilt my chin up to inspect the scratches there.

"Don't act like you didn't enjoy shoving me face-first into the dirt, Beave." I try to smile but it quickly turns into a wince as she grazes a tender spot.

"Believe me, in all the ways I've imagined getting you dirty, it's never involved the human wheelbarrow." Color paints the tops of her cheekbones as though perhaps she didn't mean to say that, but she juts her chin out a bit higher, owning it all the same. Her eyes are warm and molten, and for an instant, I lean into her touch. "Can I help you get cleaned up?" The words prickle the skin along my arms, making my chin sting even more.

I take a small step back, freeing myself from her grasp. "No, I'm okay. Besides, we only have the egg race left, and I still need to find the mayor. This one's yours, right?"

After a second, Laine nods, as though she's reluctantly coming back from somewhere far away. An overwhelming urge to join her there fills me, and I lean in close and whisper in her ear, "You gonna win this one for me?"

"Yes, boss." The words breathe out onto my neck and shoot straight to my core, making my lower belly thrum from their delicious tug. She leans back, our lips dangerously close, but her eyes flick from mine to something over my shoulder before widening slightly. "Mayor Esposito, walking alone, your five o'clock." She takes me by the shoulders, spins me on my feet, then gives me a little nudge. "I'll keep Rachel occupied, you get us an endorsement."

Us. That little word, as small as *me* but so incredibly vast in comparison. It's like an ocean I could tumble into and never surface from again.

"Mayor!" I call, wishing in vain that I'd had time to clean off my dirt-streaked face before doing this. She pauses mid-stride, and when she sees me, her shoulders tighten.

She *has* been avoiding me.

"Zoe! Lovely to see you enjoying the festivities!" Her eyes flicker to my chin before finding mine again. "You okay?"

"Yep! Do you mind if I join you for a bit?"

Her smile tightens, too. "Not at all. I was just walking over to watch the anxious people ferry eggs on spoons across an obstacle course."

"What a coincidence! Me, too."

We exchange pleasantries for a bit, me asking about her campaign, her telling me about the parking meter controversy, until we reach the egg race and take a seat in the stands. "Listen, Mayor, I have an idea to run by you."

"If this is about endorsing Bluebell Vineyards for the *showcase*, Zoe, I'm afraid my hands are tied." She gestures at the massive fundraiser going on all around us. "Into the Woods is one of my biggest supporters and more than that, it's one of the best vineyards in the southeast. I can't ignore that."

I take a deep breath. I expected this, *prepared* for this.

"Okay, but you pride yourself on embracing the unexpected and bringing innovation to Blue Ridge, right?"

Mayor Esposito nods resolutely. "Right."

"Well, you can't get more expected than Into the Woods." I hold up a hand. "Don't get me wrong, it's a fantastic vineyard, and I love Molly and Ezra Woods like second parents. But it's as traditional as they come. If you plunked Into the Woods in the middle of Napa Valley, it wouldn't make a blip on the local scene. Is that really the foot you want to put forward when wine lovers across America come to Blue Ridge? That the best we can do is the standard fare they're used to in bigger wine scenes?"

A look of potent dismay crosses the mayor's face. I'm getting to her. As if sensing danger, Rachel spots us in the stands. I wave, and fury darkens her face.

"*Or* would you rather show off a vineyard that encapsulates what makes Blue Ridge so special? Scrappy, with can't-beat views, making fun wines that represent our lush mountains."

Someone has to push Rachel forward to get her spoon, she's staring at us so hard.

The mayor follows my gaze, then shifts to where my Eager BV-ers crouch in a circle of rainbow tie-dye and face paint, cheering Laine as she accepts our team's spoon proudly. "A vineyard run by queer women with a largely queer staff, no less."

The mayor's gaze cuts to me sharply. "Your point?"

I shrug. "All I'm saying is you can show outsiders the Blue Ridge they'd expect from a southern mountain town, or the *real* Blue Ridge that would surprise and delight them, and more than anything, make them feel welcome. All of them."

The referee calls up the contestants, and Laine takes her place at the starting line, giving me a wink and a rapid pulse. *A vineyard run by queer women . . . Women*, not woman. I hadn't even hesitated before making it plural. A flush crawls up my neck.

The mayor's broad, unlined face is heavy in thought. "You make some intriguing points, Zoe."

"I do that from time to time, Mayor." I smile wryly at Rachel. She immediately drops her egg, but catches it in her other hand, glowering up at me.

The whistle goes off, and the contestants jump into action, a mishmash of slow, steady, and too fast all at once. Three eggs immediately fall off and splat to the ground. Rachel and Laine are still in it, though, speedwalking with eggs balanced precariously on their tiny spoons. For a second, it pains me to see them side by side with so much animosity between them. They're *sisters*—something I always wanted, and for a while, thought I'd had in Rachel.

"You *could* endorse both our vineyards to *Everyday Bon Vivant* and let them make the final call," I say on a whim of . . . kindness? Pity? Some sense of fair play that Rachel sure as shit doesn't have? "Just don't count us out, Mayor. I *know* we'd do you proud."

Sensing anything more would be overkill, I let the words lie, sitting quietly together as the egg race grows rapidly more vicious.

Laine throws Rachel a look from the next lane over. "Watch that rock!"

Rachel snarls back, "Quit looking at me!" But her foot snags on the rock anyway, and she almost drops the egg. "See what you nearly made me do? Lord, you're *such* a loser!"

"Oh yeah?" Laine's smile grows bigger, closing in on the last stretch, and she yells over her shoulder, "Then why you wanna be me so bad?"

Laine's remark must hit a little too close to home because Rachel splutters, trips, and sends her egg flying. The crowd gasps, watching the egg land on Rachel's own head in the most satisfying *splat* I've ever heard just as Laine crosses the finish line.

"*Oh*, my *word*," the mayor says, covering her mouth.

Poor Laine has one, maybe two seconds to laugh before Rachel steals someone else's egg straight off their spoon and cracks it against Laine's head, where it explodes in a yolky sunburst dripping into her ears.

"Excuse me, Mayor. It's been lovely catching up!" I hustle down the makeshift stands and push through the gawking crowds, trying to get to Laine, but that's when it descends into *chaos*. Eggs flying everywhere, Laine smashing egg into Rachel's hair, Rachel roaring and crushing eggs in each fist, Chance and me both trying to pull them apart. All the while the referee's whistle is wailing like alarms, stopping exactly *nothing* until an older woman shoves to the front of the melee.

"*Enough!*" she booms across the entire field day.

Ohhhhhhhh, *shit*.

"Now, this rivalry has officially gone on *too far* and for *too long*," Molly Woods says, her eyes cutting between Rachel, Laine, and Chance. "I didn't spend my life raising three children just so they can go for each other's throats like wild animals!"

"Mama!" Rachel starts, completely indignant. "What are you yelling at me for? I didn't—"

"Oh, shut up, Rachel, you *literally* have egg on your face." Molly glares at Rachel, then Laine, then Chance, standing slack-jawed to the side, smeared with his sisters' war crimes. "We are having dinner as a *goddamn* family this Sunday, and we are going to work this out, once and for all." Mrs. Woods points at me. "And your ass better be at that table, too, Zoe Brennan!"

My eyes widen. "Yes, *ma'am*."

CHAPTER ELEVEN

Just as the evening's twilight settles into a deep, husky violet among the vines, a knock sounds on my cottage door. Jitters wriggle through my insides.

This is not a date. *This is not a date!* This is, in fact, a wretched family dinner caused by egg-fueled warfare that I am attending with my *employee*. Who, despite our rocky start, might be my friend now. I can't mess that up with misplaced horny vibes. I check myself in the mirror and frown.

Is this dress *wretched-family-dinner* appropriate? It's black and patterned with tiny white daisies and hangs just past my knees. The neckline approaches my throat, but it's sleeveless, showing off the subtle definition rolling wine barrels around will give your arms. Let Rachel see that I can throw a punch if need be. I grab a pale denim jacket for the walk over and zip up my stacked combat boots. Now that I'm thirty, I refuse to fuck with laces.

The knock comes again right as I reach for the doorknob. I school my face into something casual and unassuming—something that doesn't say I've been getting ready for the last hour—and open the door.

Sweet Jesus on a biscuit with *all* the fixins.

It's a cool evening, and Laine's leaning into professorial mode hard. She's wearing a dusky blue wool blazer, its thin lapel one of those that perpetually stands up to kiss the base of her smooth neck. A dove-gray shirt underneath, buttoned to the collar, is tucked into a pair of navy-blue pants, the cuffs rolled high to show off her thick-soled boots. Her flop of golden-brown hair is wavy from the shower, and her thick-rimmed tortoiseshell glasses are back.

God, she looks cool. The town's star athlete turned studious. Is there anything sexier than a jock with an intellectual bent?

Laine must sense my inner turmoil because a blush blooms high on her cheekbones. She looks at her feet, her hand going to her hair to riffle through it as always, then stops, as though she doesn't want to mess it up.

"I wasn't sure what to wear to a painful family experience," she says, her voice bashful. *Bashful!* Can you believe it? How am I supposed to refrain from clutching her collar and smothering her with kisses? *How?*

I clear my throat, then quickly turn to lock the door. "I know, right? I tried to go for Sunday school meets contrition. Ready to walk over?"

"As ready as I'll ever be." Laine's sheepish in the way only women in their thirties who are still terrified of their mother's wrath can be. It'd be adorable, but I, too, am on the bad side of Molly Woods right now.

Laine laughs and runs her palms down her face. "*Ughhh*, I wish we were going literally anywhere else right now."

I bump her shoulder gently with my own because people who aren't on dates do that all the time. "Well, at least your mom can't ground you anymore."

"You sure about that?" Laine arches an eyebrow at me, and we both smile and drop our gazes.

"Do you think this is going to work? Forcing us all to gather to share a meal? Hash out our differences?"

Laine sighs miserably. "It never has before. Rachel's hated me for years. I don't even know why."

I snort. "Really?"

"You do?"

"Varsity tryouts your senior year!" I laugh somewhat incredulously. Does she really not know this? "You kicked her off the field."

"No, I didn't!" She looks at me bewildered. "I *begged* Coach to let her finish the tryout, but after she crushed Ava Sanchez's nose—"

"Sadie Jenkins's nose, you mean," I correct gently. "Ava Sanchez was your girlfriend."

Laine's face splits into a bemused smile. "You remember my girlfriends, boss?"

"Well, kind of hard to forget after I caught you in the kitchen with Ava's boob in your mouth, *Beave*."

Laine blinks, another piece of our shared history slotting into place for her. "That was you . . ."

"Yes, but I never—I didn't tell anyone what I saw." It feels important to clarify since a few weeks later, rumors hit the high school. Some dumbasses were snickering about Charlaine as she walked by one day, and she stopped, looked them dead in the eye, and said: "Yeah, I'm a lesbian. Now get over it."

The craziest part is, they did. Charlaine approached being outed like she did everything back then—she owned it. The snickering stopped. People got on with their lives. Charlaine got on with being gay, this time out and proud. Fucking legend.

"Oh, I know. Pretty sure Shannon McGee told everybody." Laine clears her throat. "She, uh, saw us in the showers."

Wow. Ava had a *much* better high school experience than I did.

Laine shakes her head. "So, that's why Rachel hates me so much? To this day? Jesus."

"Well, it's more than that," I add, unsure why I feel the need to lay out Rachel's case. "She was so desperate to be like you, and I think she believed that, if she followed your footsteps exactly, she would be. But that day, when you kicked her off the field—"

"—when she *thought* I kicked her off the field."

"Right, sorry. When she thought that, she felt betrayed. Like you were hoarding all your success and popularity and awesomeness for yourself. It didn't help that people teased her about her own sister cutting her from the team."

"Huh," Laine says, as if it's news to her that Rachel has always had severe Ferris Bueller Syndrome. By the time our friendship ended, Rachel had fully become the spiteful, unimpressed Jennifer Grey to Laine's charismatic Matthew Broderick, though the ages are reversed. Maybe it's harder that way. The same mix of DNA just slightly altered to produce a fundamentally different outcome, a different person, having a different, better life only three steps in front of you, but the path from your here to their there is unreachable. Despite everything, I feel a pang of sympathy for Rachel for feeling like her own path wasn't good enough.

"So . . . why does she hate *you*, then?" Laine asks. "You didn't ruin any budding soccer careers, right?"

I blow a long breath out, weighing how much to tell her. The full truth is too embarrassing, so I settle on an approximation. "She realized I had a small, totally normal teenage crush on you, and she freaked out. Hated me ever since."

"Geez, that's my fault, too?" Laine frowns. "I'm sorry."

"Don't be," I say softly. Losing Rachel's friendship was one of the most painful experiences of my life, but like her issues with Laine, it's more complicated than that. When Rachel discovered my teenage crush box of Charlaine relics hidden under my bed, covered in a meaningful hodgepodge of magazine cut-outs, full of pictures of Charlaine, poems describing my longing to know her and be known *by* her, and god help me, one of her old sports bras—that was the moment our friendship drew its last breath, but it had been sick and gasping for some time.

I can't say exactly when, but at some point, Rachel became resent-ful. For most of our childhoods, she was as ambitious as I was, reaching for success with the confidence that one day, she'd achieve everything she set her heart on. Maybe it was when her perfect grades slipped in her AP courses, no matter how hard she studied, or when her face continued to break out, despite her devotion to the fancy Clinique products she begged her mom to buy. When, no matter how much Tommy Hilfiger she wore, or how smoothly she straightened her hair, the popular girls in our grade still rolled their eyes every time she tried to sit at their table. But at some point, Rachel became more fixated with the world's treat-ment of her than her treatment of the world, and the debt she felt owed pissed her *off.*

So when her sixteenth birthday arrived, and she ran outside that morn-ing to check the driveway for the new car she'd been promised only to receive her parents' apology that *sorry, we put all our extra money into helping Cosimo reopen Bluebell Vineyards to the public, but maybe by next year, you'll have enough saved to get a used car* . . . then I, too, became yet another person to wrong her, to take what was rightfully hers. All the rides to school, the meals I ate at their house, the nights I slept in her room, even the care her parents showed me when Dad couldn't parent me, it all began to feel like tallies on the ledger of what I owed her. A few weeks later, she found my crush box dedicated to Charlaine, and that was offi-cially an injustice too many. The next day, I overheard her blaming my "crazy" father and our "shitty vineyard" for her not getting a car, and I lost it. No blows were exchanged, but they had to pull shy little Zoe Bren-nan screaming out of her ex-best-friend's face, and that was that. Our friendship was over, and our rivalry began.

We're quiet as we crest the hill and take the path through the trees. It's weedy and narrow these days, with only my dad's footsteps to walk it into existence, but when I was young, it was wide enough for Rachel and

me to race four-wheelers side by side. It feels both strange to walk it now
and like traveling a well-worn artery into my past.

That duality follows me all the way to the Woods's house set at the
back of the property, out of the public eye and nestled among the trees.
A place I've been a thousand times, maybe more. Laine straightens as we
climb the front steps, the wood bowed from rain and busy feet. Her hand
goes for the doorknob, then stops, slowly rising up to knock instead.

My heart squeezes. Does this place not feel like home to her anymore?

A chorus of voices, then the smack of children's footsteps growing louder until the door's thrown open, with Darla standing there
panting, comically confused. Little kids are so wonderfully expressive
before the world teaches them to hide their feelings. She eyes Laine up
and down.

"Dad, the lady who kept beating Aunt Rachel at Field Day is here!"

"It's me, silly. Aunt Laine." Laine can't stop herself from nervously riffling through her hair this time.

"Aunt *Char*laine lives in Cali-fornya," Darla informs her, and is about
to shut the door in her face when she sees me standing behind her. "Oh
hi, Zoe!"

Darla runs barefoot onto the porch to hug me, her little arms like a
low-slung belt around my hips.

"Hey, Dar-Dar." I feel a rush of embarrassment at Darla's enthusiastic
greeting. "Chance always brings the kids to our family events," I say by
way of explanation, but Laine just nods, her smile tight. I look down at
the dirt-smudged cheeks and bright eyes staring up at me. "This *is* your
Aunt Laine, though, Darla. I can vouch for her."

Darla turns to look at this *Aunt Laine* again. "If you say so."

With that, Darla grabs Laine's hand and pulls her inside. "I found
Zoe and somebody named Aunt Laine on the porch," she announces, as
though she's dug us up like a pair of shiny beetles for all to see.

Chance's son Benny, Darla's twin, waves at us both from the table, where he's meticulously laying out silverware beside each place setting. It makes me smile. That was always mine and Rachel's job.

"There you are," Mrs. Woods says as she hurries into the dining room with a covered dish. "I was beginning to think y'all weren't going to come." She fixes us with a stern look, but that's as far as the *you're-in-deep-trouble-missy* vibes go.

"Mom, it's not even seven yet." Laine checks her watch. "We're early."

"Charlaine! You didn't bring your pet goat, did you?" Mr. Woods says gamely, setting a large platter of fried chicken in the middle of the table. He holds out his arms, smiling fondly at his eldest daughter. "Come give your Pa a squeeze."

Laine does, and for the first time since she showed up on my doorstep tonight, her tension seems to melt.

"Zoe Brennan!" Ezra's eyes light up for me next. "Good t' see you, darlin'! Awful sorry to hear about your grandmother. How's Cosimo holding up?"

"Oh, you know my dad." I laugh a little. "Same as always, far as I can tell."

His smile grows wistful because he *does* know Dad. Molly and Ezra were my parents' best friends in Blue Ridge. We spent Sunday evenings just like this one together around this table. Mom and Molly would take their wine on the porch and talk late into the evening, while Dad and Ezra cleaned up and then hunkered down in chairs on the lawn where they'd talk crops and philosophy and, I suspect, smoke a joint. The adults left the kids to our own devices, but Charlaine and Chance usually shut themselves off in the living room to watch horror movies because they knew it'd keep us little kids away. That's how Rachel and I got so close to begin with. Our parents forged bonds between our families, and who were we to fight them?

Rachel slides into the seat across the table from me and plunks a bottle of chilled Into the Woods Chardonnay onto the table. "Sorry, Zoe. We're out of your spiked Kool-Aid tonight. Hope wine will suffice."

The nostalgia for our past disappears in an instant. My fingers tighten around my fork, an unchecked impulse away from becoming a murder weapon, when a warm hand rests on mine. I glance up to see Laine taking her seat next to me. Her hand slides off as she gives me a wincing smile. "No homicides at the table, no matter *how* warranted." Laine's eyes flicker to Rachel, turning stony in warning. A small thrill races up my exposed arms, prickling the flesh. I'm not sure if it's from the feel of her hand on mine or her being mean to Rachel. Both do it for me.

"That's right," says Molly Woods, uncorking the Chardonnay without looking. "It's my number one rule." She pours me a healthy glass first, which I want to ignore to spite Rachel, but it's a crime to waste good wine and besides, how else am I going to get through this dinner?

Rachel glares at me and Laine and rolls her eyes. "Looks like you really listened to my advice, Zoe. Did you bring the money you owe me?"

"You owe her money?" Laine asks me, then understanding pinches her forehead. "For the *goat*?"

I arch an eyebrow. "Are you referring to the two dollars and fifty-two cents, Rachel?"

"Sure." She tosses back a healthy slug of wine. "Before interest."

Ezra smiles down at me. "Zoe, as our guest tonight, would you please say grace?"

"Uh, sure." I've never understood the hospitality behind making a guest pray for everybody. It's embarrassing enough to make small talk, let alone religious supplications. "Thank you, Lord, for uh, this food tonight, and for friends, and for, uh—"

Rachel snorts. *Snorts!* At a prayer! I suck my breath in through my nose, and my voice fills with earnest conviction. "And, dear Lord in heaven, *please* bless Rachel Woods. She is but a lonely, *humble* servant of yours, with no friends or lovers of her own, and has made running her entire personality—"

Laine snorts this time, and it only emboldens me further. "We beg of you, dear, sweet Jesus, please deliver this *lowly* woman from her bitchiness—"

Ezra clears his throat loud enough to dislodge a tonsil, and I deliver a hasty "Amen."

"*Amen!*" echoes Laine.

"Daddy, what's a bitchiness?" Benny asks.

Laine leans over before Chance can respond. "Like a disease. Makes you mean."

"*Come on*, y'all," Chance says, covering his face. "Can you *not* teach my children cuss words?"

"Oh, Aunt Rachel definitely has that, then," Darla says thoughtfully, then turns to Rachel, who's so furious she can't even speak. "I hope the bitchiness goes away soon, Aunt Rachel."

"I don't have the bitchiness!" Rachel finally sputters, then points at me and Laine. "They do!"

"Will I catch it if I sit too close to you?" Darla scoots as far as her chair will go. "Sounds itchy."

"That is e-*nough*, y'all!" Molly says, exasperated, but a smile's pulling at the corners of her mouth. She loves this, I realize. Having all her kids at the table, even if they're bickering and throwing cheap shots in the name of the lord. I'm beginning to suspect she's not mad about the field day debacle at all and simply used it to get her quarreling family together. She trades a look with Ezra who, taking her meaning, says loudly, "Can someone pass the biscuits?"

We settle in, comforted by the feast before us. Ezra's homemade fried chicken, vinegary collards, baked macaroni and cheese, fresh biscuits, and honey still dripping from the honeycomb go a long way in making this evening tolerable, even if every time I lift my eyes, they're met by Rachel's icy stare. Benny and Darla are human excavators, shoveling the food into their mouths so quickly, they're done and excused from the table before I've finished my first glass of wine.

Molly sighs happily, leaning her chin on her hand. "It's so good to have you home, Lainey-belle."

"Yes, it only took, what . . . two and a half months before you came over?" Rachel stabs her drumstick with her fork and knifes off a hunk of meat. Who cuts a drumstick? "Great job 'reconnecting,' Charlaine."

"Rachel," Ezra says, a warning.

Laine's lips form a thin line as she butters her second biscuit. "It's been busy. Learning my way around Bluebell, working on some new projects for Zoe. Just hadn't found the time yet."

My eyebrows rise, but I direct my surprise to my plate. While I knew Laine sticks mostly to the treehouse in her off hours, I didn't realize that Laine hadn't come over to see her family at *all*.

"It's been a real busy decade for you, hasn't it, Charlaine? You must be plumb tuckered out." Rachel sits back, arms folded over her chest. "How many times have you come home? How many times have you called Mom or Dad? How many birthdays have you missed, how many *weddings*? Not sure we could count them all."

My mouth drops open as I glance between the twins that were once so tight, they shared clothes. Did Laine miss *Chance's wedding*? It was a small family affair so Dad and I weren't invited, but I just assumed Laine would come out for her twin brother. What was so important that it kept her away from that?

"Maybe I'd have come home more if I didn't feel like the enemy in my own damn family." Laine drops her knife onto her plate with a clang. "You've pushed me out every chance you've had."

Rachel rolls her eyes and laughs, but it just sounds mean. "Oh, get over yourself! I never pushed you anywhere because you've never been here to push. You've missed out on everything, and for what—to embarrass yourself nationally? Yet here you are after ruining your career, still expecting us to kiss your feet. No, thank you."

"Rachel, stop it this instant." Molly throws her napkin on the table. "You don't speak for this family, and you *certainly* don't get to pass judgment on how we treat one another."

Rachel's jaw clamps shut. Molly breathes deeply before addressing the table. "Now, we can talk about our feelings as a family, with love in our hearts, or we're not going to talk about them at all. Ezra, you go first." Molly takes her own glass of wine and throws back a swallow, and Ezra, flustered as a student who got called on unexpectedly, sits up straighter.

"All right." He clears his throat. "Lainey-belle, your mother and I have missed you so much, and we would love it if you came around more, understanding how it's not always easy for you to do so." He pauses and looks meaningfully at Rachel. "And that's the long and short of it. Chance, son, your turn."

"I agree with Rachel," Chance says, his jaw tense. "Until you show us you're ready to become part of this family again, I'm afraid I don't buy what you're selling here, Charlaine."

"And how exactly am I supposed to do that?" Laine tosses her uneaten biscuit back onto her plate. "Go back in time and be at your wedding? Jesus, Chance, I've told you how sorry I was to miss it—when are you going to let it go?"

"Maybe when it stops being the norm for how you treat this family. You've been gone so long, and you only come back *now* because you want something?" He shakes his head and releases a sigh. "It sucks, Charlaine."

My brow furrows. What does Laine want from *them*?

"That's *not* why I came back." Laine pushes back from the table with a screech.

"Then prove it." Chance rises from his seat, too.

"I *will*!"

They stand there, a table and twelve years of growing apart between them, glaring at each other.

"Rachel, honey, are you ready to *kindly* share your feelings?" Molly asks over the straining silence.

"Sorry, I'm fresh out of kind feelings for you, Charlaine." Rachel stands now, too. "Guess you'll just have to reap what you've sown." With that, she grabs a handful of plates and marches off to the kitchen.

Laine's eyes close in frustration, and Molly puts her arm around her oldest daughter and brushes a lock of Laine's wavy hair behind her ear. "I love you, baby, and so does Rachel. She just . . . doesn't know it yet."

That makes Laine huff, though it's sad. They walk us to the door, and then it's my turn to get hugged by Molly. I relish it, relaxing into it in a way that would be embarrassing if I thought Molly would mind, but I know she doesn't. She's got enough pure *Mom* in her to share.

"I'm sorry, Ms. Woods. I know you wanted us to get past all our issues tonight."

Ms. Woods smiles at me, runs her small hand up my shoulder. "It takes time, Zoe. I'm just happy to see you at my table, though you're never allowed to say grace again, that's for damn sure." She snorts. "The bitchiness. Y'all are too much."

"Wait, Aunt Laine!" Darla and Benny come running up the hall. "You didn't say goodbye."

"I'm sorry, lil bits." Laine kneels to give Darla and Benny an awkward high five. They miss no less than three times, all of them laughing by the end. Behind Darla, Chance stands with a shoulder pressed against the hallway wall, watching.

"The twins have a soccer game next week," he says as Laine straightens. "Saturday morning."

"Awesome. Good luck out there."

Chance rolls his eyes and starts to leave, and suddenly, I get exactly what's going on here. But if Laine senses Chance's displeasure, she doesn't show it.

"We'll be there, Chance." I nudge Laine. "Right?"

For a second, Laine looks like she's about to argue, but then understanding registers in her eyes. "Oh, um, yeah. Text me where and when?"

Chance hovers in the doorway, then nods. He puts a hand on Darla's and Benny's shoulders and ushers them back inside. Laine releases a long breath, looks at me, then adjusts her glasses. *Thank you*, she mouths, smiling slightly. Then aloud: "Ready to head home?"

The words trickle down my chest, sweet and sticky like Molly's fresh honey.

Home. With *Laine.*

I wish it were true, even though it's impossible.

CHAPTER TWELVE

This time, I'm the one knocking on Laine's door before our not-date. I may be wearing jeans with ripped knees and a faded raglan tee, but I put no less thought into my outfit for today. Why is it so difficult to strike that perfect balance of *look-how-casually-hot-I-am* and *I-didn't-try-at-all-to-achieve-this*? Whoever figures that out should run for president.

Laine answers the door, and I guess she's got political potential because somehow, she's done just that. Freshly showered and dressed in a pair of form-fitting joggers in charcoal gray and a crisp white thermal that hugs the contours of her shoulders, she looks effortlessly hot and smells amazing, the clean light scent of her soap tickling my nose from here.

"Hey." The corners of her mouth quirk in a half-smile as her eyes travel across my face, lingering on my neck before meeting my gaze again.

"Hey." I smile back, that feeling of date/not-date glitching through me all over again. "You ready?"

"You don't have to go to this, you know," Laine says as she locks up behind her.

I frown a little, stung. "Do you . . . not want me to go?"

"No, I mean, you can go if you want to, but you don't *have to* go." Laine grimaces. "I'm making this weird, aren't I?"

"Yes, you are." I arch an eyebrow. "Am I going or what?"

Laine blows out a breath. "You're going. To a kids' soccer game."

I shrug. "What else am I doing on a Saturday morning at nine a.m.? Besides, these games get pretty crazy."

"Crazy? How?"

I snort. "Just you wait."

If Laine didn't understand before, she does now as we roll through the jam-packed parking lot of the county rec center. There's a full-blown tailgate going on, with tents, zero gravity chairs, and packed coolers as far as the eye can see. We nab one of the last spots, and Laine whistles. "Damn."

I grin at her. "Right? Come on." I lead her over to a big tent at the edge of the field.

"Zoe Bee! And *ho-lee shit*, is that"—Booch, everyone's favorite country boy, presses a hand to his aproned chest, eyes theatrically wide—"*the* Charlaine Woods, #27, best forward the Gilmer County Bobcats ever did see?"

"Booch!" Laine accepts his vigorous thumping hug with genuine delight. "My *man*!" Booch is the best kind of redneck—the hilarious, loving, *we're-all-here-on-Earth-to-have-fun-so-let's-go-do-donuts-in-the-parking-lot* kind. He gets here at six a.m. on Soccer Saturdays for the primo spot. Both his kids Edward and Bella play at different points throughout the day, so Booch comes pre*pared*. His smoker's already going, making my mouth water for his famous ribs at nine in the damn morning.

Booch's eyes jack even wider. "You helping Chance coach our team? Now we're cookin' with gas, baby!" He points at Laine with his spatula. "My Bella's on your team, and she's a star in the making, Charlaine, you mark my words. She just needs some"—Booch tilts his head from side to side—"redirection from time to time, that's all."

"Naw, I'm just here to spectate, but good for Bella. What's her number?"

At this, Booch throws his head back and laughs. "They don't have numbers yet, girl, half of 'em can't count! But she's the one that looks like me with a curly wig on. Can't miss her."

We bid our farewells to Booch, but not before he stuffs our hands with homemade cinnamon rolls and cups of coffee, bless him.

Laine's eyebrows are raised high as we find an empty spot in the bleachers and settle in. "It was *not* like this when I was growing up."

"Well, when football's over, the sports fans of Blue Ridge gotta latch onto something. You're in for a treat."

We both are, I think as Laine tears off a big chunk of her roll, getting icing all over her face and laughing. She looks out on the field with unmistakable fondness. "Thanks for getting me out here today, boss. I didn't realize that's what Chance was angling at when he brought it up." Laine's smile flickers. "I used to be able to read him like a book."

"What . . . happened?" I wince a little as the question slides out. I hadn't meant to ask, but it's been bothering me ever since the family dinner. It was the first time I'd seen Chance and Laine interact since, geez, high school maybe? Them being at such odds felt like a fundamental law of my universe got Lisa Frank'ed.

Laine's shoulders stiffen. "It started when I went to UC Davis to get my viticulture degree instead of UGA with him. Chance had already decided where we'd live off campus, what courses we'd take together, which ones we'd divide and conquer on. But I wanted to see what else was out there. Not because I don't love Georgia, but because I knew I'd love other places, too. I tried to get him to apply to the same schools, but he refused, saying UGA's horticulture program was good enough for both of us." Laine licks a strip of icing off her thumb. "He called my bluff, thinking I'd cave and stay. And, well. I didn't."

I'd seen some of this play out in real time that last year of friendship with Rachel, of course. The twins preparing their college applications, a tense few weeks after Chance and Charlaine returned from a visit to UGA. But by then, Rachel was avoiding Charlaine every chance she got, so I did, too, and missed a lot of this context.

"Mom and Dad ultimately got on board, though. I'd get my fancy viticulture and enology degree, then come home to help Dad and Chance run the winemaking operations after graduation. That was the plan."

"But you didn't follow the plan."

"I did not," Laine agrees. "The summer before my senior year, I got the internship at Le Jardin. It was such a big deal—I *had* to take it. That summer blew my mind. Showed me all the things I'd miss if I came home. A chance to learn from the top experts in America, living in a queer wonderland? Zoe, do you even *know* how many lesbians live in Napa Valley?" Laine shakes her head. "Who'd want to come home and make their daddy's wine after that?"

I take another bite of my cinnamon bun to avoid answering. Because I'd done exactly that, hadn't I? The moment they handed me my diploma, I was on my way home to take over operations for Dad. I didn't want Laine to perceive me that way, though. Like there's some fundamental difference in our ambition because I chose to return while she set off to explore. I think it's easier to leave home when you don't know how much there is to lose. Your hands can reach for more when they're not busy clutching the little you have left.

"When I took the full-time position at Le Jardin after graduation, that's when *everyone* got mad at me." Laine crumples the paper napkin between her fingers. "I didn't mean to break my promise, but why'd they make me promise in the first place? Why couldn't they appreciate the opportunities I had, give me grace to live my own life?"

"Maybe because they couldn't imagine living their lives without you," I offer. "Your plans changed their plans."

"Well, that's the problem with making plans around other people, isn't it? Only person you can count on is yourself." She smiles at me ruefully, and I return it with a little sigh.

Because she's absolutely right.

"Why did you miss Chance's wedding?"

Laine sucks in a deep breath. "There was a festival. Le Jardin's chief vintner made me swear up and down I'd be there, talked it up like it would be the highlight of my career. Date was set for months. Then Chance set his wedding date, and there was a conflict. He couldn't move his date, and I'd have lost my job if I missed that festival."

"Was it worth it?" I ask quietly.

Laine snorts and takes another long, pensive lick off her forefinger this time. "They had me manning a merch table the whole time."

I wince.

"Chance didn't speak to me for months. With him and Rachel both mad at me, it made it hard to want to come home at all. I love Mom and Dad, and Into the Woods is in my bones, but I just—didn't want to feel bad anymore. No matter what I said or did, I couldn't win."

She straightens and gives me a tight-lipped smile before I can dare pity her. She doesn't realize how floored I am at getting this glimpse into how her brain works. Her inability to take constructive criticism, the way that one terrible review decimated her entire self-perception, avoiding home instead of confronting her problems with Chance and Rachel . . . it all makes sense now.

Laine Woods doesn't know how to lose.

The thought almost makes me laugh. I could teach her a thing or two about losing. You don't run a tiny, resource-poor vineyard for as long as I have without seeing your fair share of business ideas tank. There was the sparkling apple cider I begged Dad to make one harvest that tasted like cinnamon-flavored vomit. The haunted house I spent *months* rigging up in our barn that provided a mere three minutes of spooky entertainment. But then, there were the unexpected wins, too, like the time I threw a memorial to Prince, and we truly partied like it was 1999. Mom once told me that anything worth doing in this life is worth failing at. Not every idea is a winner, but they don't all have to be, either.

They just have to exist.

Laine's turned her attention to the field as the screams of true enthu-siasm ring through the air, whether to avoid the aftermath of giving such a confession or out of real support, hard to tell. Darla, Benny, and Bella's team goes first, being the youngest kids' match of the day with the collective least patience for waiting. The referee is a bored-looking teenager I recognize from the checkout line at the Piggly Wiggly. She quietly delights in taking forever to type your fruit's code in until you finally give up and put it back.

Well. This'll be fun.

The teen ref blows the whistle, and they're off, a horde of adorable kids in matching T-shirts in their team's colors. Chance is on the sidelines, already in coach mode, clapping at nothing and yelling encouragement. Laine moves to the edge of her seat, watching intently as the children stumble into a loose formation on the field.

"They're clumping out there," Laine says, frowning. She cups her hands around her mouth. "Look alive, blue!"

I raise an eyebrow. I don't know if Laine's ready for this level of soccer.

The ref's whistle *PHRRRRIIIIPTTT*s, and the game gets off to a bumbling start. Someone manages to kick the ball, and the giant clump of red and blue shirts promptly runs in the wrong direction.

"Darla, turn around! It's the OTHER way!" Laine's yelling along with the other parents, which only makes the kids more confused. Half of the team's just standing there, staring up into the stands, waiting for further instructions. "BENNY! Behind you, buddy!" Laine leaps to her feet, making exaggerated pointing gestures to where the soccer ball sits some twenty yards in the distance, completely forgotten. "The ball! Find the BALL!"

Incredibly, the game devolves from there. Laine's going hoarse from screaming increasingly frantic instructions to the point that someone cracks open a beer and passes it down the row to her, which she chugs and crumples in a minute flat. Finally, Darla gets the ball and dribbles it toward the goal. Laine is jumping up and down on the bleachers now, clapping her niece on with the kind of fervor that leads to aneurysms. "THAT'S RIGHT, DAR-DAR, YOU GOT THIS! KEEP GOING, BABY, KEEP GOING, KEEP—"

PHRRRRIIIIPTTT! "SHOELACES," the teen ref calls out.

Everybody freezes. These kids may not know the rules of soccer, but they know what *SHOELACES* means. Laine, however, doesn't.

"*Shoelaces?* What the hell is she talking about?!" Laine looks at me with sheer panic. "Darla was about to score!"

"That boy's shoelaces came untied." I point, trying to be helpful.

"*So?!*"

"So . . . these are six-year-olds," I say slowly. "They can't tie their own laces, the ref's gotta do it. It's a trip hazard."

Laine's chest heaves as she stares at me, bewildered, as though I've invented shoelaces and tripping and should perhaps be destroyed for my crimes. She whips back to the field to watch as the ref saunters over to the kid and takes no less than five excruciating minutes to tie his shoes. When she blows her whistle again, some kid steals the ball from Darla, and Laine moans.

At halftime, the kids scramble off the field for Gatorade and animal crackers. I pat Laine's shoulder. "Need a cookie, Beave?"

"I didn't expect it to be so stressful." She looks at me earnestly. "They're so . . . *bad.*"

I smile. "They're six. What did you expect?"

"Hey there, Zoe!" A silky voice lifts from down below as a long-legged lady in cutoffs and a cropped hoodie climbs the bleachers toward us. Mariah Adams, bleached blonde and tanned brown no matter what time of year, pauses in front of me, hands on her hips. "You haven't been to Soccer Saturday in ages!" She winks. "Not since you were my fan, I think."

Great. Last thing I need right now is an ex stopping by to pity-flirt.

"Hey yourself, Mariah," I say, squinting up at her. The sun's behind her, making it hard to look at her dead-on. "Let me introduce you—this is Laine Woods, my new vintner. Laine, this is—"

"The *other* team's coach," Laine says and stands abruptly, startling Mariah back a bit.

"Well, aren't you somebody's cousin," Mariah says, amused. "Competition gettin' to you, sport?"

"And *how* do y'all know each other?" Laine asks flatly.

Mariah's eyebrows raise in unison, and she looks at me. *Call off your dyke, will you?*

Mine raise right back, and I shrug ever so slightly. *She's not my dyke?*

Mariah tilts her head. *You sure about that?* But she claps her hands together. "Well, it's nice to see you, Zoe. My number's still the same, case you're wondering." She smiles extra big as she takes a step back. "Laine, good meeting you. Try not to bust a vein out here screaming, 'kay? You'll scare the children." Mariah tips her baseball cap slightly in my direction, then trots away from us.

"Jesus." Laine plops back down. "*That's* your type?" The judgment in her tone is thick and growly.

"My only type is single." It's not entirely true—Mariah's definitely sorority-girl gay and a bit of a pillow princess, which isn't my first choice in partners, but you can't be that picky in a queer community this size. Besides, she's nice, and I *did* enjoy her tan lines. "Why, you jealous?" I smirk, unable to resist teasing her.

"*No*," Laine says too quickly. "Just maybe don't sleep with the enemy next time, all right?"

"The *enemy*," I repeat, incredulous. "The single queer mom coaching her daughter's co-ed soccer team? That enemy?"

"I said what I said." Laine scowls at the field.

"Okay, what's your type then?" I fold my arms, too amused to let this go.

"Harlow."

The name slams into my chest like a bullet, taking my breath away. "Oh. Right."

Laine glances up at me then, her eyes flickering with interest at the obvious fluster she's caused. "I mean, *like* Harlow. Fun, funny, sexy. Maybe more interested in serious relationships, though. What about you? You ever going to settle down?"

"Um, me? Settle down?" The world stops spinning around me, and I'm almost thrown off into space from the sudden halt. I huff out a laugh. "I don't know, settling down's never felt like an option before."

"What do you mean?"

I try to think of how to explain what it's like being queer in a tiny mountain community, taking whatever scraps of interest I could get only to watch them fizzle out after a few hours, days, weeks. "You know when you're driving toward the Aska trails, and the road curves this way and that, never showing you more than fifteen feet ahead before turning again, and then suddenly, you hit that stretch where the road's straight as an arrow, and you can see for miles and miles, like the road goes on forever?"

Laine nods, and I blow out a breath. "My relationships never reach that stretch, where I can see off into the distance. The end's always there, right in front of me." She *hmms* thoughtfully before leaning back on her palms again. "You ever consider that maybe you've got to take those twists and turns to get to the long stretch?" My cheeks burn as I face the field once more. I start to say *no, my roads always end*, but it's giving petulant teenager, even to me.

The second half starts with a bang, and this time, it's Benny who gets the ball. Even though he's running toward the wrong goal, Laine's whooping like a madwoman, taking whatever she can get. Maybe now she'll understand the plight of being a single Blue Ridge lesbian. Ten feet from the goal, Benny starts to kick, and—

PHRRRRIIIIPTTT! The ref points to Bella, where she sits on the sidelines making dandelion wishes. "SHOELACES."

"She's NOT EVEN PLAYING!" Laine yells. "COME ON!"

The ref makes unflinching eye contact with Laine as she takes extra time tying one shoe, then, untying and retying the other one, too.

"Oh my god, the ref's fucking with me, isn't she?"

"You'll want to avoid checkout number three at the Piggly Wiggly."

With a minute left in the first half, Darla gets the ball again, and she and Benny run side by side toward the goal, the right one and everything, dribbling the ball back and forth, as twinnish as twins can be. Laine's sleeves are fully rolled up now, a fine layer of sweat dampening her forehead, as she claps like a maniac, urging those babies on. Then—

PHRRRRIIIIPTTT! The ref smiles fiendishly at Laine. "SHOELA—"

Laine leaps down and marches over to the referee and starts yelling in her face. I can't make out much, but the words *evil* and *Sisyphean* and *What did I ever do to you?!* float up before Chance comes over and joins them. At first, I think he's gonna drag Laine off the field, but now he's yelling at the ref, too, to the teenager's evident delight.

"THAT KID WAS WEARING *VELCRO!*" Chance bellows.

PHRRRRIIIIPTTT! The ref's whistle shrieks in Chance's face, then she tosses a yellow card at him. Chance throws his clipboard on the ground, groans rising from the bleachers.

Laine snatches the whistle out of the ref's hand. "You can't *yellow card* him!"

Undeterred, teen ref licks the back of a red card and sticks it against Laine's forehead. "YOU'RE OUTTA HERE, CHAMP."

It takes Booch plus three other concerned parents to drag Laine off the field. I find her sitting on my truck's bumper, sulky as the day is long. It's weirdly endearing.

"Well, well, well." I fold my arms over my chest. "Never been thrown out of Soccer Saturday before."

"You haven't been paying attention then." Laine sniffs. Her eyes flick upward as Chance, Darla, and Benny join us. The twins rush over, completely undisturbed by the game's 0-0 score, and give Laine a hug on each side. "Hey, lil bits," she says, her growly voice softening a bit. "Sorry Aunt Laine got booted out."

"You were the loudest one there," Darla says, then gives Laine a kiss on the cheek, which makes her smile.

Laine looks up at Chance, sheepish. "Sorry. I got . . . carried away."

"That's one way to put it," Chance says, chewing his gum. "Maniacal's another."

"*May*-be if you taught those kids how to stay in formation, I'd have kept my cool better." Laine stands, flint sparking in her eyes once more.

"Oh, you think you can do better?" Chance says.

"I know I can, *a—butthole*." Laine steps into his face. They used to be eye-to-eye, but Chance shot up at least three more inches during college, and it clearly bugs Laine to hell and back. "When's practice?"

Chance stares her down. "Tuesdays at five thirty p.m., *coach*."

"I'll see you then, *coach*."

With that, they nod aggressively at each other, and Laine turns and stalks off to the passenger side of my truck, just missing the first genuine smile I've seen Chance sport since she's come home.

I salute him before getting into the driver's side.

My work here is done.

CHAPTER THIRTEEN

"Bless you, Elisa. I've been trying to get an appointment with the permitting folks for weeks!" I spin in my office chair, cradling my phone to my ear. "Pass along my gratitude to the mayor, too, will you?"

"You've got it, Zoe," Elisa says.

I swear, it's like night and day out of that office ever since Rachel's field day. While Mayor Esposito ultimately put both Into the Woods and Bluebell Vineyards forward for the showcase, that's been good enough for me. Overnight, the partnerships have been rolling in, everybody excited to get on board now that we have a fighting chance of winning the spot. River's almost done with our new infrastructure, we've got a permitting appointment thanks to Elisa, and my newest business venture is soft-launching next week—the Redneck Wine Tour. Everything's coming up Brennan, except for—

"Have you heard from *Everyday Bon Vivant* yet?" Elisa asks.

I twirl my pen in my hand, hating the flush traveling up my neck because I *haven't*. I know from Olinda, former Small Business 101 student and now friend, that the *Everyday Bon Vivant* events team is coming next week because they've booked her shuttle service to pick them up in Atlanta and take them to their lodgings. I've been hoping they'd call requesting a tour while they're here, but nothing. That hasn't stopped me from engaging in a little guerrilla marketing effort, though. Olinda has agreed to reroute their trip on the way into town and feign van trouble right in front of Bluebell Vineyards an hour after our Strawberry Moon night begins. Cue devious chuckle.

Our outdoor bulb lights have all been freshly restrung, there'll be wildflower crowns for sale, and three delicious food trucks will be on-site. In a coup, I even booked Blue Ridge's best folk country outfit to play, The Genteelmen. They're difficult to get a hold of, but Killian, Hannah's ex-boyfriend, has been playing with them lately and put us on their busy schedule. It'll be a magical, flower-strewn evening, our sweet wines flowing to the heart-plucking twang of guitars and soft voices harmonizing. We'll woo the events team, I have no doubt.

I just wish they *wanted* to be wooed. I wish they'd call.

Elisa picks up on my hesitation, and in a soothing tone, says, "Don't worry, Zoe. They're not going to ignore Mayor Esposito's endorsements."

I let out a small sigh. "I hope you're right. Thanks again, Elisa."

After we disconnect our call, there's a knock on my office door, and River pokes his shaggy golden head in. "Hey, cuz, ready to do the once-over?"

I brighten. "Absolutely!"

I fish two beers from the fridge, hand one to River, then follow him as he leads me out the back patio doors into the vibrant blue afternoon, the sun dangling lazily like a marigold over the green mountains. River's crew has been working daily for the last month on the new infrastructure, but they've been saving the best for last—the viewpoints.

Bluebell Vineyards, nestled in a valley of rolling hills carpeted with forest and creeks and lush, untamed land, has always had an amazing vantage on the mountains that surround us. But not everyone is content to stroll our vineyards, gazing into the distance as they go. Some people need a destination to feel the freedom to wander, and I've long wanted to put in some seating areas to encourage people to stop and bask awhile in the beauty. As we walk up the newly graveled trail to the first overlook, my heart twinges with happiness. The platform itself is nothing extravagant.

A simple wooden stage with steps that seem to spring from the ground themselves, already flanked with beautiful budding perennials that Hannah planted herself.

But the view is nothing short of magical. The platform's few feet of elevation lifts your gaze above the vineyards sloping below to the dip and swell of mountains beyond.

"Well done, River," I say, my heart opening like a blossom toward the slowly setting sun. I take a long swig of the pale beer, its bubbles like tiny fireworks down my throat, feeling a satisfaction deep in my bones.

"Hannah sure knows how to pick 'em, doesn't she?" River clinks his bottle against mine before we sit down on the platform. The wood is sun-warmed beneath me, but the cool underside of the May breeze tickles my ankles as I let my legs dangle over the edge. He stares into the valley, a look of profound yearning etched in the lines around his eyes, like he could look and look and never be filled up for want of it all. "I love that woman so much, Zoe."

I reach over and squeeze his hand. "I know you do."

That sweet, earnest gaze lingers for a second before my goofy cousin reemerges, winking at me. "I can't help noticing that our wedding's only two weeks away, and yet, you've failed to RSVP with the name of your date. A man can only ponder for so long, Zoe. Which lucky interim vintner will it be?"

I frown and snatch my hand back. "What *exactly* do you think you know?"

River raises both eyebrows. "Well let's see. I know the woman you've held a torch for since you were a kid now lives on your property, you let her adopt a *goat*, and you've apparently consecrated your union by way of pink balloon humping in broad daylight."

"Baahlzebub isn't adopted, he's a long-term foster." I lift my chin. "And it was an innocent balloon race."

"Well, the foster goat that *you've named* ate about half your fence. Don't worry, I already fixed it, and from what I heard, that balloon would beg to differ."

"Would it now?"

"Come off it, Zoe. You got it bad for Laine, it's plain as day. What's holding you back?"

I huff out an incredulous laugh. "Okay, first of all? You need to stop listening to Teddy and Diego—"

"They're reliable sources!" River interrupts indignantly.

"You should hear what they say about *you*, man-child."

River shrugs. "Like I said, reliable."

"Second of all, Laine works here. What if I let something happen, and it went badly? Think Laine's gonna keep making my wine once she realizes what a—"

"—wonderful woman you are? Yes."

I furrow my brows. "You're a terrible interrupter, River. You've gotta work on that, or Hannah will leave your ass for *me*."

River stops to ponder that for a second. "Duly noted."

"Third of all, Laine and I have finally gotten to where we don't want to rip each other's heads off. You saw her with the pruning shears that day—she couldn't handle the tiniest bit of feedback! All that drama out west made her so afraid of trying and failing, she was barely functional, but we're working through all that. If we're going to have any shot at winning the showcase, I *need* her to come through for me." I pause long enough to polish off my beer. "I can't endanger our vineyard's future on some temporary horniness-induced insanity."

It's quiet for a beat, then two, then River gingerly lifts his hand. "May I speak now?"

I shove him in the arm.

"I'm tryin' not to lose Hannah to my spectacular lesbian cousin two weeks before our matrimony." He clears his throat. "If I may point out the painfully obvious?"

"You may *try.*"

"I don't think Laine's the only one here who's afraid of trying and failing *and*"—he lifts a finger before I can start in—"judging by the last eighteen years plus of grade A pining I've witnessed, I don't think your horniness-induced insanity is all that temporary, either."

My mouth drops open as River rises to his feet, grabs our empty bottles, and takes off toward the next viewpoint, whistling a Chappell Roan song, the *nerve.*

CHAPTER FOURTEEN

Just like that, the cool spring sun of May melts into June's stormy heat, all blue skies and boisterous clouds that dapple the roads before unleashing bursts of quenching rain. In our blocks, the buds have swelled with life, burst into flower, and the tiniest clusters of grapes have begun to form. I have to give it to Laine—after the pruning fiasco, she's been a devout student of Jamal's, absorbing his lessons on canopy management, leaf-thinning, and the dangers of powdery mildew—all things she never had to worry about in the dry, arid climates of California's wine regions but are critical to making grapes thrive in our humid, rainy mountains.

She's doing great. The pride I feel for her is of a soft and grateful sort. I miss Dad ferociously, but it's for his quiet voice, long hugs, and sad, loving eyes. It's no longer accompanied by the fear that Bluebell can't survive without him because with Laine here, I've started to believe we can.

Laine surprised me, though, when she asked to take last Friday off. "I know things are picking up right now, but I have to go back to California for the weekend." She'd cleared her throat, as if asking for a day off was unthinkable. "I need to get some things I left in storage. That okay, boss?"

"Sure, no problem." I tried to put extra kindness in my words. Le Jardin did a real number on her, and while Dad and I never take days off, we never hold our employees to that. "Will you let Josiah know so he can keep things going in the Pinot Noir blocks?"

She'd nodded, then a couple days later, left. I felt her absence keenly that weekend, my eyes sweeping the landscape for her again and again, even though I knew she was gone. Feeling disappointed anyway. Then, feeling a surge of glad relief when the lights flicked on in the Treebnb Sunday night when she returned.

I head to the back of the winery where Dad works on the red blends. Instead of his hunched shoulders, Laine's there now, and my heart warms at the sight. Her long legs are perched on Dad's thinking stool, folded on either side of her. She's wearing a white lab coat and goggles on her head, reading one of Mom's old wine journals intently. Judging by the getup, she must've been working with the sterile filtering agents earlier, but I don't really care why. She can mad-scientist in here anytime.

I rap my knuckles against a barrel. "Knock, knock."

She turns on her stool and gives me that heart-fluttering smile. "Hey, boss. What's up?"

"Darryl and Trish'll be here any minute." When her face fails to register the importance of this, I add, "For the Redneck Wine Tour?"

"Oh, right." She closes Mom's journal and places it on the table with reverence. "You know, your mom was a genius. The way she manipulated every step of the process with such intuition . . ." Laine shakes her head. "Nothing short of witch-level."

I smile ruefully. "That's my mom, wine-witch of Appalachia."

"Something to aspire to, that's for sure."

"Are you getting any closer to cracking the code for her red blends?"

"I'm trying, but so much of it depends on coaxing the grapes to the right acid and Brix, achieving the right length of fermentation, and adjusting everything else to what nature gave you that season. Your mom spoke her own language with the wine she made." Laine looks at me then, her face softening. "Have you ever read her journals?"

I wave a hand at her, but it's shaky. "I've tried, but you're right—it's like a different language. I love wine, but I've never wanted to make it myself." The words come out clipped through the sudden tightness in my throat, but it's not Laine's fault. She couldn't know how much I tried to force myself to fit into Mom's shoes exactly, to live the life she'd chosen but was cut short. When I was a kid, wine was this ocean I never knew how to cross to get to Mom. Obviously, I couldn't drink it or make it myself—I was just a kid. But I hated feeling barred off from this big, beautiful calling she loved, and that feeling magnified by a multitude after she died, made worse by my complete lack of aptitude for farming and making wine. It was only through business and marketing that I found my way across that ocean, and she was already long gone.

My fingers are gripping the wrist of my other hand, and I force them to relax. Just then, a series of loud, canned honks punctures the stillness of our countryside. It takes me a minute to realize it's the opening notes of Garth Brooks's "Friends in Low Places." The honking's followed by the sound of heavy wheels crunching over our gravel parking lot, and a megaphone announcing, "Callin' all y'all *rednecks!*"

I raise my eyebrows. "They're here."

"Listen, do you mind if I sit the tour out?" Laine smiles, but it's apologetic. "I feel bad taking time away from the blends right now."

I breathe in deeply through my nose because this isn't about the blends waiting. Laine and I have been getting along so much better since the smudge pot, but it's not because we magically solved all our differences about wine. Laine still carries around this—this *grudge* against Blue Ridge's wine region. To her credit, she tries to temper her opinions more, but even what she considers polite commentary still digs beneath my skin.

Will Blue Ridge ever be good enough for her?

Or do I have to *prove* that it is?

I give her a firm smile. "Nope. You're coming." I reach out my hand and to my surprise, she lets me pull her to standing. She's close now, so close that my breasts lightly graze the front of her lab coat. I know I should step back and make room, or at the very least, let go of her hand, but now that we're here, I can't make myself move at all. She tilts her chin down so she can meet my gaze, and the look in her eyes is so immediately attentive, so interested, it's like I flipped a switch within her to *on*.

"Is that a directive, boss?" Laine asks quietly, her lips still parted as though the question's physically lingering there. Heat floods my body. It flips my switch *on*, too.

"Yes," I breathe, unable to resist. "It is."

Laine pulls her bottom lip in. "If you make me, I'll come for you."

Her words thrum deep and low in my belly, my muscles tensing with pleasure. God, does she know what she's doing to me? She *does*. A smirk lifts the corners of her mouth, and finally, she steps back, stripping off her long yellow gloves. I suddenly feel the need to spout off all the justifications I'd planned if she'd fought back. "You need to experience other vineyards here, taste their wine. It's important to understand our scene, and besides"—I blow out a breath—"I'm nervous. I could use the company."

Laine's eyebrows flick upward, but the smirk remains. "Nervous? Why?"

An airhorn sounds from the parking lot, followed by Darryl's amplified voice: "*I said, CHOP CHOP!*"

My cheeks flare red, and I curse myself for telling Hannah once again. "Well, you heard the man. Let's go."

Laine gestures for me to lead the way. "This should be interesting."

She's not alone in her skepticism. Of all my new business ideas for Bluebell Vineyards, the Redneck Wine Tour's the one that's drawn the most excitement *and* squinty-eyed suspicion around town. We don't have many wine tour operators in Blue Ridge, perhaps because of how spread out the vineyards are, or how rowdy the clientele can get. But why not lean into both? A relaxing, comfortable ride provided by a dynamic duo, promising lots of wine and laughter and beautiful mountain views, tailored for the type of tourists who don't take wine too seriously.

Where's the wine tours for those folks?

Once I came up with the idea, I immediately thought of the perfect driver/docent pair, and I couldn't stop thinking about it until I turned it into reality. If it works, it'll bring in tour ticket sales *and* steady business to Bluebell each day the tour runs. Not to mention, the other vineyards on the route are paying us a small fee, too. We need the money, and this enterprise pays on all sides.

Laine and I emerge from the winery to a small test group gathering around the pristine sixteen-seater van. Hannah and her two best friends Kira and Mattie are here, and Teddy and Diego just shut the doors to their red Mini Cooper and are gleefully sprinting across the parking lot.

"HEAR YE, HEAR YE," Darryl says through his megaphone, a big man wearing top-to-bottom fishing gear. I'm talking cargo shorts stuffed with lures, a vest with more, and a trucker hat that says *Got Trout?* "Step right up for the inaugural Redneck Wine Tour and Unofficial Bachelorette Party for Ms. Hannah Tate!" He cackles, then slaps the side of the van like they're bros.

"It is *not* my bachelorette party, and who decided to give Darryl a megaphone?!" Hannah demands as Laine and I approach. Darryl is Hannah's stepdaddy, and judging by the flush of her pink cheeks, she's already deeply mortified. "*Who?!*"

Kira grins and rubs her hands together. "This is gonna be so *good*."

Mattie, Kira's wife, smiles in that way people do who live their life being amused by the people they love. "Trish, nice honks. Was that Garth Brooks?"

Trish, Hannah's mom, cranks the driver's side window down and hangs her elbow out. She's an older, wilier version of Hannah with hair just as wild, though it's gray instead of dark blonde. She's inexplicably wearing a blue railroad conductor's cap. "Yes, thank you for noticing! I wanted something like *Dukes of Hazzard*, but you know—not racist! I preloaded lots of goodies. This one's for you, Hannah baby!" Trish fumbles with the small device attached to her steering wheel, which then omits a honking version of "Like a Virgin."

"Good god," Hannah whispers, and Kira throws her head back and laughs.

"Trish, you got the dick necklaces, right?" Kira manages out.

"That's an affirmative, Kiki." Trish holds up a fistful of necklaces hung with plastic dicks of every color and jangles them triumphantly.

"*What?!*" Hannah looks like she might bust a vein. "Absolutely *not!*" But nobody's paying her any mind. Trish's already stowed the necklaces away, and Darryl's busy passing out tour maps. I watch our participants' expressions flicker from confusion to delight. I've already seen Darryl's hand-drawn map of the wine tour, complete with all four vineyard stops plus "See Bigfoot" overlooks and little notes, like: *Best potty, hold ur pee till here* and *By now, u will b drunk.* Over Into the Woods, he's drawn a big red X, saying: *For fancy-pants only.* The last stop is of course Bluebell Vineyards, followed by an optional fishing excursion in our stocked pond. A redneck's preferred way to sober up, Darryl's informed me.

I heartily approve.

Laine's looking at the map with an incredulous smile, her mouth slightly parted as she takes in all of Darryl's scribbles, skulls, and Bigfoots (*Bigfeet?*) lurking in the margins. She finally looks up at me. "This is hilarious," she says cautiously, like maybe that's on accident.

"I know." It's a small compliment, but the pride's rolling through me like a tidal wave anyway.

I turn to Kira and Mattie. "Y'all, this is Laine Woods. She's filling in as vintner while my dad's out of the country. Laine, this is Kira and Mattie, our good friends from Atlanta."

"Wait. Laine Woods as in *Charlaine Woods?*" Kira is awestruck. "As in, TFL?!"

"*Kira!*" Hannah grits out, and Kira claps a hand over her adorable face while mine goes nuclear with horror. Kira winces and mouths: *Sorry!*

"TFL?" Laine looks from Kira to Hannah to me for explanation. My red face must announce my guilt because her gaze lingers there, waiting.

"Erm, TFL. You know, The First Lesbian?" I mumble out. My entire body starts sweating, all at once. "You were my First Lesbian. I mean, that I knew of? Not like you were *mine*, per se—"

"Her Guiding Gay Light," Mattie cuts in unhelpfully. "The Alpha Queer, First of Her Kind. The Crush that 'Made Her Gay.'" She air-quotes the phrase with a grin, then glances around and receives the pointy end of Kira's elbow. "What—was that still a secret?"

Laine's eyebrow quirks up. "I thought it was just a little crush, boss." A sly smile plays about her mouth as she repeats my brazen lies from the night of the smudge pot. "You didn't even know you were gay."

"I didn't, until you." The words stumble out, but Laine's playful gaze softens. Her eyes trace over mine, and it's uncomfortable, being seen like this. Understood in a context I've shared gladly with a hundred strangers, but never with her, the source.

I never dreamed I'd have the chance.

"Who was your TFL?" Kira asks Laine, papering over the loaded emotional moment as we board the van. It's the least she can do since she brought this plague of vulnerability upon me. I slide into a window seat, and my heart picks up speed as Laine sits next to me. The press of her arm against mine feels warm and reassuring, like finding out she was my queer North Star doesn't freak her out.

Laine pauses to think, then smiles coyly. "Ellen."

The van erupts into laughter.

"All right now, simmer down!" Darryl says from the front of the van where he's holding an extremely large microphone. "This here's the Redneck

Wine Tour. If you in the wrong place, whew, boy! You about to get drunk! You can call me Big Daddy, and that silver fox driving is G-ma."

"Woo, G-ma!" Kira hollers. "You're not drinking today?"

"Honey, I'm as sober as they get. This granny's shootin' to live to a hundred. Y'all have a good time, though." With that, Trish tips her conductor's hat and rams the van into reverse. We lurch into motion, and Darryl clutches one of the metal poles for support.

"Damn, baby!" Darryl grouses over his shoulder. "Good thing this was a stripper van." With one arm hugging the pole, he lifts the giant microphone to his face, speaking into it so close, the bristle of his mustache hairs is audible from the speakers. "First stop, Red Clay Vineyards!"

Darryl's a natural. He knows absolutely nothing about wine, but that's part of the draw. With us huddled around him in the Red Clay tasting room, he samples the first pour. "This wine's exceptionally slurpable. I give it four *hell yeah*s."

Mattie takes a sip and ponders. "It's a three *hell yeah* for me."

The commentary gets better as the wine tour goes on.

"Now this merlot reminds me of this jar of grape jelly that sat out on our porch for too long. Five fishing rods up."

"Ooh, *blech*. I give this one three-and-a-half trout."

"This trami-what now? This Traminette is like . . . well, it's like if an angel made a baby with Willie Nelson."

Laine tastes the light, sweet Traminette, and her eyebrows rise. "You know what? I see what he means!"

The others get into it, too. Teddy describes the bouquet of a deep, smoky Pinot Noir as the smell of freshly burnt tires, and Diego agrees, giving it five *damn straights!* We spend the entire afternoon tasting and drinking and laughing as Trish weaves the van up and down the winding gravel roads through Blue Ridge wine country. The best part has been watching Laine slowly change her mind. She marvels over a fruity white blend at Jamal's vineyard, exclaiming to whoever'll listen that *who knew our native Catawba pairs so well with classic vinifera?* Doesn't hurt that, true to Big Daddy's map, we're all drunk as hell at this point. Hannah doesn't even stop Trish from breaking out the necklaces, and soon we're all bedecked with dicks.

"*Y'all!* If you mash the balls, the dicks light up!" Kira raves, squeezing a bulbous pair to Teddy's visceral horror.

"That is *not* how they work, baby!"

Mattie frowns. "Dicks or necklaces?"

Teddy balls up his tour map and throws it at her in response. It somehow lands behind him.

I can't judge, though. I didn't set out to get drunk this morning, but it started feeling strategic as the tour went on. Something's gotta calm my brain down. Between Laine's physical proximity and *Everyday Bon Vivant*'s impending visit to Blue Ridge, my blood's crackling with electricity.

"So, what's got you so nervous?" Laine asks as we board the van to head back to Bluebell. "Your leg's been jiggling all day."

"*Everyday Bon Vivant* still hasn't called yet." Just saying it aloud makes my throat tighten uncomfortably. Damn alcohol releasing all these emotions. "And they arrive tomorrow."

Laine throws a loose arm around my shoulders and corrals me into our row. The pressure sends a bolt of pleasure down my spine. "Don't worry, boss. If they haven't called you yet, they probably haven't called anybody. And don't you have some sneaky plan cooked up to meet them anyway?"

I laugh, leaning into her a little more than is strictly professional, but her body draws me in like a magnet, and I can't find the willpower to fight it right now. Not after four buckets of wine and a glorious, sunny afternoon rolling through my favorite place on earth. Besides, it's not like she's let me go yet, either. "How d'you know about that?"

"I heard you cackling about it with Olinda when she came in last week." Laine's face slides into an easy grin. "You're so cute when you cackle."

My insides somersault within me, and I briefly consider taking up witchcraft or some other cackling profession full-time. "Y-yeah?"

She boops my nose with her finger. She is *definitely* sauced. "Oh, shut up, Brennan. You know you're adorable." My entire head goes up in wild, searing flames.

She thinks I'm adorable?

"Yeah, *Brennan*," Kira says as she and Mattie slide into the row behind us. "Stop being so adorable all the time."

"You first, Kira!" I jab a finger at her. "You're *queen* of inconveniently adorable people, all married as hell."

"She sure is," Mattie says lovingly, then presses a big, messy kiss to Kira's temple, which Kira wipes off with a loud *blech!*, then resumes squeezing balls and giggling to herself.

"Goddamn drunk-ass lesbians," Teddy says, salty as ever. "You're all in love with each other, get over it!"

Laine's arm slides from my shoulders to the top of my seat back, creating a little cocoon of *us*. "Why are gay men so wise?"

"We're immune to the power of tits," Teddy says, earning a chorus of groans and flying objects from the rest of the passengers. Hannah beans him square in the head with one of her socks, which she's abandoned along with her shoes, purse, and other assorted clothing.

"You okay, Hannah?" I raise an eyebrow, waiting to see if anything good gets shed.

"Too hot," she grumbles, then lies down in the back row, dick necklace still glowing to a beat only it can hear. I snap a picture to commemorate this unofficial bachelorette party.

"So Olinda's gonna roll up with the *Everyday Bon Vivant* team tomorrow," Laine prompts, a bit glassy-eyed, but hanging in there. "Walk me through your plan."

I take a deep breath. "The vineyard's gonna be all set up for our Strawberry Moon night. The Genteelmen will be there early, playing already. The vineyard's windows will be open, and our outdoor bar set up on the patio. We'll have freshly picked strawberries to pair with Electric Daisy, and the food trucks will be set up, too."

Laine nods thoughtfully. "Sounds nice. What are you gonna say?"

"I'll feign sympathy for their inconvenience of course, offer them drinks and snacks while they wait for Olinda's mechanic to come service the van. Then I'll give them our standard tour, if they'll let me. Show off the vineyards, the winery . . . what?" I trail off and frown, interrupted by the vigorous, sloppy shake of Laine's head.

"No, no, *no*. Don't give the *standard* tour! You've gotta tell them about what makes Bluebell Vineyards *special*."

I frown harder, weirdly hurt by this. "That *is* what our standard tour's about. You don't think that shows?"

"The tour's about your valley location, the soil composition, your philosophy of everyday people drinking wine. But you never share the *story* of Bluebell Vineyards. Tell them about your mom, Zoe. Why doesn't anyone tell her story? Tell them about how your parents started Bluebell and ran it together." Laine smacks her leg with her hand emphatically. "*That's* what people want to hear. *The romance*."

I swallow. "Talk about *Mom*? Dad's never been able to handle that." The wine's making it difficult to steady my feelings, pitching me about like a ship on stormy waves. But my parents' story *is* happy, isn't it? A good one that lingers in your heart, even if it ends in tragedy. Just because Dad can't handle telling it doesn't mean I can't or shouldn't.

"Maybe it's time you start." She looks at me with such fondness, it's easy to forget we're just coworkers.

But that's all we are, I grind the reminder into my brain. Even if River's right that I'm afraid of developing feelings for Laine again, he's wrong about why. I'm not scared of trying and failing—that's already happened. We had sex, she realized who I really am, and she ended it, just like every other woman has in my life. But that was *before* we started working together. Now, my vineyard's future hinges on her staying and delivering in a big way. If we hooked up again, how would she end it then? By leaving me and Bluebell in the lurch? Staying and making me miserable? I already know what war against her is like; I can't go back to that.

Laine gets pulled into a raucous conversation about favorite celebrity queers, but I stare out the window instead, pondering what to say about our vineyard's origins, and Laine. She's always in my thoughts these days, one way or the other. The countryside swirls by until my eyes grow heavy, a deep yawn overtaking me. The van's grown quiet. When I turn back, I realize Laine's already fallen asleep, her head resting against her arm, still stretched across the back of my seat. The way her soft breath sighs out from her parted lips, close enough to dance across my own, makes my chest ache.

Okay, so maybe I *do* have a crush on Laine again. Or maybe it never ended, lying dormant all these years until a crack fissured, and now powerful feelings are flowing out of me once again, hot and molten and incredibly destructive. Wanting her is wanting to be hurt. Wanting her is asking to be destroyed.

But I *do* want her.

I turn fully to face her, resting my head lightly against the smooth cotton of her shirt stretched across her arm. She smells like sandalwood soap and sweet muscadine, and she murmurs in her sleep, a quiet rumble that I half hear, half feel against my cheek. The way her body curves toward mine feels incredibly intimate, like we're a pair of parentheses, reaching for each other across the expanse, despite all the circumstances that make *us* a bad idea. Maybe it's pathetic letting myself pretend like this, laying my head on her arm like her comfort is mine to have, but any self-consciousness I might've felt has been dulled by wine and rocked to sleep by the van's gentle ride through the Appalachian foothills.

I don't know how long I'm asleep, but when Laine shakes me awake, it's with a strong vibe of terror.

"*Zoe!* Wake up!"

My eyes flap open, head swimming with alcohol, stomach lurching. "Wh-what?"

"Olinda's van is in the lot!" Laine's face is contorted in panic as she shakes me again. "*Everyday Bon Vivant* is here!"

CHAPTER FIFTEEN

"Darryl, we need a water, *stat!*" Hannah's launched into action, staggering around like a drunken, half-dressed general caught in a surprise attack. "Someone check Zoe's face!"

"My fa—?"

Diego grabs me by the chin and peers into my eyes, then scans my face for imperfections and sniffs. "Looks good. Smells bad!

"Got it, baby!" Teddy hurriedly shoves a stick of medical-grade mint gum into my gaping mouth. Then Laine's pulling me up to my feet, smoothing down my wrinkled sundress with the heels of her hands. "You with me, boss? It's showtime!"

"Wait, WAIT! Her hair's weird, y'all!" Teddy screeches over his shoulder. "What do we do about her hair?!"

"I've got a curling iron up here!" Trish hollers back. "I can plug it into the USB port!"

"Oh my GOD, stop it!" I slap all their reaching, frantic hands away, which sends me reeling backward into my seat.

Fuck, I am *drunk*.

"They're not supposed to be here till tomorrow," I wail at the van's ceiling. Teddy tentatively picks up an errant lock of my hair, and I smack his hand away.

"You've missed ten calls and thirty-two texts." Laine hands me my phone from where it fell on the floor. "Plans must've changed while we didn't have service."

Fuck, fuck, FUCK. I take the wretched gum out and throw back the bottle of water Hannah thrusts at me, then shove the gum back in, chewing furiously. *Willing* the burning mint to dry out my brain. Everyone's looking at me nervously. They know how crucial this moment is for Bluebell Vineyards, and I'm drunk, smeared with sleep, and completely unprepared.

Well, so fuckin' what?

I'm Zoe Nicoletta Brennan, boss-bitch through and through, and I'm about to win me that goddamn showcase. I grab the headrest in front of me and haul myself to standing. "It's *ho-time*."

"Showtime," Mattie corrects.

"I said what I said!"

The van goes up in cheers as I push past them to the front. "Darryl, you go out first, and I'll follow. That way if I trip, I've got something soft to land on."

Laine pumps her fist and says, "*Yeah!*"

Bacchus must be watching over me, because my black zip-up boots carry me swiftly and confidently across our gravel parking lot to the front doors of our tasting room, where a small group of people wearing rumpled white linen and heavy black sunglasses stand looking distinctly put out. Olinda's there, too, wringing her hands, but when she sees me, relief washes over her face. "Oh, thank goodness you're here, Zoe! My shuttle broke down right there in the road, and it's going to be at least forty-five minutes until the backup can arrive to transport my guests to their accommodations." She winks at me then, with a mischievous smile only I can see. "I know you're closed for the evening, but could you find it in your heart to let us in to get out of this heat?" Olinda waves her hand at her face. "My god, it is hot, though."

"Yes, of course!" I pull my keys out of my bag with a flourish, which sends them flying through the air. Laine appears out of nowhere and catches them deftly in one hand despite being a few sheets to the wind herself.

Fucking athletes.

"So sorry to hear about your shittle troubles, *er*, shuttle troubles," I say over my shoulder as I unlock the doors, hoping to God that Tristan remembered to wipe down the counters before clocking out for the day. "Olinda has the best airport service in town. But since you're here, might as well come in and take a load off while you wait." I'm striving for nonchalance, feigning complete ignorance as to who these disgruntled fashionable people are. "Are y'all in town for a wedding? Family reunion, maybe?" *Reunion* comes out more like *roonyin*, but overall, I'm doing great. Very sober, three fishing rods up, me.

"We're here on business, actually," says a lovely older woman with silky, silver hair tied up in a simple topknot. To *be* that elegant after a long day of flying. *Jesus*, I am out of my league. "And a bit of pleasure," she adds with a laugh as silky as her hair. "This is quite a coincidence, really."

"Oh? How so?" I flip all the lights on, unable to hide my sigh of relief. The place is spotless.

Bless you, Stan. Bless you.

"We're with *Everyday Bon Vivant*. I'm head of events, and this is my team," Silver Fox says, offering her hand to me in a genteel shake. "Marisol Torres. Pleasure to meet you, Ms. Brennan."

I command my eyes to widen *just so* in amazement. "I heard y'all were looking at Blue Ridge for your annual festival! I'm so excited to meet you. What a surprise!"

Laine catches my eye and mouths, *Oscar-worthy*, and I beam.

"This is my vintner, Laine Woods. She worked at Le Jardin before coming home to Blue Ridge, and now, we're lucky enough to have her here."

Laine freezes, and I realize belatedly maybe listing off her California disaster-train exodus *wasn't* a great idea? *Shit.*

"Laine Woods?" Marisol pauses, looking at Laine thoughtfully. "I've heard your name somewhere." She taps a long nail on her chin.

Laine laughs a little, but it sounds strangely choked. "Oh, well. If you're in the wine business long enough, you get around."

"It's wonderful to meet you both." Marisol's voice is a little distant, evidently still trying to pin Laine to whatever she's heard about her. But then her friendly eyes land back on me. "We were already planning on visiting Bluebell Vineyards this week while in town. Unannounced, of course." She smiles demurely. "You understand."

"I do indeed." I don't know why I'm speaking like a debutante at her first cotillion, but here we are. "Well, I'm honored to have you here on *this* unannounced visit, though I'm sorry it's under your present circumstances. Hopefully a little wine can help?"

I sidle behind the bar, grabbing a still frozen Laine by the arm as I go. "Give us just a moment, and we'll be right back." I give the team a gracious smile, then pull Laine into the back. The door swings shut behind us.

"Laine? You've gotta snap out of it." I wave my hand in front of her spooked face. "You hear me?"

"She'll remember," Laine whispers, her eyes still trained above my head at the wall behind me. "She doesn't right now, but she will. Then what?" Her eyes flicker down to mine, fearful. "They'll write off Bluebell Vineyards as soon as they find out who I am."

I grab her by the shoulders, sinking my fingers into the firm muscles there. "No. They won't." My voice is commanding, deep. It forces her to focus on me. "We won't let them write us off. You know why?"

Laine blinks, her eyes begging me for rescue. "Why?"

I step closer, tilting my chin up, defying her crackling insecurity with a million volts of pure *boss*. "We're about to charm them out of their goddamn minds. They're going to be in love with us, with Bluebell Vineyards, with *all of it* by the time they leave here today. We're going to do whatever it takes to make that happen." Laine swallows as I run my hands along the line of her shoulders, smoothing her shirt. One hand goes renegade and tightens around the back of her neck. "*Whatever it takes*," I say, repeating our mantra from Rachel's field day. "Do you understand?"

Laine sucks in a breath, her eyes flashing heat. The alcohol's loosened up all my impulses, and I let go of her suddenly, then shake my head as if that could dispel the horniness that's descended upon me like a fog. "I'm—sorry. I—"

Laine catches me by the wrist, deliciously present once more. "Don't be, boss." She runs her thumb over my pulse point, sending a thousand shooting arrows of lust straight through my core. "Now, let's go win this thing."

We each grab a few bottles to bring out. My head feels woozy from the encounter with Laine, like I drank a bottle of *her*, and it's gone straight to my head.

We bustle back into the tasting room, and Laine, full of a sexy, new confidence, pulls out the corkscrew and begins describing the crisp acidity our grapes achieve in this climate. The team listens enraptured, and I lean on the counter, placing my chin in my hands, listening to her, too. This is going *great*. Laine is pure competence and grace. I am the picture of sobriety and good cheer. Hospitality personified. I am—my chin slips out of my palm, and my head jerks toward the counter, but I save myself before I crack my jaw open. One of the other women, a short brunette with suspicious eyes, frowns at me.

"Are you all right?"

"Yes, yes." I wave a hand at her. "Allergy season, that's all." I grab a bevy of stemmed glasses before anyone can think too long about *that* excuse and set the glasses down artfully in front of each of the events team, thanking the Universe for muscle memory kicking in. Altogether, there are four of them. Marisol; the suspicious little brunette whose name is probably Agatha (she just *looks* like an Agatha); a younger man with hip metal glasses and a tablet, positively dripping with executive assistant energy; and a softly jowled man who looks like he eats Tums by the barrel.

I push a small pour of Electric Daisy toward the nervous man first. "You must be the logistics person," I say conspiratorially.

He blinks at me with wide, owllike eyes. "How did you know?"

"You look like you're planning a hundred different contingencies right now based on this unexpected detour." I wink at him. "Always ready to save the day. Am I right?"

"Well, I—" He laughs a little, slides a finger under the tight collar of his shirt to make room for his sweating neck, then undoes the top button. "I do have an eye for detail." He sniffs the wine's bouquet appreciatively. "Like wildflowers. Lovely." He smiles shyly back.

One down, three to go.

I slide glasses toward Marisol, Agatha, and Mr. Bright Future and watch with as casual a gaze as I can muster as they sniff and sip their wine.

Marisol's smile is as kind as ever as she declares Electric Daisy a perfect refresher on a hot summer evening, but Agatha winces subtly. Laine and I both see it, and we trade apprehensive glances.

"If you're ready to stretch your legs after the long drive from Atlanta, how about a tour of the property?" Laine's tone and manner are professional, congenial, perfect. It's hard to believe the same woman was singing Faith Hill songs unironically at the top of her lungs a couple hours ago at Jamal's *Keep Calm and Karaoke* Wednesday afternoon programming. It's harder to believe she was ever scared at all. She's slipped her tortoiseshell specs on, which goes a long way toward hiding the loose, relaxed set of her face that comes from a long day sipping wine in the sun. "Zoe can tell you the beautiful story of how Bluebell came to be while the sun sets over the vineyards. It's one of the prettiest places in the world."

My insides warm with happiness. "You really think that?"

Laine glances at me, her cheeks pinking beneath her frames. "I do."

"Oh my goodness, you two are just the perfect pairing, aren't you!" Marisol exclaims, delighted. "My son just married his partner of ten years last spring. Beautiful wedding."

"Congratulations," Laine says with genuine feeling, her eyes soft at the corners, completely unshaken. "You must be so proud."

"I am! With two sons, I like to say I'm surrounded by handsome men now. Were you two married here, as well?" Marisol's smile is warm below her twinkling eyes, rendering me speechless at how quickly this misunderstanding has escalated. But I can't regret it. Marisol's vibes have gone from polite professionalism to sweet, caring, and maternal, her eyes glowing with happiness for the young queers in love.

"Um, n-no," Laine stutters out while I stare, dumbfounded. She adjusts her glasses and smiles nervously. "At least, not yet," she recovers quickly. She reaches for my hand and squeezes. My heart explodes into a gaggle of red and pink confetti, as fooled by her words as the *Everyday Bon Vivant* team.

Stupid heart, get your shit together!

"Well, lead the way, lovebirds. We can take this delicious wine with us to go."

Laine's eyebrows rise over her frames as she smiles giddily at me, then offers her arm. "Shall we?" The question's layered, and though my head is spinning on a different axis than the rest of my body, I know she's asking more than whether I'm ready to go right now.

Shall we give the people what they want?

Whatever it takes, right? I take her arm, bringing her close to me.

"Yes, we shall."

We set out on the new gravel path that winds through our vineyards. It's magic hour right now—the last kiss of sunlight gilds the rows of leafy canopies, turning green grapes golden as we make our way to the top of the hill, toward Mom's tree and the first majestic viewpoint. The blue skies are ablush with apricot and honey, pinkest where the emerald-green curve of the Appalachian Mountains presses against them in the horizon. The whole world feels vivid and alive.

"Story time," Laine says fondly down at me, and Marisol agrees cheerily. I clear my throat, looking out on the vineyards, and summon this untold story, forbidden for so long, from my heart.

"Once upon a time, there was a young woman named Julie who worked on her family's farm in the foothills of Appalachia, where she helped with a little of everything." I didn't intend to tell it like this, but the story flows out of me like a fairy tale, the way Mom always told it when I was a kid. Every night, I'd beg to hear it, and she'd indulge me more often than not, sitting on the side of my twin bed, her hand resting gently on my covers. Sometimes Dad would listen in the doorway, his eyes starry as he leaned against the frame. How I loved seeing them in love.

"Julie's favorite pastime was helping her father cultivate a small patch of merlot vines and turning grapes into rich, red wine. She longed to turn her father's hobby into her own future, but her family didn't approve. There weren't any vineyards in Blue Ridge then, and it was an untested idea whether they could work here on a large scale. But Julie believed in what she could do, so she saved all her nickels and dimes with the hopes of buying her own land one day. She worked every job she could, but it was her job at the old hardware store, the one place in town you could buy camping gear back then, that set her dreams in motion. One day, a young man came in with a shopping list a mile long, preparing for a months-long hike up the Appalachian Trail. He was dark-haired, handsome, and extremely confused, and Julie took pity on him." I stop to smile, remembering how Mom's eyes would always travel over to Dad as she told this part of the story, a gentle, teasing lilt to her voice. "He seemed to think he could carry a hundred pounds of beans on his back and make it past Springer Mountain."

Young Cosimo was an ambitious man, Dad would always add, then grin. *And very stupid.*

"It took weeks to get all the supplies he ordered into the store, but Cosimo found he didn't mind the delay. He'd graduated from college that winter and, feeling lost about his own future, had decided to hike the Appalachian Trail to find himself. He was a romantic that way, idealistic to his core, and he wasn't ready to return to his family in Italy just yet. He was looking for inspiration, and he found it behind the register at the hardware store with a name tag that read 'Julie.' He asked her out that night and every night after."

"After a short, passionate spring romance, it was time for Cosimo to depart on his hike. The weather was right, his pack was ready, but his heart longed to stay in Blue Ridge with Julie. She hiked with him to the top of Springer Mountain, and as the sun set on the rolling hills and valleys below, she told him of her dreams to start her own vineyard."

"Cosimo listened, thinking this must be his fate. He grew up in Tuscany, where every extra pair of hands were set to work in the vineyards. He had no dream of his own, but he could help Julie live hers. Wine was her dream, but Julie was his."

"They sat, surrounded by the first bluebells in bloom on Springer Mountain, and together, they picked the prettiest patch of hilly forest below them, drenched in the last rays of sun, to be their future home. He promised her he'd return, and they'd start their lives together. Julie didn't believe a word of it, of course. He was a beautiful Italian man who wore his heart on his sleeve, and she didn't believe in fairy tales anymore. So when Cosimo Rossi Giuratraboccetti appeared on her doorstep a month later with a deed, a ring, and more bug bites than you could count, Julie nearly fainted on the spot."

"He quit the hike and bought the land?!" Marisol broke in, her hand pressed against her chest, unable to contain her surprise.

I grin. "He didn't last two weeks on the AT. He couldn't stop thinking about his Julie, and fate, and the sign he'd been given. He turned right back around, emptied his savings for a down payment, and put all his romance and fate to the test. He proposed, and she didn't even have to think about it. Julie said yes."

Laine shakes her head and whistles. "Cosimo, that old dog."

Agatha scrunches her brow. "Didn't you know the story already?"

Laine starts a bit at the question, then falls back into character. "Of course! Gets me every time, though." She wraps her arm around my shoulders and gently brushes a tear off my cheek. Quietly, she says, "You're crying, boss."

I laugh a little as Marisol hands me a handkerchief with concern. "I'm sorry. I hear my mother's voice in my head whenever I tell this story. She died when I was twelve."

"Oh, you poor dear," Marisol murmurs. Even mean-faced Agatha looks chagrined. I smile weakly as I look out onto our vineyards, the gold faded into a solemn silvery lavender in the sun's absence.

"My mother Julie and my father Cosimo cultivated the land they picked on sight alone for Bluebell Vineyards, the land we're standing on today. You can see Springer Mountain, just there, in the distance. It must've been fate because our terroir is perfect for growing grapes. The hills are red clay topped with sand, providing the drainage we need to survive our rainy seasons, and the constant breeze from the mountains keeps our leaves dry and healthy. Every spring, our woods are ringed in bluebells, which gave us our name. Together, my parents founded this vineyard and filled it with their love, my mother as vintner, my father as farmer. My mother may have passed on, but not before giving me her dream, too. I've run this place with my father ever since, and now, with Laine."

Mr. Logistics wipes his own tears away. "What a *beautiful* story, and you and Laine are carrying on the tradition, just like your parents. This vineyard runs on pure romance. My *goodness*."

Laine gazes into my eyes so tenderly, it takes my breath away. "It's hard not to fall in love with this place, or the people in it."

I swallow, just barely, as her hand brushes my cheek again.

"Where is Cosimo now?" Agatha asks abruptly, then coughs into her hand as though self-conscious about her question.

"He's on an extended stay in Italy to see our family there," I respond, still locked into Laine's dreamy eyes. "Would you all like to see a picture of my parents?" I turn to face the events team, pleased to see their wholehearted delight at the idea. I pull out my phone and open a special folder of old pictures I scanned in one night when I was feeling lonely. Dad took all her pictures down after Mom passed—he just couldn't handle seeing her face everywhere her body no longer lived, but I missed seeing her smile. I pull up my favorite—a black-and-white photo of my parents when they were both young and healthy, just a few months before I was born. Dad's sitting with his back pressed against Mom's tree, his arms wrapped protectively around her pregnant belly. His chin rests on her shoulder, and she's smiling through a big laugh, as though the photographer, my Aunt Bri I think, had just said something funny. Dad's eyes are shining and gloriously happy, an expression that disappeared the day Mom found out she was sick. But here, with their whole lives ahead of them, they *were* happy. A southern girl and an Italian boy. An unlikely romance fated to be.

I float through the rest of the tour and back to our tasting room, the tide of memories making my heart swell in bittersweet longing. It feels good to tell them, to remember her here. This is her place, her land, picked by her and Dad in a moment of waking dream. Long after the wine leaves my system, I remain heady under the memories' influence and Laine's lingering touches. I know it's just for show—Marisol and the *Everyday Bon Vivant* events team are fully in love with the idea of Bluebell Vineyards, and the idea of Laine and I together, carrying that romantic legacy forward. It makes good business sense to lean into it, that's all. I should be grateful she's willing to sell it as hard as we need, though the pleasure from her touch is laced with a stinging pain.

I may not have the romance my parents did, but I have the heartache. Every good love story has both, so if you look at it that way, I'm halfway there.

Always halfway there.

The substitute shuttle arrives, but the events team opts to stay late into the evening, laughing around a table on our patio beneath the string lights with Laine, Olinda, and me, wine flowing while stories are traded. Eager to hear more Julie/Cosimo canon, the team begs me to tell them more, so I regale them about our trip to the *Everyday Bon Vivant* festival in the Finger Lakes, to which Marisol exclaims that was the first event she ever worked on. By the time they leave, Marisol feels like an old friend, and Matthew and Preston, Mr. Logistics and Mr. Bright Future respectively, are well on their way, too. Only Agatha, whose real name is Erica, remains difficult to pin down. She didn't finish her wine at the tasting, nor did she hug Laine and I goodbye as the others did when they bid their farewells.

"We'll win her over," Laine whispers into my ear as we wave goodbye from the door, making the soft down of my neck prickle. "Don't you worry."

But when? When would we see them again, if ever? Suddenly possessed, I run out into the parking lot, calling for them to slow down.

"This Saturday evening, if you don't have plans, please come visit us again. We're hosting my dear friend Hannah's wedding, and the reception will be a huge party—all are welcome." I smile, pleading and breathless, as Laine joins me. "I'd love to show y'all Bluebell Vineyards fully decked out and brimming with romance."

Marisol's mouth curves in the moonlight as she takes both my hands in hers, and without even looking at the others, says, "Zoe darling, we'll be here. See you soon!"

I clasp my hands to my heart as the now familiar weight of Laine's arm encircles my waist, fingers splayed warmly across my hip. The touch feels possessive and easy, and it sends waves of heat through my belly, radiating from each point of contact between our bodies. We wave goodbye for a second time and as the van rolls away, Laine leans down.

"I hope that was okay," she whispers against my neck, her full mouth forming each letter's shape against my taut, flushed skin. I feel how a violin in the hands of a musician must, each of my strings tightening beneath her fingers until they reverberate with high, clear music. The strong line of her nose nudges my jaw, as though she's prodding my head to fall back and stare at the nearly full moon so she can kiss her way down the sensitive skin there. If there was any doubt before about Laine's sexual interest in me, this moment's banishing it for good. She keeps her face buried against my neck until the headlights disappear into the flooding darkness of the mountain night. Breathing into me. Once again, asking me multiple questions under the guise of one. Waiting for my answer.

What *is* my answer? *Hurt me, please? Destroy me, please?* Take what I have to give, then leave when it's not enough?

The front door to my father's house opens, then slams shut, jolting us apart.

"How'd it go, lesbians?!" Teddy bellows across the parking lot. Diego hurries out after him, apologizing profusely.

"So sorry to startle you, we just tucked inside so we could sober up before driving home!" Diego throws his arm around Teddy, corralling him toward the red Mini Cooper still parked in the corner of our lot. "He's still drunk," Diego stage-whispers. "But seriously, how did it go?"

My side where Laine was pressed seconds ago feels cold without her. I find myself looking to her to answer.

"Zoe was amazing." Laine locks her eyes on mine, heat pouring through an invisible channel from her to me. "*Is* amazing." She walks backward a few steps. "Good night, boss."

I press a hand to my chest, as though her words branded me there, and watch her turn and walk away.

CHAPTER SIXTEEN

Hannah and River's wedding is in less than an hour, there are still a dozen critical tasks to do, and yet I'm here, in the winery-turned-dressing room, arguing. There's no *Bridezilla* here, no *Groom Kong*. But there is a *Teddy*.

I really should've seen this coming.

Teddy glares at the elfin ear prosthetics in my hand with revulsion, then his eyes flick up to mine. "I will bite you if you come any closer."

"*Teddy*." My heartbeat's pounding in my neck. I've grown increasingly agitated over the course of the day, not only because I want Hannah and River's wedding to be perfect, but also because of the *Everyday Bon Vivant* team's impending visit. Yesterday Jamal texted me that Marisol and company had spent a long evening at Into the Woods the night after our meeting, and apparently, it went so well that Rachel pranced through town, smug as ever, telling anybody who'd listen every detail. Whatever confidence I'd gained from Marisol's warm hugs had dissolved in the sober light of day. I was drunk, for God's sake, parading them around our property, telling them sad, deeply personal stories, pretending to be madly in love with my vintner who, only recently, stopped detesting me. What was I thinking? I've been kicking myself ever since, and Teddy's bullshit now is grating my last bit of patience down to the nub. "Put them *on*."

"I'd rather fellate Gimli!"

"You wanted to be a part of Hannah and River's wedding, and that means you're *wearing the ears!*"

"What's going on here?" River strides over, his gait excessively swaggered thanks to his own attire. The sight of my sweet, goofy cousin, forever a dreamer, manages to bring my nerves down a full notch. River's beaming as bright as the sun. His broad shoulders fill out a soft off-white linen tunic, loosely tucked into a pair of fitted leather breeches that, Hannah confessed during a late evening with the Queer Mountaineers, were the sole reason she agreed to River's *Lord of the Rings*–inspired vision for their wedding in the first place. Everybody razzed her mercilessly until she finally passed her phone around with a shirtless picture of River in the tight leather pants.

Even Teddy shut up after that.

Well. Until the ears.

"But I'm just an usher! Why do I have to be a goddamn elf, too?!"

"Because Hannah and I have a vision." River smiles devilishly, hand resting on the base of his sword's hilt. It isn't real—Hannah forbade *that* part of his vision—but the move is delightfully menacing all the same.

"Oh, don't bring Hannah into this, *Lord Dildo*! That poor girl's only mistake is marrying a dork!"

"You could be a hobbit instead," River offers, his glee multiplying. "It only requires blush, a curly wig, and giant hairy feet." River points at Maeve and Gloria, both of whom have wholeheartedly embraced the hobbit option. We had a blast one night gluing fake hair to the tops of their Crocs.

"I'm too sexy to be a hobbit, and you *know it*." Teddy grits his jaw as he grabs the elf ear-tips and stomps off, his long, silver-haired wig swishing behind him as he mutters something about *giant nerds* and where they can shove their swords.

"It's Bilbo, by the way!" River calls out, grinning. He sighs pleasantly, then throws an arm around me. "I picked the extra-big ears for him."

"Are you trying to make my life impossible?" I exhale through a smile, willing the *Everyday Bon Vivant* stress to melt away. This is River's wedding, my beloved cousin who's always been like a big brother to me, and he's marrying one of my closest friends. They're incandescently happy, and I cling to that joy, reminding myself that there are more important things today than impressing some wine folks.

"What can I say?" River shrugs, that playful smile I've known all my life dancing on his face. "I have a vision, and it includes annoying Teddy. Everything's going exactly as planned."

We clink our heads together gently and walk arm-in-arm out of the winery toward the groom's backstage tent area. Hannah has her own tent opposite, and together the effect is like a royal encampment. Guests are laughing and milling about the pre-ceremony cocktail hour, which I've set up on the patio. Tristan's in charge of that, fully rocking his dwarf ensemble and braided beard behind the bar as he pours guests glasses of frothy mead. Literal *mead*. I have a freaking *mead guy* now.

I shake my head and smile. River owes me so big. To his and Hannah's credit, though, Bluebell Vineyards has been transformed into a lovely, mystical place straight out of a fairy tale. Garlands of flowers and silvery vines drape lazily between ornate wooden posts carved by River's capable hands, making a path through the vineyard to each destination—the cocktail hour, the ceremony tucked right at the entrance to our woods, and the reception in the meadows with our property's best views of the hazy blue mountains. I'm starting to get River's point. People in black suits and satin dresses would look utterly out of place beneath the magical fairy lights and gilded lanterns dangling from the trees. Not all the guests complied with River's dress code, but the ones who did add to the ethereal bohemian atmosphere that Hannah created within River's parameters. The effect is like walking through a beautiful dream, studded here and there with straight comedy. Seeing Darryl in wizard robes with the words *Stepdaddy of the Bride* embroidered on the back made my entire *life*.

While I usually wear my own black tailored suit to weddings, this is family, and I love a reason to dress up. When Hannah and I were perusing designs for her wedding gown, we stumbled across my dress. It's a pale shade of copper, the exact rosy hue of our blush Catawba blend, and feels just as light and silky on my body as the wine does on my tongue. It's long and flowing, with gauzy sleeves that end past my elbows, neckline dipping in a perfect V that shows off my sternum. The bodice holds my breasts firmly in place. Inside-boob for the win, with nary a strip of breast tape required.

"It is perfection," Hannah breathed when I tried it on for her.

"Still want to marry River?" I flashed her a little ankle with a grin.

"*Barely.*" She looked like she meant it, too.

So yeah, I'm feeling pretty hot right now. No ears or wigs for me—River's granted me the honor of being a Middle Earth warrior queen or some such, I don't know. Just my short black hair left wavy beneath a simple crown of scarlet bergamot and several strands of gold looped around my neck. I politely declined the jeweled dagger he offered me, though weaponry could've been useful for a wedding planner.

When we reach River's tent, he grasps me by both arms. With misty eyes full of a heartbreaking love, he says, "Thank you for today, Zoe."

"You deserve this." My words are without context, but River doesn't need any. He pulls me into a gentle hug, as though he can see all the bittersweet longing that brims within me, too. It's making it hard to breathe.

"So do you," he whispers, resting his chin on my head. "Your love story is coming soon, Zoe. I can feel it."

I laugh, though the sound is unbelieving and thick with unshed tears. If I could believe it were true, maybe this weight that's rested on my chest ever since the people I loved most started leaving me would finally lift.

"Hey, boss?"

River and I turn our heads at the same time, and I quickly dash away the few tears that made a jailbreak. I tense in his arms, not breathing—not because I can't this time, but because I forget to. Laine is wearing camel-colored suede leggings that hug each muscular segment of her strong thighs, tucked into a pair of laced boots the color of cognac. The pants rise over her straight hips, where a slim white button-down is tucked in front. It's a modern shirt, but the collar is open deep, the buttons undone enough to reveal her chest tattoos. My eyes dance across the intricate pattern of wildflowers that stretches across her collarbone in either direction, kissing the tops of her breasts and disappearing beneath the cotton. I'd seen them briefly that night in Harlow's bed, but I was so drenched in mortification, I didn't register what I was seeing. A small gasp exits my lips in recognition.

Bluebells.

River glances between me and Laine, then back to me again. "Maybe it's already begun." He squeezes me one last time before disappearing into his tent.

Our bodies bring us closer, so close I could trace the dusky blooms curving over her breasts with my finger. Follow each blue-green tendril along its twists and turns, until they led me to her heart.

"Your tattoos," I murmur, wishing I could push her shirt aside to see more. To see all of her.

"The woods behind our house, in the spring. The bluebells rise out of nowhere, like a veil of blue." Laine smiles ruefully. "I always thought they were magic."

Maybe they are. They brought you to me, after all, my heart whispers. For a second, it seems like she heard. She looks at me, dazed, the small divot between her brows that appears when she's thinking pronounced beneath her doe-brown hair. The smoky plum eyeliner ringing her silt-brown eyes makes them even richer, like if the wind scattered me there, I could grow into something beautiful.

"Is everything okay?" I manage out through the tightness growing in my throat. It hurts sometimes, how perfect she is. This blend of hard lines and soft edges, the grown-up version of all my teenage fantasies. The mountain breeze ripples through my dress, bringing with it the memory of her mouth on my thighs, tongue sliding languidly across my skin until I clenched so hard it hurt. I hate myself a little for how turned on I am, just from looking at her. From remembering what, for one night, I briefly had. For showing her a glimpse of all these warring feelings within me, and for her not looking away.

"Laine?" I try again. "Did you need—"

"You are beautiful," she says faintly, the soft words interrupting me, my thoughts, the entire space-time continuum, as she takes a step forward. Her head bows down, her hand reaching dreamily upward, cupping my cheek. The pad of her thumb brushes away the last dew of my tears, lifting me up to face her fully.

"Laine, the—the events team isn't here yet." My voice is shaky and unsure.

"So?" The word blooms from her parted lips as her eyes search mine, sending warmth cascading through my entire body. "Say my name again."

"I—"

"Say it," she commands, her lips brushing against my hair. And I am molten, unsteady, collapsing into her arms as they wrap around my waist.

"Laine," I breathe, like her name is air. Her eyes flutter closed, and she groans softly in my ear. "Laine, we—work together. I need you too much. I can't afford to have some fling with you."

"Who"—she breathes—"ever said"—her lower lip skates across my earlobe—"it would be some *fling*, boss?"

My spine curls, bringing my hips flush with hers, the sweet, dull ache between my legs pulsing in time with my heart. Every professional impulse in my body flees the country. It doesn't even occur to me that I'm ready to publicly ride my vintner's thigh at my place of business until Hannah's happy laughter trills through the side of her tent, lurching me back into the present. My eyes fly open, and I press both palms against Laine's shoulders, pushing us apart. I don't have time for my feelings. Today, I am part of someone *else's* happiness, and that, like always, has to be enough.

It *has* to.

"It's time to do final setup for the ceremony because we're walking the guests over in twenty minutes," I say in one long, breathless rush. Laine's pupils are blown wide, dreamy and dark, as she considers the frantic edge to my tone. But if it puts her off, she doesn't show it. Instead, she slowly adjusts the bodice of my dress, fingers dipping beneath the fabric, eyes drinking in the way my breasts swell against the tight, constricting dip of the neckline.

"Yes, boss." She trails her index finger down my collarbone, stopping when both our breathing goes ragged. Her eyes hold mine.

"Whenever you're ready." It's a challenge, a dare, a *promise*. She turns then, disappearing into the folks of the shire .

And I finally exhale.

My thoughts are on a wild rampage as I flit through the ceremony area, but everything is perfect and thus, utterly unable to distract me from *Laine*. The wildflowers bundled with wheat and wrapped by vine hang from each row. The trail of vintage Turkish rugs Hannah's meticulously collected makes a long, mismatched path of ruby and yellow, pink and indigo, all the way to the small round dais River built at the edge of our woods. An arch formed of curling birch branches, draped in honeysuckle and small floating lights, stands on the dais ready for the magic to come.

The breeze whispers through the leaves, adding the melodic thrum of wind chimes to birdsong, and my heart yearns, *yearns*, at the beauty of it all.

And Laine. *Laine!* I'd say her name a thousand times if she asked me to. Oh god, I'm losing it.

The yearning only grows as the guests meander to their seats to the soft sounds of Killian, Hannah's ex and Bowie's father, fingerpicking Simon & Garfunkel songs on his beat-up acoustic. Trish takes her place on the dais, smiling as River joins her, then grinning with tears streaming down her face as Hannah walks down the aisle toward her, holding little Bowie by the hand and a bouquet of wildflowers in the other. Hannah is otherworldly, lit by the golden hour and the soft glow of the hanging lanterns. Her wedding dress is the color of palest champagne, a folk story of flowers spun in lace. It plunges down the front and back to reveal the swell of her chest, the strong line of her back, the tops of her summer-golden shoulders, before cascading in a waterfall of threaded blooms. Her dark blonde waves are braided away from her face and spill down her back, and she's crowned with a wreath of magnolias and silver-green thistle. But it's the look of joy, like she's found her home at long last, that lights up her entire being. The pride and love and beauty of it all overwhelms me completely.

When River picks up Bowie with one arm and helps Hannah climb the steps with the other, my chest tightens painfully. What they have is so beautiful, it almost hurts to witness it.

Could I have it, too?

"Greetings, folk of the shire," Trish says, signaling the guests to sit. "My future son-in-law made me say that." She smirks at the audience chuckling politely in their seats. "The rest, though, will come from my heart." Trish's smirk trembles, her voice catching, and I'm going to be bawling in two seconds flat.

Trish turns to her beautiful daughter with a tender look. "I didn't always believe in love, but then I had you, Hannah. From the first moment you grabbed my finger in your tiny fist, my heart unfolded into a hundred new directions, growing, stretching, multiplying, and it's never stopped, baby. You've been teaching me the meaning of love ever since.

"Our roads aren't always easy, paved with potholes and assholes and all manner of other—oh, right. This is a family event." Trish laughs, wiping her eyes furiously with the sleeves of her own wizard robes. "But those hard, dirty roads got us here today, baby. You are the most beautiful person who ever lived, and you've finally found the person who sees you as the treasure you are." Trish stops, her voice fully wobbling, to address the audience. "If y'all thought for one second I was going to give anything other than a sermon about how wonderful my daughter is, you're thicker than mud."

"You tell 'em, baby!" Darryl calls from the front row, and the audience gamely whistles and hoots. Hannah's laughing and crying, holding a grinning River by the hand, Bowie tucked between them.

"That's the real trick, isn't it?" Trish says, her voice strained with emotion. "Finding someone who loves you in all the ways you can't love yourself just yet. Who gives you what you deserve, even when you don't believe you deserve it." She smiles at Darryl, who's now openly weeping. "And if you're lucky enough to find that person, being *brave* enough to put down everything you've got and bet on happiness for once in your life." Her eyes travel across the audience, resting on mine.

"It can be so hard, can't it? To let yourself hope?"

A small sob arches out of my throat, completely against my will. An instant later, a warm arm wraps around my shoulders, and I look quickly to see Teddy standing beside me. Teddy, who faced an even larger dearth of romantic opportunities than I do now and still found his person. His crinkly eyes see all the hurt and fear I keep inside, making it easier to bear in this beautiful, painful moment. I wrap my arm around him, too, and hug him close.

"When you've been hurt again and again, believing that could change seems like the most impossible thing in the world. But it can." Trish's words feel more hopeful, more charged with power than any actual sermon I've ever heard. They feel dangerous, too, like plans of escape uttered through the bars of a jail cell.

"But not if you won't let it." This, Trish delivers in a near-whisper, and it's up to the breeze to carry it through the clearing. The collective mood has gone from joyful to touched to unspeakably tender, her words resonating within every current and former lonely heart sitting among these trees. They feel like a personal challenge to me, churning through my mind and all my bullshit, daring me to heed them. *But how?* I want to scream. *With Laine?*

My employee? The future of my vineyard rests in her hands, and I've worked *hard* to trust her with that. I've seen what happens when a heart is destroyed, I've witnessed it every day since my mother died. How could I hand mine over to someone who could crush it and my family business in one fell swoop? Laine's too powerful, and I'm too defenseless. Even if part of me wants to be destroyed, my sense of self-preservation is screaming at the top of its lungs right now. I squeeze my eyes shut, willing my life not to be such an utter travesty. Am I doomed to fall in love with the same woman in each era of my life, only to be ignored or worse, tried out and discarded, on a godforsaken loop?

The sobs crawl up my throat, begging for release, and I quickly disentangle from Teddy's arm. "I'm—I'll be fine, I just—I've got to go check on the reception."

Teddy nods. "I'll keep an eye on things here, baby."

River's holding both of Hannah's hands now, giving her his vows that not a soul in this place could ever doubt, and I can't hear a word of them over the roaring in my head. I wish their happiness didn't hurt so much, but it's like looking at the sun, and my eyes ache to be released from it. I've reached my mother's tree by the time loud cheering rises from the woods, and a wave of relief and shame washes over me. Sometimes my loneliness feels like a boulder inside of me, separating me from everyone I love. I try to ignore it, tell myself that all I need are the occasional blips of intimacy I get from Harlow or Mariah or whoever's willing to throw me a bone that day. I have family and friends who love me—shouldn't that be enough? But the boulder's always there. I wish I was strong enough to roll it down the mountain, to accept this life and the people in it. Let what I have be enough.

I *wish it were* enough.

"Zoe?" Laine's voice raises the hair on my neck, and I take a second to wipe my eyes before turning.

"Yes?"

She gazes at me long enough to tell me she knows I've been crying again. Whatever, lots of people get emotional at weddings. I'm not an emotionally stunted bad cousin and friend, choked by jealousy and loneliness to the point where other people's love feels like air I can't breathe. She reaches out for my hand and squeezes it gently. She doesn't let go.

"The *Everyday Bon Vivant* folks just arrived. It's ho-time."

Ho-time. Right.

CHAPTER SEVENTEEN

L aine leads me down toward the reception, already bubbling with guests and laughter, to the high-top table where the events team is huddled. It's surreal, walking quietly hand in hand with Laine toward them now. I've been worried about seeing the events team all week, anxiously waiting for the moment where I can win them over for good, but now, all I can think about is the feel of Laine's hand in mine. The promise, *whenever you're ready*, she made directly to my trembling heart.

The hopeful feeling blooming inside me has more to do with Laine than the showcase, and that's scarier than all of it together. The soft hope turns sharp, though, when I hear Erica's irritated tone rise above the reception's hum.

"*Yes*, I concede that it's lovely here, but there's more to the showcase than views, Marisol." Erica swirls a glass of red in her hand with clear disdain. "Like wine? Maybe you've heard of it."

"Oh, don't be such a snob. I quite like all the regional white varietals and blends they have. Sweet isn't always bad, you know."

"And the reds?" Erica pins Marisol with her gaze. The menfolk watch this exchange silently, their opinions unnecessary in this regard. My stomach clenches as Marisol's defensive expression drops noticeably.

"They're not a strength, I agree."

"Are you *really* willing to put *Everyday Bon Vivant*'s stamp of approval on such substandard wine?" Erica huffs. "Into the Woods is a better choice, and you know it."

Through all of this, Laine's grip on my hand has steadily increased in pressure. Before I can slink away, regroup, and come up with a contingency plan for how to change their minds, Laine drags us both forward with sudden conviction. All four pairs of eyes widen at once.

"Marisol, Erica!" I greet them warmly in full actress mode. Gonna play this off like we didn't just hear them trash our wine. "Good to see you! You, too, Preston and Matthew."

"We heard everything you said," Laine blurts.

Well, fuck.

Marisol looks stricken, but Erica turns to us, a smug challenge on her face. Some people just aren't happy unless they're telling you the truth, which to them, usually means whatever nasty opinion they have about you. "And? You're Napa-trained. You worked at Le Jardin. What do you have to say about Bluebell's red offerings?"

Laine breathes deeply through her nose, her eyes darting to me. With an apology lacing her words, she says, "Poorly executed, basic, and clumsy at best."

My nostrils flare. It's not that she's wrong, but can't she be less right? I wriggle free from Laine's grip, but she catches my hand again before I can pull away. She mouths *big vintner energy*, then *trust me*.

"Ha!" Erica spins to Marisol. "See? Their own vintner agrees with me."

"But," Laine interjects, pulling me closer, "there's a reason for that. Julie Brennan was chief vintner here and was known for her complex, beautiful reds. And if you knew Cosimo, you'd see how heartbroken he is over Julie to this day. He's never been able to handle reading Julie's wine journals, and because of that, he's never been able to carry on her work in that area." Laine stops, a tentative smile on her face. "I can, though. I've read everything she wrote. And she's a genius—more inspiring and insightful than anyone I worked with in California, that's for sure. And *I'm making her wines*."

Erica's challenge slides from her face, replaced by reluctant intrigue. "You are?"

"I'm working through the blending process now. They're intended to be young reds, so they'll be ready by the showcase. The whites, too. We'll have our popular offerings, but I'm bringing back some of Julie's creations there, also. With my own spin, of course."

Marisol's eyebrows rise. "There's a story there, Erica—you have to admit it."

"My mother's story," I finally speak up, my voice rusty. Maybe it's seeing River and Hannah so happy or all those hours I spent alone under Mom's tree, whispering memories of her to myself, but this feels *right*. "We're finally ready to tell it."

Marisol shakes her head, a delighted smile on her face as she looks past me to the lantern-lit paths winding through the vineyard. Their honeyed light spills against the lavender skies and hazy blue mountains beyond, a beautiful dream made real. "Julie and Cosimo's love story, set here in these breathtaking vineyards, with a fresh slate of wines representing a fusion of California winemaking principles with Georgia grapes and heirloom recipes . . ."

Marisol looks at Erica pointedly. Erica's mouth goes flat, recognizing a clear nudge from her boss to admit she's wrong. "It definitely sets a scene." Erica sighs. "A compelling one."

"Thank you," I say, truly meaning it. Everything else in my life may be on fire, but as long as Bluebell Vineyards is safe, I feel safe, too.

"Would you consider working with Into the Woods, though?" Erica asks abruptly. "Collaborating somehow? You're right next door to each other. That way, your wine offerings could be bolstered by—"

"No." The word comes out heavy and loud, like an anvil splashing into a river. Perhaps it will drag me down to the bottom with it, but Rachel doesn't get to benefit from our work after being so cruel to us.

Matthew *hmms*. "Funny, Rachel Woods said the same thing when we asked her."

"Let's just say there's a story there, too. One that only gets told after shots of tequila." I smile to dispel any lingering tension.

Marisol laughs. "Well, sign me up for that when this is all behind us."

"In the meantime, how about we take you around the property so you can see how we set up for big crowds?" Laine slips an arm around me, her fingers pressing against the soft space between hip and ribs. "Zoe's completely outdone herself with this wedding." Laine smiles down at me. She's only a few inches taller, and I fit so neatly at her side that my body believes this story of us, my heart fluttering, skin prickling with chills at her touch. My brain knows better than to put stock in stories, though, and what's a body without a brain?

A bag of dumb meat. Her fingers caress my back, and my pulse quickens. *Stop it, meat bag!*

"We'd be delighted," Marisol says.

We take them from spot to spot on the property, finding renegade parties broken off from the main group at each location. I have a feeling the revelry for River and Hannah will continue late into the night. *I'm* certainly not going to kick any of these people out. We even have the barn stocked with snacks, water, ibuprofen, and sleeping bags for guests too blitzed to drive, a giant sleepover just waiting to happen, as long as they don't mind Baahlzebub's occasional bleat.

By the time we get to the ceremony area, Marisol looks resolved, Matthew utterly charmed, Preston a little drunk, and Erica weirdly impatient.

"Finally, the restroom!" she exclaims when she spots the bridal tent.

"No!" I try to stop her, but she must really have to go because she's already through the tent flap before I can tell her that's *definitely not* a bathroom.

She freezes, her body parting the tent flaps. *"Dear god!"*

Just over Erica's shoulder, I see the beautifully carved chair decked with flowers that River made for Hannah, which he calls her throne. I *also* see Hannah's head thrown back against it, her long neck exposed, one golden brown hand tucked inside the bodice of her gown, gripping her breast. The rest of River is on his knees before her, head buried between her legs splayed wide.

Hannah's head whips up, her eyes dazed with pleasure. "Oh, *shit!*" She scrambles to sit up, but River doggedly yanks her back to his face. He deigns to give the group of stunned onlookers a casual glance over his shoulder, with the purest example of *I-don't-give-a-fuck* energy I've ever witnessed.

My eyebrows disappear into my hairline, and perhaps, space.

"O-kay!" I exclaim, "let's give the newlyweds some privacy!"

We usher a stunned Erica toward the *actual* bathrooms. The crickets trill loudly as we stand in the darkness, waiting for Erica to return, when Laine busts out a single, booming laugh.

"I'm sorry, it's just—" She wipes at her eyes. "That must've been part of his—his *vision!*"

Marisol tilts her head to the side and considers for a second.

"That was a good vision."

And then, we lose it. We *lose it.* Preston's laughing so hard, his glasses fall off. Marisol appears to have an incurable case of the giggles. Matthew's crying, and I am, too. Crying and laughing so hard, it feels like an exorcism. When we finally see the events team off for the night, rumbles of laughter still rolling through our group, Marisol pinches my cheek lovingly.

"This vineyard really does run on romance." She winks at me, and my heart lifts on fluttery, happy wings. "We'll be in touch."

The moon is almost directly over the meadows, like a lone lightbulb hanging over the dark world. It's nearly midnight, but the band's still playing though it's long past the end of their paid gig. Couples are dancing, swaying softly to the music.

"Excuse me, boss, can I have this dance?" Laine appears to my left, startling me where I stand at the edge of the dance floor. She's half in shadow, half in golden illumination, but her eyes shine brightly all the same.

"Do you really think it's a good idea?"

The corner of her mouth curves up, showing her dimple. "I'm starting to think coming to Bluebell Vineyards is the best idea I've ever had."

She extends her hand to me, and though I've been holding it half the night, I can't get used to the warm strength of her grip, her confident touch. My breath catches as it closes gently around mine, tugging me into the light.

"That's not what I asked," I say to her back as she leads me forward to a break in the crowd. I study the muscular line of her shoulders, the dip of her narrow hips, the solid ass and strong thighs gliding through this world like nothing's too difficult for her. Not this dance, not this life. Not even me.

I wish I felt that sure, too. That optimistic.

"It's what you wanted to know, though." She turns, and I start to lift my arm to hold her hand when she slides her arms around my waist instead.

I swallow, draping my own arms around her neck. "So, we're going *high school prom* here, huh."

"That all right, Chop Chop?" Laine smirks, and maybe it's my imagination, but the heat in her fingertips seems to kick up a notch, as they find the divots in my hips and hold on tight.

"Okay, Beave," I say through my rapidly drying throat. Does she fluster me like this on purpose? "Still your boss."

"Right," Laine says. "About that. I have a confession to make."

My heart skips a few turns at, you know, keeping me alive. "What?"

"The red blends I'm working on *are* great," Laine says, her eyes fully latched onto mine. "If you like the taste of old shoe."

I huff out a laugh, which turns into a groan. "But you swore to the events team that they're amazing!"

"They *will* be amazing. They're just not there yet."

"How do you know?"

Laine's face softens. "Because of you, Zoe. You're the reason I believe in what I can do again." Her hands slide around my hips to the small of my back, holding me there. "It wasn't easy, trying to make something new after"—she releases a deep breath—"after my wine project at Le Jardin tanked. I felt so adrift, but you've helped me find my way back." The corners of her mouth twitch. "My guiding gay light, if you will."

I groan again, this time burying my face in her shoulder. "I'm gonna kill Mattie."

"Please don't," Laine says through a smile, using the opportunity to wrap her arms around me tighter. "Your friends are amazing."

We sway together, my head on her shoulder, her hands anchoring me to her beneath the full moon. The whole town will be talking about us after tonight, but I don't care. They're used to seeing the arc of my romantic exploits, the initial interest building until something inevitably punctures the balloon, and it fizzles out, leaving me holding nothing once again.

No *one*, once again.

"Tonight's been hard on you, hasn't it?" Laine murmurs into my hair.

"Yes." I don't explain, and she doesn't ask me to.

"For me, too," she whispers. Her hands bring me closer until our hips meet, her head dipping toward mine. My fingers ache to touch her hair, the memory of it like suede in my mind. "I know you're a fighter, boss, and I love that about you. But it's time for you to stop fighting us."

Her full lips kiss my forehead gently, in that little space between my eyebrows, where lines form when I'm thinking too hard. Like I'm doing right now.

"Laine," I breathe. "I don't—I can't—"

"You're scared."

I pull back so I can meet her dark hooded eyes. "Yes."

"Listen to me, Zoe." Her hands slide up to cradle the back of my neck. "I'll never leave your vineyard high and dry. I *won't*. No matter what happens between us, I will give Bluebell everything I have until you no longer need me." One hand drifts along my jaw, her thumb light upon my chin. "But if you don't let me kiss you right now, I think I might die."

Her words strike my heart like a mallet to a gong, its reverberations ringing through me. I search her eyes and see the truth of her promise reflected there, and the dam of my resolve comes crashing down. My hands tighten around her neck, and I pull her to me, my fingers snaking up into her hair, pulling there, too, as our mouths crush against each other. She moans into me as I taste her, tipping her into my mouth so I can drink her up, licking, lavishing, and sweet Jesus, *having* her, all to myself.

Laine, Laine. My Laine.

"Yours," she whispers back, and only then do I realize I murmured the words aloud.

The kiss may begin with our lips, but it flows through me like a rich, ruby wine, warming my insides with its fullness and heat, tweaking the buds of my breasts before puddling deep in my core, pulling deliciously between my legs like a finger, like a hand, beckoning me to *come*. She said she'd stay until I no longer needed her, but does she realize that *until* may never come? In this moment, I'm convinced I'll need her for the rest of my life. And that maybe, I always have.

I break away from her mouth, panting, but my fingers refuse to relinquish their grip. Her face fills my frame of vision, her lust-blown eyes starry and sparkling. Her lips are parted, bee-stung from the crush of my own, and I can't stop myself from diving in once more, taking her bottom lip between mine, sucking, scraping it lightly against my teeth.

"*Fuck*, Zoe," she says, her hands still cradling my head.

"Yes, let's." I breathe her into me. "*Now.*"

I pull Laine by the hand through the glow of the lanterns until night envelops us. My cottage appears ahead, the porch light a beacon, promising relief from the unrelenting desire as soon as I get her inside and onto my bed. My couch, my floor, the kitchen counter. It's negotiable.

I thrust the key into the lock and have the door half open when Laine spins me around, pinning me against the door with her body. Her mouth leaves a treasure map of kisses down my throat, my collarbone, the hollow between my breasts.

"Zoe," she murmurs, running a hand down the front of my dress and cupping my pussy through the gauzy layers, making me clench. "I want you *so bad.*"

"I want you, too." Inside preferably, but frankly, that's also negotiable. "But *some*one won't let me open the door." I smile, lips parting as Laine slides down my body, pressing her hot mouth to my core through my dress and wrenching another moan from me. "How—are we going—to make this bad decision—if you won't—"

"This isn't a bad decision, boss." Laine curls her fingers around the back of my knees, making them weak. "This is the best decision," she breathes the words into my dress, purring against my aching pussy. "*Mmm.*"

"You're right," I pant, canting my hips toward her lush mouth, holding her there with my hands. "I should've added *casual sex with the boss* to your job duties ages ago." Her chin is pressed firmly against my clit, each movement bringing me closer, and I think I could *come* like this, if she would just—

Laine's hands stop their slide midway up my thighs, and she looks up at me. "What if I want more than that?"

"Laine. You can have *anything* you want right now."

But she doesn't move or smile wickedly or rip my panties off or *any* of the things I desperately want.

She frowns.

"Zoe, this isn't just casual sex. I *like* you."

I blow out a frustrated breath, my ass wriggling in her grasp as if to say, *come back!* "Okay. It's not casual sex. Just please, come inside." Maybe it's not dignified to beg, but now that I've made this bad decision, I want to reap every last orgasm I can from it. I wriggle some more, but Laine's hands are not persuaded to resume their advances. Instead, she runs one over her mouth, eyes squeezing closed, before standing before me.

"I can't come in."

"What?! *Why?*" I say with all the chill of someone screaming *fire* in a crowded theater.

"Because you're trying to write this off as some fling, and I won't let you. You think that us fucking will get me out of your system." Her eyes fall to my mouth, pouting and completely pissed, and frames it between her strong fingers, stroking the corner of my lips hard with the pad of her thumb until they part for her. "Don't you?"

"*Yes.*" The damning confession comes out in a whisper. But come on, we could never have a *real* relationship. Laine told me her first day here that she won't relocate to Georgia, and Bluebell Vineyards is my home, my job, my identity—I can't leave. Sex is what we can have, and I want to *have it.* Now. Then maybe I could think clearly for the first time since she showed up at my vineyard. For a second, I think her ridiculous decision to blue bean us both might crack as she runs her thumb along the smooth, wet rim of my lower lip, a strangled sound of want emerging from her own mouth.

"Well, I'm going to do more than just fuck you, Zoe Brennan." The words nearly send me to my knees, but Laine's eyes flash up to mine, pinning me there, utterly under her control. "I'm going to court you."

I blink. "*Court* me? What is this, the 1950s?"

"You don't believe that I'm crazy about you, and you need me to prove it. So, I will." Her smile is amused and indulgent, but her hand's still grasping me firmly by the chin. .

"You know what's very convincing? Coming inside." I reach for her waistband so I can yank her against me.

With one swift movement, she pins both my wrists above my head. My nipples tighten viciously as she presses her chest against mine, holding me against the door. I legit *growl*. The feeling of being trapped here, in her thrall, desperate to fuck her yet watching her withhold that from me is *so* hot it's utterly infuriating. "God*dammit*, Laine! Court me in bed, then!"

She slides one hand free, running it down the inside of my arm to caress my cheek while her other one keeps me pinned in place. "You deserve more than that, Zoe, even if you're afraid that's not true." She runs her thumb over my flushed cheekbone. "You've made me confront my fears. Now it's time for you to confront yours."

With that, she lets me go. My jaw burns with the imprint of her heat my arms collapsing to my sides, freed from her grip against my will. I stare at her, furious, as she steps backward into the night, her eyes never leaving mine. . I rush to open my door and step inside before I do something humiliating, like beg her to change her mind, *again*.

"Goodnight, boss," Laine says softly, though it's clear right now who's really in control.

"Good *night*." The voice doesn't even sound like mine. Angry, breathy, *needy*. Is this who she makes me become?

I slam the door behind me. She wants to *court* me? After she system-atically removed each of my defenses until I crumbled *riotously* horny into her arms, she tells me she's going to *court me*? God, the power she yields over me—it's terrifying.

I stand before the window, looking out into the vineyards, but my lights are on, and all I can see is my reflection overlaid upon the black night. I don't know if she's out there, still lingering in front of the fruit-heavy vines. The grapes round and plump, getting sweeter every minute they spend in the sun before they're ready to burst.

So, I don't know if she sees me unzip the back of my dress she marked with her mouth so fiercely, letting it slip off my shoulders and fall in a heap at my feet. When I dip my thumbs beneath my panties' waistband, I see only myself as I slide them slowly down each hip, turning just enough that the curve of my ass is the first thing exposed as I pull them gently off. I don't know if she sees me slip a finger between my split, so warm and wet and *aching* from an evening spent resisting the pull of the energy between us.

But the thought that she might be standing there still, those burnished bronze eyes watching me through the window, sends chills licking across my body. I face the window fully now, watching myself give me what I want, even if Laine won't. My clit tightens, swells, and I lift one leg to give myself more access, propping it up against the windowsill and working faster. Laine, cupping my pussy and telling me no. Laine, pinning me down, watching me squirm with heat dripping from her eyes. Now I can't see my face, obscured by the fog of my hot breath against the glass, but I see the rest of me, trem-bling beneath my roving hand from the threat of oncoming release. I don't know that she's out there, wanting me back, I don't.

But I *feel* that she is.

I come *hard*, one hand braced against the glass while I press the other against where I ache most, clenching and releasing with short bursts of breath until my orgasm peaks and finally, *finally* tapers off, a heavy splash transformed into ripples traveling across the surface of a lake.

I step back from the window, run my hands down my face, exhale into my palms.

Laine might be powerful, but goddammit, *so am I.*

CHAPTER EIGHTEEN

My eyes snap open like those roller window shades, and I heave up to a sitting position on my bed.

Laine.

Did I . . .

I cover my mouth with my hand, a horrified laugh bouncing against my palm. *I did.* Drunk on emotions, lust, and a whole lotta wine, last night I exacted what must be the strangest form of revenge ever. My cheeks heat as the memories roll over me. Laine's finger skimming down my collarbone, her hair in my hands as I pulled her into my kiss, the taste of her thumb in my mouth, the sweet release I felt after punishing her for making me want her *so bad.*

I launch out of bed.

The shower's cool water does nothing to release the steam that's been building inside me ever since Laine looked at me yesterday with stars in her eyes and told me I was beautiful. Scarlet petals from my hair collect in the shower drain, as trampled now as my resolve to stay the hell away from her. If anything, the magnetic pull I feel toward her has tripled in strength, quadrupled, filling me with the desire to hunt her down and make her *pay.*

So much for Laine's ideas of courtship. I want *contact, release,* to excise her from my brain so I can finally think again. Sure, Laine talked a big game, but she was barely able to resist me last night. I just need to drag her off her high horse and into the mud with me, and maybe that'll shake this ridiculous notion of courtship out of her head. She's leaving as soon as Dad comes back, she said so herself! What's the point in dating when she knows it's going to end? I can't even pretend to understand what her motives are, but the sexual tension's been building for months now—any more and I'll go insane. It's a liability, a distraction. It cannot be borne a moment longer. I've got to crumble her resolve so we can fuck and this meaningless fling can run its course, like they always do.

I root through my bathroom drawers until I find it—a palette of face paint left over from last year's family picnic. An evil grin blooms on my face.

It's on, Laine Woods.

Twenty minutes later, I pull into a spot at the nearly empty rec center lot and throw my truck in park. I check my lipstick in the mirror, then the sparkly #27 glitter-painted on my cheek. Satisfied, I grab my bag and head off for the girls' middle school soccer practice.

Laine's out on the field, too busy running drills with the gangly tweens to notice me saunter up and lean over the fence. Once she started coaching Darla and Benny's team, word got out that the prodigal daughter of the Gilmer County Bobcats had returned. It was a matter of days before the middle school reached out to Laine and asked her to fill in while Coach Wilkinson's out on paternity leave.

"That's it, Desiree!" Laine claps. "Excellent pass!"

A lanky girl sporting long rainbow socks covering her shin guards beams at Laine from midfield, and something hot and fiery explodes inside my chest. It didn't occur to me until now, but these girls have *Laine* as their adult mentor—ambitious, talented, capable, *queer* Laine. I would've done anything to have a mentor like her growing up. Someone to show me that effort makes you stronger, that there's power in being true to yourself, even if others aren't ready to accept you that way.

But then again, I did, didn't I? Because I had Laine, too.

My eyes mist up, *goddamn* emotions, and I frantically try to wipe the tears away before they ruin my face paint. Of course, Laine takes this moment to glance over her shoulder and see me at the fence, swiping at my eyes.

Dammit, this is *not* the *you-teased-the-wrong-bitch* energy I came here to display!

A smile breaks out on Laine's face as she adjusts her glasses, making sure that yes, it's really *me* standing here, painted up like her biggest fan. She waves, then holds up a finger.

"Take five, team!" she shouts, then breaks into a brisk jog around the far corner of the field before circling back to where I'm standing. In her hand is a small bunch of wild-grown goldenrod and dandelions, and my heart trembles within its cage.

"Milady." She grins and proffers the makeshift bouquet to me over the fence. I take the flowers, willing myself to quit being so goddamn *charmed*.

"Do I have any say in this," I murmur, more to the flowers than to the gorgeous butch soccer coach who gave them to me. "This whole courting thing?"

"Hmm." Laine tilts her head. She's wearing a faded blue baseball hat that I recognize as Chance's. My heart pinches with affection. "Not really, no."

I take a step closer to where she's leaning on the fence, smiling slyly behind my flowers. "Then I guess I'll just have to make this hard on you, huh."

"After last night?" Laine whistles. "I'd like that very much." Her brown eyes smolder, and I feel every inch of my body as she sweeps them over me like fingertips. If there was any doubt she saw my act of revenge in the window, it's gone now. A small, pleased huff of laughter escapes me. I like surprising Laine—displacing her expectations of me provides with a rich, satisfying feeling of *winning*. What's more, I enjoyed surprising my*self*. Last night, I followed my instincts, giving myself permission to explore what *I* wanted.

And it was *hot*.

I step even closer, until we're in kissing distance.

"You're gonna rue the day you decided to court *me*, Laine Woods." My voice is low and dangerously flirtatious, but Laine just smiles and reaches out a hand to gently cup my painted cheek.

"No," she says simply. "But I rue all the days I didn't."

I've been standing in our parking lot for a hundred years. At least that's what it feels like as the old-timer in the pale yellow button-down consults his clipboard *again*. Though his sleeves are short, Mr. Tommy Sumney of the Gilmer County Licensing & Inspection Department still wears a brown tie covered in tiny, jumping trout. Mr. Sumney does not forego *professional attire*, even in the blazing heat of an early-August afternoon. I learned this the hard way as he viewed the thin straps of my black tank top with disdain when he first arrived for our appointment. It's been downhill ever since.

"You sure I can't offer you a glass of water, Mr. Sumney?" I fan myself with my hand. "It's a million degrees out today, and I'm afraid I've had you traipsing all over creation." Sometimes it helps switching to ultra southern mode with the older folks.

"No, ma'am." Mr. Sumney looks up over the rim of his wire-framed spectacles. "I do not fraternize with supplicants."

I squint at him. "Do you mean . . . applicants, sir?"

"No, ma'am."

I raise my eyebrows. O-*kay*.

"Is there any other paperwork you need, sir? I've prepared a binder with supplemental materials for your convenience if that would be helpful. Estimated power and water usage, for example, restroom trailer rentals and their locations, updated certificates of insurance—"

"Did you fill out the form?" he drawls, still looking at me over his glasses.

"Yes, sir . . . that's how I got this appointment."

"Then that's all the paperwork I need"—he pauses to click open his pen—"unless I *ask* for more."

Sweet Jesus, deliver me from this old white man on a power trip.

"You don't know the date of the event?"

"No, sir. As I explained in the application, I'm not sure whether we'll be selected to host the showcase yet."

His droopy eyes drift up to regard me. "You tryin' to get a jump on the competition?"

I have a feeling the truth's the wrong answer.

"No, sir! It's just I have a deep respect for the hard work you do at Gilmer County L&I, and I look to your office not only for permission, but *guidance*, for how to run an event so large. I'm sure you could teach us a thing or two about how it's done." I poke him playfully in the arm, which was the *wrong* thing to do. His Eeyore eyes bulge from their sockets.

"*Miss Brennan*. If you do not know how to run an event this large, I will be *forced* to deny—"

"Well, if it isn't Grandpa Tommy!" Laine's voice slides over my sweaty back like cool water, providing instantaneous relief.

Mr. Sumney's mouth does the weirdest thing: it *smiles*. "Coach Woods! It's awful nice to see you."

"You, too, Tommy. Did you see your grandbaby's pass at last week's game? That girl's got a heck of a kicking foot."

Mr. Sumney beams as though Laine pointed a spotlight directly on his balding, sunburnt head. "She gets it from my wife." He smiles shyly.

"Oh, you're here from L&I, aren't you? I didn't realize we lucked out and got the best inspector this side of the county!" Laine gently pats Mr. Sumney's back as he chuckles, steering him toward the tasting room.

"Now you listen here, sir, it's too hot to do business without a cold glass of lemonade in front of you. Or can I get you something with a kick of its own?"

Mr. Sumney laughs. "Coach Woods, you are a *troublemaker*. I'll have that lemonade with a side of gin since you suggested."

I stand there, shocked, as Laine singlehandedly saves our permitting inspection with the power of athletic charisma.

"Miss Brennan, you better close that mouth of yours, or a fish'll fly in," Laine calls over her shoulder and winks, setting Tommy Sumney off into a gale of old-man chuckles.

What in the *world*?

I'm rooting around in the back room for my bottle of Hendrick's when the door swings open behind me, and a pair of hands slink down to my waist.

"You found Grandpa's gin yet, boss?" Laine asks, and it shouldn't sound sexy, but it *does*. She settles her hips directly behind mine and presses, *firmly*, against my ass. My eyes flutter back as I bite back a groan. She works one hand between us, dragging her thumb from my pussy up the seam of my pants until my back arches in response. I grab the dusty bottle of gin from the lower cabinet and spin around, hoisting myself up on the countertop and pulling her between my legs by the shirt.

"Is that any way to court a lady, Coach Woods?"

Laine grins. "Well, tonight's our first date. What's the harm in starting a little early?"

I run my hands over her strong shoulders, sliding them along the hard triceps bracing her against the counter. "Now I hope you won't think this too forward, but instead of a corsage, I can think of something I'd like more."

Laine leans back, exposing her throat. "Tell me."

"A permit." I smile, handing her the bottle of gin.

Laine grabs me by the strap of my tank top and pulls me toward her. Our faces are inches apart, my lips parted and breathless, when she leans into my ear, nose brushing its shell.

"Yes, boss." The words are wickedly hot, undoing something in my belly that flows like melting wax through my core. She releases me, winks, and saunters out the door.

Mercy.

"Just what I always wanted!" I hold the store-bought bouquet to my chest, along with the stamped permit tucked within its blooms.

"See? Courting can be fun." Laine twists me back and forth by the hips in front of her.

I've never felt so deliciously pursued by someone before. Ever since the wedding, Laine's made it no secret that she's dying to throw me into bed, which thrills me with every groping kiss stolen in the storage room, or pressed against the thrumming metal tanks in the winery, or that one time in the barn while she was feeding Baahlzebub. But it's the little gestures—the notes tucked beneath my coffee mug, a new pack of my favorite pens on my desk, a midnight text sharing a video so funny that I *had* to text back, our conversation going so late I fell asleep with my phone nestled to my chest—that I have no experience with. Laine's version of courting heats me from the inside out, exciting and touching and absolutely *terrifying*. I'd feel safer if this was just sex, some tryst that'd fall apart before I could develop real feelings, but Laine, damn her to hell, knows that. She lured me out of hiding by my desire first, and once she got me good and exposed, she strapped a collar around my neck and set about domesticating me, one dish of cream at a time.

I didn't realize how hungry I was until someone decided to feed me. And even though it's scary, knowing that any meal may be my last, that based on my long, long history, this *whatever it is* with Laine has a couple of months left at best, how am I supposed to walk away now that I've had a taste of what it's like to be full?

I've floated along this entire week in a horny dream state, and after what Laine managed with Grandpa Sumney today, well.

Business wins are my love language. I snap a picture of the permit, then text it to Marisol.

"Extremely important question," Laine says as she slides behind the wheel of my truck. She insists on driving tonight on the strong condition I don't hang out of the window. "Ice cream before or after minigolf?"

"Minigolf?" I laugh. "Our courtship's beginning with minigolf?"

"It's beginning with every date I should've taken you on in high school." Laine leans over to waggle her eyebrows at me. "Plus, I'm *amazing* at minigolf. Branson dyke, remember?" She rests her arm along the back of the truck's bench seat and around my shoulders. "Got to impress my new lady."

"Show her you can provide." A wry smile rises on my face.

"That's right. First comes minigolf, then comes marriage, then comes Zoe with a—"

"Whoa, stop right there!" I twist in my seat to face her. "Are you going to make me wait until marriage?"

Laine smiles and jostles me by the shoulders toward her. "Maybe."

"Laine Woods, are you secretly a *prude*?!"

Laine arches an eyebrow while her lips curve in a smirk. "You *do* remember how we met, don't you?"

"The first time? Or the second?"

"You remember the first time we ever met?" Her right hand caresses my shoulder, playing with the strap of my sundress.

"The first time I saw you, at least."

"Tell me."

I close my eyes, summoning the picture of Laine I've thought of a thousand times. "You were in the meadow behind your house, lying on this old picnic blanket staring up at the clouds. Your hair was fanned out behind you, and you looked so . . . thoughtful. So serious. I remember staring at the sky all afternoon trying to figure out what you were thinking about."

We're quiet for a long moment. Then Laine shakes her head. "You were so gay. Like, right out the gate."

"Hey!" I laugh, leaning into her touch. "Well. Yeah."

"I wish I'd known," she says softly, and we're quiet again, all the way to the ice-cream shop.

It's an early August evening in Blue Ridge, the air thick with unspent rain. We eat our ice-cream cones one-handed down Main Street, because Laine won't let go of my other one. She pauses mid-sentence to lick my scoop, then kiss me with summer-sweet lips for so long, a cold tendril of melt weeps down my fist before she lets me go. She licks that, too. My heart is aloft, beating above us, watching how Laine laughs at my stories, how she teases. When she smiles at me, she feels like home, if home was what I'd always desperately wished it would be.

When we reach the minigolf course, she makes a big deal of picking out our clubs just to make me laugh.

"We could make it interesting." She squints one eye at me.

"You already said you're amazing! Why would I make a bet I'm sure to lose?"

"If I win," Laine continues as though she didn't hear me, "I get to take you out next Friday night. If you win, you get to pillage my body."

We shake on it.

By the fourth hole, Laine's kicking my ass so hard, there will be no pillaging.

Fucking *athletes*.

She's pretending to help me with my swing when a loud, crackly voice clears behind us.

"Charlaine Woods, is that you?"

Laine straightens, and if Mrs. Peterson, our former high school principal, notices how swollen Laine's lips are, or the lush mark on my neck she was leaving, she politely does not comment on it.

"Well, hey there, Mrs. Peterson. How you doing?"

"I'm just fine, the good Lord does provide." Mrs. Peterson presses her hand to her chest. "I heard you were working at the Brennan place. Hey there, Zoe." She gives me a knowing glance that has me adjusting my hemline on reflex.

"Yes, ma'am," Laine says, leaning on her club like a dapper gent with a cane.

"Our shining star, back in Blue Ridge." Mrs. Peterson tilts her head as if she's trying to work out an algebra equation that doesn't add up. "I have to say, I'm surprised."

Her words are innocent enough, but the subtext is clear: *You of all people were supposed to make something of yourself.* Judging by the stiffness that's gripped Laine, she heard Mrs. Peterson's meaning loud and clear, too.

I wrap my arm around Laine's tensing back and squeeze. "Well, that's the thing about stars, Mrs. Peterson. They shine in our skies, too." I purposefully look over Mrs. Peterson's shoulder. "Is that your grandson dunking children in the waterfall?"

"Oh, my! Good seeing you, dears." She hustles off, a principal to the end.

Laine exhales, and I squeeze her a little tighter, leaning up to whisper in her ear, "Your worth doesn't come from your job title, where you work, or where you live, Laine. You are worthy, just as you are."

Laine turns to look at me, her tawny eyes a dark, smoky black in this poorly lit tropical jungle course. She drops her club, then takes mine and throws it down, too, and gathers me up in a kiss so scandalous, it takes my breath away. Kids are oohing, adults are shushing, and the poor teenager on duty takes a solid minute to get up the nerve to tap Laine on the arm and remind her this is a family-friendly establishment.

When we break apart, Laine leans her forehead against mine.

"I wish I'd *known*."

CHAPTER NINETEEN

The summer days pass in a haze of heat and Laine, Laine, *Laine*. Courtship, as it turns out, is an extraordinarily horny endeavor, though true to Laine's word, she refuses to let me "get it out of our systems."

Tonight, under the stars, lying on a bed of old blankets and pillows in the back of my truck while some action movie plays in the background at the Swan Drive-In, I'm putting that to the test, my new favorite pastime.

I push Laine back and climb on top of her, shamelessly grinding against her lap.

"What are you *doing* to me, baby?" Laine's hands travel down my sides, over my clothes, her lips slightly parted, distracted by the view of her thumbs rubbing circles where my hard nipples strain against my T-shirt. She's guiding me against her, the friction between us building into a threesome of Laine, me, and the jeans between us, dragged along for the ride.

"What? We're parked in the back of the lot, and besides, it's misty out. The place is deserted." I peek over the truck's rim in both directions before lifting my shirt over my head. But growling, Laine pulls my hands away. Under Laine's rules of courtship, kissing is allowed as well as all manner of groping, but no nudity or getting off or *anything* that would stop the high-pitched hum of need that's reverberated through my body ever since the wedding.

I drag her hand between us, gasping as her knuckle presses hard against where I'm aching for her. "Can you feel how wet I am for you, Laine? Don't you want me, too?"

Laine groans as she palms the hot underside of my jeans, giving me the heel of her hand before roughly grabbing me by the waistband. "Don't *you* understand that once I get my hands on your pussy, I'm never letting go?" She yanks the rim of my jeans, rocking me against her, groaning again. "Are you prepared for how *hard* I'm going to own your pussy?"

"That's not very PC of you, Laine Woods." My breaths are shallow, light-headed from need.

"There's nothing PC about what I'm going to do to you, boss."

This time, I'm groaning as she pulls me down until I collapse against her chest, soft breasts and hard nipples, and I feel like I'm going to go mad with wanting.

"Come on, Laine, hasn't there been enough courting yet?" I pant into her neck, sliding my palm down the exposed planes of her stomach, fingers dipping below her waistband. "You're not going to be here forever." I try, but there's no hiding the note of melancholy that creeps into my voice. Laine must hear it, too, because she grabs me by the wrist, then twists her body, dismounting me so that we're facing each other on our sides.

"Now, how do you know that?" She lifts the hand she caught like a criminal mid–break-in and kisses each of my greedy fingertips, slowing down my thundering heart with each deliberate brush of her lips.

"You told me, day one. You're not relocating to Blue Ridge." I swallow against the knot forming in my throat. "Has that changed?"

"I don't know," Laine says. "But I don't need to know right now, either. I've committed to you and Cosimo that I'll be your vintner as long as you need me. Once that's done, if a good opportunity opens up here, then of course I'd consider staying. But none of that changes how I feel about you, Zoe, and I refuse to let what's unknowable dictate what I do now." She runs her hand up and down my bare arm, her dark eyes lit by stars. "And I want *you*, boss."

It's not a promise she'll stay, but hope resonates through me all the same. I tug her close, wanting her more than ever. "Then stop courting me and *have* me."

"Didn't anybody teach you your ABCs?" She smiles at me crookedly. "Always Be Courtin'? That's the secret to happy relationships, according to my Papaw."

"You can court me forever if you're putting out. *When?*" Not quite begging here, but if there's one thing I've learned since Laine showed up in my vineyard, it's that dignity is overrated.

"When you admit that you're crazy about me, and when you believe I'm crazy for you, too."

Laine's words lodge into my chest, fitting neatly into a hole that's been there for as long as I can remember. But then they expand, filling every crevice and dusty corner until my heart aches.

"Can you admit that yet?" she asks quietly.

I haven't told Laine I've never been in a real relationship before. It makes me feel defective, like I'm missing parts, and that's why I keep getting returned to the store. How would I know what love is, and whether this growing tide of feelings Laine draws from me is the same thing? I've been infatuated with her for most of my life, only for her to show up now and show me the *real* Laine, all grown up, flawed and insecure, different from what I thought, but also, profoundly the same. My mouth opens, but nothing comes out.

"Then there's more courting to do," Laine says simply, wrapping me in her arms.

When my alarm starts wilding out at five a.m., I wake up with a grin. It's my favorite day of the year—Bluebell's Community Harvest Day. As a kid, it was like a surprise Christmas where there were no gifts, and you worked all day in the hot sun with your friends and family.

Ahh, *bliss.*

I've always loved the frenetic energy of harvest, which usually spans over four nonconsecutive days driven solely by when the grapes reach their peak. Right now, in mid-August, only the white crops are ready for picking. Our red crops will go fully nuclear in September, and we'll spend the day laughing and shearing grapes all over again. There's a short window at harvest—you've got to pick the grapes at exactly the right time. One day past optimum, and the sugar levels could go out of control. Too early, and the grapes' tannins will punch you in the face. In the vineyard business, you learn early—when the grapes are ready, you've gotta be ready, too.

So when Laine knocked on my office door yesterday with the results of the day's Brix readings, I dropped everything and sent the beacon out to every friend, family member, and former student I know. Of course, only twenty or so can help us pick grapes all day, but we need every pair of hands we can get. We're entering the heaviest period of a vineyard's work, the crush from August through November where grapes are picked, sorted, cleaned, and de-stemmed before the highly precise fermentation process begins. When Laine herself will transform from farmer into alchemist, coaxing our grapes into their higher calling. Though she's incredibly busy, she refuses to pause our courtship, insisting that the vineyard can't control our lives. It's been refreshing, if disconcerting, seeing someone establish healthy boundaries with vineyard work and forcing me to do the same.

I march across the dewy grass between rows of plump Seyval Blanc, grassy green and lush with their coats of frosty bloom, just *begging* to be picked. Laine's already setting up for the day. Her table's stocked with sunscreen, water, block assignments, shears, a huge stack of buckets, and enough gloves for a small gardening army. She also has coolers filled with Electric Daisy because Community Harvest involves a lot of day drinking. Also accidents, because drunk people handling shears is always a fun time, but Laine's ready for that, too, with four first aid kits lined up and waiting for ouchies.

God, is there anything hotter than preparation?

"Good morning!" I say brightly, the sight of her behind the table with a worn, red bandanna around her neck my personal utopia. *God*, I love a butch in a bandanna.

She glances up at me, her smile lighting up my heart like the sunrise as she sets insect repellant on the table. "Morning, boss."

Mmm. I sigh, wishing I could push her down between the vines, but the screech of tires rips my attention away, announcing Booch's big black truck as it comes roaring into our gravel lot. "Zoe Bee!" Booch hops down from the cab. "Are. You. Ready. To. SNIP?!!" Booch is a Community Harvest regular and a total beast with shears. He beats his chest like Tarzan for a hot minute, then gives me a bear hug as our parking lot steadily fills with cars, trucks, and even a motorcycle or two.

Trish pulls up next with the Redneck Wine Tour van loaded with friends and family. We have about thirty people here, ready to usher a season's worth of hard work from nature's arms into our buckets and have a damn good time doing so.

"Welcome to the 2025 Bluebell Vineyards Community Harvest Day!" I yell through cupped hands to a wave of hoots and hollers. "In case you're new here, these are the rules: 1) shear grape clusters at the top; 2) don't cut off any fingers; 3) like grapes go with like, no mixin' 'em up; and 4) whoever fills the most crates by the end of the day wins!"

"What's the prize?" someone yells from the back.

"Maeve, please show the contestants what's behind door number one!"

"This here goat," Maeve announces, parading Baahlzebub out on a fancy red leash. Try as we might, we still haven't gotten anyone to adopt him, so this is our last-ditch effort to *give* him away. I've allowed his foster situation to continue here under one strict condition—Laine's solely responsible for his care, and he can graze in our fallow field that's fenced in properly or be locked up in the barn like he's gold in Fort Knox, no other freedoms permitted. His horns are too sharp and his morals too loose for anything else.

"He will eat anything," Maeve says by way of sales pitch.

There's wary grumbling from the onlookers as Maeve's already tried to punt him off on most everyone here, but Booch looks pumped. "Yeah! A goat!" He claps his hands, then whoops.

Might have to rig it so he wins.

"Anything to add, Coach?"

"That I do." Laine's arms are crossed over her chest, a surly tilt to her chin. "Do *not* smush my grapes, and we won't have a problem." She points at our volunteers one by one, warning in her eyes, then breaks into a grin. "Happy Harvest Day, y'all! There's also a bottle each of Bluebell's full line to the industrious winner!"

Cheers go up once more, and with the scream of Laine's whistle, our troops go wild. I join her behind the table, helping to distribute assignments and supplies to the volunteers.

"Okay, what can I do for you now?"

"Hmm," Laine rubs her chin, pretending to think. "My lips are feeling a little dry. Parched. Untended, you could say."

"Oh, are they?" I smile, sidling up to her, letting her hook her fingers in the belt loops of my shorts to reel me in the rest of the way. "I could help with that."

She closes her eyes and puckers up, and it's about the cutest thing I've ever seen. But it doesn't stop me from grabbing a water bottle and tilting it over her lips.

Her eyes blink open in surprise as the splash of cool water dribbles down her chin. "*You*—"

But I'm already there, kissing up every trace of my little prank, until I cover her laughing mouth with my own. Her hands dive into my hair, holding me to her, and I feel so *happy*.

A van plastered with angel wings and the Franklin Second Baptist Church of God logo rolls up, and Ms. Betty appears from the driver's side door, followed by her entourage of church biddies.

"Hey there, Ms. Betty," I say, genuinely surprised. "I didn't know the prayer circle was helping out today."

"We're here on a mission from God," she replies serenely. "It don't involve wine." She lifts a finger. "That's for later."

"Ms. Betty lost her partial plate during Hannah's reception," an old lady with thick trifocals offers from the back. "The Lord will lead us to it."

"*Oh.*" My eyebrows raise of their own accord. "Do y'all need help?"

But the biddies are already on their way, disappearing into the fields like very old Children of the Corn.

Laine and I grab gloves and shears and join our friends in the vines. The morning passes in a blur of laughter and the sticky-sweet smell of ripe grapes. There's something so special and intimate about sharing the vineyard's work with her. This place that brought my parents together, this land we've lovingly cared for ever since, this life's work that's clutched me so tightly, I haven't always been able to breathe. Laine helps me bear my family's dreams, keeps me company in what's always felt like such a lonely endeavor. It's not a trap when I choose to be here.

The good vibes flow all morning, as does the wine. People are getting so sloppy I call the food truck to come an hour early, but I can't argue with their productivity. Drunk people are happy people, and happy people work hard. We've already made our way through the Seyval Blanc and Chardonnay, and we're a good way into the Traminette, too.

"I'm hungry!" Darryl moans, then dangles a cluster of grapes over his mouth and takes a bite like he's Bacchus and the hot lady feeding him, all at once. "*Ugh*. Why do these grapes taste so bad!"

"They're not wine yet, you drunkard!" Trish says, our sober granny once again. "Go sit in the shade and drink two bottles of water, or I'm divorcing your ass."

"The taco truck'll be here soon, I promise!" I keep checking my watch. It's almost noon, and. Darryl's not the only one munching on grapes, no matter how many times we announce wine grapes aren't for eating.

Someone screams. "THERE'S BEEN A MURDER!"

"Good lord." I run toward the newest disaster, Laine and others quick on my tail.

"I HAVE FOUND HU-MAN RE-MAINS!" It's Booch screeching this time, perhaps the drunkest of all. When we reach him, he's hunched to the side, his hands braced against his knees, looking like he's seen a ghost and decided to vomit about it. He points a shaky finger at a deep burrow where something white and shiny shimmers within. I get on my knees and peer down into the darkness, starting a little when I see human teeth grinning ominously up at me.

"Someone tell Ms. Betty we found her teeth!" I call out. I slip on a glove and lean down to fish them out.

"You sure you should be doing that?" Booch asks, a tremor in his voice.

"Just some dentures, Booch. Not like they're attached to someone." I laugh a little as I reach inside, then reach further, looking up at the sky as I grasp around, trying to find the teeth. Suddenly, pain lights up my entire arm.

"AHHH! SON OF A *BITCH!*"

I yank my arm wildly from the burrow, but it doesn't budge. "I'm STUCK!" I scream as zapping bolts of agony shoot up my arm and into my shoulder. No less than four drunk people tackle me from different angles, yanking my remaining appendages like a good old-fashioned quartering.

It doesn't work.

"Get off her!" Laine barrels through the unhelpful drunks pawing at my body. She slams down to her knees, wraps her strong arms around my waist, and pulls. My arm pops out, and I go spilling backward. A miniature black cloud rises from the burrow.

"BEES!" Maeve screams, but those aren't bees. They're wasps, yellow jackets to be precise, and their stings hurt worse than anything because their venom's made from the black blood of Satan himself. I should know since my right arm belongs to them now.

What happens next reminds me of a nature documentary featuring a stampede of large, bumbling, inelegant creatures, elephants or bison perhaps, racing away from a pack of predators. Only this time it's eight drunk people trying to get away from mean-ass yellow jackets hell-bent on revenge. Laine drags me up to standing, my bad arm dangling by my side, and hauls me out of there, which I'm grateful for because all I can comprehend right now is *pain*.

When we're safely away, Laine lays me down on a picnic blanket, panic etched across her face.

"Trish! We need you over here!"

I whimper, tears coursing down my cheeks. It still feels like they're crawling all over me, phantom stings piercing my skin again and again. I keep checking, but all that's there is the rapidly swelling cuff of angry red arm exposed between my glove and shirtsleeve.

"You're not allergic, are you?" Laine's hands fly over my body, checking for more stings brushing my hair back off my face, eyes searching for more danger. She pries the teeth out of my clenched fist and throws them over her shoulder, like it's their fault I got mobbed by nature's henchmen. Somebody yelps and swears as the sound of fake teeth collides with a head, and I sob out a laugh.

"N-no," I manage, right before Trish shows up with the first aid kit and several ice packs. I'm incredibly grateful to have a retired nurse on the premises.

"Okay, let me at her." Trish kneels on my other side. She examines my bad arm gingerly as she gently swabs the stings out with peroxide relief hitting as soon as she encases the welted flesh in ice packs. "Ten-some-odd stings in all. You're a lucky lady, Zoe."

"How is she lucky?" Laine demands. "Her arm's swelling up like a water balloon!"

Trish arches an eyebrow. "She'll be fine. Now go get me a bottle of Electric Daisy." When Laine just sits there, chest heaving, Trish says, "Go on now."

Laine glares at her, then launches to her feet and skulks off, returning with an icy bottle from the cooler.

"Pop the cork," Trish instructs, and again, Laine grudgingly obeys.

"Now take three big swallows and chill the hell out," Trish says, her lips pressed into a flat line. I laugh a little, then moan as the movement jars my arm.

"Shouldn't we take her to urgent care?"

"With this many stings, if she were going to have an anaphylactic reaction, it'd have already started." Trish turns her attention back to me, gentleness replacing the no-nonsense attitude she undoubtedly perfected after decades of handling upset family. "You feeling dizzy, baby? Any difficulty breathing?"

I shake my head and wince.

"I really think—" Laine begins, but Trish cuts her off like a sword through butter.

"Here's what's gonna happen. You're gonna sit with Zoe and keep an eye on her for the next half hour. If anything changes in that time—her face starts looking puffy, any wheezing or whistling when she breathes, any changes at *all*—you can throw her over your shoulder and cavewoman it all the way to urgent care. Until then, she needs to take it easy and keep the ice packs on. Got it?"

Laine screws up her lips, then nods brusquely.

"Good." Trish stands and brushes her hands down her legs. "Now, I've got other patients to help. I think Booch's gone and put himself into shock. Call me if you need anything, baby." She winks at me, then disappears into the throng of crying drunk people scattered about on folding chairs, waiting their turn.

Laine rocks on her heels, blows out a short breath, then plops onto her ass. Five seconds later, she's back on her heels. The nervous energy she's putting off could fuel a power plant.

A smile curves across my face.

She glances down at me and squints suspiciously. "What're *you* smiling about?" Her eyes widen. "That's not a symptom, is it? *Trish*—"

"No!" I laugh. "I'm fine. It's just . . . you're—"

Adorable.

Hilarious.

Mine.

My throat tightens, but it's no allergic reaction. At least, I don't think so. I start to sit up, but Laine pushes me back down. "Where the hell you think you're going?"

I sigh and smile at her from where I'm beached on the blanket. "This is an awkward way to have this conversation."

"What conversation?" Laine crosses her arms, looming over me still.

"About us," I say softly.

"*Us?*" Laine's jaw is locked tight, but when I try to readjust my arm and let out a small cry, she goes soft and concerned as she helps me get more comfortable. Her gaze meets mine. "What do you mean?"

"Are you happy here, Laine?" I swallow. "With me?"

"Am *I* happy here? Is this a joke?" Laine blinks down at me. "*Yes*, Zoe. Happier than I've been in years. Maybe not right now—right *now* I'm pretty pissed because I asked you *months* ago to let me get the exterminator out here, but *you* said that bees are a natural part of the ecosystem, which, okay, they are, but yellow jackets are unnatural tools of the devil, and now *look* at you, lying here, jacked up *to hell*—"

My phone buzzes in my back pocket. I try to lean up onto an elbow, but without even breaking her tirade, Laine pushes me right back down.

"—your one arm lookin' like Popeye's, and you can't even move!" Laine presses the palms of her hands against her cheeks and groans. "You could've gotten so hurt, Zoe!"

The buzzing grows persistent, but I can't get it out of my back pocket. "Laine?"

"*And now* you ask me if I'm happy? Well, I'll be happy once you let me fry those little assholes—"

I glance down at the screen of my smartwatch and see the name flashing on the screen.

"*LAINE!* It's Marisol!"

Her mouth falls open, and I lift a butt cheek, my bad arm now a useless ice cube. "Get my phone, it's in my back pocket!"

She hovers over me and plucks it carefully out of the back pocket of my jeans.

"Accept the call! Hold it up to my ear!" Laine fumbles with my phone, cursing before she shoves it so close to my face, it smooshes my nose. "LAINE! *Jesus!*"

"Sorry!"

This time, the facial recognition unlocks the screen. "Hello? Marisol?" I breathe out in a rush.

"Zoe, darling, you've got the showcase!"

Laine screams. I scream. We all scream for life-changing business opportunities.

"OH MY GOD! Thank you so much!" I yell into the phone while Laine holds it clumsily to my ear. "We won't let you down, Marisol!"

Her delighted laughter rings up from the receiver like tinkling crystal. "I know you won't, darling. Now, go celebrate because tomorrow, there's work to do."

"Yes, ma'am!" The line disconnects, and I snatch my phone from Laine and chuck it to the side.

"WE GOT THE SHOWCASE! WE GOT THE FREAKING SHOWCASE!"

I grab her by the front of her shirt and pull her down to me roughly, closing the distance between us with a demanding kiss. I pour every damning truth I have into the kaleidoscope slide of my lips on hers: *I want you. I need you. I'm terrified of you leaving.* But perhaps the most dangerous of all:

"Laine Woods, I'm crazy about you."

She pulls back for just a second, eyes wide. *"And?"*

I laugh. *"And* I believe you're crazy for me, too."

I've always thought Laine was beautiful. Since that day in the meadow when I found her lying among the wildflowers, to her rumpled Umbro high school days, to the wine scientist in goggles blending our varietals. But right now, she's incandescent, like a new sun in my sky, beaming out in every direction. She smiles at me, removing every doubt in my heart.

"Oh, thank *God!*"

Her lips are warm and fierce on mine, and she pulls me tight against her until our chests are locked together.

"Does this mean our courtship's finally over?" I ask, laughing into her kisses.

She breaks away from me just far enough to frown at me. "Our courtship isn't *over*, boss. It just means other things have begun." She smiles at me wickedly and takes my mouth again while a bunch of happy, silly drunks hoot and holler around us, and the world falls *away*.

CHAPTER TWENTY

After we wave goodbye to our friends and watch the last taillights disappear into the settling dusk, it's just me, and Laine, and a deep, joyful contentment that's flowed through my body ever since Marisol's call, whispering *we could* and *we did* and *we will*.

When Laine's eyes find mine, their rich, golden brown has gone as dark as the sky. I feel like I could wander inside them and never find my way back.

I entwine my fingers with hers. "Come on."

"Where we going?" Laine pulls my hand to her mouth and kisses my knuckles softly, one by one.

"You'll see."

I lead her into the fallow field, where a large tub sits waiting, its wooden slats pointing straight into the air, ending roughly waist high. Strands of bulb lights ring the tub's perimeter on flower-pot poles. They sway lightly in the mountain breeze, casting their flickering light across the scene I've set.

"No . . . ," Laine's eyes widen as she runs her hand reverently over the rim of the giant wooden barrel River built for a previous Community Harvest. "Is this a replica from the grape-stomping scene in—"

"*I Love Lucy*, yep."

Laine laughs returning my big, happy smile, then peers inside. "It's filled with grapes!"

"It's the unusable stock. We usually host a grape crush the night of the first Community Harvest, but after the *Everyday Bon Vivant* news,

I decided these grapes are just for us." I smile, strangely nervous that Laine won't understand why this tradition means so much to me. Why sharing it with her, and only her, means so much more.

Nobody makes wine like this anymore—have you seen people's feet? But the weighty tradition connects me to this ancient art that's existed long before I was born and will last long after I die. It's comforting, being a part of something eternal. Joining my mother there, in the crush of grapes, the pour of wine, where she still lingers. Mom's hands under my arms, lowering my tiny body onto the crushing pad, laughing as I laughed, delighting in my delight with each popping burst beneath my little feet. I find her memories waiting for me each time I step inside and share that delight with friends, letting their laughter fill me where I'm empty.

I want to join Laine there, too. In the eternal. Infuse this tradition with *her* and *now* and all the happiness I feel.

"Oh my god!" She hauls off each of her shoes and socks in a funny hopping-stumbling-run straight for the grapes. "I've always wanted to do this!"

My own smile stretches as she swings her legs over the edge and lands with a squish. Laine swipes at her hair dangling in front of her eyes, laughing as she squelches through the grapes beneath her feet. "This is *so—weirdly—satisfying!* Coming in?"

She holds out a hand, her twinkling eyes a gift only for me. I want to memorize this perfect image of her. Laine, calf-deep in a wooden barrel filled with lemony yellow and pale green grapes. Her strong thighs holding her steady, the rivets of muscle fascinating me before disappearing beneath a layer of black bike shorts that honestly? Should be illegal for the workplace. I've been staring at the peach of her ass all day. Her thin gray tank kisses her everywhere I want to, revealing the inky bluebells etched into her skin, the muscular set of her shoulders, and the heady contrast they make with the swell of her breasts. Her body is a topographical map, with dips and valleys and long expanses of smooth skin I know are there and wish I could see, wish my fingers could travel across. And her face?

It's beautiful. Without any effort and after a long day of sweaty work that began at dawn, Laine Woods is still unfairly, incomprehensibly beautiful. The day's sheen makes her high cheekbones glimmer, and her lips are full and lush and alive. More than that, I love how this edition of Laine is transposed on all those that came before, from teen soccer star *Char*laine, to grown Laine glimpsed on her rare visits home, to Napa-snob Laine who made faces at each of our best-selling wines. And now, *this* Laine, her eyes lingering on my face like I'm the sunrise, and she's gotten up early just to see me. Happy-to-be-here Laine.

My Laine.

Before I can second-guess it, I whip out my phone and take a picture of her standing in the grapes she grew for my family. For *me*.

"Hey, you sneaky little paparazzo. Get in here, or I'll drag you in myself."

I huff out a laugh, though the thought of Laine putting me *anywhere* leashes my desire and *yanks*. "Oh, will you now?" I kick off my shoes and socks, abandon my phone and keys, and launch myself into the barrel. Not trying to brag, but I've been known to do cannonballs in here. I tumble straight into Laine, and we're both laughing as I yip and curse and knock her off balance into the grapes.

"Save me!" I yell theatrically as my head starts to sink below the surface. I reach a hand above the skim of grapes and burble loudly for dramatic effect since there's almost no juice in here yet. Laine yanks me up, pulling me to where she sits, back propped up against the barrel.

"Save you?" She pants with laughter as I struggle to right myself before falling into her again. "I should let you drown for taking me down like that."

Our chests are pressed together, me lying halfway on top of her. Even without moving, the grapes continue to pop beneath us, little bursts tickling the tops of my thighs and stomach. I glance up at her, not quite breathing from the proximity. Laine's eyes are dark and playful.

"Laine?"

"Yes, baby?"

"There's something you should know . . ." I clear my throat, then retrieve a cluster of grapes that tangled into a crown upon my head and hold them up to the light.

"I play dirty." Then I resolutely squash them right into her ear.

Laine gasps in outrage, and I can't help it, I *giggle*.

Her eyes narrow and an evil smile blooms on her face. She flings the grape cluster to the side and pulls me back down. "Oh, it's *on!*"

I've never participated in a mud-wrestling match before, but I'd guess it's something like this as Laine topples me sideways in a spray of bursting grapes. This time, she's on top of me, though her torso is splayed across my hips like we're a human plus sign. She's so strong it's no contest at all, but like I said, I play dirty. I smush more grapes into her face, and she sputters, spitting them away and laughing hysterically as she tries to maintain her pin on me. I wriggle out, sliding easily in the slick, juicy grapes, my nipples burning they're so hard from the symphony of sensations against my body. The press of Laine's hot skin slipping against mine, her tight, furtive grips around my wrists, the full, heavy weight of her across my lap, then landing between my legs, and the pressure there, good *god*, it's all I can do not to drag my aching core against her. Our laughter is heady as tears stream down our faces, our wriggling and shoving losing steam as other impulses heat and begin to sizzle.

If Laine's eyes were dark before, they're positively molten now, and I feel their heat burning across my face, my neck, the juice dripping down my V-neck shirt, into the tunnel between my breasts.

"Wait a second," I say breathlessly, then shove up to sitting. "There's something else I want to share with you."

Laine reluctantly lets me go, then helps me to my feet. She's looking at me like she doesn't know whether to trust me or pin me down again, lest I try more bullshit.

I wade over to the edge, then reach behind the barrel for the bottle of wine and two glasses I'd stowed there.

"Is that—" Laine takes the bottle gently from my hands, one of the last three of my mother's famous reds. She glances up at me with a tentative hope. "Are you sure you want to open this?"

I run my hand up and along her arm until it rests on her shoulder, then trail the other one up to meet it around her neck. "We have a lot to celebrate."

"Zoe Brennan, as I live and breathe," she says, almost purring as I draw her closer. "Are you courting me back?"

"Maybe." I grin. "Though my idea of courting involves a lot more fucking."

Laine's jaw tightens, her eyes smoldering and serious as they pin me with her gaze, and I feel the responsive kick of giddy desire deep in my belly. She places the wine and glasses carefully back out of the vat, then grabs me roughly by the hips, pulling me closer. My mouth falls open in a gasp the instant before she takes it with a fierce, unyielding kiss. Across my body, synapses crackle with energy, pulsing the heady, delicious news like a heartbeat through every bit of my core: *Laine, Laine, Laine, Laine.*

One of her hands travels down my ass, grabbing the low curve where cheek meets leg. It's a tender spot, and her possessive, commanding touch weakens my knees. Her other hand pushes between us, finding my pussy and squeezing it roughly through my shorts. I moan, my body responding to the gruff, physical expression of her desire.

"You've been torturing me all fucking summer, boss," Laine urges into the shell of my ear. "Do you know how bad I've wanted to do this to you?" She squeezes my pussy again, and the hot ache blooming there tells me I'm already slick and wet, ready to be punished for my transgressions. "How many times I've wanted to turn you around and throw you against the bar, slide your panties down, and devour you?"

I gasp as her hand dives beneath the front of my shorts, finding my throbbing clit and offering the hard, unforgiving heel of her palm to it.

"That night in your window, Zoe, I swear to god." Her middle finger slides inside me, hooking into me, trapping me.

As if I'd ever want to leave.

"You fucking ruined me that night," she says hoarsely into my ear, punctuating each word with a bite. "*Ruined* me. Do you understand?" I'm trapped, but she is, too, locked in and around my body, pumping into me mercilessly as though making me come into oblivion is exactly the revenge she's looking for.

"I—*yes*," I confess as I clench around her finger. She slides another in, and I suck in my breath, trying not to buck against her. But the hand on my ass urges me forward, her fingers driving deeper within, while mine curl against her neck, crazed with the desire to own her body the way she's owning mine. The first time, our sex was tentative, exploring, then fell into a delicious stride as our bodies learned each other. Beneath the blindfolds, we were equals, removed from our history together, from my idolization and her indifference. But now, the woman ravaging my body is *Laine Woods*, and this time, our past charges the very air I'm gasping, mingling with our present, too.

It's *amazing*.

My frozen fingers turn to sharp points, and I drag my nails up and into her hair. Her mouth falls open, and her eyes flutter back for an instant before returning to mine, even hungrier than before. How many times did

I imagine this? Not the sex—when I was in high school, I barely comprehended what that would entail—but her looking at me, *seeing me*, like this. I feel like an invisible woman, finally given shape and color and recognized at last, and it's the rest of the world's turn to be forgotten.

Her eyes fix upon me like I'm the one thing that matters, and I'm *hers*. She commands me with her hands to come for her, seizing control over me and gripping it tight. And this, *this*, is the sex I've imagined when she walks into the winery like she owns the place, her tanned skin gleaming with sweat. Laine in charge, just like she's always been.

But *I'm* the boss now.

I pull her head back by the hair, and sink my mouth upon her long, luscious neck. She tastes like sun and sweet and *Laine*, like every horny thought I've ever had, and the long, low moan she gives when I run my teeth across her collarbone gratifies me in a primal place, puckering low in my belly. And just like that, the dynamic changes. Now she's in *my* thrall, doing *my* bidding, as I trace the tattoos stretched across her chest with my tongue, kissing and biting in response to the fierce ache she's building inside me.

"Do you know how much *you've* tortured *me*, Laine Woods? Making me want you so bad I *hurt*, then telling me no?" I yank down a strap of her tank top, and her dark eyes flicker to the movement, almost nervous, but her hands keep striding against me, too intent on making me come.

"Well, you can't stop me now." My voice is edged with fierce petulance, the words thrilling me because *they're true*. I yank down the other strap. "You won't."

"I won't," Laine whispers. "*I won't, baby.*"

I slip my hands down the rim of her shirt, the hard knot of her nipples dragging against my sticky palms, and it almost sends me over the edge. Laine Woods here, with *me*, working my pussy like *that's* the job I hired her for. Her breasts in my hands, then my mouth, crimping in pleasure from the firm press of my tongue. I'm in utter, delicious control. The Zoe I was, who I *still* am sometimes, would happily lie beneath the crushing weight of Laine's desire and let it pulverize me, squash me like grapes into a glorious nothing, then beg, weeping, for more.

But the Zoe I am now has other inclinations. The kind that want to dominate, command, break down the myth of Laine that's ruled me half my life and consume it piece by piece.

Because the real thing is so much *better*.

As I close my lips around a perfect nipple, the final string is strummed within me. The orgasm trembles, shudders, then explode throughout my body, like a bomb detonated in a steel box. I don't know how my skin contains these waves of pleasure streaming outward. I don't know how I'm still standing. I rock into Laine's chest, the hand cupping my ass steadying me, but still she refuses to let me go. Her palm feels part of me now, devoured by my flesh, and the brief second it's gone sends me reeling until her rock-hard thigh takes its place. I moan in relief as I grind against her leg, pitiful with wanting. She grips my hips, pulling me down onto her as she drives into me, the pressure so hard it feels like I might split with ecstasy.

When the pleasure threatens to overwhelm me, I push her off, which only kicks the desire in her eyes up more. We're battling each other again, this time with our bodies and needs instead of words and opinions on wine and how to prune a goddamn vine. Each gasp of the other is a blow, each trembling touch an opponent faltering, and when I yank down the rim of her bike shorts and fall to my knees before her, spreading her legs till her crux is revealed, hard, wet, and *mine*: victory.

Her hands dive into my hair, pulling from the roots, the pain mixing with the pleasure of making her cry out. I suck her clit greedily, grabbing her ass and holding her to my face.

"You are mine," I whisper into her, half delirious with the want spiral-ing through my body. *"Mine. Mine. Mine."* I punctuate each pronounce-ment with a flick of my tongue, circling for the kill as she grips my head and forces me closer. Maybe it's not normal to bring this kind of com-petition to sex, this battle of wills and power grabs, but Laine and I have been fighting against each other one way or the other since she got here. Against each other's views, wants, and needs. Against our *own* wants and needs. Against our past selves and perceptions of the other and perhaps even our own futures. Against our fears. It's been a battle to get this far, but unlike any other fight I've had, I've never enjoyed the ring more. When she thrusts against my mouth in a wild, fierce release, the moan she releases becomes my proudest achievement.

Fuck honor roll, I made Laine Woods *come.*

And this time, she knows it was me.

When we lie back in our bed of squashed grapes, Laine's arm nestled behind my neck, the fight's gone all out of me. Out of us both, judging by the way her fingers dance lightly on my skin and the tilt of her head rest-ing against mine. I'm too tired from the long day of harvest and evening of wildly cathartic sex to spin out, which is my normal go-to after a par-ticularly delightful round of orgasms. But tonight, the animal of my anxiety is resting. Maybe somewhere deep inside my brain where it likes to cower, it realizes that catastrophizing would be too easy, too fruitful, too enormous for the dwindling reservoir of energy I have right now. I already depended on her for the livelihood of my family's legacy; now I've thrown my stupid heart into the mix, too. But while these thoughts usu-ally send my heart racing, all I feel now is sleepy and content, warm in the press of her embrace. Maybe this is the peaceful resignation that comes in the face of annihilation, when you're helpless to stand by and watch the beginning of your own end.

But, maybe not, a small voice insists inside of me.

"Tonight's been perfect," Laine murmurs into my hair, making my scalp prickle all the way down my neck.

"Mmm," I agree. "One thing's left, though. To make it perfecter."

"Perfecter?" Laine says through a smile I can hear.

"When you're already in the realm of perfect, and yet there's more to delight." I stand and reach over the barrel's edge until I find the bottle of my mother's red. "Perfecter."

She nods. "Consider it entered into the Laine Lexicon."

The cork comes off with a satisfying *thunt*, and the rich, almost leathery smell of tannins long mellowed fills my nose. Laine's eyes roll back in her head as she takes a deep pull of the aroma.

"This is going to be *so good*," she says when her irises reappear, then scrambles to sit up properly, giddy. I'm glad she recognizes the gravitas of this situation and is appropriately thrilled.

I for one cannot speak. Opening a bottle of this wine is as close to a religious act as I get. The tawny garnet slides down the bell of each glass, glazing it in a smooth, jewel wash of red. As it pours, its rich aroma lifts around us—black cherry and tart red plum, the smooth, mineralish air of crushed gravel, followed by cedar and cream. And the taste is more than the refined balance of acid and sugar, of heady tannins long tamed and spicy oak, and it's more than the feel of its serene swim down my throat, the heat efflorescing through my cheeks. It's the taste of summers long gone, spent in the shade of my mother's favorite tree. It's her fingers in my hair, braiding the strands back while I read The Boxcar Children and pondered whether I could survive on my own, too, not knowing how soon I'd be forced to do just that.

I close my eyes and let the wine loll across my tongue bringing me back in time as it always does. It's the smell of my mother's clothes after a long day in the winery, pressed against my nose in the first hug after school. It's the sound of my father's unburdened laugh, the scent that lingered in his tickling mustache when he kissed my forehead goodnight. This wine is from better days I no longer have access to. From seasons long gone, made by hands that no longer create. It is finite. This portal to my family's past, to our happiness that once was, is closing more with each swallow.

I open my eyes and find Laine's.

"Do you feel it, too?" The words come out choked through my tight throat. "The magic?"

Laine puts her glass down and takes my face in her hands, brushing the tears from my cheeks with her thumbs. "It's amazing, Zoe. Unreal. Perfect, perfecter, perfect*est*. Like you."

And she kisses me, the memories traveling between our lips, bitter and sweet with a full, luscious body all its own. When she pulls away breathless, she touches her forehead to mine, hands still cupping my face. "What are you so afraid of, baby?"

A million things. But most of all: "This," I answer, too tired to be anything but honest. I rest my cheek in her palm. "Needing you. You leaving." *Like everyone else*, I think. "And at times, Rachel." We both huff at that, but the joke doesn't wash away the truth of my admission, or the unfettered view of my intense vulnerability it provides.

"I can't imagine *ever* leaving you," Laine says softly, brushing a stem from my hair. "This is all I want." Her finger skims lightly along my jaw, desire flowing through the small, simple touch.

"How can you know that, though?" I laugh a little through my swollen throat as her finger traces its way down it. "This just began."

"No, it didn't," Laine says. "It began fifteen years ago. It's just now getting interesting, is all."

I want to believe her, but flowing beneath these feelings swirling between us is a deep current of fear that refuses to be banished overnight.

But maybe, with time, it *could*.

"Now." Laine's voice turns all business as she leans back against the barrel, then taps both hands to her chest, indicating for me to *come here*. She gives me that wicked smile.

"Shut up and sit on my face, boss."

CHAPTER TWENTY-ONE

My eyes fly open, the primal terror at being awoken by a foreign sound *in your lair* sluicing through my veins. Someone's in my cottage. Did I lock the door?

I clutch fistfuls of sheets in both hands, as if I could defend myself with bed linens. The fear drumming in my ears turns into something else—the rhythmic patter of water.

The shower's on. Someone's . . . humming?

I suck air in through my nostrils, exhale a shaky laugh.

Laine.

I'm not being murdered, I'm being *morning after*'ed. I prop myself up on one elbow to peer through the door to my bathroom, and yes, that's definitely Laine's voice. Singing . . . Willie Nelson?

Well, this is a first. People have stayed over before, sure, but no one's ever partook of the *facilities*. It's usually a quick kiss to the cheek and a promise to text later, the words half cut off by my front door swinging shut. It's the only practical option, really, since my cottage is so small.. If you only have room for yourself, you can't notice how there's no one else.

The knobs squeak off, and Laine steps out, her singing unmuffled by the shower curtain. A smile quirks up the side of my mouth.

She sounds *terrible.*

"Good morning." Laine steps into my bedroom wrapped in a towel that's too small. My hair towel, I realize. It takes me a second to place it since it's currently revealing *her pussy.*

"Good morning," I rasp out, throat dry as she strides toward the bed. I pull the sheets up and over my bare breasts, suddenly self-conscious of my sticky, juice-covered skin, but Laine's having none of it. She climbs onto the bed knee by knee, then pulls me to her, hard. I let out a little gasp as I slide easily toward her, helpless as a turtle on its back, until the firm press of her thigh greets the growing ache in my core, separated by a thin layer of cotton. There, poised high between the legs that she spread, Laine sports a look of satisfaction that curves her mouth, heads her eyes. She presses my knees down until they're flat against the bed until I'm stretched wide open beneath the sheet that still separates us. She falls onto her hands on either side of my head, my hair towel fired for its lackluster performance and flung into the distance.

"Very good morning," I amend, breathless.

Her eyes are greedy as she gives the line of my jaw a long lick, then gently pulls the sheet down from my clutching fingers, exposing one breast at a time. "This sheet's not allowed, boss." Her tongue travels down my collarbone, then dips between my breasts. Every unshaven hair on my body is standing fully erect, like a roomful of hands shot into the air, screaming *Pick me!!*

"I'm filthy, Laine," I murmur. "I'm covered in grape must. Let me shower first, I'm so stick—*ohhh*." I break off suddenly when the wet tip of her tongue reaches my nipple, traces its circumference there.

"Filthy," Laine breathes against my ferociously tight bud, then licks, hard. "*Mmm . . .*" Her thigh grinds against me, or maybe I'm grinding against it, like I'm thirteen all over again and discovering the beauty of a nice, round bed knob. "Sorry, boss. Shower's not allowed, either."

Turns out, the only thing that *is* allowed is a pair of mind-bending orgasms, one for each of us.

The list of novel experiences continues throughout the day and into the next week, too. Not just sexual acts, either, though there have been *many* of those. On Saturday, I woke up to find my trash had been taken out. At first, I thought it had magically disappeared, or that I sleepwalked it all the way to the winery, but then I spotted Laine whistling her way through the vineyard, hauling my bags of trash away like a very confusing Santa. Then on Monday, I got a text from Federico's Auto Shop, informing me of my upcoming oil change appointment for the vineyard's truck. So when Laine shows up at my office door in the middle of my weekly paperwork marathon with two milky iced coffees and a pair of chocolate croissants, and plops down in the chair in front of my desk, I'm almost not surprised.

Almost.

Laine catches me staring at her from over my croissant. "What? Do you like almond better?"

"What's going on, exactly?" I whisper from behind the safe, predictable layers of flaky croissant she inexplicably bought for me.

Laine wipes a crumb from her mouth. "With the fermentation? Well, the whites have already gone through primary—"

"I mean, here. With us?" I take a huge gulp of coffee to avoid having to say more.

Laine's brow relaxes, then arches into a bemused smirk. "We're having a midmorning snack, boss."

"In a casual way? Or an . . . exclusive way?" I sound like a dork, but it's been two weeks of consistently amazing sex, like, *on the daily*, which is a new record for me, but in conjunction with all these small, thoughtful gestures? I thought I understood the rules of courting Laine, but this feels like new territory.

Maybe she *is* going to murder me. I scoot my office chair back on its wheels on instinct.

Laine takes a long pull from her iced coffee, rolling the straw between her still smirking lips, then slowly rises. She comes around my desk to stand over me, separating me in my rolling office chair from all my responsibilities, and slides one perfect half of her ass at a time onto my desk. Her legs are naturally spread apart, but the space between them draws my gaze like a magnet to steel. It's an effort to flick my eyes back up to hers. The look on her face is a knowing, silky confidence that heats each area of my body in a cascade of tumbling sensation. We've already had sex once today, and yet . . .

She reaches for the croissant loosely dangling from my hand, places it to the side, then pulls me by the armrests into the V made by her legs. She stops only when her thighs surround my shoulders. The familiar smell of *her* mixes with the tart grapes she's been handling, and I want to bury my face in the warm denim of her jeans and breathe it all in. She stops me, though, cradling my head in her hands, her fingers pulling me by the hair gently, gently back, until my vision is filled with her, top to bottom.

"It's in a very serious way, boss." Her fingers tighten in my hair, and I gasp as she runs the back of one hand down my cheek, my neck, before yanking me closer to her. All it would take is a small squeeze to put me in a headlock with her thighs.

If this is murder, so be it.

But the squeeze doesn't come, and her grip on my hair gentles. My scalp tingles with pleasure from the conflicting sensations. With her free hand, she reaches for the croissant and brings it to my lips, nudging them open. I obediently bite into the flesh, the pleasurable tang of chocolate and salt on my tongue mixing with the building ache in my pussy, and I moan as she watches me, as though the lick of my lips is a fascinating mystery.

"I'm going to take care of you, Zoe Brennan," she says, her voice faint as she intently watches me swallow, then nudges my mouth again. "You're mine."

Sex in my office? Check.

Involving *croissants*? Didn't see that coming, but *check*.

Reaching the absolute pinnacle of my desire and longing and—

happiness?

I sit back in my office chair, caffeinated, sugared, and thoroughly wrung out.

Check, check, check.

It's terrifying, but each time the fear buoys in my chest, I feel Laine's fingers pulling my hair, hear her sultry, commanding words: *You're mine.*

And . . . I am. At some point, Laine hooked a steel cable into my core, pulling me utterly, helplessly into her wake. Laine could straight up destroy me if she wanted, but that makes whatever this is so much more *satisfying*. All the protections I've built around my heart blunted the hurts caused by others, but they blunted the good feelings, too. I've never felt anything like the sweet, swoony rush I get when Laine takes me in her arms and tells me how smart I am, how talented, how incredibly sexy. I've been desired before, but Laine's wants are on a whole new level. The steadfast devotion she puts into her work is lavished upon me, too, now. If I'd known as a lovelorn teenager—staring at her best friend's older sister from across the dinner table, the lunchroom, the vast expanse of life and experience that separated me from *Charlaine Woods*—that inside the girl I idolized was all *this*?

I'd have followed her anywhere.

A knock on my office door shakes me out of my romantic reverie, Tristan's blurred outline visible through the milky glass window. I quickly glance around, but there's no evidence of the pastry sexual awakening that occurred here earlier, and all my clothes are buttoned, zipped, and right-side on.

"Come in."

The knob turns, then Tristan's shoving the door open with his hip, his arms full of teetering boxes. He takes one look at me and rolls his eyes. "You have sex hair."

I run a hand over my head, smoothing the snarls. Crumbs fall onto my shoulder, and Tristan's frown grows. Oops.

"Erm, what's in the boxes, Stan?"

One auburn eyebrow arches but he lets me change the subject. "I was cleaning out the storage room, and I found these." He pauses to swallow, looking suddenly unsure. "There's some pictures of your parents in here, when the vineyard was starting out. Wanna see?"

"Really? Yeah!" I put a bright smile on my face, and relieved, he lifts the lid of the first box and hands me an old brittle clipping.

It takes my breath away. My mom and dad, arm in arm, standing in front of the original Bluebell Vineyards sign that Dad painted by hand. Behind them are our vineyards, or where they would be, one day. In this shot, only a fraction of the property has been cultivated so far. The headline reads: BLUE RIDGE—AMERICA'S NEXT NAPA? which makes me smile. The article goes on to detail my parents' story—how they met, how they picked the land, and how their first growing season was going. Bluebell Vineyards was one of only two vineyards in the North Georgia mountains back then, and nobody knew if the great Georgia wine experiment would succeed. But while reading the words, my eyes are drawn up again and again to my parents' beaming faces. This couple had no sad future waiting. It was all open fields under big blue skies, red clay and rolling hills. My finger brushes over their faces, holding the memory of this moment in time for them.

"Is there more?"

Hours pass as Tristan and I pore over every relic he's uncovered. It softens my heart, seeing the history of Bluebell Vineyards laid out before me. A picture of my mom, laughing from behind the bar. Dad mopping the winery floor, mouth open, undoubtedly singing along to some bad European techno. An idea's building inside me, but the details are out of reach. I feel that tickling sensation whenever a good idea's about to hit.

"Could you scan these pictures, Tristan? Digitize them so we can blow them up big, maybe as projections?"

Tristan's brows draw together. "Yeah. Why?"

"What if you did an art installation for the showcase? My parents' story and the history of Bluebell Vineyards and surrounding areas, but with your modern eye? Something beautiful and cinematic, something we could project against our walls, the forest—"

"The barn, the surface of the pond." Tristan plucks my thread from the air and keeps it spinning, the cadence of his voice picking up to match mine. "The west hill, even. It has the right slope—we could project images onto the vines themselves after dark."

"What if you could make it like—like a walking tour through the property, with little vignettes projected for people to experience?" My heart's picking up speed.

Tristan's eyes meet mine, and I see the same spark igniting his own creativity. Suddenly he stands, his hands still full of pictures. "Hey, do you mind if I head out early tonight? I wanna do some research on this."

"Go for it." I smile, feeling prickles of excitement at this new take on the local showcase's theming. *Everyday Bon Vivant* wanted me to imbue my parents' story into our vineyard's experience, and I could do that and more, situating my family's narrative among the area's stories, too. Because this festival is about more than Bluebell Vineyards—it's about Blue Ridge. The next Napa? No, maybe not, but it's a one-of-a-kind place with one-of-a-kind people.

I want to share our stories.

I once read an article about how partners share stress, that it ping-pongs back and forth between them with greater intensity until there's a constant *thwap-thwap-thwap* between your heart and brain and theirs, and you want to throw yourself into a lake to escape it.

As a confirmed spinster, I never thought that would happen to me.

I *also* never thought it would involve Soccer Saturday.

"THAT'S RIGHT, DAR-DAR!" I scream from another plane of existence where I, Zoe Brennan, *desperately* care about the outcome of the peewee soccer league final championship. "GO, BENNY, GO!" At this point, I'm just screaming general encouragement. I don't know what the hell is going on. While Laine's addition to the coaching staff has made some mild improvement—the children scatter every time she yells *CLUMP!*—it hasn't done anything to decrease the overall chaos of six-year-olds attempting team sports. All I know is that it's 1-1, we have somewhere between ten seconds and five minutes left, and I haven't sat down for the entire second half.

The vibes are *intense.*

But Darla has the ball, and Benny's at her side. Every time she dribbles a little too hard, Benny's there to bring it back under their joint control, just like Laine's worked with them out in the yard. As the youngest Woods twins approach their team's goal, the oldest Woods twins are clutching each other, waiting with gripped fingers on each other's biceps. Darla swings back to kick, and *bam!* The ball hits the post and bounces off, but Benny catches the rebound and kicks it in before anyone can do anything about it.

I'm . . . not sure you can do that in soccer? But even the teen ref is cheering. The goal brings Chance and Laine back to life, and now they're jumping arm in arm before Chance runs out on the field and scoops up his kids, one on each side, and spins them wildly.

Laine, on the other hand, is now on top of the Gatorade table. I shake my head, laughing with the sweet relief we're sharing now.

Fucking *athletes!*

After the game, the entire Woods clan is partying in the parking lot. Molly and Ezra are proud as punch and have gone full tent, handing out those gooey little Hawaiian roll ham sandwiches and a play-by-play of Benny and Darla's best hits. I'm happily waiting my turn to congratulate Laine and Chance after the crowd of parents dissipates when a figure sidles up beside me. I glance out of the corner of my eye and nearly choke on my eggroll.

Rachel stands there, arms crossed tightly over her chest.

After a pause, I resume chewing. Slowly.

"Congratulations on getting the showcase," she says, each word like the individual blow of an ice pick landing in my skull.

"You do not mean that."

"I don't," she agrees. "Just another thing you've stolen from me. You owe me twenty dollars now, by the way."

I turn on her. "Me, steal from *you?* Are you fucking with me, or just delusional enough to think you came up with the idea for field day—"

"—oh, *please*—"

"—Lantern Fest, Water Wars, Books and Barrels." I tick off each of the events that Rachel stole from me, repackaged, and subsequently ruined over the years. This could go on for a while, but then an arm wraps protectively around my shoulders, and Laine appears. She smells like sweat and clementines and looks ready to throw down.

"Is this relative bothering you, Zoe?" Laine asks. I shake my head, and she gives me a long, lingering kiss hello, which catches the entire family's attention. I guess this is Laine's way of announcing that we're "courting."

Direct, to the point. I like it.

Rachel's face transforms into an open-mouthed frown. "Are you *kidding me,* Charlaine?"

Laine breathes deeply through her nose but doesn't look at Rachel when she addresses me. "I can't come home just yet, boss. My folks are calling a family meeting after the tailgate today. Can I meet up with you tonight?"

"Absolutely, Coach." I give her a firm smile, trying to show everyone here that I could care less about Rachel's open disgust at us being together. It's a little harder to ignore how Molly and Ezra are staring at us, with dismay. Even Chance looks uncomfortable. It drives a cold wedge into my heart, biting into the warm parts of me all the way home. Ever since Laine came back to Blue Ridge, I've been fighting hard to feel like I'm good enough for her. That Bluebell Vineyards is good enough for her—hell, that *Blue Ridge* is good enough.

Does her own family disagree?

CHAPTER TWENTY-TWO

I t's a long day in the tasting room, but I live for the busy season. Friends, townies, tourists of all types—from posh Atlanta gay couples to Georgia families that save up for their yearly trip to the mountains—Bluebell Vineyards is decked out with happy faces today. The sweet fizz of Electric Daisy and bubbling conversation, punctuated by the constant swing of our doors opening, has kept me so occupied, I've almost managed to forget the weird incident at the tailgate.

Almost.

I wish Laine would return and fill me in on this mysterious family meeting. On the heels of *Everyday Bon Vivant*'s picking us to host the showcase, it makes me feel unsteady somehow, which is silly because Rachel may have zero qualms about fighting dirty, but the rest of the Woods are above that. Plus, why would they loop Laine in if they were up to something unsavory? It makes no sense.

And yet, the weirdness bubbles in my stomach until closing when Laine's strong arms wrap around my waist from behind, her nose nuzzling my ear. "Mmm," she says into my hair. "Best boss ever."

My eyes flutter closed as the wave of serotonin floods my system. "Laine," I murmur back. She spins me around in her arms and presses kisses all over my face—the corner of my mouth, the hollow below my cheekbone, the tip of my nose.

"Are you angling for a raise or something?" I laugh as her kisses move down my sensitive neck, tickling me there. "Come on, tell me about the family meeting,"

She stops, chin tucked between my cleavage, to look up at me. "Now?"

"Please."

Eyes still locked on mine, she licks beneath the rim of my low V-neck, giving me goose bumps all over, before extricating herself from my chest. A soft, contented smile settles on her face.

"My folks want to cut me into the family business officially. There's money set aside that could fund something for me."

My eyebrows rise. "Whoa. Rachel's okay with that?"

"She was outvoted. It doesn't matter if she likes it." Laine brings my knuckles to her lips, the heat of her breath reaching deep inside me, tightening my nipples, dipping low into my belly. "I told them I'd think about it. That I wanted to discuss it with you first."

I exhale shakily, my heart squeezing with such *love*, tears pop into the corners of my eyes. "You did?"

"Mm-hmm."

"Does this mean you'd stay in Blue Ridge after my dad comes back for sure?" The idea of it flashes through me, the first glimpse of a long road ahead appearing through the trees.

"I . . . don't know yet." Laine kisses the palm of my hand, but it doesn't hide the reluctance in her voice.

A kick of fear lands square in my heart. I pull my hand away.

"You still don't think Blue Ridge is good enough, do you?"

You don't think I'm good enough.

Laine pulls me into her arms. "Hey, no, Blue Ridge is amazing, you've shown me that. A cut of the family business means obligations I haven't had up to now, that's all. I don't want to work at Into the Woods, I don't want to work with Rachel *at all*, and I'm ready to make my own wine for once. It would all come down to whether I can find the right opportunity here to do that while still contributing to the family business somehow." She runs the long, straight bridge of her nose against my jawline. "And if I don't, well . . . we could always go somewhere else together."

"Go somewhere else? What are you talking about?"

"I don't know." Laine pulls back from my neck, her dark eyes hungry over her flushed cheeks. "I want to take you to Oregon. Or California. Show you all the places I love. Follow our ambition and opportunities and live happily ever after." Her thumb parts my lips until she feels the wet there, then leans in and bites, pulling my bottom lip into her mouth and kissing me deeply. It's hard to think while she's lighting up my body like this, fear alternating with love and hope and shamefully, a burst of wild excitement at the idea of leaving Blue Ridge with Laine. Somewhere I wouldn't be responsible for holding up the weight of my world alone. Where I could take a day off from time to time. Where I could just *be*.

But who would *I* be then? Without Bluebell Vineyards, and Dad, and the singular purpose I've had ever since Mom passed away? The anxiety yawns open like a canyon, and just like that, I'm tumbling down its steep walls, scrabbling to stop my fall and hang on.

I break away so I can look at her, needing us *both* to hear me. "I can't ever leave Blue Ridge, or my dad—it'd break his heart for good. You know that, right?"

She sighs, her eyes full of gentle understanding as she brushes my hair behind my ear. "All I know is that it doesn't matter where we are, because I'm yours, Zoe." She drops to her knees before me, sliding her palms over the curve of my hips as she goes. She's still murmuring *yours, yours, yours* as she lifts my skirt, presses her mouth against my panties, and breathes. She stops to look up at me, eyes wide and flooded with desire.

"And you'll *always* be my boss."

I'm lying in the crook of Laine's arm, half drowsing on the floor of our tasting room on a makeshift bed of linens, when a loud pounding from outside wakes me cold.

Is someone . . . *knocking*?

It's after midnight. We've been closed for hours. I hoist onto my elbow, listening, adrenaline spiking my blood. The pounding comes again, this time from farther away.

"Wake up." I jostle Laine in the ribs. "Someone's outside."

She squints open an eye, then another, as the pounding grows louder. "Is that—from the winery?"

Another noise, something heavy falling, the stomp of feet, makes us both scramble up, pulling on clothes as we go. "Did you lock up?" I grab an empty wine bottle from the recycling to reuse as my weapon.

"I don't remember." Laine's bleary-eyed but awake. She grabs the bat we keep behind the counter, and together, we ease toward the winery. She squeezes my hand before she throws the door open. The lights are already on.

"For the *love* of God, *ugh*!" A figure sways near our aging base wines, reeling backward from the threat of Laine's bat. "It's me, your sister." Rachel glares at Laine before dumping her gaze on me. "And your—your—Rachel!"

I don't know what I was expecting—a wine burglar? Baahlzebub on the prowl? But definitely not Rachel, drunk as a skunk and smelling like the last flat swallow of beer.

"*Jesus*." Laine lowers her bat. "What are you doing here?"

"I've got somethin' to say to you!" Her giant purse is capsized on the floor, its contents scattered around like a very strange Easter egg hunt where the best prizes are lipsticks and Keto bars. "And also, tryna find my keys." Rachel straightens, but her eyes slide closed like the move's made her dizzy. "I've seen it a hundred times.

"We've got a puker!"

Rachel heaves over and gags, and Laine snatches her by the arm, dragging her away from the tote of base wine that's holding her up, its cover half-off.

"Not near the wine! *Jesus!*" Laine yells, her face scrunched in disgust as she pulls the cover back on the base wine. "You're blitzed."

"Well, *you're* a bunghole," Rachel replies, then gives us a crooked smile of triumph.

Laine runs her hands over her face. "You didn't drive here, did you?"

"Just Dad's golf cart. It's fine." Rachel gestures behind her at the wall. That cart's probably in a ditch somewhere.

"Anyway, quit changing the subject!" She lobs a finger at Laine, then clears her throat as though she's about to launch into a rehearsed speech. "You have some nerve, Charlaine! You disappear for the last ten years, then come home on your ass, acting like you're too good for everything while begging your family for handouts!"

Rachel wobbles on her feet, anchored only by her big, glaring eyes. "That money was set aside for *me*, for *my* new project! But noooo, evvvverybody loves the lesbians! Give *them* all the money! Nobody gives a shit about Rachel! Or Rachel's brewery. Or what Rachel cares about!"

"You're opening a brewery?" I ask, unable to resist probing Rachel's third-person confession for truth.

"I was *trying* to!" Rachel gestures at her beer-splashed outfit, like that explains anything. "Not anymore! And all so Charlaine here can buy up some decrepit vineyard in the middle of nowhere and make *more* bad wine? Yeah, real great business plan, fam!"

Vineyard? What vineyard? I blink, then turn to Laine, but she's looking straight at Rachel, fury glinting in her eyes. "You're drunk and spewing nonsense, Rachel. I know you hate me, but that doesn't change the fact that I'm a member of this family, too! You were outvoted, okay? Deal with it!"

"I *won't* deal with it! How can I when you both keep taking everything I've worked so hard for?" Rachel's voice breaks.

I rear back. "What have *I* ever taken from you?!"

Rachel points at me so hard, she staggers. "You said *no*. *Everyday Bon Vivant* asked if you'd collaborate with Into the Woods for the showcase, and you said *no*!" Rachel's hands ball into fists, even as tears stream down her cheeks. "After everything we've done for you, you ungrateful bitch!"

"Whoa!" Laine forces herself between Rachel and me. "You need to stop talking to her like that, Rachel, so help me God."

"*You* said no *first*!" I yell over Laine's shoulder, like the beginning of every fight I witnessed at good old Gilmer County High. "Marisol told me so!"

"That's right!" Rachel puffs out her chest like that's something to be proud of.

So she's aware she's a hypocrite. Great.

"I'm tired of carrying your sorry ass, Zoe Brennan! But the *one time* you could give us something back, you say no? Well, fuck you! You wouldn't even have a vintner right now if it weren't for us and Charlaine sucking so hard!"

"That's it." Laine's jaw grinds as she grabs Rachel by the arm. "I'm taking you home."

Rachel allows herself to be pushed out, but not before yelling over her shoulder, "She's gonna hurt you, Zoe, don't you see that? She hurts everybody who loves her! Wait, I don't have my keys—"

But Laine's got Rachel's purse and she's leading her toward my truck, and me?

All I've got are questions.

CHAPTER TWENTY-THREE

'm already in bed when Laine returns from dropping Rachel off. She climbs in beside me, wearing her boy-short briefs, a tank top, and a look of concern. We face each other, back in our parenthesis form, the first unease in months swirling between us.

She runs a hand up my arm. "You okay?"

I bite my lip in and nod. "But, you're buying a vineyard?"

"Not buying, not right now. Just looking for that next opportunity, remember?" She smiles sadly. "Business has been so good, my family has capital to grow. There's a couple of competing proposals on the table now that I'm back, and Rachel's furious about it, that's all. She wants to open a brewery she'd manage on her own, but I put forward a few properties to consider instead. Existing vineyards looking to change ownership, places with good, established vines where it'd be easy to step in and get to work right away."

I frown, trying to imagine both things. Laine running an expansion of Into the Woods is easier to picture, but Rachel? Drinking *beer*?

My mind runs over every rumor and bit of gossip in the local wine scene. "But there aren't any properties like that for sale around here. Are there?"

"No, but I'm keeping an eye out." Laine's hands fold over my hips, tugging me to her. "And none of this matters right now, anyway. We've got the showcase to plan, and I have to deliver on a delicious slate of reds for my demanding—"

She presses a warm, breathy kiss behind my ear.

"sexy—"

Her lips trail down my throat, teeth scraping into a bite where my shoulder meets my neck.

"—*ferocious* boss."

Laine pulls me on top of her, until my legs are forked over her lap, stretching me apart. Her index finger runs along the outside of my panties.

With great effort, I push her hand away. "Laine, I—" But the words don't come.

"You need to hear more." Laine's hands encircle my wrists. "You're nervous, and you won't feel better until you know every detail so you can run through all your worst-case scenarios and figure out how to protect yourself from them." The pads of her thumbs run over my pulse points. "From me."

I'm still wearing my T-shirt, but I feel completely naked. "Am I so easy to understand?" I mean it as a joke, but it comes out too soft.

"You're a language that I'm learning, Zoe." A stripe of bright, moonlight falls over her face, so serious and intent. "Maybe I can't speak you fully yet, but I will. I want to *dream* in you." Her hands slide down to braid her fingers with mine. "But until then, please believe me when I say there's nothing you need to worry about. These are just the twists and turns, boss, but I promise there's more road for us up ahead."

I blink, my eyes welling from the magnitude of how much I want to get to that straight line of road with Laine.

"I believe you," I finally say. Or I want to, at least.

I lie down on top of her then, letting someone, for once, bear the full weight of me.

After that, the days move by in a blur, filled to bursting with preparing for harvest and the showcase. It's the nights that slow down long enough for me to savor them. Nights spent in Laine's arms, sleeping beside her, reading beside her. It's unbearably endearing to find Laine with her thick-rimmed glasses on, propped up in bed poring over grape history. *Did you know that the Norton variety was almost lost during Prohibition?* she'd asked last night, and I smiled and shook my head. *Fascinating,* she murmured, then lit up once again with the next interesting fact. *Did you know, did you know, did you know?*

Did *I* know?

How easy this would feel? Falling into step with Laine as though our strides were perfectly matched to carry us from our shared past to some future destination?

No. I didn't know feeling this way was something I could expect from life. Other people fall in love; I just fall.

When I wake, Laine's already up and gone. She's next-level busy right now, and While it's amazing to watch her in her full glorious vintner element—guiding the slow, steady fermentation of the white wines, monitoring the fast and furious fermentation of the reds, pressing, filtering, racking over and over again—I have a to-do list a mile long, too. The showcase is in two weeks, and despite my careful planning, there's no avoiding the crush of work that always comes right before a big event. By the time I get to my office, Matthew, aka Mr. Logistics, has called twice and left seven text messages. It's like having a very concerned second head looking over all my planning and coordination efforts and *tsk*ing nonstop. The man thinks of *everything* that could go wrong. *When was the last time your septic system was serviced? Have you changed the batteries in your fire detectors? Who's your linen rental provider? Have you purchased special event insurance, or is your general policy sufficient? Are you making time for self-care? Can't burn out now!* 😉 The questions go on and on, and after every call, I have a new set of tasks to add to the ones still waiting from the day before.

I sigh into my coffee cup and set about destroying my to-do list. Around eleven a.m., a knock on my office door interrupts my hundredth email of the day.

"Yeah?"

The door opens, and Josiah sticks his head in.

I frown and fully disengage from the keyboard. Josiah's one of our longtime vineyard hands, but I can count the number of times he's entered my office during the workday on one hand.

"Hey, Zoe, you got a minute?"

"Sure, what's going on?"

He wrings his faded orange ball cap in his hands so tightly his knuckles blanch. "Laine pulled down some white samples today. There's something—off about 'em."

This statement looks like it's costing Josiah years off his life. Usually, he's all smiles, tipping that ball cap for every woman, elder, and that one time, the TV as it flashed an image of Queen Elizabeth II. He and Laine took immediately to each other, so I know this isn't mean-spirited. It must be extra hard for him to bring it to me.

"Did you share your thoughts with her?"

"I tried to." He shakes his head forlornly. "She says it's on purpose, but that ain't what Georgia Girls is supposed to taste like. I been helping Cosimo make that wine for the last ten years, and it ain't never tasted like . . . that." His usual smile twists into a disgusted wrinkle across his face, and *fear* shoots through my veins.

I squash it down. Laine's committed to a more organic style of winemaking, meaning less sulfur dioxide treatments throughout, giving an earthier quality to our wines. Maybe that's all it is—a slight change to a well-known wine can feel momentous to a trained palate. I'm hoping it's just Josiah's long familiarity with Georgia Girls that makes any deviation from the standard product feel distasteful, and simultaneously terrified that Laine's iteration of our best-selling crowd-pleaser will turn off our long-time customers, too.

"Thanks for telling me. I'll check on it." I give him a weak smile, letting him leave first. The way he looks both ways down the hall tells me he's as nervous as I am to challenge Laine on her winemaking. God, how's *this* going to go?

I wander into the vats area, the smell of fermenting yeast overwhelming even with the exhaust system on full blast. "Laine?" I call for her again, then feel her arms slip around me.

"Hey, boss!"

I force myself to face her. "Can we talk?"

She leads me by the hand with a wry smile to the quieter end of the winery, where the samples are conveniently still laid out. It's a testament to her confidence that she doesn't look fazed at all. If the roles were reversed, and *my* girlfriend asked *can we talk?* I'd have already dissociated from my body by now.

"What's up?" She brings my hand to her mouth, sliding a finger between her lips. "I don't have time for a quickie, but if you try to convince me . . . I might."

"Are these the samples?" I ask, though I already know they are. "Can I try?"

Laine's playful expression shifts a little, and then *she* appears, Beave, my chief vintner, shoulders thrown back, exuding a competence that turns me on more than her sucking my finger, and that's saying something. "Sure. In fact, I was just about to try the new red blend." Her eyes spark with the energy of expectation, that feeling the moment before your test scores load when you don't know how you did, but you *suspect* you aced it. "I haven't tasted it since I made all those changes to it inspired by your mother's journals—it's been killing me to give it enough time to get over the bottle-shock period. Wanna start there?"

She looks so excited, I can't help but feel it, too. *Please, let Josiah be wrong.* "Absolutely." I force myself to smile as she grabs the sample bottle and uncorks it, pouring us a glass of each. Already, the color is mesmerizing. This is a young red, fresh and fruit-forward, the color a pale ruby filtered by sunlight. If nothing else, Laine's blended our bases into a beautiful wine.

The wine slides against the glass, leaving a wake the color of sunsets that promises a healthy alcoholic content. I bring the glass to my nose, sniffing lightly, then deeply in.

"I'm getting ripe strawberries laced with black currant, pomegranate, the forest after it's rained."

"*Yes!* I get wild roses, strawberry jam, a field in early spring," she says, the excitement in her voice growing. Unable to wait any longer, Laine closes her eyes and lets the wine kiss her lips. The liquid beads on the shell of her mouth before slipping in and down. It's mesmerizing to watch—the thinking divot between her brows faint, then disappearing altogether as her eyes open, widen, and gleam. "It's . . . *Zoe,* stop staring at me and try it!"

I laugh a little, lost in the happiness that's rising on Laine's face like the morning sun I finally tilt the glass up, letting the wine tumble across my lips, pool into my mouth, splash against my tongue. My brows quirk up as the flavors dance across my palate. Balanced, its tannins rich but neutralized, creating a fuller body on my tongue than it has any right to have—everything I could want in a young red wine and more. It's not my mother's red blend, but it is, perhaps, its daughter. The similarities are there as much as the differences. I've only ever tasted my mother's reds in their tawny old age, after mellowing in their bottle homes for years. Laine's version has a delicious bite, softened by the faintest touch of sweet—like the wild blackberries I'd find along the creek at summer's edge. Tart and light, a waking dream, and so, so *complex*. I sip again, trying to hang onto the feeling of it and all the memories it's evoking as it trails down my throat. Fresh spring and lazy summer, crisp fall and the deep grey of winter—this is the kind of wine that takes your moment and builds upon it, whenever it is.

"Laine, it's . . . perfect."

Laine grabs me by the hips, then sinks one hand into my hair, pulling until my chin tips up to take her fevered kiss. The taste of her hard work, her genius mixed with my mother's, of Bluebell Vineyards and all it can give the world, is shared between us. The press of her velvety mouth is as tart and sweet as the wine. "Really?"

"I love it, Laine. It's incredible."

I love you, Laine. You're incredible.

Both thoughts swim through me, both true.

She laughs as she presses her forehead against mine. "God, I'm so relieved. After all those promises I made *Everyday Bon Vivant* . . . I'm so glad I came through for you, baby."

"You did." The smile she gives me is achingly tender as she brushes a loose tear from my cheek with the soft pad of her thumb.

"With a little help from your Ma." She throws her head up to the ceiling. "Thanks, Ma!"

My own laugh bubbles up at that, rising through the heady mix of emotions I'm making space for in my life now. Vulnerability. Love. Trust.

Yes. *Thank you, Mom.*

Laine gives me some of her seltzer water and a hunk of baguette she keeps on hand for palate cleansing, but even still, I'm not prepared for the switch to the Georgia Girls sample. I hold up a hand, spit the wine into the bowl, then take another long drink of seltzer.

"Okay, let me try that again." Laine nods, but her demeanor's changed, too. She watches me closely. I sniff the wine first, and there are all the telltale smells—honeysuckle and peach—but they seem muted somehow. A different presence rises above them, elbowing in at the table. Earthier, different. When the mellow golden wine slides over my tongue, the earthiness is present in the taste, too. All the things I love about Georgia Girls take a back seat to this new flavor, and the effect is disconcerting.

I clear my throat. "This tastes a little . . ."

Off.

Wrong.

Flat-out bad.

"Different," I finish weakly. Laine's fully on edge—I see it in her stance, the pinch of her shoulders. "What's making that . . . difference?"

"I cut back on the sulfur dioxide treatments, to give Brennan's offerings a more organic vibe. That'd help us stand out in the Blue Ridge market, give us a modern edge that'd appeal to eco-conscious consumers."

"But don't the sulfur dioxide treatments prevent bad yeast over-growth that can . . . affect the taste? Could that be what's causing this, uh, flavor?" I don't have the heart to openly criticize what she's done to Georgia Girls. After all, this is next year's batch—it has a whole year after fermentation to settle and develop. Real criticism is premature at this point. But at the same time, Josiah's right. Georgia Girls has never tasted like this, not at any juncture of its process. The bottom of my stomach drops out.

"Yes," Laine grudgingly admits, "but I—"

"Should we do a sulfur dioxide treatment now? Head off this taste before it really digs in?" I know I've cut her off, but my courage is rapidly dwindling, and I need to get this out before the bliss I've been swimming in ever since that night in the grape-crushing barrel convinces me to stay quiet.

Laine frowns, and it feels like I've done something wrong. "I don't think we should give up and turn tail at the first sign of something different. We discussed this—the wines will taste slightly different with more organic processing, but not worse. If anything, it will elevate Bluebell's classic offerings."

I bite my lip, the fear of tanking an entire season of our best-selling wine warring with my desire, my *need* to trust her on this. Finally, I nod. When Electric Daisy, C'est la Grigio, and the rest of our white wine samples present the same off-putting musty taste, I keep my mouth shut. I'm going to trust Laine. It's just Bluebell Vineyards entering our hippie lesbian era, the wine equivalent of hot ladies with hairy pits.

It's gonna be fine.

Laine's relief at getting through all the samples with no more criticism from the peanut gallery is evident, and she shoos me out as soon as we're done. No objections from me. It's the first time we've butted heads over our professional differences since we started shacking up, and it's left us both feeling shaky.

I step out into the warm October afternoon and force my shoulders to relax. The faded red boards of our barn stand in stark contrast to the bright blue of the afternoon sky. The rolling mountains have finally started to let go of summer, their dying leaves crisping into the reddish brown of a good Irish ale. Our vines have begun to turn, as well. Soon they'll retreat into their roots and cozy up for the long winter's sleep. Baahlzebub's out in the field, munching away, and I join him at the fence, rubbing the space between his horns while he chews.

"What do you think, Bub? Will it be okay?"

But the damn goat just butts my hand to keep the rubs coming, no answers in sight. I'm still scratching his bristly fur when beyond the fence line, a figure appears in the trees, walking down the old trail between properties toward us.

I raise a hand over my eyes. "Mrs. Woods? Is that you, or some malevolent specter?"

"Hey there, Zoe!" Molly Woods calls out. "No, it's me—left Rachel at home!"

We both belly laugh at that as she draws closer, an envelope tucked under her arm. "Laine left this at the house the other day, so I thought I'd drop it by. Is she in?"

"She just left for the back fields, but I'll give it to her for you."

"I bet you will." Mrs. Woods passes me the envelope, smiling. "You know, you've always been a part of my family, Zoe, one way or the other. First as Rachel's closest friend, and now as Laine's sweetheart, which Ezra and I cannot be happier about."

My brows flicker together. "I—I'm touched to hear that, but at the soccer game, when y'all found out that we're together, why did you look so . . ." I struggle to find a word that's not accusatory.

"Unhappy?" Molly smiles wistfully. "I'm sorry that's how it appeared. We were more surprised than anything. It's just, we know how tied you are to your mama's vineyard. But if anyone can make long distance work, it'll be you two! It sure is a beautiful property. Once she gets the new vineyard up and running, who knows? Maybe—"

But Molly's words fade against the loud buzz filling my head. I rush through some excuses about needing to get back to work, accepting her hugs and promises to return for another family dinner soon. I'm barely inside my office when I undo the clasp of the envelope, slipping the documents out. The first is a legal description of a plot of land for sale, with pictures attached. A small vineyard rolls out before me on gentle green slopes, its address in Dundee, Oregon. The vines are shabby and unkempt, long neglected, but the property is beautiful. A rehab project, then. Notes are scribbled in the margins in Laine's blocky, precise handwriting, including an amount circled with the words *down payment?* beside it, then *earnest money paid September 15*, which was weeks ago.

I blink down at the words, willing them to disappear. I check the date against my memory. September 15th . . . that would have been a few days after we found Rachel in the winery, a few days after she'd promised me there was nothing planned yet, that I had nothing to worry about.

A few days after she *lied* to me.

Does she think she can convince me to leave everything behind? That I can just walk away from my vineyards, my dreams, my family?

A worse thought hits me in the stomach, taking my breath away.

Or does she know that I can't, and she's going to leave me anyway.

A vibration in my back pocket interrupts my increasing panic, but the calling number is unavailable. I almost let it go to voicemail, but a niggling sense of dread makes me answer.

"Hello?"

"Ciao, Zoe? It's your Uncle Paolo."

I scramble to hold the phone up to my ear better, as though that will make the overseas connection clearer. Anxiety drums against my insides, tapping relentlessly against my pulse points, the back of my neck, my sternum. "Uncle Paolo! Is everything okay?"

The line is quiet for a beat, then Uncle Paolo's words hit me in tall, rushing waves.

Nonna passed away this morning, Zoe Nicoletta.

Your father—he needs you.

You must come as soon as possible.

CHAPTER TWENTY-FOUR

The cell phone drops from my hand. A steady stream of sound rises around me, filling my ears, blocking everything else out. Laine rushes in from outside, and only after her arms wrap around me do I realize that great, tearless sobs are barreling out of me. She's cooing soft, soothing questions at me, asking what's wrong and promising she'll make it better without even knowing what's happened.

But she's leaving, isn't she? After all her promises to include me in her decision, she's taking her family's money and leaving. I break free from her embrace, still gasping for breath.

"Zoe, *please*. Talk to me!" Laine reaches for my face, taking it between her hands. "I wanna be there for you, baby, but you've got to tell me what's going on!"

Her words sting like a rubber band snapping against my tender heart.

"How are you going to be there for me in Oregon?" I hoarse out, my vision narrowing down to her. My Laine, who's been planning her escape from Blue Ridge all summer, who lied to me. Who, it turns out, was never *my Laine* at all.

Laine's eyes widen, confusion and more telling, dismay settling on her face. "What do you mean?"

"You're buying a vineyard."

"*What?* That's not—"

"I saw the documents, Laine!" I jab a finger at the envelope, its contents spilled out across my desk. "You've been planning to leave for months! That weekend trip you took to California—that was really to Oregon to see the property, wasn't it?"

Laine's jaw flexes, her eyes making quick calculations between doubling down on a lie and finally owning up to the truth. "Well, *yes*, but—"

"You lied to me—*why?* So you could use me for a job and sex, then leave me here?"

"No!" Laine's voice is vehement. "When Cosimo gets back, I won't have a job. What am I supposed to do then? I'm a *vintner*, Zoe, you helped me believe that again. I want to make my *own* wine, run my *own* vineyard. This opportunity opened up, and I thought if I could get everything ready for us there while giving *you* enough time to realize we're meant to be together, that when the time came, you'd come with me. We could run the vineyard as equals, baby, a place that could belong to us *both*. Is it so wrong to want to do what I love *with* the woman I love?" Laine holds her hands out to me, her eyes beseeching me to hang on to the life preserver she's offering. But what good is a life preserver in the middle of the ocean with no boat waiting to rescue me, no shoreline in sight?

"I can't leave Bluebell Vineyards." The statement barrels out, my ever-present reflex that kicks her words away from my heart. "And you *know* it!"

"I know that you believe that," Laine says softly. "You see me, Zoe, but I see you, too. You've been unhappy here, and for *so long*. You've chained yourself to this vineyard as though it deserves your life more than you do, but that's not true. You *can* leave. You can have a different life with me. You can let yourself be happy."

"I can't leave my family! I have obligations here, I'm part of something *here*. Bluebell is the one thing I have, and you're asking me to turn my back on it!"

"It's not the one thing you have, Zoe. It's the one thing you choose." Laine's voice crumples at the edges, and it rips my heart in half. "Even over me."

"Then don't make me choose!" I beg. "*Why* are you making me choose?!"

"Because I shouldn't have to give up my dreams to be in this relationship!" Laine finally yells. "I want both!"

I swallow, the painful ache in my throat metastasized throughout my entire chest. "Then that's that. You won't stay, and I won't go."

"Do not *do* that, Zoe! Do not give up on us!" Laine's eyes burn. "We can make it work, if you just *try*—"

"How?!" I demand.

"We'll do long distance, then!" Laine pulls at her hair. "We'll keep trying until—"

"How many months do you think we'll make it once you leave?" My voice trembles in the face of our oncoming reality. "Are we going to talk on the phone every night? Text each other all day long? How many plane tickets can you afford a year? Three? Four? How long before your trips home become little islands of time that grow farther and farther apart, and the visits turn into just sex? Sex I'll be too weak to say no to because—"

Because I love you.

Because I've always loved you.

"Because I'm *pathetic*!" I hurl the word at her, willing her to see me as I really am. "It'll be like Harlow all over again, *no strings attached*! Well, I'm all strings, Laine, a messy, tangled knot of them, and those strings keep me here."

Keep me trapped here.

"This is why I didn't want to tell you yet! I knew you'd use Oregon as proof I don't love you so you can throw us away, because despite everything I've done to show you how I feel, it's still easier for you to believe that I'm lying than believe that someone could love you. Well, I love you, Zoe, and I won't let you tell me I don't. When Cosimo returns, *then* we can figure out—"

My dad. I press a hand to my chest, as though I can brace my lungs from the outside in, willing them to expand properly. Laine's form swims in front of my eyes.

"Zoe, you need to sit down. I think you're having a panic attack." Laine takes my arm, and I snatch it out of her hands, then stumble. With a grimace, she grabs me around the waist and hauls me into the tasting room, taking no heed of my flailing arms. I sag against her, struggling to breathe, and let her set me down in a chair. She returns a second later with a glass of water and squats before me.

"Drink this." Her tone brooks no argument, so I take the glass and try, but my hand's shaking so hard that water spills down my chin. Laine steadies the glass before I drop it altogether. "Now tell me what's going on."

"It's my Nonna," I finally gasp out. "I just got the call that she's— she's—passed away, and my dad's not—handling it well." My voice breaks, remembering the vacant expression my father wore for years following Mom's death. I *knew* he wasn't strong enough to go out there alone, to live alongside another person he loved and watch them die. "He needs me out there, but how can I go? The festival's only two weeks away—there's so much to do, how am I going to get it all done, how can I—"

Laine gathers me in her arms and shushes me against her shoulder, and I let all the questions resolve into wordless gasping sobs again. Landing the showcase was a dream come true, our big chance to break free from our suffocating financial position. The one thing, ironically, that could've maybe made Laine's dreams of taking me away possible. But how can I manage the showcase and bring my broken father home, too?

"Here's what's going to happen." Laine's hand is firm against the back of my head, the pressure there helping to stifle the fear burgeoning in my chest. Fear for my father. Fear of ruining our vineyard's big chance. Fear of not being enough, of never being enough, to hold up the world around me. How am I going to hold it together now?

How am I going to hold myself together *without Laine?*

"I'm going to buy us some plane tickets. We'll get on the next flight to Italy, and then—"

"We can't both go to Italy, Laine!" I yank my head back and disengage from her arms. "I'm not even sure I can go!"

"Of course we can go," Laine says firmly. "Nothing's more important than being there for your family, not even the showcase." She tries to pull me back to her chest, but this time, I don't let her.

"What do *you* know about being there for your family? You left them before, and you're going to leave them all over again!"

Laine swallows. "I did. And I know now it's a mistake, choosing work over the people you love, and I'll never let distance come between us again." A thin current of hurt spikes her words. "But that's a mistake you don't need to make, too."

Is she talking about me and Italy, or me and her? Because Bluebell Vineyards has never been a choice for me. It's all I have. It's all I've ever been given.

The tears come then, finally, and I let them pull me down, down, down.

In the end, Laine handles everything. She alternates checking on me with calling in favors from our friends, finding my passport, and booking my travel arrangements while I lie curled up in bed, falling apart. The tears break me down, but they put me back together again, too. When the heaving sobs finally stop, I'm exhausted and devastated, but I'm also breathing normally again, and the imprisoning spiral of my thoughts has slowed from mad carousel of terror to the stable, sleepy swings of a pendulum. Back and forth, up and down, the grief and fear rise within me, then retreat again.

We don't talk much. She holds me, though, all night long, and in the small hours of the morning. I lie there, memorizing the feel of her skin against mine. The warm brush of her breath across my neck. The weight of her arm resting on my hip, fingers splayed across my stomach. Her body is so relaxed lying atop mine, as though it's easy for her to trust in my solidity. As though she doesn't live in fear that I'll disappear. Maybe because she knows that I can't. Like Rapunzel trapped in her tower, I'm as much a part of this vineyard as its wine.

At the unholy hour of four a.m., Teddy comes ripping into our parking lot like braking is for amateurs, my ride to the airport. Laine and I are outside waiting for him, the small suitcase she packed waiting by my feet like an obedient dog. Teddy comes to a stop right in front of us, his window rolling down. He's wearing his gold wire aviators propped on his head even though the sun won't rise for hours.

"Get in, loser, we're going to Italy!"

I huff out a confused sound. Teddy pops the trunk, and there's barely enough room for my small carry-on amid a suite of matching designer luggage.

"Um . . ." I stand there, frowning at his open trunk. "Teddy?"

"Once I decided to take your mopey ass to the airport, I thought, why stop at the boring part?" he yells over his shoulder. "You need me and my sunshine, Zoe. Now get your ass in."

I turn to Laine. "Did you do this?"

Laine shrugs one shoulder, the corner of her mouth quirked up to match. Her eyes are dark and tired, though, worn thin from the weight of my despair. "You won't let me come with you, but you never said Teddy couldn't." She takes me by the wrists, pulls me to her, and after a second's hesitation, kisses me.

Teddy lays on the horn.

Laine locks her eyes on mine, pushes my hair behind my ear. "You take care of *you*, Zoe. Leave the rest of the world to the rest of the world, okay?"

I nod, a hollow promise. It all falls on me, one way or another.

Her goodbye's still lingering on my lips as I close the car door.

Teddy exhales loudly and throws us into drive. "*Finally.* Jesus."

"Thanks for doing this, Teddy," I say quietly to his profile, framed by the dark mountains beyond.

"What, canceling Mr. Gibbons's root canal? Gladly." Teddy turns on his blinker for a split second before jutting into the next lane. "That old bastard can go to the twisted sadist down in Jasper for all I care."

I sigh against the window at the world rushing past us.

"But, Zoe?"

"Yeah?"

"You better have TSA pre-check, so help me God, I will *not* wait for a bitch."

By the time we're settled into our assigned seats, two middle ones in the long middle row on a massive plane *stuffed* with loud, excited high school students on a field trip, Teddy's had two spiked coffees, a small meltdown in the Popeyes line, and a full recovery when he found the newest Alexis Hall rom-com at the bookstore. I'm *infinitely* glad he's here. The world's indignities and insults never land as hard when Teddy's there to chew them out for me.

Something in my expression stops him from diving into his book, though. With a sigh, he closes it and takes out his earbuds, aka *teen-murder-prevention devices* as he calls them.

"All right, Zoe. Out with it."

"Huh?"

"Your fears. Your worries. Everything that's troubling your pensive little mind."

"Hey," I frown. "My mind is really big."

"At least ten inches, sure, whatever." He rolls his eyes. "Point is, let's get it out, right now. This is all part of the *Teddy Does Italy* package. Free therapy."

I start to argue. Push away my own needs, like always, but I'm too tired to pretend, and there's too much wrong to keep it all bottled inside, so I pick the biggest thing, the thing that's scaring me the most.

I blow out a deep breath. "I'm really worried about Dad."

Teddy's face is serious. "That makes sense. He didn't handle your mother's death well, and you're worried the death of his mother will bring all that old dysfunction back."

I nod, my pulse picking up in tempo just from hearing him say it aloud.

"Okay, let's play out that scenario," Teddy says, his matter-of-fact tone bracing. "We get there, your dad's extremely distraught. What will you do?"

"I—don't know. Take him home?" I breathe in for four, out for six, willing my lungs to stop constricting in my chest.

"Well, that's not that hard. We know how to pack a bag and buy a plane ticket. Then when we get home, let's say he's all jacked up. Then what?"

I blink. "Um. Get him into therapy?"

"Right!" Teddy nods encouragingly. "That takes making a call. Maybe finding an insurance card, not that they'll pay anything, the bastards. We can do that, right?" He puts a hand on my shoulder, squeezes, and all I can do is nod again.

"They don't teach therapy in dental school, but I think I understand all the same," Teddy says, his voice softer than usual. "The first time your dad checked out, you were a helpless, scared kid who'd just lost her mom. You needed your dad to take care of you, and he couldn't. But you're not that kid now, Zoe. You're a grown woman, and your dad's mental state can't threaten your survival anymore, even if it *feels* like it will, in here." He taps lightly on the space above my heart.

I sit with that for a moment. The panic and fear I've been feeling both come from the same dark blot in my heart. When I think about it, most of my hard feelings originate there. The anxiety that edges every venture that's not business, the resigned feeling of doom that escorts every romantic attempt I make, the loneliness.

"How long does it take for a bruised heart to heal?" I swallow, my throat tight.

"I don't know." Teddy takes my hand in his. "But it'll go a lot faster if you stop pressing your thumb into it all the time."

I shake my head, annoyed at how simple he makes it sound. "What does that even mean, though? Just . . . stop hurting?"

Teddy rolls his eyes and smiles. "You're such a little storm cloud, Zoe Brennan! You're so sure you're meant to suffer that you live your life waiting for the next bad thing to happen."

"But bad things *do* happen, Teddy!" I'm tempted to list each of my life's tragedies as proof to wipe that smug expression off his face when he surprises me by nodding vehemently.

"They sure do! So what good does it do worrying all the time when they're *not* happening? You're living in what Brené Brown calls the *stress rehearsal*, baby, but no amount of worrying can prepare you for life's real punches." He leans close to my face. "So. *Stop. Flinching.*"

I sit back with a loud exhale, and the two teen girls sitting in front of us snap back to their normal seated positions, as though they haven't been gaping at us through the gap between seats.

"Hope she's listening," one says as she puts her AirPods in.

"Love that growth for her," the other replies, then leans her seat back right into my legs.

"Teddy, just one more thing."

"What is it, baby?"

"You read Brené Brown?"

Teddy sticks his index finger straight in my face. "You bet your ass I do."

CHAPTER TWENTY-FIVE

Cobblestones are quaint as hell, but I'd give my soul for a smooth, paved sidewalk right now. Instead, I'm dragging my little carry-on and Teddy's huge suitcase up a steep alley in the outskirts of Montepulciano over a thousand little speed bumps.

"Mamma mia!" Teddy cries beneath the rest of his luggage. "Prego! Ragu! Newman's Own—"

"Teddy," I wheeze out. "Stop that. It's obnoxious."

"That's a," Teddy says louder. The spry asshole isn't even winded. "Spicy meata-ball!"

I groan. While Teddy's no-nonsense energy kept me from fear-spiraling all day, I don't know what I'll find waiting for us at Nonna's house. Dad, listless in a chair? The aunts, uncles, and cousins I barely know all in black and silently weeping? What if Nonna's body is in there? Do Italians perform wakes? I'm ashamed of how little I know about my culture, and worse, how little I know my family.

"This the place?" Teddy asks as I stop in front of a house with red shutters. I stare at it for a long minute, trying to reconcile it against a memory of my Nonna's house, but . . . there's nothing there. I glance down at the instructions on my phone, but the notes I took read like abstract poetry.

"I, um. I—" I try to clear the feelings out of my throat, but the words warble in there, stuck.

"Hey, look at me." Teddy grabs me by both shoulders, forcing my attention on him. "You're freaking out, but remember—you're not alone here, and our to-do list for tonight is very short: find your family's house, pee, be there for your dad. Okay?"

I swallow and try to breathe. "Okay."

Teddy nods curtly, then snatches my phone from my hand. "Now let me figure out where the hell we are, you're absolutely *dumb* with grief."

Teddy leads the way down the lane, and I follow gladly behind, dissociating into the sights of this small, medieval city. Its walls are the color of Chardonnay, but beneath the sunset sky, everything's turned a coppery rosé. I drink it in, this place where generations of my father's family lived, worked, loved, and died. It's a strange feeling to be reunited with a place where your roots grow so deep, yet you know so little. Like the confusion you feel when a stranger calls your name, looking expectantly at you, asking with their eyes, *do you remember me?*

But you don't. You really, really wish you did, but you don't, and the embarrassed disappointment flows between you both.

Finally, Teddy stops in front of a low garden gate, the peach-colored stone house beyond hugged by ivy. An arched green door sits at its middle, half open.

Teddy gives me a bracing smile. "Okay, this is it, and even if it isn't, I'm peeing here, anyway." He pushes me forward. "You first, bambino."

"Bambin-*a*."

"Bambin-*x*."

Fair enough. I take a deep breath and open the gate. Images of my father at his worst in the days after Mom's death flash through my mind. When I found him passed out drunk on our kitchen floor, and I screamed because I thought he was dead. Standing in front of our bathroom mirror before the funeral, a long cut on his cheek from shaving bleeding freely into our sink. Lying in bed, clutching her pillow and crying so hard he threw up. Even worse, the silence that followed all that outward despair, that lingered for years. The interminable quiet of our home.

"Hello?" With an uncertain hand, I push the door open all the way. This home, however, is *not* quiet.

"*Qualcuno ha visto Fredo?*" A woman in a black Britney Spears sweatshirt barrels down the staircase directly in front of the door. "Fredo?! Where is that little shit!"

"Lucia, *relax*!" comes a thoroughly unconcerned voice above the general din, speaking Italian, English, and even a bit of French. "He'll turn up by suppertime."

"He stole my cell phone again, so I will *not* relax!" Only then does Lucia, one of my many cousins, clock me standing there on the threshold. Her angry face transforms into a wide grin, and it's shocking how much we look alike.

"*Dio mio*, Zoe's here, Zio Paolo!" Lucia envelops me in a big, perfumed hug, then thrusts me away almost as fast. "Have *you* seen little Fredo?"

I blink. "Ah, nope."

"That little *shit*." Lucia stomps past me, pausing only to eye Teddy and his bags. "Ooh, *bello*, I love your luggage!"

"Why, thank you!" Teddy says, hand pressed coyly to his chest. He leans in. "If I see Fredo, I'm getting your phone back. I got you, baby."

Lucia nods, satisfied, an alliance formed between them quicker than you can say *prego*. Then she's out the door and screaming for Fredo down the lane.

Uncle Paolo appears, tall and handsome as ever. "Zoe Nicoletta!" He kisses me on both cheeks. "I am so glad you are here."

"Me too." He smells like leather and the newest Hugo Boss cologne, the familiarity like solid ground. "Where's Dad?"

Uncle Paolo pushes me back gently, eyes flickering over my face with a sad, tender smile. "He's in the kitchen, where else? I'll take you to him.

But first tell me, who is your friend?" Paolo lifts an eyebrow as he takes in Teddy's Nike tracksuit, matching sneakers, and suite of bags lining the walkway. "I thought you were for the ladies, Zoe?"

"*Ugh*, please! I am her very dear *friend* who is for the *gentlemen*." Teddy brushes off his shoulders as if to get rid of Uncle Paolo's misplaced heterosexual assumptions. "I'm Teddy."

"*Un altro omosessuale!*" Aunt Cecilia says as she bustles past, arms full of blankets. "It's Club Europa in here!"

Uncle Paolo rolls his eyes and grins, then steps aside to let us in. "Welcome to Club Europa, eh?"

It takes a solid fifteen minutes for Uncle Paolo to escort us from the front door to the kitchen due to the nonstop parade of laughing relatives, questions as to mine and Teddy's relationship status, shocked proclamations of *More homosexuals? Welcome!*, and lots of hugs. The relief at the happy, bustling atmosphere inside my Nonna's house is only skin-deep, though, because everywhere there is evidence of why we're all here. The house is jammed full of people, but not my grandmother. Instead of Nonna, piles of flowers and bottles of her favorite amaretto sit in her armchair by the window. Suitcases and bags spill from the corners and line the hallway from all the family in from out of town. Somewhere, someone is crying.

I silently plead that it's not Dad.

When I duck beneath the low arch of the doorframe into the kitchen, I spot my father's shoulders hunched over a simmering pot on the stove. He's not crying, though. A strange, humming sound is coming from his throat.

He's . . . *singing*?

"Dad?" I let my purse fall to the floor.

He drops the spoon in the sauce and whirls around, joy dancing in his bright eyes. His cheeks are fuller now, rosy from the kitchen heat, and his beard looks shinier, too. His hair is neatly trimmed and pushed back in classic silver-threaded waves, his pants sharply tailored, his button-down crisp and protected beneath one of Nonna's old aprons. Evidence of Uncle Paolo's cosmopolitan influence is clear as day. "Zoe Nicoletta!"

"Dad?" I repeat dumbly in the face of this gorgeous older man who shares the same eyes as my father, but not much else. He takes me into his arms and squeezes, rocking from foot to foot in a long embrace. One hand cradles the back of my head as he murmurs *Zoe Nicoletta* and *my little Zoe* over and over again, and then *I'm* the one crying because I've missed him so, so much.

"Oh, it is so good to see your beautiful face." Dad releases me to hold my chin, turning my face this way and that to get a good, long look at me. "Being in love looks good on you, bella."

"What?" I sputter out a tearful laugh. "What are you talking about?"

Then Dad shocks me even more by throwing his head back and laughing, too. "Zoe Nicoletta, surely you knew I would be checking up on you?" He waggles his eyebrows, which, I swear to god, I have *never* seen him do. "Still mad I hired Laine without asking?"

"Okay, that's it. What's going on here?" I gesture back and forth between us. This is *Dad*. He's supposed to be *sad*. It rhymes, even! "I came here to be with you because you needed me, but you seem fine."

"I knew you would come for me, Zoe Nicoletta, but more than anything, you needed to come for *you*."

"What are you talking about?"

Just then, Uncle Paolo busts in, his arm wrapped around a disbelieving Teddy's shoulders, promising him a glass of Montepulciano's signature Brunello di Montalcino that's worth staining your teeth for. Teddy looks intensely skeptical.

Paolo releases Teddy and slings his arm around Dad instead. "Doesn't your father look so well here, Zoe Nicoletta? Back in his homeland, surrounded by family, in the kitchen where he belongs!" For the first time since I've arrived, Dad's smile falters, and he gives Uncle Paolo a strange, loaded look before shaking off his arm and returning to the sauce.

"I hope you both are hungry," Dad calls over his shoulder.

We eat and drink late into the night, crammed in across three rooms loaded with food, wine, and laughter. Any awkwardness I felt at not knowing my own family wears off after the second glass of Brunello, happily drifting in and out of the roar of conversation and hilarious family politics. After dinner, I lose Teddy to Uncle Paolo and some of the other cousins, who excitedly discuss the possibility of going to the *real* Club Europa later that night. I'm not exactly sure where Teddy and I are supposed to sleep until Aunt Cecilia announces she's waking the butcher down the street who, for some reason, will help us solve this problem. When she shows up triumphantly brandishing a ring of old keys ten minutes later, I realize it's because Teddy and I will be staying in the little apartment above the butcher shop that may or may not be a part-time meat locker.

I do *not* share this information with Teddy.

After the first wave of cousins leaves for their homes and hotels, then the second, I pull up my messages to text Laine. Up until now, everything I've sent has been by way of update, opting for nice, safe facts. *Checked in. On the plane. Arrived.* Now as I stare at the blinking cursor, the facts no longer feel quite as safe. *I'm sorry for freaking out. I love you, too, and I've never felt so scared in my entire life.* More than anything: *I don't want you to leave.*

I close the messages app and sigh. Dad finds me on the couch between aunts listening to a heated debate over club football teams I can barely follow. He places his hand on my shoulder. "Zoe Nicoletta, come have a glass of wine with me, yes?"

I follow him into the back garden, lit overhead by the same string lights Dad likes at home. "Did you put these up?"

"Nonna loved sitting among her flowers, but the summer heat would get to her. I hung these up so we could enjoy the evenings out here after the heat of the day had passed." He smiles ruefully. "She gave a lot of feedback."

I smile, imagining Dad on the stepladder while Nonna instructed him from her chair. "She must've loved having you here."

He nods, then takes a sip of his wine. "She did," he says. "I've loved being here, too." His eyes watch mine carefully, but I'm not sure why. I'm glad he doesn't regret leaving home for the last seven months. All my fears of finding Dad broken by grief have been eradicated, and the relief is overwhelming.

I swirl the wine in my glass, remembering how Lucia and Teddy pounced on Fredo the moment the scrawny fourteen-year-old stepped into the house and fleeced him of the stolen phone. "We need to be better about visiting, Dad. Everyone's great, and it's so beautiful here." Beyond the garden fence, the city's ancient walls loom, the stone town like a jaunty cap upon this rolling mountain's head.

"You should visit more, that is true." Dad clears his throat. "But I won't because, well . . . I've decided to stay."

"*What?*"

Dad puts his glass down, then leans forward and puts his head in his hands. "I want to stay here, Zoe Nicoletta. Indefinitely. Forever, maybe."

I laugh, though it's anything but amused. "I don't *understand*, Dad. You've said nothing about this before now, you got Uncle Paolo to lure me out here saying *you needed me*, so I drop everything to come out here and save you only to find you're abso-fucking-lutely fine and having the time of your life, and now you want to leave home forever?"

"I want to be with my family, Zoe, I—"

"*I'm* your family, Dad!" I jab my heart, hard, with my thumb. "Me! Your daughter!"

Dad sighs and runs his fingers through his waves. "I understand why you're upset. This is all coming as a big shock to you, and it will take some time to get used to the idea." He says this with *zero irony*, even though it's almost verbatim what he said when he told me he was going to Italy in the first place.

"God, Dad, could you be any worse at communicating?!" I clench my jaw to keep from crying. I'm so goddamn tired of *crying*. "Maybe I wouldn't be so shocked if you'd actually talk to me." The tears come anyway.

"I'm sorry, Zoe Nicoletta. I've handled this all wrong." Dad rubs his hand over the day's stubble, morose for the first time since I arrived. Of course, I caused it. Or his crushing sense of fatherly duty to me, anyway.

"Why, Dad? Tell me why you want to stay." I sniff, wiping my eyes on the back of my sleeve. "Really fucking explain yourself for once."

Dad breathes in deeply through his nose. "I will—*try*, Zoe Nicoletta. It doesn't come easy to me, but you deserve the best I can give." He clasps his hands together, the string lights flickering across his thoughtful face.

"Moving back here, to a place where I existed before your mother, it's woken up a part of me that I'd long forgotten, Zoe. I feel . . . lighter here. More myself than I have in decades." He pauses, really *searching* for a way to make me understand without making me feel bad at the same time.

"*I* make you sad, don't I?" There it is, the question that's loomed over me ever since Mom died and Dad stopped looking at me. I've never spoken it aloud, afraid that it would give the words truth. But I'm too tired right now for anything *but* the truth—I just want to know. "I remind you of Mom."

"No!" Dad sits up straight with a flash. "Zoe Nicoletta, you are my dearest thought. You are the sweetness that runs through my life like a river. Yes, I see bits of your mother in you—the way you laugh when something surprises you, how you always look for the moon. But they don't make me sad. I cherish these glimpses of my beloved when they appear. Mostly, I see *you*, Zoe Nicoletta. My sweet, brilliant, lonely Zoe." He touches my cheek gently. "But that last part's changing now, isn't it?"

He brushes my tears away, not waiting for me to answer. "Great loves change us. One minute, you are yourself, growing straight up into the sky. But then, someone comes along that challenges the sun for your attention. You grow toward them, entwining your life with theirs, sharing the same water, soil, air, and light. You hold them up as best you can, and they do the same for you. Until one of you no longer can stand." He smiles then, though his eyes fill with tears. "And the other one has to let go. I've never been good at letting go, my Zoe, and I'm afraid I've never taught you how to, either."

I open my mouth to respond, but a small sob comes out instead. Dad gathers me in his arms and holds me close. "It can be scary, letting yourself need someone, especially when you've lost someone you needed so much before. We both know loss, Zoe Nicoletta, but where we've gone wrong is fearing it. The truth is, when I first came out here, I was not okay. Seeing Nonna so weak terrified me, and the guilt of all the years spent not visiting her in healthier days ate me alive. I was so afraid of losing her that I was wasting the time we had left."

Dad holds me back far enough so he can look at me, his eyes shining and tender. "It was Nonna who set me straight, Zoe Nicoletta. Even in her illness, she could see I was committing the same sins I did when your mother got sick. Wasting her time by counting the minutes we had left together, mourning each one as it slipped from my fingers instead of using that time to love her. What a miserly way to live." Dad shakes his head, his lips pressed in a grim line. "If I could go back, Zoe Nicoletta, I'd do things so differently with your mother. I'd be there for her, really *be there*, instead of mourning her before she even passed. And I'd be there for you, too. I'd show you that we are strong enough for great love, even when it entails great loss." His smile is forlorn, laden with the relieved exhaustion that follows when you're finally allowed to set down a heavy burden. "I am so sorry I wasn't there for you. I am even sorrier that I taught you to fear love, instead of cherishing it. My only consolation is that you've found love, anyway, and together, you and Laine can run Bluebell and keep your dreams alive, too."

I love my father, I always have. Even at his lowest and most broken, I never begrudged him the pain he felt, or how it took him so far away from me. It'd be like blaming a tree for being struck by lightning, then judging it for its charred, ruined trunk. Sure, it was once a beautiful tree that gave you shade and fruit, but bad shit happens, and this stump of a father is all that remains.

I never expected him to grow back. I never thought he could.

But he did. He has. He *is*.

And it's going to change everything.

Well, that's the problem with making plans around other people, isn't it? Laine's words come back to me

Laine wants to run her own vineyard, make her own wines, be her own vintner. Something she's wanted *forever*. All that's holding her back from her dreams is her promise to stay at Bluebell until Dad comes home, and now, he never is. Would she accept Bluebell Vineyards in place of the fresh start in Oregon? Can I let her change my mother's vineyard enough to make it hers, too? It's a huge request, asking her to change her plans for me to stay on and live season to season at my struggling little vineyard. Dad did that for Mom and look what it got him—a twenty-year depression and an identity crisis he's only just now confronting. I can't *expect* Laine to hang up her dreams and stay in Blue Ridge forever any more than I can expect Dad to.

But can I *hope*? I take a long pull of my dwindling wine, letting the plummy burn clarify against my tongue, considering what that would really look like. *Feel* like. Laine, taking over for Dad permanently.

"Won't you miss the vineyard?"

"The vineyard, yes. You, more than anything. But making wine? No."
Dad laughs softly. "That was more of my refusing to let go, I'm afraid.
Your mother begged me to sell Bluebell before she died."

I choke on my actual breath. "She *what?*"

Dad nods, swirling his wine. "She didn't want us to stay at the vineyard out of grief. She wanted us to make new lives for ourselves, follow
new dreams. Maybe even here, in Italy." He closes his eyes and slowly
shakes his head. "She knew *exactly* what would happen if we stayed at Bluebell, and I'm so sorry, Zoe Nicoletta, because I chose that life of grief for
us, anyway."

I sit back, stunned. Mom wanted to *sell* Bluebell Vineyards? Just like
that, the cornerstone of my whole reality, the basis of every big decision
I've ever made, sifts through my fingers like sand. This whole time, I've
been guarding her vineyard with my life, bartering days, weeks, months,
and years to keep her dreams safe from the passage of her own time. But
I see all of that for what it was now.

My choice.

It was always just my choice.

"At the very least, I should've hired another vintner years ago, someone with real passion for the work. I simply could not bear another person
taking your mother's place, though." Dad reaches over and pats my hand.
"The beauty of that work falling to the woman *you* love is not lost on me.
Life is funny that way, bella."

How his words squeeze my heart.

"I'm going to miss you so much," I whisper, and this time, I take him
into my arms and hug him tight.

CHAPTER TWENTY-SIX

Nonna's funeral was on an orange October afternoon in the small church up the lane. She'd been very specific in her wishes—cremation, a short Mass, and a long party—and we complied. After we opened her house to friends and family to visit her urn, Dad and his brothers and sisters scattered her ashes in her garden and surreptitiously around her favorite spots in Montepulciano, as she'd instructed. It seemed a little weird to want your earthly remains at your favorite fishmonger's stall, but the fishmonger removed his hat and held it to his chest as they did the deed, even saying a few words remembering Nonna for her kindness and impeccable taste in seafood. It was a beautiful day and a sad day, all wrapped up in love for the woman she'd been, the family she'd created, and the life she'd lived.

I'm profoundly glad I came. I only wish I'd done it sooner, so I could have more memories of Nonna than the precious handful I gathered during my childhood. Taking time off from the vineyard, traveling here, visiting relatives—I wish I'd made space in my life to *experience* my life and the others in it, long before now. All my fears of leaving Bluebell Vineyards in the hands of my friends have come to naught. The love and support so freely given by my community has been nothing short of amazing, leaving me choked up and humble. Hannah's jumped in on festival preparations with truly unhinged positivity. Tristan's called in moonlighters to cover tasting room shifts for the next week and is attacking the vineyard's normal paperwork with gusto and ease. Even Matthew at *Everyday Bon*

Vivant has pitched in, commandeering my to-do list like a pirate greedy for logistics.

And Laine. Even though I panicked, and showed her, yet again, that I struggle to believe in her love, she's been there for me, supporting me from afar. Before the plane takes off, I send the text I should've sent every minute I've been away.

Zoe

> I love you, Laine Woods. Everything will be okay because we'll make it okay.

Somehow, my brain adds quietly.

The attendant walks by, and I hurry to turn my phone off, settling in for the long flight home. The sprawling metropolis of Rome disappears as our plane lifts above the thin sheaf of clouds. I sigh, and Teddy turns in his seat and squints at me, as though he's assessing my mental health.

"So . . . ," Teddy begins. "Lots to process. Should we start with how you're going to tell Laine everything as soon as you get home, or how sexy Cosimo looks in Italian menswear?"

"*Jesus*, Teddy, can you *not* sweat my dad to my face?"

"No," Teddy replies simply. "I cannot. Guess we better start with Laine then, hmm?"

I heave another sigh, effectively trapped. "Look, I want to tell her everything, but I don't want her to feel pressured to stay out of guilt to keep my struggling vineyard afloat. I want her to *want* to stay, you know? If she knows Dad's never coming back, how will *I* know that—"

"That she's staying out of love for you while *also* staying because that decision will truly make her happiest, without secretly holding it against you for the rest of your lives?" Teddy arches an eyebrow.

I grimace. "Yes?"

"You won't! You can't know that. And this isn't some test you can give her to see if she passes or fails."

"*Test*? I don't *test*—"

Teddy leans his head back and groans. "I've developed a theory about you, would you like to hear it?"

"Not really," I grumble, now regretting getting seats together.

"Understandable, personal growth is always a drag when it's happening to you," Teddy says, drumming his fingers on the armrests. "But I'm going to tell you anyway because I love you, and I'm tired of watching you sabotage your life."

Teddy stops to clear his throat, and then, in a tone he usually reserves for discussing money, he says, "Zoe, my dear, you are a beautiful, whip-smart, delightful little coward. You're terrified of being hurt and even more terrified of being loved. So instead of putting your neck out and showing someone how *you* feel, you withdraw and wait for them to prove how much they like you."

I rear back. "I do not!"

Teddy looks down his nose at me, and without breaking stride, continues. "Maybe your suitor is brave, so they text you first, ask you out. You have a good time, you go home, but then, you do it all over again. You wait for them to prove to you, again, how they feel. And if they don't text you, if they *dare* wait to see if you'll initiate contact first? You chalk it up to another rejection, the one you were so afraid would happen that you willed it into existence. It's like giving them a never-ending test that, even if they pass it, you force them to take again and again, every day. Do you see the problem with this approach?"

Is that really what I do? A dozen tiny relationships click through my mind like PowerPoint slides, throwing themselves into the ring for reassessment. Did Kai really ghost me? Or did she ask me on three dates and

wait for me to take a turn doing the asking? Have I really willed each of
my many rejections into existence?

"Jesus," I hiss out, then unscrew the cap off the mini wine bottle he
hands me. He must've shaken down the attendants when we boarded the
plane. "What the hell have I done?"

"Tried your very hardest to protect your heart," Teddy says matter-of-
factly. "Have you ever heard of your inner firefighters?"

"Huh? No," I mumble, still trying to process the bomb he's dropped
on me. "Firefighters?"

"Inside every person is a team of firefighters. They're trained to put
out fires and save you, even if they destroy everything else in your house.
Sometimes the damage they cause trying to save you is worse than
whatever made you summon them in the first place."

"What are you saying? Is this more Brené Brown?"

Teddy reaches over and places his hand on my arm. "I'm saying you
have a large, robust team of firefighters, Zoe Brennan. A whole sexy calendar's worth." He smirks. "Maybe you should try giving them a night off
sometime, eh? Maybe a whole year."

I bite my lips, and after a long second, nod. "So how do I do that?"

"You've got be vulnerable, baby. Go home and tell Laine everything.
What you really want, and what you're afraid of, lay out all your options.
No more secret tests. Then, let *her* decide what she wants to do next. You
don't get to be her boss on this one, and if she chooses to be the Cosimo
to your Julie, then that's *her* choice that *she* gets to make, just like your
dad did. But Laine can't make that decision without all the information.
You've got to be brave enough to give it to her."

I take a deep breath, then exhale slowly and place my hand over his
and squeeze. "Thank you, Teddy. For being here. For knowing me."

"It's an honor and a privilege, and sometimes, a goddamn circus, and
I've loved every minute of it. Just don't mess this up, all right?" Teddy

leans back in his seat and closes his eyes. "I like that bossy butch know-it-all wine snob."

Me too, Teddy. Me too.

The longer the flight goes on, the more restless I am to see Laine. Now that Teddy's convinced me of the path forward, I'm dying to tell her everything, to apologize for how I acted and present *Bluebell Vineyards* and *me* and *forever* to her and beg her to stay. Laine hasn't texted much over the days I've been away. I keep telling myself it's because she's beyond busy orchestrating the secondary fermentations for the reds, finishing up the blending and bottling of our whites, and holding down the fort at large as we prepare for the showcase, which is now a mere eight days away. But I can't help feeling intensely vulnerable about breaking down in front of her the way I did. I haven't had a panic attack in decades, but my protective skin slipped off that night, exposing the raw animal of hurt I've kept leashed and hidden away.

If she ran from me now, after seeing all that? I wouldn't even blame her.

I've reached out to Tristan and Hannah, too, both of whom have been quick to reassure me everything's fine, but not much else. It's strange, honestly. Like they're all conspiring to create a real separation between me and the vineyard.

I mean, how *dare* they? Also, well played, because I finally get just how much I've let Bluebell rule my life and the consequences of my conscious submission to its never-ending work.

And all this time, Mom wanted to *sell* it.

As soon as we touch down in Atlanta, I turn off airplane mode but frown when I see that Laine hasn't texted me back. It's seven p.m., which is normally when she takes a dinner break, so I call her but the phone rings and rings. A small spurt of fear erupts in my chest that continues to grow as we deplane, get all four of Teddy's bags and file a missing claim for mine because somehow, my single suitcase has been lost, and find our car in the economy lot. She doesn't answer any of my calls or texts.

Is she okay? Did she fall into a vat? Suffocate from the toxic carbon dioxide pumping out of our fermenting reds?

Or . . . did she leave?

Did she assume Dad would be with me and leave as soon as she could, saving herself from having to break it off to my face? Teddy doesn't even bother trying to call off my emotional firefighters or whatever for the last hour's drive, letting me place call after call to everyone in my phone, looking for answers and finding none.

I can't get ahold of anybody. What the *hell* is going on?

By the time Teddy pulls into our parking lot, it's almost ten, and my chest feels too small for the heart pumping erratically within it. The car is still running when I throw open my door and run up to the winery, where the lights are all on, the exhaust system thrumming loudly.

"Laine, are you in here?" I call as soon as I open the door.

I'm not sure what I expected, but it wasn't a half dozen people dressed in hazmat suits surrounding Laine, who's loping back and forth like an agitated wolf. Her hands hang by her sides, fingers splayed wide yet clenched in place like claws. She's the only one wearing normal clothes, though they're wrinkled and dirty, like she hasn't changed in days. She spins on her heels when she hears my voice, her eyes red and ruined.

"Zoe, baby," she says, her usual deep, smooth voice scraped raw. "I've fucked up so bad."

"Brettanomyces," Jamal confirms from behind the clear plastic face panel of his hood. "The numbers are completely out of control." He drops the sample vials in a baggie, the pity radiating off him in waves. "I'm so sorry, y'all."

"Brettanomyces," I repeat dumbly, still trying to process the information thrown at me in the last five minutes. "But Dad always tests for it—that's part of our precautions to keep it out of the wine." I turn back to Laine. "Did you follow the standard hygiene protocols?"

Laine nods vehemently. "To the letter! Only—"

"Only *what*?" My voice comes out sharper than I mean it to, but reality feels like an avalanche right now, breaking away in huge, head-crushing chunks, coming down on me all at once. The panic I've felt all evening finally has something to feast upon, tainting me the same way Brettanomyces has our entire line of wines for next season. I don't know much about the fermentation process, but I know about Brett—every wine person does. It's an opportunistic, nasty yeast that, once it infiltrates your vineyard, is incredibly difficult and expensive to get rid of. Brett takes a good wine and reduces its fruit, flattens its acids, and robs it of its texture and mouthfeel. But worst of all is what Brett does to the *smell*, the *taste*.

Vomit.

Band-Aids.

Manure.

These are just a few of the descriptors a Bretty wine garners. It's responsible for ruining entire vintages, entire seasons, and if you're poor enough, entire vineyards.

"Well, I didn't do *all* the sulfur treatments—like we discussed, remember? A more natural approach?" Tears stream down Laine's cheeks, but I don't think she realizes it. Her voice thickens, and she squeezes her eyes shut. "If I had, it would've stopped it. *Fucking stupid*, Laine. *Stupid*." She smashes her open palm against her face. The vitriol in her voice razors my heart, and I grab her hand, holding it in mine, as if that could protect her from her own self-loathing.

"You don't know that for sure. Sulfur treatments don't kill Brett—they just weaken it. This infestation grew so quickly, whatever the source was might've been too strong even for the sulfur to combat." Jamal puts a suited hand on Laine's shoulder to comfort her, but I can't help feeling like Laine and I are in a plague ward for two.

"And it's in all of our base wines for next year?" I try to swallow, but my mouth has gone bone dry. Which is ironic, because if *any* of our wines were made dry, they wouldn't be so susceptible to a Brett infestation. It's the residual sugars in our sweet wines that Brett loves so much.

Jamal nods. "It's been in every tote I tested. It wasn't in any of Laine's new red blends, though, or any of the reds and whites ready to sell this season."

The sigh that leaves my body trembles on its way out. Somehow, one season's worth of wine will have to cover the expenses of running Bluebell for *two* years, until the next batch of base wines are ready to blend and bottle, and that's assuming we're able to get the Brett infestation under control by then. I've always known it'd take only one calamity to bring our small vineyard to its knees, and now it's happened. How can I convince Laine to stay now? This isn't the Bluebell Vineyards I was planning on asking her to trade her dreams for, but she's so racked with guilt, she'd probably spend the rest of her life in a dungeon if I asked her to. The last of Dad's bottled wines are safe, but everything Laine's produced, save the new red blends, weirdly, is chock-full of Brett's farm-ass polyphenols.

I frown, mulling that over. "Why would the new reds be safe, but everything else not?"

Jamal shrugs. "The new red blends have been bottle-aging since late July, correct?" When Laine nods, he shrugs again. "The infestation must've occurred after that. Since it's not in last season's wines, either, this is a new problem. Did anything out of the ordinary happen since August? Any visitors to the winery that might've brought it in on their clothes?"

One second passes, two, and *boom*. The realization hits, its implications rippling outward in shock waves. My eyes widen.

"Rachel!"

CHAPTER TWENTY-SEVEN

While Laine and I drowsed on the tasting room floor, the security footage shows Rachel lumbering into the winery, knocking into everything, then leaning over an exposed tote of base wine with what must've been a contaminated stirring rod and swirling it ferociously until Laine and I walked in and unknowingly cut the Brett sabotage short. Not that it did us any good. Brett spreads so perniciously, all it would've taken was Rachel walking in with Brett on her clothes, and she'd probably have been able to affect most, if not all, of our base wines for next year. The direct contamination with the stirring rod just made it move on a faster schedule.

I don't know *what* to do about it. Call the cops for trespassing? Get on the phone with Kira and put together a devastating lawsuit of business sabotage? Hold her down while Laine pours a bottle of Georgia Vomit Girls down her throat? I alternate between a fury too big for my body and a crushing desolation that *anyone* could hate me this much.

The thing is, I'd started to think that maybe Rachel still cared about me. She *had* tried to warn me about Laine all summer. It seemed like she'd been watching out for me, in her own toxic way.

But the footage is unambiguous. She practically threw herself into that tote, which Jamal confirmed was ground zero as far as Brett goes. Its readings were the highest of all.

I lower myself onto the winery's floor, propping my elbows on my knees, and breathe. Our entire season of base wines is both contaminated and irreplaceable. When Laine realized something was wrong yesterday morning, Tristan spent the day calling every vineyard in the southeast to see if anyone has surplus base wine they'd be willing to sell, but it's too far along in the season—everything's been sold or slated for use. Our short-term looks even worse. We'd have to thoroughly decontaminate the winery before we host anything here, or else we could spread it to every vineyard in the area. That kind of effort takes weeks, months even. How can we gather that much manpower in just seven days?

Can we even *afford* to?

Every free dollar I had, I put into the showcase, not to mention all the money I already owe Teddy for the infrastructure improvements. We'd have to buy hazmat suits and industrial cleaning supplies, plus throw away every barrel we have and start over from nothing. A winery with no grapes, no barrels, no money, is a winery with no *wine*. No future.

I huff out a breath as I scrub my bleary eyes with the palms of my hands. The biggest problem I had five hours ago—how to ask Laine to stay—is the *one* problem I no longer have. Because what's left to stay for now? Me and my wreck of a vineyard? My mother's dreams, which I've treated like an inheritance at best and a sentence at worst, instead of seeing them for what they are: an excuse.

An excuse to hide from life by burying myself in work.

"Zoe?" Jamal places his hand on my shoulder, but even through his thick glove, I can feel his warmth. "What do you want to do?"

What *do* I want to do? Give up and go to Oregon with Laine? She's barely made eye contact with me since I got home and is currently slumped over my father's worktable, but I have no doubt she'll do anything I ask her to right now. For her, this is the Hayseed Vintner all over again, only this time the failure's been feeding on nuclear waste and has morphed into Failure-zilla, bigger and deadlier than ever.

This could *ruin* her.

The realization that Laine will carry this failure around for the rest of her life—whether here or in Oregon or somewhere else, letting it define her and keep her small—makes me lift my head.

I can't let that happen. I *won't.*

I'm Zoe fucking Brennan, and goddammit, I know how to lose. I know how to try and fail and *keep* trying and failing, until I *win.*

I stand up so fast that Jamal flinches.

"I want to get to *work.*"

I put out the bat signal to everyone I know, explaining the situation and what I need from them. Jamal, bless him, stays up with Laine and me into the wee hours of the morning, running scenarios for how we could fix this. We come up with one possible solution—an intense round of sterile filtration bookended with heavy sulfur treatments—and hold our breath as Laine pours us each a small tasting glass of the first batch it produces, sometime around three a.m.

"Okay, boss." Laine tentatively passes me a glass, her bloodshot eyes filled with hope and fear in equal measure. "Bottoms up."

Jamal watches nervously from behind his hood. This task is mine and Laine's alone. I lift the glass first to my nose and . . .

"Nothing," I announce, then sniff harder. "I smell nothing."

Laine smells hers, too, and nods. "A light scent of the alcohol itself, maybe. Nothing else."

We share a flutter of a smile. Not that that's *good*, per se. Wine should smell like wine. But my heart beats a little faster, fueled by relief that at least it no longer smells like Baahlzebub's stall. I lift the glass again, this time to my lips, watching Laine mirror my actions.

Here goes nothing.

Laine gags before I do. I can't even swallow it, choking it back out and into my glass. "Oh *god.*"

"Like, sixty proof—*Band-Aid* water," Laine splutters, wiping her mouth before gagging again. I guess Jamal feels left out, because he turns and gags, too.

"We have to dump it." Laine's face collapses in misery.

"Fuck that," I croak, still pressing a hand to my roiling stomach. "Haven't you heard of wine slushies?"

Her misery melts into horror. "Wine slushies?! With *that*?!"

I clap her on the back. "There's my Napa snob."

Jamal tilts his head, considering. "Not a bad idea . . . That sangria slushy mix could make gasoline taste good."

"Well, now we know what we're serving all winter." I smile grimly, then clap my hands as if to say, *next!*

By dawn, we have a plan. It's not pretty, and it requires calling in every favor I've got, but I'll be damned if I'm going to let Rachel's sabotage destroy everything Laine and I have worked so hard for.

She doesn't get to destroy *us*.

We agree to meet back at seven a.m., giving us a few short hours of sleep before the real work begins. I'm so grateful to Jamal I could cry, but I settle for a long hug through his hazmat suit. Then, Laine and I walk back to my cottage under skies the color of denim. I slip my hand into hers, and she begins to cry.

"*Shh*, Laine, everything's going to be okay." I pull her close among the sleeping vines in the cool, damp stillness where night greets morning. And I realize I really believe it. Because I know now that *this* is my saving grace. It's her. And me. And the beautiful, terrifying, completely worth-it risk of a great love. Not my family's vineyard, my work, not even my dreams, inherited, adopted, or otherwise.

"Zoe, I'm so sorry. About keeping Oregon from you, about the infestation, about everything." Laine's voice rumbles and scrapes through her throat. "I know it was Rachel that contaminated our wine, but it's still my fault. She was so furious with me, she took it out on Bluebell, and if I'd followed your dad's protocol, we might've prevented the worst of it. I don't care what I have to do to make it happen, but I'm going to decontaminate the winery before the showcase and Cosimo gets back. And then, I'll—I'll leave, if that's what you want. Just please, believe me. I'm so sorry for ruining what you love most." Her voice shatters on the words.

I brush a soft lock of her hair behind her ear, tilting my head back so I can take her all in, every ragged breath, every tear, every earnest, loving bit of her. How could I have ever doubted this woman's devotion? "That's not what I want, Laine. You haven't ruined anything because *you're* who I love most." I run the bridge of my nose along her jaw before placing a light kiss in the hollow beneath her ear. "All we have to do now is try. Can you do that for me?"

She wraps her arms around my waist, crushing me to her, her head dipping to press her cheek against mine. "I *will*."

A hope-starved heart hurts to the beat of its own blood. You get so used to the ache of not expecting that you see the world through a pain-colored hue. You don't know the true color of happy or recognize all the shades of love.

Until one day, you do.

Laine holds me, tells me that she loves me, whispers into my hair how much she missed me these few days apart, and when we rise a few hours later, I swear the sun glows brighter than ever, a fat peach gilding the world just for us. The sky's bluer, the chilly air fresh and tart. When Jamal shows up with a rainbow of trucks, cars, and even Trish and Darryl's redneck tour bus in our parking lot at seven a.m. sharp, it takes my breath away.

I blink, wondering if I'm still dreaming as Jamal and half his team start passing out hazmat suits to a growing line forming behind his truck. My bat signal worked and then some—just about everyone I know is here to help scrub down the winery. River, Hannah, Maeve, Gloria, Teddy, Diego, Trish, Darryl, Gus, Martha, Ms. Betty and her whole horde of merry spinsters, Killian and the Genteelmen, and, I realize with a deranged laugh, about half my exes. The *Everyday Bon Vivant* team is here, too, Marisol looking foxy in her *gettin' dirty* clothes while Matthew bustles over, his arms loaded with shopping bags full of industrial cleaning supplies. Their extended team mills behind with walkie-talkies strapped to work belts, which I find inexplicably impressive.

"Hope you don't mind we phoned in some reinforcements." Matthew smiles and sets the bags at my feet. He catches me staring slack-jawed at all the kindness flowing into Bluebell Vineyards, and his eyes go soft. "We fight for our vineyards, Zoe. And our friends."

I could kiss him all over his meticulously shaven cheeks. I'd been scared to tell Matthew and Marisol about the Brett infestation last night—what if they called the showcase off before we could even *try* to save ourselves? But I see now that once again, my tendency to expect the worst from people led me astray. Behind him is an army ready to eradicate the Brett teeming across every surface, stirring rod, and barrel in our winery.

My heart squeezes as hope bursts in. When my eyes catch Laine's, she looks at me as though to say, *see how much love you have in your life.*

And for once, I'm seeing.

CHAPTER TWENTY-EIGHT

Our army of Brett-killers storms the winery like it's Satan's toilet. I've never seen so many people viciously scrubbing at the same time in all my life. Cleaning, relocating anything salvageable, then cleaning some more. This goes on at a fearsome pace all morning, with waves of people coming and going, until a delivery car shows up with a trunkful of pizza, and Marisol announces it's lunchtime.

I'm about to have my third slice when my phone buzzes from my back pocket.

WARNING, it's that bitch Rachel

Can you meet me in 10 min at Fort Queens?

WARNING, it's that bitch Rachel

I heard about what happened.

The words hit me like bombs, setting off bursts of anger and hurt that electrify my blood. I shove the half-eaten slice of pizza in my mouth and leave it dangling there so I can type back.

Zoe

about what happened? Don't you mean what you DID?!

WARNING, it's that bitch Rachel

Just give me a chance to explain.

No, thank you. Unless you're going to tell me you'll fix everything so that my family's vineyard won't be driven to financial ruin, I'm not interested.

WARNING, it's that bitch Rachel

I'm going to fix everything so that your family's vineyard won't be driven to financial ruin. Now, meet me in 10 min. You know the spot.

I blink at my phone's screen, trying to process the words, then give up and thumbs-up her message instead.

"If I don't come back in twenty minutes, call the cops," I say to the feasting people camped on our patio. A few grunt in acknowledgment, which is good enough for me.

This time of day, the October sunlight hits the woods at an angle, illuminating the autumn foliage like it's lit from within. I follow the old trail through the burning orange, until I find the remains of our wooden playhouse, Fort Queens. Its planks are gray and splintered from rain, and I run my finger across the fine rind of lichen coating its door.

"Hey."

I nearly jump out of my skin. "*Jesus*, Rachel!" I spin to find her, sitting in her vineyard's old golf cart where it's parked/crashed ten feet behind me off the trail, its fender in full contact with a tree.

Rachel takes a deep breath. "First of all, it was an accident. I didn't even piece together what happened until Mom and Dad got your text this morning. I know it looks bad—"

"You're on camera frantically stirring the infested wine like a witch at her cauldron." I cross my arms. "It looks *real* bad."

"Just listen!" She groans. "Earlier that day, at the family meeting when Chance, Mom, and Dad decided to vote Charlaine back into the family business, they also promised her the money set aside for my expansion project."

"The brewery?"

"Yes. Well, a microbrewery," Rachel amends. "It'd be a restaurant, too, with a board game menu where folks could order beer and what games they'd like to play at their table. We'd even have a sommelier, but for games, where you'd tell them what you're in the mood for, and they'd bring you the perfect game." Rachel's eyes have gone a bit starry talking about it, and my gut twinges for her on reflex. It's a good idea. A great idea, even. And kudos to her because for once, it wasn't *my idea*.

"After the meeting, I stopped by my brewer Ethan's workshop to tell him everything was off. We were upset, and we started drinking all the beers he'd been working on for our microbrewery, and you saw the—the aftermath."

"When you were shit-faced."

"Well. Yes." Rachel clears her throat. "I got a ride back to Into the Woods, thinking I'd beg Mom and Dad to change their minds, but then I remembered how Charlaine kissed you that morning at the soccer game, and I realized—you must not know about her plans to leave. You'd *never* endanger your vineyard by having a fling with your vintner, which meant you must've gone and fallen in love with her, not knowing all the while she was planning to *leave* you! I couldn't believe she was screwing you over like that." Rachel grips the steering wheel of her cart hard enough to make her knuckles turn white. Her eyes flicker up to mine. "You weren't listening to my texts, so I decided to tell you myself."

That's why Rachel came over, to warn me out of *concern* for my heart? My throat tightens.

"I had no *clue* Ethan had been experimenting with Brettanomyces in his workshop. If I'd gone looking for Chance or Mom and Dad like I'd planned, I would've infested our own winery instead. I just—happened to go to yours."

"Then why the stirring? What were you doing to our wine, Rachel?"

Rachel covers her face with her hands. "I lost my keys, remember? When I dropped my purse?"

"In our *wine?*"

Rachel nods. "At least, I thought so. I'd stumbled into that tote and knocked the cover off by accident, and when I went to put it back on, my keys slipped out of my purse into the wine. I was trying to find them with the stirring rod when y'all showed up." She gestures at the parked golf cart she's sitting in. "Carterella is stranded here until I do."

I stare at her, trying to parse out the emotions on her face. Is that guilt or a convincing replica, meant to fool me into not suing her ass?

"Oh, come *on*, Zoe," Rachel says, exasperated. "If I truly wanted to sabotage you, don't you think I'd have done a better job at it? I'm not *sloppy*."

Honestly, that *has* occurred to me, too. From a childhood playing board games together, I know that Rachel is cunning and ruthless, but that night, she literally knocked on all my doors *before* she let herself into the winery and started messing around. The work of an amateur. Not Rachel.

I slide onto Carterella's bench seat beside her and hold my head in my hands. "Goddammit. I believe you."

"I'm really sorry, Zoe," she says softly. "And I'm even sorrier that I've given you so many reasons to believe I'd do such a thing. I've talked it over with my family, and we all agree it's only right that Into the Woods replaces all the base wine lost by the Brett infestation with our own. I know the terroir is different, but we had a great year, and Chance assures me that it'll work for y'all's purposes."

I whip my head up. "Really?"

"I told you I had a plan to keep you from financial ruin."

"Why?" The word falls in the forest like a dead tree, loaded and heavy. It's all the *why*s wrapped into one, not just why she's saving our asses now after being so resentful for doing that in the past, and Rachel knows it. Why did she abandon me?

"I could ask you the same thing."

When I look at her, I feel such an amalgamation of feelings, of times long gone and worse, times never had. "What do you mean?"

Rachel sighs. "Why Charlaine, Zoe?" she says, meeting my gaze. "Why not me?"

My head rears back so hard it's a good thing it's attached to my neck. "Um," I sputter, dumbfounded at the direction this has taken, "first of all, you're not gay, Rachel, and second, *you're not gay, Rachel*." I wouldn't speak so surely about someone's sexuality if I didn't know it with every fiber of my being, but Rachel is deeply straight. Her first crush was on Burt Reynolds. *Burt Reynolds!* He was probably sixty, and she was twelve, but she printed out pictures of that mustachioed alpha and plastered them all over her bedroom.

But . . . could I be wrong? *Is* there some connection between Burt Reynolds's chest hair and eventually realizing you're a lesbian?

"I *know* I'm straight!" Rachel's eyes tear up. "You two have rubbed it in my face every chance you got!"

"You'll have to explain yourself because I sincerely don't understand what you're talking about."

"When we were kids, it was me and you, *always*. I had nobody else, but it was okay because you liked me. Even though I had zero hand-eye coordination and played sports for shit, and I wasn't pretty, and I was a huge nerd who chewed up her pencils and played board games and had a crush on Alex Trebek—"

"And Burt Reynolds," I add, because now I can't get those hairy chests striped with low toner lines out of my head.

"Do you know how hard it was, being in Charlaine Woods' shadow? You were her fan, but I was her wannabe, the little sister who couldn't compare. She was great at everything, and it all came so easily to her—she just *was*, and the way she was, was *right*." Rachel swallows. "But I was all wrong. I thought that one day, I'd get to be just like her. I'd magically run faster, make the soccer team, look hot in shapeless Umbros, too." She lets out a bitter laugh. "But I never did, and you saw all of that, knew I'd never be Charlaine, and you still loved me, Zoe. We were a united front on everything, even her. Especially her. She was perfect, and we were in awe of her together. Intimidated by her, *together*. But then she was outed, and I thought, wow, Laine's finally gonna have to pay for being who she is. But even being a lesbian didn't change a thing! Gilmer County in the aughts? Was she invincible or something, I mean, *come on!*" Rachel clenches her fingers, then releases them one by one. "Laine has never, not once, experienced any repercussions for being who she truly is. She's not stuck in a prison of her own unacceptable, unlikable, unpopular personality. She gets away with everything, and no matter what, everyone will always love her more than me." Rachel's eyes well up again. "Even my best friend."

"I didn't love her more than you, Rachel," I say quietly. "Just overnight, you made hating Laine your number one priority, and all that hate squeezed out the best parts of you. You never wanted to play Settlers of Catan anymore or lay in the fields reading mysteries together. And I think"—my throat tightens—"I think you knew I was gay before I did. And when it started to show, you hated me for it."

"I did," Rachel admits, "but not because I hate gay people or anything. I hated it because it felt like Charlaine was stealing you from my team and putting you on hers, because you're right, I'm straight as hell! And I felt so incredibly"—she throws her hands in the air, searching for the right words—"*uncool*. So dumb. So basic." She looks down at her lap. "So left out."

"You do know you're in the majority, right? White, cis, heterosexual?"

"In the world of people I cared about, I wasn't. I even tried it once."

"Being gay?" My brow furrows. "You did not. With who?"

Rachel shrugs. "Some girl on my hall freshman year at UGA, but her mouth felt . . . I don't know. Too small."

"Too small?" I laugh, and even the corner of Rachel's mouth quirks up. I've heard many explanations for why women aren't attracted to other women, but lacking a cavernous mouth is a new one. But the laughter dies in my throat because we're still sitting here, the mountain of Rachel's feelings and all the hurt they've caused lodged between us. "I still don't understand how you could just walk out of my life, Rachel."

Rachel's head slumps forward against the steering wheel. "If I could've stopped talking to my family back then, I probably would've. When my parents gave your dad the money they were going to use to buy my new car, I just felt so . . . *unimportant*, you know? Like everyone else's needs mattered more than mine. Even if I followed the rules to a *T*, I still couldn't win. My parents would always love everyone else more." Her voice breaks, and she wipes the tears trickling down her cheeks furiously away.

It all makes sense now. Rachel embedding herself in her family's business, still chasing her parents' approval, pitting herself and Into the Woods against our vineyard every chance she got. The way she attacks Laine for leaving their family, for breaking the rules Rachel treats like commandments and still getting away with it. How she must've felt to hear that, once again, her family had decided to back someone else's dreams over hers when they voted to give Laine the money set aside for Rachel's microbrewery. How badly it must've hurt that when Bluebell was picked for the showcase, I refused to share it with her.

"Jesus, Rachel. I'm—I'm so *sorry*."

Rachel sits up, her face pink with tears. "You are? Why?"

It's not that Rachel's perception is right—Molly and Ezra adore Rachel and her bitchiness and always have. But it's easy to see how she'd feel wronged. It's easy to see all the hurt and anger living just under her skin. And after all these years, it's still easy to see *her*.

"I just—wish I could've been there for you." I give her a sad smile, full of regret for how we got here.

"I wish you could've, too." Rachel's face buckles in on itself, her raw sobs undoing something in my own heart. "I'm so sorry I pushed you away, Zoe."

In a slow-motion undoing of reality, I wrap my arms around her and let her cry against my dirty T-shirt as she spews apology after apology for the Brett infestation, every stolen idea, every mean word, every day we've spent apart. She pulls away suddenly, her face streaked with mascara tears. "But one thing I'm *not* sorry about is warning you off Charlaine! She's no good, Zoe! She's selfish, puts her career first, and uses people who love her to get what she wants."

"That's not true," I say quietly.

"She lied to you! She made you fall in love with her, and the whole time she was planning on leaving for Oregon!"

I consider Rachel's accusations—weren't they my exact thoughts a week ago? What do I understand now, so clearly, that I didn't then?

"Sometimes you've got to ride the twists and turns before you get to the clear stretch of road." I squeeze Rachel's hand in mine. "Thank you for looking out for me, but, Rachel, you owe it to Laine *and* yourself to let go of this story you've believed about her all these years. It's not true, and it's poisoning how you feel about everyone in your life. Including *you*."

Rachel's sobs have reduced to hiccups, her eyes fixed on mine. I can tell she wants to argue in that way where your heart's saying one thing, but your mind's unable to back it up, so you sit there in resistance, wondering what the hell the right answer is.

"Did you know that day at varsity tryouts Laine begged the coach to let you finish?"

"*No.* Charlaine was the one who kicked me off the field," Rachel insists. "She humiliated me in front of everyone!"

"She tried to help you, but the coach overruled her. That's what I'm talking about. You have this . . . *lens* you see Laine through, and it distorts the truth in ugly ways. You've got to let it go."

She stares at me, emotions passing over her face as she battles versions of Laine in her mind, and we're silent for a few minutes.

I check the sun, then my watch. "I need to get back. We still have a winery to decontaminate if we're going to make the showcase."

Rachel nods. Will our conversation today serve as a truce, where we peacefully go our own ways? Or could it be the beginning of something different? I slide out of the semi-crashed golf cart. The impulse to say my goodbyes and keep walking, to let Rachel make the decision of what comes next, presents itself, but the desire to have learned something from all this pain and upheaval is even stronger. Where Rachel falls in my heart is just a big, old ache that I'm so tired of feeling. I come around to her side of the cart and offer her my hand. Surprised, she lets me help her up.

"Rachel, I'm in love with Laine, and she's in love with me, too. Whatever comes next, we're figuring it out together. Can you get right with that?"

"Guess I have to," Rachel says, then blows out a breath. Tries again. "Yes."

Maybe it'd help if she realized that what I love about Laine now was part of what I loved about Rachel back then. The fierce grip on life. The ambition. The great calves.

Maybe if she realized that I see her, too. Then *and* now, and I'm still standing here.

"Come on. Let's go find your keys." I squeeze her hand, then pull her toward the winery.

"Then you've got some toilets to clean."

CHAPTER TWENTY-NINE

Some days, you wake up knowing the day is destined to become filler. Part of the yawning blur that sweeps you between the major touch points of your life.

But some days are *magic*. You open your eyes, and the air feels charged with potential. Each minute stands by, ready, waiting, *wanting* to become a memory.

When I open my eyes the morning of the showcase, I already know I'll remember today forever. Dawn whispers in through the cracked window, the crisp feel of fall like the cool of my mother's hand pressed against my forehead. Maybe it is. All these years I've felt sewn into this place, stitched tight by the thread of her blood in my veins, but Mom never wanted that for me. She only wanted me to be happy, to find my own way like she found hers. By climbing a mountain with her great love, looking out onto the world together, pointing, believing, that where they dare set their sights, happiness would follow.

I'm happy, Mom. My heart lifts the words in the hopes she'll hear them. *I'm climbing this mountain. I'm finding my way.*

And I swear I smell wildflowers in October.

I stretch and wrap my body around Laine.

"Mmm," she murmurs, covertly removing her retainer and tucking it under her pillow. "Good morning, boss."

I pretend not to notice, because I love her.

"Good morning, Beave." I kiss the words across her bare shoulder blades, leaving a trail of goose bumps in my wake. "Would you care to make it a *great* one?"

Laine finds my hand tucked around her stomach and brings it to her mouth, kissing the tip of each finger. She spends a little extra time on my thumb, wrapping her lips around it and giving it a long, slow suck that plucks me deep inside. With her other hand, she reaches behind to grab my thigh and drag it over her, grinding me against her hip in the process.

Guess that's a yes.

Laine shifts until she's on her back, looking up at me as I straddle her. She likes it this way, working me from below while watching me come for her above. Like she's the conductor in the orchestra, watching the ballet on stage surge to the music she creates. I don't mind starring on this stage for her. After all the years I spent desperate for Laine to look my way, feeling her hot, dark gaze trained on me now is a power I never imagined I'd have. One that's borne from loving and being loved and resting in the faith that whatever tomorrow brings, it's worth it.

It's all *so* worth it.

After, we walk hand in hand through the rows of vines until our respective to-do lists require us to go in different directions. It's early, but our friends and family begin to arrive, ready to help execute their parts of the showcase. There's a world of tasks to be conquered before our doors open at five, and it's up to us to conquer them. Laine leans down for a long, slow kiss before letting me go, like we have all the time in the world.

Maybe we do.

"I love you," I murmur as she presses a final kiss to the top of my cheekbone. Her face hovers close to mine, her eyes the rich, tawny brown of the acorns scattered across our forest's floor. She feels as much a part of this place as I do. Her hand cups my cheek.

"I will never, *ever* get tired of hearing you admit that." Her face splits into a cocky grin. "Now, chop chop, Chop Chop. We've got a ho-case to throw!" She sends me off with a smack on the ass and my own eye-rolling grin.

As for my day, it goes smoother than apple butter thanks to Hannah. She took over planning while I was in Italy, then kept on while I worked day and night with Laine on getting the Brett infestation under control. She's got a real knack for sweet-talking our vendors into better deals—extra speakers for the PA system, local snacks for our VIP swag bags, bathroom trailers upgraded to deluxe. They even have *bidets*, for God's sake. She shows up at eight a.m., my angel of business largesse, ready to help me destroy the remaining to-do list. By two, we've pretty much got 'er done.

"Damn, Hannah," I say, wiping the sweat off my brow after we finish setting up the kids' play area she conceived, planned, and sourced all on her own. "You're really good at event planning, you know that?"

Hannah gives me a loose grin. "You know, I think I'm pretty good at a lot of things these days."

We cheers to that just as Maeve's white animal rescue van rolls up, with its big Cheshire cat logo grinning on the door.

"Ahem, what?" I ask as Maeve throws open the sliding door, revealing a maze of crates filled with animals.

"It's our petting zoo/adoption station!" Hannah says brightly, then runs over to help Maeve. I frown at the fenced-in section at the edge of the kids' area, feeling utterly had as Tristan leads Baahlzebub from our barn over to the pen. He throws his head back and brays to the others like, *Daddy's home, bitches.*

"Whoa! What's *he* doing here?"

"He's still up for adoption, remember?" Hannah places her hands on her hips, eying me suspiciously. "Why, Zoe Brennan. Have you gone soft on Baahlzebub?"

I don't know why she'slooking at me like that. I'm just cuddling his head. "No . . . it's just—"

Hannah tilts her head. "Hmm?"

"He'suseful. Sometimes." I scrounge for exactly how. "He eats—weeds!"

"He also ate Rachel's car. And half your fence."

"He's a growing boy!" I clutch him tighter, and he *baa*s.

Hannah huffs, then removes the ADOPT ME! tag from Bub's collar and replaces it with the ADOPTED! one.

"We just had our first adoption of the day, people!" Maeve announces, then points at me. "No take-backsies, Zoe."

"No take-backsies." I sigh as Baahlzebub gives me a long, goaty lick. I don't even vomit about it.

"What is this?" Matthew appears by my side, with his truly preternatural ability to zero in on undiscussed developments. He checks his clipboard, probably looking for the word *Hell-Goat*. Finding none, he repeats his question louder, a slight panic to his voice. "That fencing looks suspect. Are these animals insured?"

"Fully insured, sir," Maeve says, puffing out her chest.

"Calm down, everybody, the showcase's gonna go off without a hitch!" Hannah says with a kitten in her arms to an almost-immediate backlash of groaning in stereo. "What?" she asks, genuinely puzzled as she delivers ear scritches.

Matthew's eyes flutter closed as he takes five deep breaths. I place my hand consolingly on his arm. "You just jinxed us, Hannah. You *never* say that kind of thing before an event!"

Hannah rolls her eyes. "Y'all are as bad as Killian with that superstitious business. It's gonna be *fi*—"

We cut her off with loud booing.

When Tristan finishes bar setup, we run a final check through the art installation's wiring. It was no easy feat figuring out the placement of projectors around the vineyard and how to power them, but the early test runs have me giddy to see the final product. With doors set to open at five, just as dusk begins to drape across the sky, we decide to go live at four thirty with the big reveal for all the people working our event tonight. I even manage to flag Laine down.

"Come on, take a minute with me," I say, pulling her into my side. "I want you to see this."

She's already changed into her fancy clothes for the evening—a pair of trousers that hug the long, lean line of her legs, a pale blue button-down, and a wool blazer with the narrow lapel flipped up in the back. She's got her tortoiseshell glasses on, that just-showered smell lingering around her, and I want to lick her top to bottom. Judging by the way she's looking at me, the feeling's mutual. I'm all fixed up now, too, wearing a slim, black suit, the pants cropped high to show off my ankles. The jacket's fitted with strong shoulders revealing the white silky shirt beneath unbuttoned to reveal what else? In-between-boob. With my bold red lips and black winged eyeliner, Laine can't look away. She fingers the dainty, hair-thin golden chain hanging in loops around my chest. The way the metal trawls across the delicate skin there makes my nipples tighten viciously.

"Yes, boss." This beautiful, sexy wine scientist looks at me like she wants to drink me up. Like she loves me.

And the best part is, I know she does.

"Now, folks, this installation is meant to be experienced the way a night of good stories always is—at your own pace, with laughter and talk and sharing in the simple act of memory," Tristan announces to the small group of helpers. He presses something that looks like a Power-Point clicker, and a whoosh of gasps rises from the crowd as the vineyard lights up. Over a dozen projectors going at once, their images stretched across the forest, the hills, the vines themselves. A picture of my mom at the hardware store, waving behind the counter. My father, tiny beneath a massive hiking pack. A long-arm shot of their heads pressed close together at the top of Springer Mountain, our untamed land in the distance. The newspaper clipping announcing Bluebell's opening. Small cuts of family videos are interspersed with the static shots, too. Dad chasing toddler-me down the Chardonnay vines, our faces lit up in silent laughter. Me blowing out six flickering birthday candles. Mom and Dad slow dancing at a vineyard event, when the patio was just grass with the moon hung above them.

All these images, flickering, distorted by the trees, or the ground, or even the barn roof they stretch out upon. The past overlaid the present, giving a feeling of place that's heavier than the here and now. The story of my parents, my family, and now, *us*. Laine sucks in a breath as I lead her toward the pictures of young Zoe mirrored beside pictures of young Laine that Molly supplied. Then there's Laine with her goggles on, me behind the tasting bar; Laine holding me up while I laugh wildly in front of the Redneck Wine Tour bus. Our own slow dance at River and Hannah's wedding, a candid shot Tristan took.

"Zoe, baby, it's incredible." Laine hugs me closer and presses a kiss to the top of my head. "Thank you for making me a part of this magical place."

I lean up to kiss her cheek. "You make it even better."

The installation is beautiful, but even better, it's *interesting*. The crowd of workers stands in awe for a few moments before people head off to explore whichever vignette calls to them most.

"All right, everyone! Doors open in THREE MINUTES!" Hannah announces through Darryl's camouflage megaphone, swiped from the tour bus. "To your stations!"

Laine spins me around to give me a soft, tender kiss. "It's ho-time, boss."

I smile, kissing her once more before giving Hannah the signal and throwing my arms wide. "Let the ho-case begin!"

The wine starts to *flow*.

And it's magic, this bright October evening. The moon's not quite full, but it hangs in the darkening sky like a spotlight shining down on Blue-bell, on *us*, us from heaven above. The vignettes look amazing, folks happily ambling along our bulb-lit trails, glasses in hand, oohing and aahing over every chapter of this love story. On the autumn breeze floats the sweet scent of woodsmoke and the rich, heady smell of wine. Everywhere is happiness, and I soak it all up.

"There you are!" Marisol squeezes past the crowds gathering at the cheese tent for the tastings. A worried crease lines her brow.

"What is it?" I ask.

"We received a last-minute press pass request." Marisol wets her lips. "From Benjamin Soren—the wine critic from *Vinitopia*. He's here."

My eyebrows shoot up to my hairline. "The one who wrote the Hayseed Vintner review about Laine?"

Marisol nods glumly. "I've been trying to find her before she stumbles into him by accident."

I cross my arms, a keenly edged protectiveness within me ready to do battle. "I'll look for her, too."

"Just remember, his words can't touch either of you after tonight." Marisol squeezes my arm. "Everything is perfect, Zoe. I'm so proud of you both, and I hope it's not wrong to say it, but I know your mother would be, too."

The air lifts the tips of my hair gently, and I place my hand over Marisol's and squeeze. "Thank you, Marisol. For everything."

I jog off, texting Laine as I go, but find her first, glorious and grinning behind the bar dedicated to her new line of reds in the tasting tent. She's pouring glass after glass, graciously accepting the heaps of praise from her customers. A sour note twists in my stomach at the thought of telling her Soren is here. But if he catches her unaware, or worse, says a *single* goddamn thing to her, I'm not sure how either of us will handle that.

Probably with a bottle of our boldest bludgeoning varietal.

I'm still making my way toward the bar when a hand taps me on the shoulder. I'm ready to make a quick excuse so I can get to Laine, but it's Mayor Esposito.

"Zoe!" Her politician's smile is brilliant, full of pride for Blue Ridge and glee at the mass of wine tourists entering town. "Congratulations, darling!"

"Oh, thank you, Mayor. I've just—" I make a little pointing gesture toward the bar, but she throws her arm around my shoulders, reeling me in.

"Whatever it is, it can wait. You *must* meet this wine buyer. She selects the full inventory for Publix, and she's crazy about Laine's new Pinot Noir blend!" She spins me toward an effusive redhead who already has her hand outstretched to shake mine. When I finally extricate myself from the exciting, if extremely poorly timed meeting, my heart stutters in my chest.

I'm too late.

Benjamin Soren, slouching all his weight onto one leg, holds a wineglass under his nose like a fishbowl he's reluctantly sniffing. It's Laine's favorite of her new red blends, appropriately titled Redemption Red. Laine's standing there watching him, her jaw clenched. She's trying to play it cool, but you don't have to be in love with her to see all the signs of distress. Marisol's beside her, watching Soren warily, a protective hand on Laine's shoulder.

My first instinct is to run over and rescue her before this guy can disturb Laine's hard-won peace of mind. Soren doesn't know how much is riding on his good opinion. Not that it matters in Blue Ridge what he thinks, but it matters to *Laine*. I can't bear the thought of him damaging the confidence she's painstakingly rebuilt grape by grape ever since his cruel words soured her on her life's true passion. But something roots me to the spot.

Soren lifts the glass to the pinched line of his discriminating mouth. You can tell he's prepared to hate it by the faux regret already playing across his miserable face.

Fuck this guy! My feet unlock, and I stomp over there, ready to lay him out.

But then, he tastes it. The smug expression slides off his face, replaced with surprise. Not delight or approval, but genuine surprise. He rolls the wine around in his mouth, thinking. By the time I reach Laine's side, she doesn't seem to be breathing, still hanging in limbo for this man's opinion.

Soren swallows, blinks. Looks at Laine. His face softens, brow furrowing. "I'm so sorry, Ms. Woods."

Now Laine's wearing the same surprised expression. "Sorry? For what?" she croaks out.

"For all those things I said about your abilities in my column. I take them all back." His dark eyes look so humbled, I actually believe him. "This wine is incredible," he says in awe. "Bright and interesting, so *nuanced* for such a young red. How did you manage such complexity so quickly?"

Laine deflates, her head lolling back in sweet relief, and laughs. Tears roll down her cheeks as Marisol, arching an eyebrow Laine's way, speaks for her. "I'm sure Ms. Woods will share a bit of her inspiration and technique with you shortly"—Laine guffaws—"just as I'm sure *you* will cover Laine's incredible work here and this beautiful showcase in the next edition of *Vinitopia*, complete with a retraction of your prior incorrect statements about Ms. Woods." Marisol fixes her steely gaze on Soren, who nods dumbly before drinking from his glass again, all of us standing in a dazed orbit around our star, who *may* be mid-supernova, not sure.

When it's clear Laine's laughter isn't stopping anytime soon, Marisol deftly ushers Soren away to meet some other local vintners so Laine can lose her shit in peace.

"Babe, *babe!* Are you having a breakdown? Do I need to call for an ambulance?" I say it the way Darryl always does, *am-bu-lance*, which only makes her laugh more.

"I'm just—so—*God*, I was terrified!" Laine says through her laughter. "And for what? While I was standing there, waiting for this boogeyman to deliver my sentence, it struck me how dumb it was that I cared so much about what one asshole with a platform said about me. And then, after all the times I tortured myself replaying his insults over and over in my mind, for him to *love it?* To take everything he said *back?!*" Laine straight up hoots, and now we're getting looks of concern.

"Okay, baby." I smile at the onlookers and wrap my arm around Laine's shoulders so I can corral her still-shaking body out from the tasting tent and into the beautiful moonlit night. Our night.

Once I get her out of the crowds, her manic reaction to the release of all that toxic stress finally dies down, but the smile on her face stays. Languid, loose, and *free.* I lead her up to the tip-top of the vineyards, where we can gaze down upon all we've accomplished together beneath my mother's tree. I laid out a blanket here earlier, with a small lantern, a bottle of Laine's red, a corkscrew, two glasses, and, god help me, a *shoe box.*

"Aww, babe." Laine looks at the spread before us, touched. "How'd you know I'd need an escape plan?"

"I didn't." I smile and get down on my knees and take her hands in mine. Looking up at her, the stars framing her beautiful face that's etched on my entire history, I'm struck by how lucky I am to be here, with this woman I've always loved. From sighing over the newspaper clippings I kept of her secreted away in my crush box to the night where even beneath a blindfold, my body somehow already knew hers. Knew that when I felt her hands trace my neck, slide down the swell of my shoulders, grasp me around my waist, that I was home, that I was safe. That within those hands, I belonged to somebody.

And at long last, somebody belonged to me back.

"Laine, I've got some things I want to say to you." I tug her by the hands till she's down on her knees, too, facing me. Her eyes are waiting for me to begin. So, with a deep breath, I do.

"I've never been in a serious relationship before because I'm a chicken. I tried Le Jardin's famous Pinot Grigio once and hated it. I'm absolutely terrified of change in all forms, unless I thought of it, and then it's the best idea ever." I smile wearily. "I'm simultaneously phobic about commitment *and* flings because I guess I'm just . . . phobic? And I have a hard time believing anyone could ever love me because"—I swallow—"until recently, I thought nobody ever had. But I can be a real dumbass."

A slow smile breaks across Laine's face, traveling like the first rays of sun across the ocean. "Are you done?"

"Not yet." I blow out a breath, knowing I have to say the biggest thing, the scariest thing, but also knowing it'll be okay. "I'm fully, deeply, indelibly in love with you. I know you put money down on that spot in Oregon, but I desperately want you to stay. I get that it's always been your dream to run your own place, and I have nothing to offer you here except for a small family vineyard. But I do have an opening for a permanent vintner if you're interested. Also, I know about your retainer."

"There's no retainer. *Now* are you done?"

I arch an eyebrow. "There is absolutely a retainer. Also, I love you like crazy."

Her smile turns into a grin. "You said that already."

"I'll say it every damn day of our lives, if you let me."

Fireworks shoot off from every cell in my body as she cups my face in her hands. "Yes, please," she whispers as her eyes fall to my lips.

"I love you, Laine, and I'm pretty sure I always will." I lean my forehead against hers, our breath mingling in eddies between us. "Also, one time, I stole your sports bra, but in my defense, I was sixteen and going through some things."

"*Really?*" She leans back to stare at me incredulously.

"Really," I confirm. I pick up the box from the blanket and shake it. "It's in here."

"What *is* that?" She eyes the decoupaged box with such amusement, I almost abandon ship, but you can't shove the proverbial teenage crush box back under the bed once your teenage crush sees it. "Is that—"

"Shut up, or I won't show you."

"Yes, boss," Laine says, darkly playful.

I raise an eyebrow, daring her to make me regret this. "It's . . . about you." I slowly remove the lid, then slide it over to her, fully aware that this may cross the line from *it was just a crush* to *intense baby psychopath.*

But really, weren't we *all* intense baby psychopaths at sixteen?

Laine's amused smile dips, then flickers out, replaced by something more difficult to name as she gingerly picks up newspaper clippings of her soccer days, her honor roll announcements, a wallet-sized picture day photo from tenth grade. Candid pictures from parties Laine and Chance threw when their parents were out of town that Rachel and I were grudgingly allowed to attend so Rachel wouldn't rat them out. Laine doing a cartwheel drunk on red wine. Laine laughing on the couch surrounded by her soccer friends.

And a dingy old sports bra.

God, this was a *terrible* idea, this was—

"This is amazing," Laine says, her eyes twinkling as she stares down at my box of relics. "You absolute weirdo. Why are you showing me all this now?"

"I'm done hiding from you, Laine. I've been so scared of losing you, I haven't let myself relax since you got here. But I realize now I was doing the same bullshit with you that I've done to everybody since my mom died—waiting for you to leave me. And maybe you still will one day, but it won't be because I held back how I feel about you. For better or worse, you're getting it all. The good, the bad—"

"—and the stolen underwear." Her smirk is contagious.

"Who said I was giving that back?" I reply indignantly as she tugs me into her arms. "Oh, thank *God* the bra thing didn't scare you off."

"Scare me off? No way," Laine murmurs against my neck, sending waves of giddy heat down my belly. "You can have this one, too, if you want." She bites at my pulse point. "You little freak."

"Hey! I'm a big freak now," I say, the words increasingly breathier as her full lips brush open kisses down my collarbone. "But, Laine?"

She stops, nuzzling my neck. "Yes, baby?"

"The whole reason Dad's decided to stay in Italy is because that's where his dreams lie now. I know I've asked you to stay, but I want to be clear— I'm not asking you to stay on at Bluebell in his place. I want you to keep following *your* dreams, just like my dad's doing, and not feel beholden to mine."

Laine frowns. "What if I want to stay on, though? What if I want to be your vintner and your person and your everything? What if my dreams are just making wine and making you happy, and the details don't matter?"

"Laine Woods, we both know you're ready to be the boss, but let me finish, will you?" This time, I brush a lock of her hair behind her ear, unable to stop the smirk on my face. "You want your own place, where you have the freedom to make your wine without some boss-bitch in the tasting room hampering your style."

"And what do you want?" she asks gently.

"I want you, but also, *freedom*. I want to be able to take a week off to see my dad in Italy without it hurting our business. I want to travel to lots of places, actually. I'm thirty years old, and I've barely seen the world.

Health insurance would be nice, too, plus the ability to save for retirement. I want to be able to *rest*, Laine, and stop worrying every damn day that this season will be the vineyard's last."

I take a deep breath, then finally say what's been on my mind ever since Italy.

"You're looking for land of your own. Well, share *my* land. You want to make your wine? Be my guest, though I'm partial to—"

"Electric Daisy and Georgia Girls," Laine finishes, smiling.

"I want to go into business with you, Laine Woods." I look out at all I have, heart sparkling, and I'm ready for it to be more.

I'm ready for it to be *ours*.

"I want to sell a stake of Bluebell Vineyards to Into the Woods, to you." My words falter as her eyes pour over my face, drinking me in. "For us to run it together, as co-bosses. What do you think?"

She tells me *yes* in the fierce press of her mouth on mine. She says *I'll stay* when she lowers me to the blanket, hand cradling the back of my head like I'm the most precious thing in the world. She says *I love you* and *I love you* and *I love you* as we spill onto the blanket, out of our clothes, out of everything that's ever held us back.

Here, in *our* vineyards. Our home.

We curl up together beneath a blanket, staring up at the stars visible through the branches, little fish glimmering in a big, dark pond. My head tucked under Laine's arm, tracing my finger across the bluebells inked on her soft chest, feeling in her heartbeat like it's my own. Down below, the party rages on, though I could stay here forever, as happy as I've ever been.

"I can't wait to go into business with you, babe," Laine murmurs into my hair, then throws a hand into the air over us. "I can picture it now: *Boss N' Beave's Wine Depot*."

I arch an eyebrow. "Laine."

"Lil' Napa!"

"We are *not* rena—"

"Bluebell Woods," Laine says, still chuckling as she pulls me closer with both arms. "How about that?"

I smile into her neck, her soft hair tickling my skin. "It's *perfect.*"

When our phones' buzzing becomes near constant with texts demanding to know where we are, we reluctantly begin to dress. After a few minutes, Laine's still rooting around the blankets, though, naked from the waist up.

It's a great look.

She straightens suddenly, her hands on her hips, a suspicious tilt of her head. "Hey boss . . . you see my bra anywhere?"

My arm squeezes around my crush box, and her eyes narrow.

"What?" I give her my most innocent smile, which quickly turns wicked. "You *said* I could keep it."

THE END